S0-HJI-333
LIGONIER PUBLIC LIBRARY
LPL00000004849
WITHDRAWN

Mark the Sparrow

Books by Clark Howard

The Killings
Mark the Sparrow

Mark the Sparrow

by Clark Howard

The Dial Press 1975
New York

Copyright © 1975 by Clark Howard
All rights reserved
No part of this book may be reproduced in any form or by any means without the prior written permission of the Publisher, excepting brief quotes used in connection with reviews written specifically for inclusion in a magazine or newspaper.
Manufactured in the United States of America
First printing
Library of Congress Cataloging in Publication Data
Howard, Clark.
Mark the sparrow.
I. Title.
PZ4.H848Mar [PS3558.0877] 813'.5'4 75-2367
ISBN 0-8037-5431-0
Book design by Paulette Nenner

For my son
Steven Brian Howard

Mark the Sparrow

One

It was Tuesday morning and it was warm. The Los Angeles *Ledger* offices were sticky; the air conditioning had gone out again. Outside, it was drizzling a thin, undetermined rain. The air on the street and the air inside the building were equally saturated, and the *Ledger* staff was wilting an hour after the day shift started.

In the newsroom, Robert Cloud could feel perspiration across the small of his back as he leaned forward at his desk to type. He was an ordinary-looking young man, ears slightly too large, hair in need of trimming. His only outstanding feature was his eyes, unusually brilliant for gray, and icily intense when he concentrated. His fingernails looked bad: chewed down to the quick; even the skin showed signs of having been bitten at occasionally.

Cloud typed rapidly, with four fingers. He was doing a story on an early-morning freeway collision; one driver had been killed. He was in the middle of the last line when a copyboy spoke to him over his left shoulder.

"Hoskins wants you in his office right away."

"*Mister* Hoskins to you, kid," Cloud said. "Wait a minute and you can take this." He finished the last sentence, dragged the paper out of the machine, and handed it over his shoulder. "Better start showing a little respect for the day editor, or you won't last long around here. Mr. Hoskins insists on proper respect; even his wife addresses him as Mister."

"I'll try to remember that," the copyboy replied indifferently. He took a cigarette from Cloud's pack on the desk and lighted it. "You want in for the World Series pool in the composing room?"

"No. Those guys in the composing room are a bunch of thieves; they grab off the good numbers ahead of time. How much is it?"

"Buck a number, pays off a hundred."

Cloud fingered a dollar bill from his pocket and held it over his shoulder.

"Try to get me a decent number for a change, will you?"

The copyboy headed for the city desk with the story, and Cloud went toward the day editor's frosted-glass office. Cloud had seen Lew Lach, the paper's top feature writer, go into Hoskins's office several minutes earlier and had not seen him come back out. So Cloud was in for some legwork. That was always the way when you were new on a paper; you had to spend half your time birddogging news-hustlers like Lach: seasoned pros who would *make* news if they couldn't find any. Cloud had been through the routine on three papers already in the five years since he finished school.

He tapped on the door. Inside, he found Hoskins pacing the floor, talking. Cloud could tell from the suspiciously attentive expression on Lach's face that he was paying only token attention to the pearls of wisdom delivered by Hoskins. Quickly, while the day editor's back was to him, Cloud eased into a chair next to Lach.

"So there's this punk, see," Hoskins was saying, "and he's up on a dozen or so counts of armed robbery, kidnapping-with-bodily-harm, and sex perversion. That makes him an A-Number-One candidate for the little green gas chamber upstate. So what does he do? What does this punk do when he's going on trial for a capital offense? He decides to conduct his own defense, that's what he does."

Hoskins turned and paced back toward them, appearing not to notice Cloud. As he walked and talked, he chewed juicily on a half-smoked cigar held professionally between his teeth. Cigars were the only thing in the world that anyone had ever heard Hoskins admit he liked.

"Now, I can't blame him much for deciding to be his own lawyer. Right now there's not an attorney in this town worth his weight in bullshit. Which is about all they use in courts nowadays," he added, coming dangerously close to smiling at what he considered his sage humor. "There hasn't been a good defense lawyer since Darrow and there hasn't been a decent prosecutor since Dewey." Hoskins paused and scratched his upper lip, skillfully avoiding the cigar.

"All right, so maybe this punk has got a good idea, after all. He's got nine women on that jury, and everybody knows there's nothing any goddamned dumber than a housewife pulling jury duty. Now personally, I don't think they're going to let this boy off the hook. He's a four-time loser now, and if this was any other state except California, he'd already be doing life as an habitual. On top of that, he's on trial in old Carl Lukey's courtroom, and everybody knows Lukey is the state's hanging judge.

"Still"—he took the cigar from his mouth and waved it in the air—"there's always the chance that one of those dames in the jury box will wet her bloomers over this punk and talk the rest of them into an acquittal; so maybe he goes free. And that"—he jabbed the cigar at Lach—"is what we're looking for."

Hoskins sat down in his ancient swivel chair and leaned back precipitously. He extracted a large, ornate timepiece from his vest pocket.

"The jury has been out for about three hours now. They won't reach a verdict until after lunch because the lunch is free. Hop over there and get a quick interview with the punk, just enough to size him up. Then wait for the jury to come in. If they spring him, see if you can pick out the one that wet her bloomers and get an exclusive that we can build up for a nice page one. If they don't spring him, just put together about two-columns-by-a-half for the back of section one. Of course, if you see anything we can put a little whipped cream on, maybe we'll throw in a short feature on Sunday. You got all that?"

"I'm not sure," Lach said blandly. "Would you mind going over it again?"

"Get your ass moving," Hoskins growled. He turned to jab his cigar at Cloud. "You. Go with him, give him a hand."

"Let's go, pal," Lach said, walking out of the office. Cloud followed, not having spoken a word.

In the elevator, Lach said, "So what have you been doing lately, pal?"

"Nothing earthshaking. Piecing, mostly. Little rewrite here and there. Covered a wreck on the freeway this morning."

"Bodies?"

"One."

"Female?"

Cloud nodded. "Yeah."

"Young? Built?"

"Yeah." Cloud wished he hadn't mentioned it. A couple of people in the newsroom had already told him about Lach's interest in young, physically attractive dead women. There was even a story that Lach had paid another reporter two hundred dollars to let him take over his assignment to cover the Marilyn Monroe suicide, just so he could see the body.

"Get any pictures of the girl?" Lach asked.

"Yeah."

"Maybe I'll take a look at them when we get back."

"Sure." With Lew Lach it really didn't fit. To look at him, you'd think he stepped right out of *Front Page*. He was small and Cagney-like, a seasoned war correspondent before Cloud was even born. He had gone ashore with the first wave at Normandy, had been aboard the observation plane when Nagasaki was devastated, and probably had seen as much combat as the average infantryman. And still, Cloud thought, he has a thing about looking at dead young women.

Downstairs, they checked out a car, then drove over to the Hall of Justice. Lach parked in the police lot, flipping the visor down to show the PRESS permit. It had begun to drizzle more strongly on the way over; now they hurried into the big gray building as the downpour started in earnest. Lach stopped at the jail office for passes to the top-floor detention room.

"Ever been here before?" he asked.

Cloud shook his head. "I've only been in L.A. a couple of months. I haven't hit the courtroom circuit yet."

Lach led him over to the jail elevator. "All defendants not out on bail are kept in one big tank up here when court's not in session."

They stepped off the elevator into a long, narrow area separated from a large jail dayroom by a floor-to-ceiling wire grille. Several visitors stood talking to inmates at various places along the grille. A guard sat on a high wooden stool at each end of the area. A third uniformed man occupied a small desk off to the side.

"Hiya, Oscar," Lach said to the man at the desk, handing over their passes. "I saw your boy in that Notre Dame game last weekend. Looks like you've got an All-American in the family."

"Takes after his old man," the guard said, smiling. He glanced at an overhead clock and scribbled the time on their passes. "I wasn't half bad myself, you know, back in the old days."

"The kid's already better than you ever were."

"An insult I'll gladly accept," Oscar said soberly. He leaned over to a public-address amplifier on the wall. "Whitman, Weldon, to the grille!" he ordered, his voice blaring statically from two speakers in the dayroom.

"We'll take Number Eight, Oscar," Lach said, walking away.

"As if I didn't know."

Lach chuckled. Cloud followed him to the middle of the grille, where a large white eight was painted on the gray floor.

"Always take Number Eight if you can get it," Lach told him. "There are fifteen spots, and eight is the farthest from the guards. Puts the guy on the other side more at ease."

"Makes sense." Cloud lighted a cigarette and looked around idly. Once again he heard Oscar speak commandingly into the public-address system.

"Whitman, Weldon, to the grille! Number Eight!"

Weldon Whitman was sitting in a corner of the big bullpen, sharing sections of a newspaper with two other prisoners, when he heard his name over the loudspeaker. The two men with him stopped reading at once and looked over at the grille. Whitman neither looked up or moved.

"Who is it?" he asked after a moment.

"Two guys. One old, one young."

"Fuzz?" said Whitman.

The prisoner studied the visitors clinically, then shook his head. "Not fuzz," he ruled.

Weldon Whitman carefully folded his part of the newspaper and laid it aside. His mouth opened slightly as he turned casually and scrutinized the two men, considering whether to go over and talk to them. With his lips parted, Whitman appeared to be sneering; an illusion created by his nose, large and prominently hooked, which so overshadowed his upper lip that it accentuated a very slight, possibly unintentional smirk. As if to draw attention to both his nose and his smirk, Whitman's thick black hair formed a severe widow's peak that pointed like an arrow directly down to both of them. Overall, he had a tough, even sneaky look; but at the same time there was something about him, some very elusive quality, that quietly asked for sympathy. It may have been simply that, with his mouth open slightly, he seemed a shade dumbfounded—almost as if he needed someone's guidance, someone's protection. Anyone's. Like a child sometimes needs an adult—any adult.

After a moment's contemplation, Whitman stood up and walked toward the grille. He walked with a swagger that looked practiced, yet suited him. He was dressed for court: a cheap blue suit tight at the shoulders and too short in the sleeves, and a drugstore tie with too much green in it. Impassively, he stepped up to the Eight-spot.

"You Weldon Whitman?" Lew Lach asked.

"Yeah."

Whitman's voice was moderately deep, slightly hoarse, perhaps from his week of speaking in court. There was a hint of defiance in the single word he spoke.

"Lach and Cloud of the *Ledger*," the older reporter said. "How about an interview?"

"Sure." Weldon Whitman, smiling a half-smile, took out a cigarette and lighted it. "What do you want to know?"

"Well, to begin with, what do you think your chances are of getting off?"

"Not so hot," Whitman answered frankly.

"Oh?" Lach raised his eyebrows. It was the first time he had ever known a defendant in a capital case to publicly take any position other than the adamant belief that justice would triumph and he would go free. Lach was caught off guard. "What makes you think that?" Lach asked.

"They've decided to railroad me, that's why," Whitman said.

"They?"

"The judge," Whitman said, his lips tightening briefly. "And the D.A."—he began counting them off on his fingers—"the witnesses, the city police, the county sheriff—"

Lach shot Cloud a quick look: Same old bullshit.

"You pleaded not guilty, right?" asked Lach.

"Right," Whitman nodded. "I didn't pull those jobs. The law is trying to clean up their unsolved-crimes file and they're making me their patsy."

"Sure," Lach said. "What made you decide to represent yourself in court?"

"Simple. I don't have money for a private attorney and I don't trust the public defender's office."

"Well, that's a switch," Lach said lightly. "Most of the time you guys swear by the public defender's office. Mind telling me why you don't trust them?"

"Who pays the public defender's salary?" Whitman asked.

"The county, naturally."

"And who pays the district attorney's salary?"

Lach nodded. "The county. Okay, I get the drift."

"I thought you would," said Weldon Whitman confidently.

Cloud, watching and listening closely, pursed his lips slightly. You couldn't really blame Whitman for having a theory like that, he thought. He had heard accusations of collusion between the offices of the district attorney and the public defender.

"Okay, how about a little background info?" said Lach, taking out his pocket notebook. "How old are you?"

"Twenty-seven."

"Married?"

"No. Not anymore. I was."

"Where's your ex?"

Whitman shook his head. "Forget it."

"Sure," said Lach. Cloud saw him write *wife* and underline it twice. If Whitman were acquitted and the case became front-page news, Lew Lach would find the ex–Mrs. Whitman wherever she was.

"You've done time, haven't you?"

"Yeah. I've been the whole route. Chino, San Quentin, Folsom."

Even Cloud, a newcomer to California, knew the route he meant. Chino was the honor farm for first-offenders, the nationally known prison without walls. San Quentin was a maximum-security prison for second-timers, and housed the state execution chamber and Death Row. Folsom was the big joint, the high walls, the last stop for long-termers and those so tough they had to be kept in almost perpetual solitary confinement.

Whitman had been the route, all right, Cloud thought. All in twenty-seven years, too. That might be some kind of record.

"On parole now?" Lach asked.

"Yeah." Whitman dropped his cigarette to the floor and stepped on it.

"When did you get out?"

"The second week in May."

Lach frowned. "The second week in May? You were picked up for this beef in June, weren't you?"

"Yeah. June twenty-third."

"For Christ's sake," Lach said incredulously, "you mean you were only out six weeks?"

Whitman nodded solemnly, his mouth tightening again as if silently cursing his luck.

"Well," Lach shrugged, "that's the breaks, I guess."

Whitman looked at Lach intently but did not respond. Cloud glanced at the older reporter, thinking there were times when Lew Lach was just a little too insensitive to suit his taste.

"Is there anything else you want to know?" Whitman finally asked in a quiet voice.

"I guess not," said Lach, flipping his notebook closed. "See you downstairs in court."

As Lach started toward the elevator, Robert Cloud impulsively held back for a moment. Whitman paused too, as if he wanted to be the last to leave.

"How are you fixed for cigarettes?" Cloud said, a little awkwardly. "I could have some sent up."

Whitman was as surprised at Cloud's words as Cloud himself. At first his mouth just hung open in its characteristic way, and he stared at Cloud openly, unguarded, for the briefest instant; then his eyes narrowed slightly and Cloud knew he was scrutinizing him for a motive, a reason, for the offer.

"No strings," Cloud said, embarrassed now. "I just thought—"

"Thanks anyway," Whitman interrupted. "I've got enough."

Cloud nodded. "Good luck downstairs," he said. He turned and followed Lew Lach to the elevator.

Weldon Whitman walked away from the grille and headed back for his corner. One of the prisoners sitting in a group on the floor reached up and grabbed his sleeve.

"Hey, Whit," he said, "we're smuggling a cocksucker up from Tier Two tonight. He charges three bucks and you can pay in cash, cigarettes, or commissary chits. Interested?"

Whitman thought about it for a moment, then said, "Check with me later. I want to see how it goes this afternoon first."

He walked on. If he got lucky this afternoon and beat the death rap, he might just celebrate by treating himself to a blow job.

If he got lucky.

Mark the Sparrow

Department Four of the Criminal Division of Superior Court reconvened at two o'clock. It was merely a technical reconvention, however, since Judge Carl V. Lukey remained in his chambers to await the pleasure of the jury.

The rest of Department Four's staff were at their appointed positions: the court clerk shuffling papers at his desk, an elderly court reporter—wearing a hearing aid, which Cloud thought unusual—going over his notes at a small table near the witness stand, and the uniformed bailiff sitting at the end of the jury box, his chair tilted back, reading an afternoon paper. The prosecutor and his trial assistant lounged at one of the counsel tables, talking in quiet, idle undertones. A dozen or so spectators had wandered in and taken seats in the public section.

Whitman had been brought to a small lockup immediately behind the courtroom. He would remain there until a verdict was reached or until the jury was locked up for the night, in which case he would be returned to the county jail until court opened the following morning. The general consensus, however, was that the verdict would be reached sometime during midafternoon.

Lew Lach and Robert Cloud had entered the courtroom shortly after two o'clock and walked down the aisle to the front row left, marked PRESS ONLY. Cloud did not recognize any of the three already sitting in the row, but Lach apparently knew them all—or at least they knew Lach, for each of them waved or bobbed his head in acknowledgment of his arrival. He and Cloud took the two end seats, and Lach at once lighted a cigarette in complete indifference to several NO SMOKING signs. Cloud saw the bailiff glance at Lach and then resume reading his paper, apparently unconcerned.

"That's G. Foster Klein," Lach said confidentially to Cloud, indicating one of the men at the prosecutor's counsel table. "He's the D.A.'s hatchet man. He and old Judge Lukey keep about twenty of those thirty death cells occupied up at San Quentin."

Cloud studied the man Lach had indicated. G. Foster Klein was short and stocky, the kind who looked short and stocky even sitting down. His hair was straight and black, almost slick. There was something crisp and sharp about him, an attitude of alertness and formidability. This was belied, but only slightly, by his rather pudgy cheeks, which looked as if they had the capacity, even the inclination, to become florid. This minor characteristic did not, however, detract at all from the imposing impression the man usually made: G. Foster Klein, chief prosecutor of the largest county in the state, a master of trial strategy and an expert in the complicated, often ambiguous field of criminal law.

"Why do you call him a hatchet man?" Cloud asked.

"Because in eighteen years of prosecuting killers, kidnappers, and rapists, he's managed to get death sentences forty-one times. That's a lot of bodies." Lach nudged Cloud with his elbow. "Incidentally, for your own information, he's also a publicity hog. Loves the press. Which makes him a good man to know."

Cloud nodded. Then he turned his attention from Klein to a large chart on an easel facing the jury box. "What's that thing?"

"Don't know," said Lach. "Looks like some kind of breakdown of the charges against the punk."

"Think I'll take a look." Cloud pushed through the low swinging gate into the business side of the courtroom. "All right if I take a look at that chart over there?" he asked the bailiff.

"Go ahead. Long as you don't move it."

Cloud walked over to the chart. Several sheets of posterboard had been put together to form a surface perhaps six feet wide and four feet high. The lettering was hand drafted, very precise, starkly black. The words and sentences and the accusations they formed were bold and commanding, a harsh recapitulation of the charges made by the state against Weldon Whitman.

Cloud's eyes moved slowly down the list. It read like a one-man crime wave. There were eight charges of armed robbery and one of attempted robbery; one burglary and one grand theft auto; one assault with a deadly weapon and one assault and battery; four counts of kidnapping, two sex-perversion charges, and one attempted rape.

Cloud shook his head. Weldon Whitman was accused of doing all that—*in a single three-week period.*

"Hard to believe, isn't it?" said a pleasant, even voice. Cloud turned to see G. Foster Klein standing next to him.

"Almost too hard," Cloud said. He held out his hand. "Robert Cloud of the *Ledger*. You're Mr. Klein, I believe."

"Yes. I thought I noticed you in the press row earlier," Klein said, shaking hands. "If you have any questions about the case, I'll be happy to help you."

"Did he really do all this?"

"He did it, all right. Come over here and let me show you something." Klein led Cloud to his counsel table and picked up a thick, bound file. "This is the record of testimony given at the preliminary hearing in the case of the People of the State of California versus Weldon Carpenter Whitman. Let me recap it for you—"

G. Foster Klein began paging through the transcript.

"On a Saturday night early in June of this year, a lone gunman entered a Pasadena menswear shop and held it up for around eight hundred dollars. The proprietor later identified Whitman in a police lineup, identified a stolen sport coat Whitman was wearing when apprehended, and identified the type of automatic pistol used in the robbery and found on Whitman at the time of his arrest.

"Ten days later, also in Pasadena, an automobile was stolen from a young housewife while she was shopping. That car was the vehicle Whitman was driving when he was captured by the police.

"Four nights after the car theft, a family consisting of husband, wife, and daughter were returning to their home, again in Pasadena, and had just driven their car into the driveway when they observed a burglar climbing out of their bedroom window. The burglar escaped but was later identified by the family as Whitman after they saw his picture in the newspaper.

"Less than nine hours after *that* incident, at about five o'clock the next morning, a man and a woman driving on a lonely stretch of highway up near Malibu were forced to the side of the road by a car with a red spotlight, which they assumed to be a police vehicle. As it turned out, it was a car being driven by a lone gunman; he had put red cellophane over the spotlight. The gunman robbed the people of eighty dollars. The driver of the car identified Whitman in a lineup, and identified the type of automobile and gun used in the holdup."

Klein paused and glanced up to be sure Cloud was listening. Then he continued relentlessly, almost as if addressing a jury.

"Approximately sixteen hours later, between nine-thirty and ten o'clock that night, a man visiting here from the midwest was out with a woman on a date. They were parked up in the hills off Mulholland Drive, in the lovers'-lane section that looks down on the lights of Los Angeles, when a car, again with a red spotlight, pulled up behind them. They were approached by a person whom they first assumed to be a policeman, but who turned out to be a holdup man. The visitor was robbed of forty dollars. The woman with him was slapped across the face by the holdup man when he thought she was looking too closely at his appearance. Both victims identified Whitman in a lineup.

"Twenty-four hours later, at about nine-thirty the following night, a divorced woman named Doris Calder was on a date with a man she works with. They were parked at another section off Mulholland Drive. Similar events took place: the car with the red spotlight; an approach by a person they assumed to be a police officer. In this instance the gunman robbed the man of forty-five dollars, took his car keys so that he could not leave the scene, and forced Mrs. Calder to accompany him back to the car with the red spotlight. Once in the gunman's car, the woman was robbed of six dollars which she had in her purse, and was then forced at gunpoint to commit a perverted sex act by copulating the gunman's penis with her mouth. Both victims of this incident identified Weldon Whitman as the gunman."

Again Klein paused to look up. He was satisfied that he still had Robert Cloud's undivided attention.

"Around midnight of the following night," he continued, "a similar incident occurred involving another man and woman parked on one of the lovers' lanes. In this instance the man was robbed of twelve dollars. Whitman was also identified by this victim.

"Three nights later, also around midnight, a young college student and an eighteen-year-old high-school girl named Glory Ann Luza were returning from a dance and parked on still another of the lovers' lanes off Mulholland. They were approached in the same manner by a solitary gunman who emerged from a car equipped with a red spotlight. Incidentally, by this time the newspapers and the police had dubbed him the Spotlight Bandit because of his method of operation. Now, in this particular Spotlight Bandit crime, there was only an attempted robbery, since neither the college boy or the girl had any money. Following the attempted robbery, the gunman then ordered the Luza girl into his car and drove away with her. He drove around with her for approximately a quarter of an hour, then parked on a deserted dirt road somewhere in the foothills. There he forced the girl, at gunpoint, to commit a perverted sex act by copulating his penis with her mouth. After that, he forced her to completely disrobe and get into the rear seat of the automobile. After disrobing himself, he attempted unsuccessfully to rape the girl. Although he wasn't able to rape her, he did force the girl to participate in a sexual orgy lasting approximately two hours. After that, he drove her down out of the foothills and released her." Klein looked up at Cloud and tapped the open page of the transcript with his finger. "Both the girl and her escort made positive identifications of Whitman in a police lineup."

"He's certainly been identified by enough people," Cloud said.

"Want to hear how he was captured?" Klein asked.

"Sure."

Klein thumbed through the pages to another part of the testimony. "On the evening after Glory Ann Luza's ordeal up in the hills," he said, "a lone gunman entered a small menswear store in Redondo Beach and ordered the proprietor and one male clerk into a back room. When the proprietor hesitated, the gunman struck him across the face with his gun. After taking their wallets and locking the two men in the back room, the gunman looted the store of two hundred dollars in cash and approximately five hundred dollars in merchandise.

"Whitman was captured about an hour after the clothing-store robbery, with the merchandise still in his possession. The car he was driving—the one stolen from the Pasadena housewife—was spotted by a police radio car. When they attempted to stop him, Whitman accelerated. The officers went after him. After a wild chase through the streets, the officers finally were forced to ram the stolen car in order to stop it. Whitman leaped from the car and they had to chase him on foot until they were able to forcibly subdue him. He fought like a wild man even after the officers got him handcuffed."

Cloud shook his head thoughtfully. "Almost sounds like the guy's crazy."

"No. No, he's not crazy. He's a hardened, confirmed, incorrigible criminal. And a three-time loser on top of it." Klein tapped the thick transcript again. "Incidentally, the proprietor of that menswear store also identified Whitman in a police lineup."

"What about the clerk?" Cloud asked.

"He wasn't able to make a positive identification," Klein said. "However, we had adequate circumstantial evidence in lieu of an identification:.Whitman had the clerk's wallet in his pocket at the time of his capture." Klein picked up a partly filled glass of water and drank a swallow. "At any rate, that particular incident isn't one that we're emphasizing in this case. The two we're concentrating on are the ones involving the Calder woman and the Luza girl. Those are the two that will send Whitman to the gas chamber."

"I was wondering about that," Cloud said. "I'm not too familiar with California law; I've only been in the state a couple of months. How can you ask for the death penalty without a murder?"

"The kidnapping statutes," Klein explained. "The law states that when a person is kidnapped for the purpose of robbery, and as a result of that kidnapping suffers bodily injury of any kind, that it is a capital offense. Come over here, I'll show you—" Klein led Cloud back to the big chart. "Right here," he said, indicating the crime shown next to the name of Doris Calder. "He kidnapped this woman by forcing her to move at gunpoint from her companion's car to his car; the kidnapping was for the purpose of robbery because he stole six dollars from her purse; and she suffered bodily injury by being forced to commit an unnatural sex act." Klein leaned closer to him and lowered his voice. "Incidentally, that's Mrs. Calder in the front row across from the press section."

Cloud saw a shapely, rather hard-looking but not unattractive woman in her late thirties. She had bleached hair that on her was very becoming, and was wearing a dress that accentuated her wide shoulders and excellent breasts.

Turning back to the chart, Cloud saw that Klein's finger was now next to the name of Glory Ann Luza.

"Here's an even better example," the prosecutor said. "The kidnapping is much clearer in this case, since he actually removed the girl from the scene and drove around for fifteen or twenty minutes. And although there was no actual robbery—the girl had no money with her—the crime was still begun for the *purpose* of robbery, and that's all the statute requires. And, of course, the girl suffered the same bodily injury as the other victim: forced participation in a perverted sex act."

Cloud nodded again. "What about the other two kidnapping charges? The recap shows four."

"Yes, the other two are technical kidnaps," Klein explained. He pointed to the last two names at the bottom of the chart: Edward Fields and George Roland. "The proprietor and the clerk in the Redondo Beach clothing store. The two men were moved at gunpoint from one room to another."

"That's stretching the law a bit thin, isn't it?" Cloud asked pointedly.

"Perhaps," Klein smiled. "But in a case like this, with a criminal as dangerous as Whitman, well, we feel that the end justifies the means. This is an extreme case, Mr. Cloud. The public must be protected from someone like Whitman."

Before Cloud could comment further, the bailiff walked over to them. "Excuse me, Mr. Klein. Jury's coming in."

Suddenly, Cloud was standing by the chart all alone. G. Foster Klein was back at the counsel table speaking briskly to his assistant. The court clerk was clearing off his desk. The old court reporter with the hearing aid was clearing his stenotype machine. New spectators were filing into the courtroom and the bailiff was directing them to be seated quickly before the judge resumed the bench.

Robert Cloud returned to the press row to rejoin Lew Lach.

Silence descended upon the courtroom as its high priest, the Honorable Carl V. Lukey, judge presiding, resumed his place on the bench. A moment before, all eyes in the room had been on Weldon Whitman being brought in from the holding cell; now they turned to the slight wisp of a man known throughout the state as "the hanging judge."

Carl Lukey was nearing seventy. His oval face was a mass of deep, dry wrinkles. His eyes, small, slitted, keenly piercing, beady, were made to seem more so by the enormity of his ears. The dome of his head, bullet-shaped, was sparsely covered by irregular lines of black hair combed straight back. As he seated himself at the bar of justice on this particular day, he was in his twenty-ninth year as a judge of the Superior Court. He was already a legend.

The judge's eyes swept the courtroom. The spectators were quiet and attentive. Bailiff in position. Court recorder at the ready. Clerk standing by. Prosecution present. Defendant present. Everything as it should be; his domain was in order.

"Bring in the jury," the judge ordered in a raspy but firm voice.

The jury filed into the jury box: nine women first, then three male jurors, one of whom took his place in the foreman's chair. The judge, who had leaned his head back and stared at the ceiling while this shuffling of feet was going on, straightened when it subsided and silence returned. He faced the panel of twelve.

"Have you agreed upon a verdict, Mr. Foreman?" he asked.

"We have." The foreman rose from his chair and handed the court clerk a sheaf of paper slips folded neatly and clipped together. The clerk took them to the bench and handed them up to Lukey.

Silence hovered heavily in the courtroom as the judge unclipped the slips and examined them one by one, in order, comparing them with his copy of the indictment. His expression did not alter in the slightest; it was an old, familiar routine to him. He had long since lost count of the number of men who had gone from his courtroom to eternity.

He handed the slips back to his clerk. "The clerk may read the verdicts as returned by the jury," he said formally, settling back in his high leather chair.

"We, the jury," intoned the clerk, "impaneled and sworn in the above entitled cause, do, upon our oaths, find the defendant, Weldon C. Whitman, guilty of robbery, a felony, as charged in Count One of the Indictment, and find it to be Robbery of the First Degree."

Robert Cloud, from the nearby press row, saw Weldon Whitman's shoulders drop.

"We, the jury . . . find the defendant, Weldon C. Whitman, guilty of grand larceny of an automobile, a felony, as charged in Count Two of the Indictment."

Briefly, a moment of possible hope.

"We the jury . . . *not guilty* of burglary as charged in Count Three. . . ."

But after that, only defeat.

"We the jury . . . guilty of robbery as charged in Count Four . . . Count Five . . . Count Six. . . ."

Then, the ultimate blow.

". . . guilty of kidnapping for the purpose of robbery, and find that the person so kidnapped did suffer bodily harm, and fix the defendant's punishment at death."

All that followed was anticlimactic: Sex perversion, guilty. Robbery, guilty. Assault and battery, guilty. Attempted robbery, guilty. Assault with a deadly weapon, guilty. Kidnapping again, guilty. Another death sentence.

"Now they can gas him twice," Lew Lach whispered. Cloud glanced distastefully at him.

The clerk continued to read. Sex perversion again, guilty. Attempted rape, guilty. More counts of armed robbery, all guilty. Two more kidnapping charges, these the two technical ones; guilty with a recommendation of life imprisonment.

Then it was over. Almost before Cloud knew it, he was listening to Judge Lukey commend, thank, and discharge the jury, and set two weeks from that day as the date for the formal sentencing of the defendant. He ordered Weldon Whitman back into custody of the sheriff. Then he adjourned.

After Lukey left the bench and entered his chambers, the spectators began to disperse. Lach and Cloud stood up as a sheriff's deputy led a handcuffed Weldon Whitman around the defendant's counsel table. The prisoner passed within a few feet of the two reporters. Whitman glanced briefly at them but did not speak. Cloud felt a sudden strong desire to again say something to Whitman—anything, a word of some kind—but with Lach there he did not. Then Whitman was past them and being taken back to the depths behind the courtroom.

"Well, that's it," Lach said, lighting a cigarette and moving into the aisle. "A good afternoon shot. Could've got the whole story on the phone. Hoskins and his bright ideas about one of the jury broads wetting her bloomers. Shit!"

Cloud followed, saying nothing. As he started to turn up the aisle, he noticed Doris Calder step over to the railing and speak to G. Foster Klein, who bent his head toward her so that she could speak privately. She whispered to him for a moment. When she was finished, the dapper little prosecutor raised his head and smiled intimately at her. Doris Calder patted his hand briefly and walked away, her mature, excellent bottom moving nicely under its tight skirt. Klein, smiling, watched her walk all the way up the side aisle.

Cloud, frowning, watched Klein.

Two

The girl who opened her apartment door for Robert Cloud at eight that evening was a natural redhead. She did not fall within the two most common varieties of redheads: her hair was not the flamboyant, ultra-red so common among showgirls, nor the washed-out red of very pale, very freckled girls. This girl's hair was a rich, healthy red, deeply dark, with a sheen to it that could have been produced only by nature.

She wore her hair either in a severe bun at the back of her head—a style she imagined made her look the part of the young teacher of fourth-grade children that she was—or gathered back over both ears and held together with a single clip at the nape of her neck—an effect which emphasized her round, girlish face and made her look shorter, sexier, and younger than her twenty-six years.

Her only other exceptional feature was her bust. It was not overly large for her figure, but her breasts were pronounced and firm, always sharply defined no matter what she wore over them.

Between the hair and the breasts was a rather usual face—not *un*pretty by any means, but without the hair and the breasts, it would not have drawn many second looks.

The girl's name, which Cloud loved, was Laurel.

"Hello, newspaperman," she greeted him with a smile.

"Hello, schoolteacher." He removed his slightly damp raincoat, hung it on a hook next to the door, and glanced around the little apartment. Laurel's roommate was nowhere in sight.

"Where's Nancy?"

"Fifth-grade teachers' conference."

"How convenient," Cloud said.

"Isn't it."

They came together easily, fluidly, and kissed a long, satisfying kiss that was just moist enough to be delicious.

"How late will Nancy be?" Cloud asked when their lips parted.

"Not too," Laurel said. "Another hour, about." She reached down and felt his erection. "Want me to take care of that for you?"

"How?"

"You know how."

She took his hand and led him to the couch. When he was

sitting down, she knelt on the floor between his legs and opened his trousers. He watched her slip out of her sweater, then laid his head against the back of the couch and closed his eyes. He felt her fingers close around him, and drew in his breath slightly as her hand began to move up and down, slowly at first, then faster. And faster.

When he ejaculated, she reached for a box of tissues on the end table and used them to wipe the hot substance of him from between her breasts.

"You've been faithful to me," she said. "I can tell by how much you came."

Cloud sighed. "When are we going to stop playing hand-and-mouth games and go to bed together like two adults?"

"Didn't you like it?"

"Of course I liked it. But that's not the point. Do you intend to stay a virgin forever?"

She rose, picking up her bra and sweater. "I have to wash," she said. She went into the bedroom, her tight marvelous tits barely moving as she walked.

Cloud and Laurel had known each other for three months. He met her his second night in Los Angeles, at a pool party given by a college friend of his. It was a singles party; everyone kept sizing everyone else up until they found someone who fit. Cloud had been sitting on the edge of the pool when Laurel and Nancy came up and sat down beside him.

"You look like a teacher," Laurel said. "Doesn't he look like a teacher, Nancy?"

"No, he looks like a furniture mover."

Laurel giggled and Cloud thought she might be a little drunk or a little high. "Don't mind Nancy," Laurel said. "She's got a thing about furniture movers. That's because she likes big chests. You've got a big chest."

"So have you," said Cloud.

"I know." She giggled again. Then she reached and took his hand. "Which one of us is right? Teacher or furniture mover?"

"I'm an unemployed newspaper reporter," Cloud said.

"Unemployed!" Laurel all but shrieked. "You poor darling! How long has it been since you've eaten?"

"An hour or so, I guess—"

"Well, we'll take care of that right now," she said, standing

"I didn't mean it that way," he said. "I'm sorry if I put it badly."

Laurel bit her lower lip briefly and looked away from him. "Hell," she said. She expelled a short, impatient sigh. "I'm sorry too." She forced a smile and shrugged. "I just have some very definite ideas about money and security, things like that."

Cloud reached over and took her hand. "I guess I'll have to give some thought to becoming successful."

Laurel drew him over to her and they kissed. While their lips were together, they heard the apartment door opening. Laurel's roommate walked into the room. Nancy was a bouncy, freckle-faced young Texan who took everything in stride. Without pausing, she dropped her coat, kicked off her shoes, and headed for the kitchen.

"You two lovebirds want coffee?" she hollered behind her.

In his cell at the country jail, Weldon Whitman sat on the floor against the back wall, staring at nothing. It was not yet nine o'clock and the cell doors were still open, although the tier was locked at both ends. Whitman had been sitting alone like that, in sober thought, since supper. Several inmates who knew him had glanced into the cell, but seeing that he was back there on the floor by himself, they had gone on and left him alone. Now, thirty minutes before lockup, one inmate came by who did not leave him alone.

"Hello," he said in smooth voice, coming into the cell. "Are you Whitman?"

The condemned man looked up, the shadow of his hooked nose as usual emphasizing the unintentional sneer. "Yeah, I'm Whitman," he said.

"I'm Roy. I'm visiting from Tier Two."

Whitman studied him for a moment. He was in his middle twenties, fair and blond, with a delicate, well-cared-for-body, and eyes so light they would have been more suited to an albino. He raised his eyebrows when he talked.

"They said you were supposed to let them know about me," he said. "Since they didn't hear from you, and since I *do* have time, I just thought I'd check. I do have to get back to one of the quad cells by lockup, though; I have to tell the screw I got on the wrong tier by mistake. Otherwise, when they take the count down on Two, my God, they might think I've *escaped!* Wouldn't that be a lick?"

"Yeah, wouldn't it." Whitman sighed quietly. "Sit down, Roy. Take the bunk there, where you'll be comfortable."

"I wouldn't think of doing that," his visitor said. "I'll just sit right down there on the floor with you—" He sat opposite Whitman, facing him, the toes of their shoes almost touching. Leaning forward and hugging his knees, he said, almost in awe, "You got the max today, didn't you?"

The max, Whitman thought. The maximum sentence: death. "Yeah," he answered quietly. "I got the max."

"God!" said Roy. He wet his lips. "How did it feel?"

"Like shit."

The eyebrows went up. "I *guess.* Down on Two, everybody was saying they maxed you twice."

Whitman nodded silent confirmation.

"God!" Roy said again. He leaned a little closer, practically bending over his own knees. "Do you think they'll really gas you?"

"Maybe. They're sure going to try."

"The dirty, dirty bastards," Roy hissed. "Honest to Jesus, sometimes I simply cannot *stand* the fucking establishment!"

Whitman smiled his crooked smile. "I guess it can't stand us either. Otherwise we wouldn't be in here."

"Oh hell," Roy said, "it's getting to where *I'm* in here as regularly as some of the guards. I mean, it's to the point where you can't even give *private* blow jobs anymore without getting busted. Would you believe, this is my fifth—no, my *sixth*—fall in two years. And I think I'm going to do a little hard time on this one. The other five raps they reduced to lewd and lascivious behavior and I got off with jail time. Of course, there was nothing else they *could* do; all they had every time was somebody with his joint out. No physical contact, you know what I mean? But this time, *well!* The dirty motherfuckers took a Polaroid shot that shows me with four inches of this guy's unit in my mouth. So they hit me with a sex-perversion charge." Roy clasped his hands together dramatically. "No, I don't think there's a doubt in the world that I'll get a felony conviction out of this one."

"Too bad," Whitman said.

"But isn't this silly of me." Roy reached over and put his hand on the inside of Whitman's thigh. "Here I am bitching about something like that when you've just been maxed twice. Listen, let me hang the blanket up and take care of you. For free, I mean. I'd like to, really I would."

Whitman nodded and Roy got up and pulled the blanket off the bunk. Using two safety pins that he was never without, he pinned the corners of one end of the blanket around opposite bars in the door and let the other end of the blanket hang to the floor. The cell at once took on a more subdued atmosphere.

Roy stripped off his shirt, folded it neatly, and laid it on the bunk. His upper body, like his face, was fair and delicate. His chest was smooth and hairless, and his nipples had been artificially darkened. He had no hair under his arms.

He sat back down on the floor and put his hand on Whitman's crotch. "How do you like it, Whit? Lying down or standing up?"

"Doesn't matter," Whitman answered. "Whatever's best for you."

"Well, listen, this floor *is* on the rough side. Why don't I sit on the bunk and you can stand. That way you can move your hips if you want to."

They got up and took the positions Roy had suggested. Whitman reached out and braced both hands against the wall. He felt Roy unbutton his jail denims and gently lift his dick and balls out of them. He was flaccid, almost shrunken.

"I don't seem to excite you too much," Roy commented primly. "You do *like* me, don't you?"

"Sure, I like you, Roy."

"You're sweet," the homosexual cooed.

Whitman felt the first lick, felt Roy's circled thumb and forefinger move up and down on the soft skin. He closed his eyes and tried to think erotic thoughts. Roy's fingers and tongue played with him for awhile. Then, soft, he was in Roy's mouth and could feel himself being rolled from cheek to cheek and sucked on. He opened his eyes and looked down, thinking that the sight might stimulate him to an erection. It did not. He remained loose.

Finally he reached down and touched Roy's shoulder and gently broke their connection. "Let's skip it. I'm not going to be able to hack it." He buttoned his fly and sat down on the bunk next to Roy. "I was trying, but I keep thinking about the fucking gas chamber."

"I thought so," said Roy. "Maxed twice. Who wouldn't be thinking about it!" He drew his knees up and bowed his head against them. His eyes grew moist. "The dirty cunts," he said bitterly. "The dirty, dirty cunts! They fuck up everything in the world!"

The homosexual began to cry softly, and when he did, the condemned man next to him patted his shoulder reassuringly.

Laurel, Nancy, and Cloud were having coffee in the kitchen. Cloud had been telling them about Weldon Whitman.

"During two of the lovers'-lane holdups," he said, "after robbing the man, he took the woman back to his car and forced her to perform what the state defines as a perverted sex act. That's what he got the death penalty for. Twice."

"What on earth kind of perverted sex act was it?" Laurel asked.

"Its legal name is oral copulation."

"I presume that means fellatio."

Cloud nodded. "Yes. Fellatio."

Nancy looked incredulous. "You mean to say they can send a man to the gas chamber for *that?*"

"Not by itself, no," said Cloud. "But the law considers it sex perversion and says it's a form of bodily harm when a woman is forced to do it. The law also says that when a person is kidnapped for the purpose of robbery, and subsequently suffers bodily harm, that it can be punishable by death. The law was actually written to cover kidnappings for ransom. As a matter of fact, in California that particular statute is commonly referred to as the Little Lindbergh Law. Whitman didn't kidnap anyone for ransom, but his crime did fall within the legal requirements of the statute, so they tried him for it. And they convicted him." Cloud poured himself half a cup of coffee. "Somehow I can't convince myself that the court is being completely fair with Whitman."

"Well, everything must be legal," Laurel ventured, "or the court couldn't have done it."

"Legal and fair aren't necessarily the same thing," Cloud said. He thought briefly about the way G. Foster Klein and Doris Calder had conversed so intimately after the trial. It was hard to believe that the chief prosecutor would be indiscreet enough to be involved with a witness in a capital trial. Even a mediocre defense lawyer, Cloud felt, would be able to make collusion out of that. But then, Whitman had been his own lawyer; he had not had the opportunity to observe what a conventional lawyer, free to remain in the courtroom after adjournment, would have observed. And *that* could explain Klein's lack of caution in his brief encounter with Doris Calder.

"Well, I don't know if it was legal *or* fair," said Nancy, interrupting Cloud's thoughts, "but it sure seems like a stiff price to make a guy pay for forcing a woman to give him some head. Personally, I don't think I'd even testify against him if he didn't hurt me any other way." She smiled a mischievous smile that lighted up her freckled face. "Especially if he was Burt Reynolds, you know."

"I can imagine who'd do the forcing in that case," said Laurel. She rose and took Cloud's hand. "Come on," she said, "I don't want you around her when she starts thinking about giving head to Burt Reynolds."

Laurel and Cloud went back to the living-room couch. He put his head in her lap, and she played with his hair and traced his eyebrows with her fingers while they talked.

"You seem a little preoccupied," Laurel said. "Are you still thinking about that sex-perversion thing?"

"In a way. But mainly I was thinking about Whitman himself. For some reason he just doesn't seem to me to be the sort of person who would force a woman and a young girl to go down on him. I can believe he'd do everything else, but somehow the sex crimes don't seem to fit him."

"Why not?"

"I'm not sure. He impressed me as a tough, cocky, swaggering young punk. A confirmed hoodlum. I can see him spitting in a cop's face, pistol-whipping someone, even shooting someone. I just *can't* see him sexually abusing a woman at gunpoint."

"Well, I don't understand why you're so interested in him in the first place," Laurel said rather impatiently.

"I can't explain that either." A look of perplexity came over his face. What *was* there about Weldon Whitman that kept the now-condemned man so relentlessly on his mind?

He sighed quietly and looked up past the underside of her breasts at her face. "I can probably swing a couple of tickets to the Ella Fitzgerald concert Thursday night. Do you think you could get out of your counseling for one evening?"

"No, Rob, I can't," she said. There was just the slightest trace of nervousness in her voice. "I've told you before that I can't. I need the extra money."

"We might not see each other until Sunday, then," he said cheerlessly. "I'll be on nights Wednesday, Friday, and Saturday."

"Damn," said Laurel.

"My sentiments exactly," Cloud agreed.

At eleven o'clock, Cloud kissed her goodnight several times at the door and went home. Laurel turned out the lights and went into the bedroom. Nancy was propped up in one of the twin beds, reading *Cosmopolitan*.

"I just took a test and my answers indicate that I'm sexually irresistible," Nancy said.

"Did you cheat?"

"I *always* cheat on sex quizzes," she drawled. "And speaking of sex, did you give that poor guy any tonight?"

"Only with my hand."

Nancy shook her head disapprovingly. "Why in the hell did you ever tell him you were a virgin in the first place?"

Laurel, holding the sweater she had just taken off, sat on the side of her bed. "I don't know, Nan, I really don't." Her voice was tired. "I just liked him a lot from the very start. But I knew if I went to bed with him, I'd end up wanting to explain why going into me was like throwing a crowbar into an empty warehouse."

"Oh, come on now, it can't be that bad, honey."

"Well, it seems like it," Laurel said emphatically. "It may interest you to know that my lover from the Beverly Hills Tennis Club is hung like the proverbial horse. And don't forget that he's been putting it to me on Monday and Thursday nights for more than three years now. For a gal who's never been married, I'm pretty well used."

"Laur, there's nothing *wrong* with that," Nancy said. "It wouldn't matter to Rob. Besides, if you stayed away from it for a week or so, he probably wouldn't even be able to tell."

"He wouldn't be able to tell the first time, but he would the second," Laurel said. "And it *would* matter. He really believes I'm a virgin, Nan. Tonight he even mentioned marrying me. What am I supposed to do, turn around now and say it was all a joke, that I've been putting him on for three months?"

Nancy thought about the dilemma for a moment. Finally she said, "Look, you like the guy, don't you? I mean, really like him?"

"I'm crazy about him," Laurel said.

"Well then, why don't you just stop seeing Ralph?"

Laurel and she had met Ralph Blevins three years previously when Nancy's father had given her a membership in the Beverly Hills Tennis Club. Nancy and Laurel had signed up for Saturday lessons. Ralph Blevins also played on Saturdays, usually with his partner. Blevins was the personal business manager for a number of actors. He and his partner, an accountant, had a prosperous business in Beverly Hills. Blevins also had a wife and two children, but that had not kept him from introducing himself to Laurel and subsequently beginning an affair with her.

"I said, why don't you just stop seeing Ralph?" Nancy repeated. "Lay off the sex for a while, then start with Rob, and later on marry the guy."

"I'm not sure I want to marry him," Laurel told her. "In a way, I'm afraid to. I'm used to Ralph now. Used to seeing him, used to the things he buys me. It wouldn't be easy with Rob. He's irresponsible. We wouldn't have any money." Her eyes grew pleading. "Ralph *has* been good to me, Nan."

"Oh, sure," Nancy said sarcastically. "He's been great. Bought you some very nice jewelry. Takes you out for fancy dinners. Sends you flowers on Christmas and New Year's Eve and the other times when you're alone and he's home with his wife and children. And for that he gets the same treatment that he'd have to pay a hundred bucks for with a whore."

"It's easy for you to look at it that way, Nan," Laurel accused. "You've always had everything you wanted. You don't know what it's like not to have . . . *things* . . ." Her shoulders slumped and she tried to blink back tears that were starting. Nancy got out of bed at once and came over to her.

"I'm sorry, honey," she said miserably, putting her arm around Laurel's bare shoulders. "I didn't mean to get so heavy with you. I just hate to see you screwed up like this." She opened a drawer of the nightstand and got out Laurel's pajamas. "Here, you get these on before you catch cold. I'm going in the kitchen and make us a couple of nice stiff drinks. Maybe we can figure a way out of this mess for you."

For a long moment Laurel did not move. She sat very still, holding the sweater on her lap, with her pajamas on top of it, staring for no reason at the *Cosmopolitan* Nancy had left lying on her bed. The woman on the cover was cool and poised, her complexion flawless, lips, eyes, nose, teeth, all perfect, her expression one of complete confidence and assurance. She was "that *Cosmopolitan* girl" and her life was totally and completely under control. She looked up at Laurel as if she ruled the world.

"Fuck you," Laurel said, and threw her sweater in the woman's face.

Then she started blinking again, but not rapidly enough to stop the tears that ran down both cheeks.

Three

Two weeks after Weldon Whitman had been found guilty, Robert Cloud returned to the Hall of Justice for the sentencing. He walked down the wide fifth-floor corridor to the thick double doors of Department Four of the Criminal Division. Opening one of the doors an inch, he peered inside. The courtroom was practically empty; there were three spectators in the public section, and that was all: no judge, no clerk, not even a bailiff. Cloud closed the door and fingered a cigarette from the pack in his coat pocket.

He had no reason, really, for being there that morning. Weldon Whitman's conviction had rated only ten column inches of space the next day. The sentencing, a procedural formality, would rate no space at all. As far as the reading public was concerned, the story was dead. To Robert Cloud, however, it was still alive. Weldon Whitman and G. Foster Klein and Doris Calder had all intruded upon his thoughts with disturbing regularity since the day of the verdict.

Cloud had not told anyone at the paper that he was going to Whitman's sentencing; he had merely called the city desk and said he would be late that morning. He was really not even sure *why* he had such an irresistible urge to be there. He had questioned Lew Lach about the ritual of sentencing, and learned that one of two things would happen: either the punk, as Lach referred to Whitman, would be sentenced to death, or the judge would recommend mercy and sentence him to life in prison. Cloud wondered if the outside chance of seeing Whitman beat the death sentence was what he hoped for that morning.

Crushing out the cigarette under his foot, he opened one of the doors and looked into the courtroom again. A uniformed deputy was sitting near the railing, and Weldon Whitman was waiting, alone, at the defendant's counsel table. Cloud pulled the door open and went inside.

"I'm Robert Cloud of the *Ledger*," he said, showing his press card to the deputy. "All right if I talk to your prisoner?"

"Long as you stay outside the rails," the deputy told him.

Cloud nodded and moved along the empty row of press seats until he was as close as he could get to the counsel table. As Cloud approached, Whitman turned in his chair to face him.

"Remember me?" Cloud said by way of greeting.

"Sure," Weldon Whitman answered, his mismatched lips curving into that irregular grin, and a sneer that, this time, was obviously innocent. "You're the guy who offered to buy me some cigarettes. I should have taken you up on it; I ran out a few days ago."

"The offer's still good," Cloud told him.

"Well, thanks, but I guess I'll just quit." Whitman's grin widened grotesquely. "Maybe if old Judge Lukey finds out about it, he'll think I'm putting down my bad habits and go easy on me."

"I thought you were the guy who didn't have any bad habits," Cloud remarked. "I thought you were the guy everybody was out to frame."

"Come on, buddy," Whitman answered easily, "I never claimed to be an angel. I'm a burglar and a stickup man and a lot of other things. But I haven't done anything that rates the gas chamber."

"Do you think there's a chance the judge will set aside the death penalty?"

"Are you kidding?" Whitman's grin was replaced by an expression of utter astonishment. "Man, you sure don't know much about Lukey, do you?"

"No, I don't."

"Well, let me clue you in on something, then. Do you know what the cons up at San Quentin call Condemned Row? They call it Carl's Place, because Lukey keeps it populated most of the time. This guy hands out death sentences like a traffic judge hands out ten-dollar fines. Hell, he wouldn't let me off with life if I was his own kid."

"He's that bad, huh?"

"Bad? Listen, you hang around the Hall of Justice long enough and you'll find out for yourself." Bitterness crept into Whitman's voice and he said flatly, "Lukey is the worst killer in California. That's why they tried me in his courtroom; that's why they threw every lousy unsolved case in their files at me and assigned the chief prosecutor himself to handle the case. They knew I'd never get off if Lukey was the judge; they knew he'd give me the gas pill."

"You make it sound like they're going to an awful lot of trouble to get you," Cloud said. "What makes you so important to them?"

"Look at my record," Whitman told him. "I've been a thorn in the law's side since I was a juvenile first-offender. I've probably given the law in this county more grief than any six other guys put together. And the thing about it, the thing that really gets to them, is that I've never backed down from them, see? I've never copped out and I've never crawled for the bastards, not once. I tell them to go fuck themselves every time they try to make me crawl." Whitman's eyes turned to piercing black dots. "Sure, they're going to a lot of trouble to get me. What happens to me is important. Important to *them*. I'm the punk they can't beat, see? As long as I'm alive, every cop in this county is a loser, because every time I make a fool of one of them it reflects on all of them—and believe me I've made fools of them more than once. The only way they *can* beat me is to kill me—and that's what this trial is all about."

Cloud studied Whitman soberly, wondering how much was truth, and how much simply egotism. Whitman had served time in Chino, San Quentin, *and* Folsom, so he'd undoubtedly given the police considerable trouble along the way. But the rest of it—? Cloud found it difficult to believe that the city police, the county sheriff, the district attorney, and the Superior Court would all be involved in such an elaborate conspiracy simply to teach Weldon Whitman a lesson in respect for the law. Especially by sending him to the gas chamber. Still—one never knew.

The door to the judge's chambers opened, and the court clerk and G. Foster Klein strode briskly into the courtroom. Cloud glanced around. Several more spectators had entered, and the bailiff had appeared and was having them remove their hats and extinguish their cigarettes. Presently Cloud noticed a tall woman pass through the rails and begin setting up a stenographic machine at the court reporter's table.

"I got one lucky break," Whitman said. "The court reporter at my trial died before he could complete the transcript. I might be able to get a new trial because of it."

"You mean the old man with the hearing aid?"

"Yeah. Keeled over three days after the trial ended. One of the deputies said it was a heart attack."

"You call that a lucky break?" Cloud said. "An old man dying like that?"

"That's not what I meant," Whitman replied, his voice growing cool. "I meant it was a lucky break that he didn't get around to finishing the transcript *before* he died."

Cloud felt himself flush slightly. "Sorry," he muttered, and shifted his gaze away from the condemned man's flat, hard stare. What in hell am I trying to do? Cloud wondered. That was the second time in just a few minutes that he had tried to discredit Whitman. He saw that Whitman was still staring at him. "I misunderstood you, that's all," he said.

"Forget it," Whitman said.

A buzzer sounded; a moment later the chamber door opened and Judge Lukey emerged. "Everybody rise!" the bailiff ordered. "Department Four of the Superior Court is now in session, the Honorable Carl V. Lukey, judge presiding. Be seated and remain quiet in the courtroom!"

The aged jurist ascended the bench and opened a single manila folder. "State of California versus Weldon Whitman," he announced. "Is the defendant present?"

Whitman rose behind the counsel table. "Present," he said simply.

"State present?" Lukey asked.

"Present, your honor," Klein said from the opposite table.

"This being the time and place set for judgment and sentence in this matter," Lukey intoned, "is there any legal cause why such judgment and sentence should not now be pronounced?"

"The defendant is absolutely innocent of the charges," Whitman said for the record.

"That," countered the elderly jurist, "is a personal opinion of defendant and does not constitute legal cause. Anything else?"

Whitman remained silent.

"Very well then," said Lukey, "there appearing to be no legal cause contrary to sentencing, it is the judgment and sentence of this court that you, Weldon Whitman, be delivered by the sheriff of this county into the custody of the warden of the state penitentiary at San Quentin, and there, at a date and time later to be fixed by this court, be by him put to death in the manner prescribed by law: to wit, the administration of lethal gas."

Robert Cloud, listening, absorbing each precisely spoken word of the judgment, felt his mouth go suddenly dry and found that, although he wanted to and tried, he could not swallow. It was a strange and distasteful experience for him, to sit and listen to one man tell another that he must die, and not only tell him he must, but also where and by whose hand and how. In an instant it all seemed barbaric, venomous, almost blasphemous, as if an invasion had been made into the domain of God.

And, Cloud realized, it was not yet over, for Judge Lukey was still speaking. Frowning, the reporter leaned forward a fraction. His lips parted in incredulity as he became aware of a reiteration of the exact words intoned so emotionlessly a moment before; and he grasped then that the judge was sentencing Whitman to death a *second* time. He recalled Lew Lach's crude observation: *Now they can gas him twice*.

Is this *right?* Cloud wondered. Is this good law? The man hasn't killed anyone; he hasn't taken the life of another human being. Is this punishment *just?*

He tried to moisten his lips, but his tongue was dry and thick and useless to him. The judge's voice continued to flow into his head and register words like banner headlines in his mind. Down the list of charges the jurist's monotone went, sounding heavily with doom. For the third and fourth kidnapping charges the convicted man received two life sentences without possibility of parole. For the two sex-perversion charges, fifteen years each; for the attempted rape, five years; for the auto theft, three years; for the assault and battery, two years; for assault with a deadly weapon, five years; for attempted robbery, two years; and for the eight charges of armed robbery, a total of eighty years. All to run consecutively, which meant that in the event the death sentences were not carried out, the prisoner would have to serve one hundred twenty-seven years *before* beginning his life sentences.

This is incredible, Cloud thought. This isn't justice; it's some grotesque parody of justice. Even if Whitman *were* guilty of every charge in the indictment, did this punishment fit his crimes? Two death sentences, two life terms, more than a hundred years in other sentences—and for what? Robberies? Hardly. Assaults? One woman slapped across the face, one man hit in the jaw with a gun barrel. Brutal, yes, but certainly not gas-chamber offenses. Kidnappings, then? Not the two technical incidents; those were ridiculous. And the other two? They were real enough; but did the victims actually suffer bodily harm? Was being forced to commit an act of fellatio that irreparable, that permanently damaging?

One thing was certain, Cloud decided: any harm done to the victims was by no stretch of the imagination as final as a trip to the gas chamber. That was *final* final.

Was it just? he asked himself again, more demandingly. Was it right? Did society require so stringent a revenge? He recalled a quotation of Francis Bacon: *Severity breedeth fear*. . . .

"The court stands adjourned!" Judge Lukey announced with a crack of his gavel. It was all over. The judge retired from the bench without so much as a *May God have mercy on your soul.* G. Foster Klein, there only to announce his presence at the proceedings, picked up his briefcase and walked briskly up the aisle, followed by his assistant. The court clerk and stenographer began gathering up their papers. Spectators moved toward the big double doors. The deputy came over to handcuff Weldon Whitman.

"Well, that's that," Whitman said to Cloud. He held his wrists out to the deputy.

"Where do you go from here?" Cloud asked.

"Up north," Whitman said resignedly. "Up to Q, to Carl's Place, where they keep the animals pending slaughter. But my case goes to the capital. Death sentences get an automatic appeal hearing by the California Supreme Court. That's the state's way of protecting its citizens from people like Lukey and Klein."

"What do you think your chances are?"

"Poor right now," Whitman replied clinically. "But they'll improve. When the Supreme Court turns me down on the automatic appeal, then I'll try to raise some money to file a writ of error on the basis of an incomplete trial transcript. They grant new trials in civil cases when the transcript isn't complete; maybe they'll do it in a criminal case, too. It's never been tried before, but it's a chance."

"You seem to know the law pretty well," Cloud observed.

Whitman grinned engagingly. "Have to," he said. "Nobody else is going to look out for my interests."

Cloud stared thoughtfully at Weldon Whitman. Was that the reason, he wondered, why he himself was interested in the case?—the fact that nobody *else* was interested in it? Did he decide to be friendly toward Whitman just because he was all alone? Or was there some deeper reason, some *intuitive* reason that had not surfaced yet? Something had drawn him to Weldon Whitman—something as demanding as it was inexplicable.

"Let's go, Whit," he heard the deputy say. Cloud looked up, and his eyes met Weldon Whitman's.

"Good luck," Cloud said.

Whitman nodded. "Thanks," he said simply.

Cloud watched as the deputy led the chained, twice-condemned man through a rear door. He was now alone in the big courtroom. Sighing, he walked out into the corridor.

On his way to the elevators, Cloud noticed a blonde woman entering one of the other courtrooms. He was almost certain it was Doris Calder, one of the main witnesses against Weldon Whitman. Curious, he walked over to the open courtroom door. He watched the woman go halfway down the aisle and take a seat. When she was settled, she turned her head slightly; it was Doris Calder.

Cloud stepped to the side of the doorway and looked at the posted docket for that particular court, Department Two. The neatly typed agenda of the proceedings for that day was displayed behind the glass door of a small bulletin board. Cloud scanned the list of names. Near the middle of the page, he read:

People vs. Calder, Billy—Grand Theft (Auto)

Frowning thoughtfully, Cloud went back to the door and looked at Doris Calder again. Her eyes were turned toward the jury box, where two rows of defendants, under the watchful eyes of a trio of deputies, had been brought in from the holding cell. Cloud wondered which one was Billy Calder, and how they were related. As he stood there, a bailiff came over to close the doors. Cloud stepped into the courtroom and sat in the last row.

Department Two was handling the final dispositions of felony cases which had been referred for probation reports. It was routine work, and the judge, much younger, more energetic than Lukey, began calling cases as soon as he sat down, and dispatched them with speed and efficiency. In the middle of the fifth case, Cloud noticed G. Foster Klein quietly enter the courtroom and walk down the aisle. He paused next to Doris Calder for a moment, and they exchanged brief, whispered words. Then Klein continued on past the railing and sat down at the prosecution's counsel table.

Ten minutes later, the judge called, "People versus Billy Calder." A boy of about eighteen came out of the jury box and stood before the bench. Her son, Cloud thought. The boy was joined on his left by a deputy public defender, and on his right by G. Foster Klein representing the state.

"Billy Calder," the judge said, "you have been found guilty of grand theft of an auto, and upon a motion of the public defender's office, your case was remanded to the county probation department for a recommendation. That department, after a study of your case, has recommended in favor of probation. The court·will now hear further motions by the defense."

"Defense moves that the court accept the recommendation of the probation department," said the public defender.

"Prosecution?" the judge inquired.

"The state has no objection," G. Foster Klein said.

"No objection at all, Mr. Klein?" the judge said, his brow pinching slightly.

"No, your honor," Klein said smoothly. "The state has read the probation officer's report and feels that the defendant is an acceptable candidate for probation. The state makes no objection to the public defender's motion."

"Very well, gentlemen," the judge said, with what Cloud thought was a hint of judicial resignation. "Billy Calder, having been found guilty of grand theft of an auto, you are hereby sentenced to serve two years in the state penitentiary. Said sentence is suspended on condition you serve the said two years under the jurisdiction and guidance of the Los Angeles County Department of Probation. So ordered by this court."

The judge closed the file and passed it down to the court clerk. Klein spoke briefly to the public defender, then escorted Billy Calder past the rails and up the aisle. Doris Calder rose and joined them, and the three left the courtroom together.

Isn't that cozy, thought Cloud. Weldon Whitman's prosecutor, one of the chief witnesses against him, and the witness's son, a car thief. Just one big happy family.

He left the courtroom to hurry to the newspaper.

Four

Hoskins leaned back in his ancient chair and looked first at Lew Lach, then at Robert Cloud. As he turned his head from one to the other, the fat black cigar clenched between his teeth acted almost as a direction-finder for his line of sight.

"What the hell were you doing there in the first place?" he asked Cloud. "You weren't on assignment."

"No, I wasn't," Cloud admitted. "I went there on my own."

The cigar pointed to Lach. "Did you know about this?"

"Not until a little while ago, when he asked me to come in with him to see you."

"You think there's anything to his theory?"

Lach shrugged. "It's like I told him: I *doubt* it."

"*Why* do you doubt it?"

"I think Klein's too smart to get mixed up in anything unless he's covered."

"What do you say to that?" Hoskins asked Cloud.

The younger man shrugged. "What can I say? I'm new around here, remember? Lew says the guy's smart; maybe he is. But for somebody smart, he's coming awfully close to a conflict of interest."

Hoskins considered that for a moment while he took three quick puffs on his cigar. Grayish-blue smoke flowed across his desk. Cloud shifted in his chair slightly to avoid the full impact of it.

"Conflict of interest is always a good angle," Hoskins said at last. "I'll go along with Cloud on this one; I think we should at least look into it." He flipped on his intercom. "Wilma, get me Mr. Klein of the district attorney's office."

In less than a minute, Wilma's voice came back announcing that Klein was on the line.

Hoskins picked up the phone. "Mr. Klein? Hoskins, editor of the *Ledger*, here. Something has come to our attention regarding a possible conflict of interst in a couple of criminal cases you recently participated in. Wonder if I could send a couple of my people down to discuss it with you? Naturally we don't want to print anything without hearing both sides of the story—"

Lach and Cloud exchanged looks. The old line, they both thought. It worked nearly every time.

"Well, I'd rather not go into it over the phone," Hoskins said. "Some of these matters can be pretty delicate—"

The hint of mystery. Not many people could resist it.

"Yes, right after lunch will be fine," Hoskins said. "Your office. Fine. We appreciate the cooperation. Goodbye."

Hoskins hung up and immediately put the cigar back into his mouth. "You heard the appointment. I want both of you there. And I want the interview handled in a mature, businesslike manner. Remember, we are not making allegations, nor are we asking the chief prosecutor to justify or explain any facet of his personal life except as it might have influenced the outcome of these two criminal cases. Is that clear?"

"Clear," said Cloud. Lew Lach grunted and nodded.

"Lach, you're the senior man on this assignment, but I want you to let Cloud ask the questions. You can start the conversation, using our stock disclaimer, then turn it over to Cloud. If at any point the thing begins to look real good or real bad, either jump in with him or pull him out. Got it?"

Lach grunted again and got up to leave. Cloud rose and followed him to the door.

"One other thing," Hoskins said. "Remember that the publisher of this newspaper has supported the incumbent district attorney in the last two elections. Any indiscretions on the part of the chief prosecutor are going to reflect directly on the district attorney. So if you have to start digging during the interview, be sure it's into something solid. I don't want anything *made* out of this."

"Check," said Lach. When they got back out in the newsroom, Lach turned to Cloud in mild irritation. "Goddamn it," he said, "if I'd thought the old bastard was going to buy the story, I wouldn't have gone in with you. I was going to help Streeter on an assignment this afternoon. The Malibu sheriff's boys found a Chatsworth College co-ed strangled out on the beach. I was going down to the morgue and take a look at her so Streeter would have a description for his story."

"Mr. Klein is expecting you, gentlemen. He's in his office with the district attorney." The secretary rose from her desk and led them to Klein's office.

As they followed her, Lach leaned over and whispered to Cloud. "He's clean. If he wasn't, he wouldn't have his boss in there."

"Unless his boss isn't clean either," Cloud whispered back. Lach shook his head in exasperation.

At the door to the office, the secretary knocked briefly and without waiting for an answer took the two reporters inside. Klein came around his desk to meet them.

"Good to see you, boys," he said genially, shaking hands. "Let me introduce you to our district attorney—"

The district attorney was a dignified, gray, scholarly-looking man. He was cordial and at ease, seeming not in the least disturbed by the possible existence of a conflict of interest at the top level of his staff.

"I asked the district attorney if he'd mind sitting in on this," Klein said as the two reporters took seats in front of his desk. "Since I work directly for him, I thought he should have the benefit of hearing firsthand whatever you have to say."

"That's a very good idea, Mr. Klein," said Lach. "One thing we certainly don't want in a matter such as this is any sort of misunderstanding."

"Of course not," Klein said, smiling. "I'm sure we're all agreed on that."

"And we want to emphasize," said Lach, "that the *Ledger* is in no way making an accusation of any kind. We merely want to clarify whether a certain set of circumstances does or does not constitute a conflict of interest."

"That sounds fair enough to us," said the district attorney. "Shall we get on with it?"

Lach looked at Cloud. The younger man wet his lips and leaned forward slightly. "Mr. Klein, you personally prosecuted the Weldon Whitman case, I believe."

"Yes, I did," said Klein.

"And Whitman has been sentenced to the gas chamber."

"He has, yes."

"One of the main witnesses against him was a woman named Doris Calder, is that right?"

"Yes, that's correct."

"Are you acquainted with Mrs. Calder other than as a witness for the prosecution in the Whitman case?"

"I'm not sure I understand you," Klein said.

"Do you know her personally?" Cloud asked. "Do you have a relationship with her outside the courtroom?"

Klein smiled tolerantly. "I really can't see where that's any of the *Ledger's* business. However, in the interest of resolving this matter, I'll answer you. Yes, Mrs. Calder and I have been seeing each other socially. I am a bachelor; she is divorced. There's no reason why we shouldn't see each other if we want to."

"Do you feel that it is proper conduct for a man prosecuting a capital case for the state to have a personal relationship with one of the key witnesses in that case?" Cloud asked.

"I don't see why not," Klein said easily. "As long as it doesn't alter or affect the testimony."

"But how do you *know* it doesn't affect the testimony?"

"We have the transcript of the testimony given at the preliminary hearing, Mr. Cloud," the prosecutor said patiently. "Any defense lawyer would be able to tell if there was a significant difference between that and the trial testimony."

"But Whitman didn't have a lawyer," Cloud said. "He conducted his own defense."

"By his own choice and *against* the advice of the judge," Klein pointed out. "At any rate, it's a moot point. You're welcome to examine *both* transcripts at any time, and see for yourselves that the testimony of Mrs. Calder was virtually identical in both sessions."

Cloud glanced at Lew Lach. The older reporter looked away. Cloud wet his lips again. "Is it possible that your relationship with Mrs. Calder might have affected her testimony *before* the trial?"

"You mean her testimony at the preliminary hearing?"

"Yes."

"Hardly," said G. Foster Klein. "You see, I didn't know Mrs. Calder until *after* that hearing. We met for the first time when I interviewed her in preparation for the trial."

"And you don't think that your personal relationship with her in any way influenced what she said or even *how* she said it at the trial? You don't think that personal relationship in any way helped you convict Weldon Whitman?"

"I am convinced that it did not," Klein stated unequivocally.

"I am likewise convinced, gentlemen," the district attorney said. Like Cloud, he leaned forward slightly as he spoke. "As

Mr. Klein pointed out, the two sets of testimony can be compared on the point of *what* Mrs. Calder said. As to *how* she said it, I'm certain that Judge Lukey, being aware that it could be construed as a reversible trial error, would not have permitted any open hostility toward the defendant." He smiled patiently at Cloud. "Is this the basis of your paper's conflict-of-interest suspicion?"

"Not quite," the reporter answered. "We would also like to clear up the matter of Mr. Klein's intervention in an auto-theft charge against Mrs. Calder's son Billy." Cloud turned to Klein. "You did intervene to keep the Calder boy out of prison, didn't you?"

"I did not," Klein replied stiffly.

"You appeared in court with him," Cloud challenged.

Klein folded his hands on the desk and pursed his lips briefly, as if trying to control himself. "Mr. Cloud," he said, "let me give you a recap of the Billy Calder case in chronological sequence. Then you tell me whether you think I intervened. First, the crime. Billy Calder and two other boys were walking down the street one afternoon when they noticed a man park a new sports car at the curb and leave the keys in it. On impulse, they hopped in the car and went joyriding. They were caught in less than an hour and locked up. Two of the boys were taken to juvenile detention because they were several months short of eighteen; Billy Calder was two weeks *past* his eighteenth birthday, so he went to the city jail.

"At the preliminary hearing for the Calder boy, and the juvenile hearing for the other two boys, all three pleaded guilty. The Calder case was put on the Superior Court master calendar for sentence assignment, and all three cases were remanded to the probation department for study and sentence recommendation. This was done routinely, since none of the three had any previous criminal or delinquency record. Also as a matter of routine, a deputy district attorney was assigned to handle the cases for the state, and a deputy public defender was assigned to defend.

"All the events I just described," Klein emphasized, "occurred after Mrs. Calder had been kidnapped and violated by Weldon Whitman; after he had been captured and identified by her; after she had testified against him at his preliminary hearing; and *before* Mrs. Calder and I met. At the time that we did meet, when I was preparing to prosecute Whitman, Mrs. Calder told me about her son's predicament and indicated that she was worried because it seemed to be taking so long for the probation report to come back. I explained to her that it was not unusual for probation reports on first-offenders to take a long time returning to the court, since on a first-offender the probation officer had to start from scratch. I offered to make a call for her while she was in my office, to check on the status of the boy's report. I called the head of the probation department and he had the boy's record pulled. It indicated that the investigation had been completed and that a recommendation had been in favor of probation. I then checked my own staff and found out which deputy district attorney was prosecuting the matter. I called him and inquired what his recommendation would be. He told me that, subject to my approval, he did not intend to contest the probation department's recommendation. He also told me that a Superior Court trial date had just been set that morning, and he gave me the date and department. I related all this information to Mrs. Calder. Naturally, she was enormously relieved."

Klein unfolded his hands and leaned back in his chair. As he had been telling the story, his voice had become less stiff and more instructive, as if he were addressing a jury. His tone was calm, precise, exact.

"Due to the crowded court calendar," he continued, "the date for Billy Calder's sentencing was still six weeks away at the time I checked on it for his mother. During that period I brought the Whitman case to trial. I also began seeing Mrs. Calder socially. The Whitman case was successfully concluded after seven trial days. Coincidentally, the date set for his sentencing was the same date set for Billy Calder's sentencing. Since I was required to be present for Whitman's sentencing, and since I had not up to that time had the opportunity of meeting Mrs. Calder's son, who was being sentenced directly next door an hour later, I had the Calder boy's case transferred from the deputy district attorney who had been handling it to me, and I represented the state when Billy Calder was sentenced. During that representation, however, I did nothing that the deputy originally assigned to the case would not have done." Klein removed an immaculately white, neatly folded handkerchief from his inside coat pocket and blotted his upper lip. "Now then, Mr. Cloud," he concluded, "do you think I *intervened*, as you put it, in this matter?"

Before Cloud could answer, the district attorney spoke. "Whatever Mr. Cloud's opinion, or the *Ledger*'s," said the distinguished-looking man, "I want to go on record as saying that in *my* opinion you did *not* intervene in any measurable significance, and I do not consider your conduct in any way conflicting in interest."

"Thank you, sir," Klein said. He looked at Robert Cloud again, then at Lew Lach. "Well, gentlemen?"

Lach shrugged. "It was something the paper felt obligated to check," he said by way of concession.

"We understand," the district attorney said. "The *Ledger* is a responsible publication; it *should* look into any matter involving possible malfeasance on the part of any public official. And I want to commend you and your editor, Mr. Hoskins, for the ethical manner in which you handled the entire affair. I'm afraid the other two papers in town would have put it on the front page first and done their investigating later."

We would have too, Cloud thought, if our publisher hadn't supported you for election.

"Well, no hard feelings," Lew Lach said.

"Of course not," the district attorney assured him, smiling. The four men stood and shook hands all the way around, then Lach and Cloud left.

"Are you satisfied now, Walter Winchell?" Lach asked as they waited for the elevator.

"I guess I'll have to be," Cloud said. "But whether there was or wasn't any conflict of interest, whether Klein is or isn't straight as an arrow, and whether all of the witnesses were or weren't right in their testimony, I still can't help thinking that Weldon Whitman is being shafted. The punishment he's been given just doesn't seem fair."

Lach merely shrugged. "Who ever said life was fair?" He looked at his watch. "Listen, it's still early and the morgue isn't far from here. How about running over there with me so I can look at the body of that dead girl for Streeter?"

"Sure," Cloud said without enthusiasm. Why not? he thought. Might as well visit the dead. He didn't seem to be doing much good for the living.

Five

Weldon Whitman went north to San Quentin in white coveralls and chains.

He sat in the back seat of an unmarked car, a uniformed police officer on each side of him, his wrists cuffed together, his ankles shackled, and a restraining chain connecting the two links and then encircling his body.

The trip began at six o'clock in the morning, two weeks after the sentencing. The car was driven alternately by a sheriff's lieutenant and a sheriff's sergeant; they stopped only for gas or to change drivers. The changes of drivers were accomplished on side roads next to open fields, and the men also used those opportunities to urinate. When they were hungry they ate sandwiches prepared by the jail kitchen. They drank water and coffee poured into disposable cups from thermos jugs. Throughout the four-hundred-eighteen-mile trip, there were twelve checkpoints which had to be radioed to California Highway Patrol stations. The man next to the driver kept a loaded sawed-off shotgun on his lap at all times.

The car arrived at San Quentin at three-thirty in the afternoon. It was passed through the reception gates into the small arrival yard. Whitman's leg-irons were removed so that he could walk into the waiting room of the processing unit. The prisoner and his guards were met by a deputy warden, a guard lieutenant, and a service guard. The deputy warden signed Whitman's delivery papers, and the sheriff's lieutenant released him from his handcuffs and torso chain.

"This way, Whitman," the guard lieutenant said. He and the service guard led Whitman through a door marked RECEIVING, into a second room which contained green wooden benches and a tripod-mounted camera in front of an adjustable stool. An inmate in blue denims stood near the camera. He glanced professionally at Whitman's height, then lowered the stool three turns.

"Sit on the stool and face the sign," the lieutenant instructed.

Whitman sat. Two floodlights bathed his face. His eyes sought out the sign, slightly off to his right: a hand-lettered card which read LOOK HERE. It was stuck over the pubic area of a black woman with huge breasts posed obscenely with her fleshy legs spread wide.

In seconds the picture had been taken and the lieutenant

was giving him further orders. "Strip off your coveralls and throw them in the laundry basket. Put your shoes in the wooden box next to it."

When Whitman was naked, the lieutenant called him over to a white square painted on the floor.

"Listen carefully and do exactly as I tell you," he said. "First, lift your arms all the way up with your hands over your head." Whitman did so and the guard carefully examined his armpits. "All right, bend your head forward and run your fingers through your hair. Okay. Put your arms at your sides. Open your mouth, wide." He shined a penlight into Whitman's mouth, then clipped it back to his shirt pocket. "Lift your dick up. All right, now lift your balls. Now turn around, bend over, and spread your cheeks. Okay, let's see the bottoms of your feet. Good. Now spread your toes apart one at a time." Finally it was over. "Get a set of blue coveralls from that shelf and a pair of shoes from the bin. Sizes are marked on each section."

Whitman selected his clothes and dressed. Then he was led out a rear door and across a small, grass-lined yard to a building marked DISTRIBUTION. Inside, at one end of a long counter, Whitman was issued his cell supplies: two unbleached muslin sheets and one pillowcase, two brown wool blankets, a toothbrush and a package of tooth powder, a bar of soap, a set of earphones, and a book of San Quentin rules and regulations.

Carrying his cell supplies, Whitman was directed to the other end of the counter. There, a tall, hawk-nosed convict glanced at stenciled size numbers on the sleeves of the coveralls and the toes of the shoes Whitman had selected. Without turning around, he reached behind him and pulled out of a bin two sets of underwear and two sets of blue denims. As he started to reach under the counter for a pair of high-top, lace-up work shoes, the guard lieutenant stopped him with a shake of his head.

"Slippers," he said in a neutral tone.

The hawk-nosed convict looked curiously at Whitman for the briefest of moments, then moved down the counter to a special bin and selected a pair of bluish-gray felt house slippers that only the men on Death Row wore. He put them on top of the clothes and piled it all on top of Whitman's cell supplies.

"This way," the lieutenant said. In single file—the lieutenant leading, then Whitman, then the service guard—they left by the rear door of Distribution and walked down three wooden steps into the big yard.

The yard was a long, blacktopped rectangle, bounded on the inside by outer cellblock walls, and on the outside by the forty-foot-high prison wall. It was now late in the afternoon; half the rectangle was in shadow, half in waning sunlight. Since it was approaching suppertime, the yard held, at that moment, about twelve hundred men.

A walkway, separated from the yard by a foot-wide white line painted on the blacktop, extended the length of the yard next to the cellblocks. Along this walkway, Whitman was taken by the two correctional officers, carrying his pile of newly issued belongings with the soft felt slippers riding the top of the stack.

The men on the yard nearest to the Distribution steps all paused: since he was entering the prison alone instead of in a group, he was no ordinary prisoner. And when they saw the felt slippers, they knew at once where he was going. Turning to the men nearest them, they passed the word.

"Death-House fish," they said in stiff-lipped prison whispers. "Death-House fish," the whisper spread. "Death-House fish." Like water running from a crack, the word flowed the length and breadth of the yard.

As Whitman moved along the walkway, he was met by the stares of men who received the word, passed it along, and then fell silent. Slowly, the word reached the end of the yard far ahead of him and stopped. An unnatural blanket of quiet came over the twelve hundred men: voices ceased speaking, feet ceased shuffling, the grunts of men using exercise equipment stopped, the snap of dominoes on the asphalt halted, even the sound of their collective breathing seemed suspended in the presence of the man carrying the soft felt slippers.

The walk to the opposite end of the yard took three minutes. Once there, the trio went around the corner of South Block to a locked sally port into a separately fenced section of the prison. Unlocking the steel door, they passed through to the side of the Condemned Row building. The lieutenant pressed a button next to the single side door of the building. The door slid open pneumatically and the three men entered a small isolation foyer. The door slid closed behind them; a second door, in front of them, opened. The men passed through the second door into a dead-end corridor. To their left was a door which opened into an enclosed walkway leading out back to the execution chamber. To their right was an elevator to the second and third floors of the building. The men boarded the elevator; the lieutenant spoke into a microphone.

"Lieutenant Swain, Correctional Officer Bruder, and arriving inmate Weldon Whitman, to the third floor, please."

The elevator door slid silently shut, a soft whirring sound began, and the car started to rise, slowly but smoothly. On Three the car came to a soft stop and the door opened.

A guard captain with bull shoulders and a big, square head stood waiting for Weldon Whitman. He wore a short-sleeved officer's shirt open at the collar. His neck and arms were thick, the latter heavy with curly gray-black hair. On the top of his head was an iron-gray crewcut, so precisely trimmed that it looked artificial. He stood with his hands on his hips, facing the elevator door.

"I'll take him from here, Swain," the big captain said. He flicked his eyes to Whitman. "Step out."

Whitman moved out of the elevator onto Death Row. He waited there with the captain until the elevator door had closed and his escort was gone.

"I'm Captain Dukes," the big man said. "I'm in charge of this entire building. Follow me."

They walked down a spotlessly clean white corridor with a concrete wall on one side and floor-to-ceiling bars on the other. Beyond the bars was a second corridor, eight feet wide, running the length of Death Row: a long tier of thirty cells, separated by wire grilles into groups of ten. When they got to the end of the middle group, the Twenty Section, Dukes unlocked a door in the bars and took Whitman into the cell corridor. As they walked along that corridor, other condemned men came to the front of their cells to look at Whitman. Presently Dukes stopped and signaled a guard in a bulletproof-glass control booth. A second later, the master locking bar at the top of one of the cells disengaged from the cell door.

Dukes slid the door open. "This is you. Cell Twenty-two. Put your belongings on the bunk and step back out here."

Whitman entered the cell. It was larger than any he had ever seen: about eight by nine, he judged, almost square. The usual basin and toilet fixtures were mounted on the wall and floor; a cot, table, and chair, all steel, were bolted to the floor. Whitman put his prison issue on the cot and stepped back out.

"Strip off the coveralls and shoes," the captain ordered. He waited until the prisoner had obeyed. "Roll them together and hand them to me." After he had tucked the bundle under his arm, Dukes said, "You'll be kept in this cell around the clock except for two hours in the morning and two hours in the evening, when you'll be let out into this corridor. Meals are served in your cell from a steam table at nine-thirty and four; you can eat or not, it's up to you. You get up when you want to, sleep when you want to; the place stays lighted twenty-four hours a day just like it is right now. The earphones plug into a jack next to your bunk; there's a three-position switch for three different stations that are on from seven a.m. until midnight."

Whitman, naked, shivered slightly. Dukes gave no indication of noticing. They both knew that he could have had the prisoner strip *after* the talk, and they both knew why he had not. Captain Dukes was establishing his authority.

"Books are available from the prison library. You can order them from a catalog the morning service guard has. There's also an approved list of newspapers and magazines you can subscribe to if you have any money on deposit. In the morning you'll be issued stationery and a pencil; you can send out twelve letters a month, and receive as many as are written to you. You can have four visits a month, two hours each; a form will be given to you in the morning for you to list people for the warden's office to approve as visitors.

"As far as sanitation goes, we like to keep the tier as clean as possible. You're responsible for cleaning your own cell; the corridors are cleaned by mainline orderlies. There's a shower room at the end of the corridor; you're allowed to use it every other day. There's a surveillance window in it so you'll be observed all the time you're in there. No jacking off is allowed in there; do that in your cell. An inmate barber comes in twice a week to shave you. He uses a locked safety razor and the job is done under guard out here in the corridor. The same barber cuts your hair every twenty-one days." Captain Dukes rubbed his chin thoughtfully. "That's about it, except for one last thing. If you're caught in a homosexual act with any other inmate on the tier, both of you will be put in separate segregation cells away from the rest of the men on the tier." Dukes bobbed his chin at Cell Twenty-two. "Okay, get in there."

Whitman walked naked into his cell. Dukes closed the door after him and signaled the control-booth guard. There was the sound of metal against metal as the master locking bar moved back in place at the top of the cell door.

Weldon Whitman stood next to his cot until Dukes had walked away. Then he took everything off the cot except one blanket; with that, he lay down on the bare mattress, curled his legs up, and covered himself. He was shivering.

This is Death Row, he thought over and over again.

He felt an empty sickness in his stomach, and a dryness in his mouth. He huddled into a tighter ball under the rough wool blanket. Its coarse texture felt scratchy against his skin; the odor of some kind of disinfectant or moth spray invaded his nostrils. He sneezed, twice. He blinked his eyelids several times. He took a deep breath, bit his lower lip tightly, and exhaled through his nose. No, none of that shit, he told himself. No crying.

But despite his efforts, a single tear managed to break through.

To keep from dropping into the depths of depression, he forced himself to concentrate on the next morning, when he would be issued stationery for his twelve letters per month. The first letter he would write was to the head librarian of the state law library in Sacramento. The second was to a reporter in Los Angeles named Robert Cloud.

Soberly, he began to compose them in his mind.

Robert Cloud returned to his apartment after working his fourth night shift in five days. It was Tuesday and he had not seen Laurel since the previous Wednesday. As a result, Cloud was not only tired, but at the moment very irritable.

As he entered his apartment, snapping on the light and tossing his raincoat on a chair, he noticed several pieces of mail the cleaning lady had put on the coffee table. Because he was irritated about the job, and had a headache, and wanted a cup of coffee, and hadn't seen Laurel for five nights, he ignored the mail and went directly to the kitchen to take care of the easiest problem: coffee.

Waiting for the water to boil, he thought about Laurel, and how very badly he wanted her, even though, last time, he had accused her of being a wanton tease. But that had been momentary anger and frustration: she was not a tease; that was clear from the difficulty she sometimes had in mustering her last bit of self-control. He knew that she wanted him inside her as badly as he wanted to *be* inside her. But something always held her back; some last-second resistance swelled up in her, causing her to panic. When he saw the hint of fear in her eyes, he simply stopped trying and let her finish it whatever way she chose.

He mixed some instant coffee and carried the cup into the living room. He settled down on the couch, lighted a cigarette, pulled his tie loose, and glanced through the mail. The usual: two advertisements, a monthly statement from the men's shop, and an overdue notice from the main library. But there was also a plain white envelope, hand-addressed in pencil, postmarked the previous Friday at San Rafael. Cloud slit open the envelope raggedly with one finger and removed the blue-lined writing paper; across the top was imprinted CALIFORNIA STATE PENITENTIARY. At the bottom of the page was a neat, precise signature: *Weldon Whitman.*

Cloud sat back on the couch and read:

Dear Mr. Cloud:

Recently we met briefly on two occasions—just before I was convicted and again on the day I was sentenced to die. Both times you seemed to have more than a passing interest in my case. Ordinarily I do not trust the motives of newspaper reporters, but in this instance I felt that perhaps you were concerned with the lack of justice in my conviction, rather than how many lines of copy I was worth.

If I was mistaken, you can throw this letter away without reading further. On the other hand, if my judgment of you was correct and your interest was sincere, then I would like to invite you to visit me here on San Quentin's condemned row. My purpose for extending this invitation is to discuss a project which you might find both interesting and profitable. You can see me any weekday between 10 a.m. and 3 p.m.

Sincerely,
Weldon Whitman

Cloud was at once annoyed and pleased. His annoyance stemmed from Whitman's caustic comment about newspaper reporters collectively; at the same time he could not help being pleased that the condemned man had made him an exception.

Cloud put the letter on the table before him and pondered it as he drank his coffee. A month ago to the day, he had listened to Judge Lukey sentence Whitman to two deaths and more than three lifetimes in prison. Cloud didn't know how fast the California Supreme Court operated, but he doubted if enough time had passed for a review of Whitman's sentence. He had seen nothing about it in the paper, and he could not have missed it; Hoskins made him proof every line of the news section every day.

Cloud lighted another cigarette and slowly read Whitman's letter a second time. He tried to visualize the condemned man. To his mild surprise, he was unable to piece together a complete face for Weldon Whitman. Cloud recalled nothing about Whitman's hair, nothing about the shape of his face. He could not remember Whitman's ears, his eyebrows, his cheekbones—nothing except the eyes and the hooked nose and the imagined sneer.

Odd, he thought. Here he was, a newspaperman trained to observe and mentally record everything that passed before him, yet he could not picture the whole of Weldon Whitman's face, not even after seeing him three times, up close in well-lighted rooms, and twice talking with him face to face. Yet other people, the victims of the Spotlight Bandit, who had seen their assailant only briefly in darkness, had positively and without hesitation identified that same face under oath in a court of law.

Cloud leaned his head back against the couch. His mind was troubled and he seemed to be searching for something: unidentifiable, elusive, but relentlessly vexing.

An explanation, perhaps, that was far too slow in coming.

Six

The plane gradually lost altitude after it crossed the mountains, and finally slipped out of the high cloud formations.

Robert Cloud looked out the window at the patterns of cultivated land patches. He had been out of bed less than four hours and airborne for slightly less than an hour, but it seemed as if much of the day should already have passed.

At seven-thirty that morning he had been sitting again on the couch with a cup of black coffee, studying Weldon Whitman's letter. Tired after a night of restless sleep, he had not noticed the fatigue; he had been concentrating, almost grimly, on a way to settle in his mind once and for all the plaguing thoughts of Weldon Whitman. He had finally decided that the only way to do it was by seeing Whitman and talking with him. On Death Row. Today.

Cloud committed himself to the decision with two brief phone calls: one to leave word that he would not be in to work today, and the other to reserve a seat on the nine-thirty commuter flight to Oakland.

The flight upstate took barely an hour; Cloud had just finished the morning final of the *Ledger* when it was time to fasten his seat belt for landing. He had made a return reservation on the four-thirty flight and had no luggage, so when the plane landed he went immediately through the terminal and found a taxi to take him across the bay to the prison.

Cloud saw the prison the first time from a distance as his taxi cruised across the Golden Gate bridge. Leaving the bridge, the taxi followed the edge of the bay to the prison compound's front gate; through the fence Cloud could see the big wall. He was impressed, not so much by the physical appearance of the institution, as by thoughts of the mass of humanity being kept there. It was the first time he had been so close to a penitentiary, and he viewed it with mixed feelings of awe and curiosity.

Cloud paid the driver and followed signs to the visitor's section of the administration building. There, he filled out a short form required of visitors, sat down in a neat, sunlit lounge while his request was processed, and gazed out a large window at the manicured lawn and rows of bright flower beds spread richly before the administration building. Almost a pleasant place, he thought. Except for the wall. Looking up, he saw one corner of that massive barrier; perched upon it was a sterile-looking steel tower with ominous gun ports opening at intervals around its frame.

Cloud had just lighted a cigarette when the clerk came over and asked him to please accompany a uniformed service guard to the deputy warden's office.

"Anything wrong?" Cloud asked.

"No, sir," the clerk replied. "Just routine. All first visits with condemned inmates must be approved by the deputy warden. Then your name will be put on the regular visiting list, so there won't be this much red tape next time."

Cloud nodded. Next time, he thought. Would there be a next time?

He followed the guard and presently was ushered into the office of the deputy warden.

"My name is Harvey Lewis, Mr. Cloud," a pleasant, well-groomed black man behind the desk said, rising to shake hands. "Won't you sit down?"

"Thank you." Cloud took one of three chairs that faced the desk in a neat, prisonlike row. He watched Lewis shuffle several loose papers into a stack and put them aside.

"I'm sorry to detain you like this, Mr. Cloud," he said, smiling and folding his hands. "The visiting regulations for condemned inmates are naturally somewhat restrictive."

"I understand," said Cloud. Lewis leaned back in his chair and studied the form that Cloud had filled out.

"I see you're a reporter, Mr. Cloud. Ordinarily the various papers notify us in advance when they want to interview a condemned prisoner. That gives us the opportunity to clear the interview with the inmate involved."

"I'm not here as a representative of the paper," Cloud said. "This is a personal visit."

"Oh." For just an instant the deputy warden's brow pinched in a tight little wrinkle directly over his nose. Then he smiled again, quickly. "I see. May I ask whether Whitman knows that you are coming?"

"No, he doesn't," Cloud said. "However, I am here at his request." He showed Lewis the letter Whitman had written him. Lewis read it thoughtfully, his brow pinching again and remaining furrowed throughout the reading. When he finished he handed the letter back to Cloud.

"Since you aren't here on newspaper business," Lewis said, "there's no question of authorization for a press pass.

I'll just have an ordinary visitor's pass made out for you." He rose and extended his hand again. "Nice to have met you, Mr. Cloud."

Five minutes later Cloud was with another service guard, walking briskly across the very wide prison courtyard toward the Condemned Row building. Set off by itself in a far corner of the yard, as isolated as possible from the main body of the prison, the building housing the condemned was made of dull red brick laid in rough gray cement. Three stories high, narrow, with no ornamentation whatever, at first it seemed like a bleak, old-fashioned warehouse. Only after approaching it more closely did Cloud realize that its bleakness was not an illusion; only then did the uniqueness of the building come to the surface. Only then was it clear that the structure truly *was* designed for the living dead—for this place, Cloud suddenly realized, had no windows, no windows at all. He stopped and stared at the building.

"It's always the same," said the guard. He had been watching Cloud carefully. "Always the same with every first-time visitor. They always notice that part of it last. And most of them stop and stare."

"What's the reason for it?" Cloud asked. "Why aren't there any windows?"

"Don't know." The guard shrugged. "But there must be one. They say there's a reason for everything in here."

Cloud silently followed the guard into the main floor of the building. He waited in a small reception room just inside the entrance while his escort passed his visitor's permit to an admittance guard across the hall. He felt an odd awareness of his surroundings, as if being as close as he was to death was somehow precarious and threatening. He was almost physically relieved when a correctional officer arrived to take him upstairs.

They rode to the second floor in an elevator electronically operated from a master control inside the armory. Cloud stepped from the elevator directly into the visiting room, and another correctional officer closed the door of a second elevator beyond the wire grille and ran it up to the stairless third floor.

There were no other visitors. Cloud chose a chair midway between two guards at the ends of the long, grille-divided visiting table. Seeing a metal ashtray nearby, he drew it over and fingered a cigarette from his package. He had lighted it and just taken his first deep drag when the door of the second elevator reopened and Weldon Whitman stepped into the room.

Whitman walked tall and straight down the line of chairs on the other side of the grille; the condemned man had gained weight since Cloud had seen him last. Whitman was lighting a cigarette, and when he got to the chair opposite Cloud, he sat down, pulled an ashtray in front of him, and dropped a used stick match into it, all in one seemingly perfect fluid movement. Then he just sat for a long moment, staring at Cloud thoughtfully, before he finally spoke.

"You came quick, Mr. Cloud," Whitman said in a stiff, formal tone. His voice still had the same deep throatiness Cloud now remembered, but it had lost its hoarseness and was much sharper, much clearer of word.

Cloud studied Whitman for a moment. The condemned man's face was as blank as a clean sheet of paper. Cloud was not certain just what Whitman expected him to say.

"Yes, I did come quickly," Cloud replied neutrally. He let his words drop off into silence.

"Would you mind telling me why you came at all?" Whitman said.

His curt question struck a chord of irritation in Cloud. "I'll be happy to," the reporter replied evenly, "just as soon as you tell me why you *asked* me to come."

A faint hint of a smile crossed Whitman's crooked lips. It lasted for only the briefest of moments, but long enough for Cloud to see it and to catch a quick sparkle of amusement in the prisoner's otherwise cool eyes. Cloud looked back at him with a flat gaze that must have clearly told Whitman that his visitor did not share his amusement. After a moment Whitman shrugged almost shyly.

"Once in a while," he said, very quietly and soberly, "a guy in my position gets to where he thinks maybe *everybody* wants to see him dead." He flicked the ash off his cigarette and took a quick drag. On his face now was the same puzzled, almost lost expression Cloud had seen that first day back at the county jail. Whitman wet his lips. "When a guy's never seen more than half a dozen friendly faces in his whole life, it gets to be hard for him to recognize one when he does see it."

It was a simple comment, simply stated. Yet the words, coming from Weldon Whitman at that moment, in that place, had a gut-affecting impact on Cloud.

"All right, Weldon," Cloud said quietly. "Let's start over again."

"Listen, call me Whit, okay? Weldon is kind of a screwball first name." His voice was eager, and he was obviously relieved.

"Okay, Whit." Cloud relaxed a little. "How are you getting along?"

He shrugged. "Not bad, considering. As they say upstairs, I've stayed in better hotels."

"I guess. Have you heard anything yet on your automatic appeal?"

"Not yet. It's still too soon. I figure to hear around March or April. They'll probably set my date for sometime in June."

"Your date?"

"My execution date."

"Oh." Cloud put out his cigarette, avoiding Whitman's eyes for a moment. "It doesn't sound like you expect the appeal to be in your favor."

"I don't. I've been doing some checking on automatic appeals to the Supreme Court in death-penalty cases in this state, and I found out that for the most part it's just a legal formality. The court is mainly interested in making sure that the defendant hasn't been denied any of his constitutional rights. They don't go into questions of evidence or testimony, things like that. I'm pretty sure that they'll affirm my sentences just the way old Hangman Lukey gave them to me."

"How do you manage to check into things like that when you're stuck away in here?"

"Correspondence," Whitman said simply. "That's my only link with the outside world now, and believe me I intend to make the most of it. I already wrote a letter to the head librarian at the state law library in Sacramento. I explained my situation to her, told her I didn't have a lawyer or any money, and asked if I could borrow law books through the mail. I told her I was interested in reading summaries of Supreme Court decisions on death-sentence appeals."

"And she sent you the books?"

"She did better than that. She researched the whole thing for me and sent me a Xerox copy of a legal brief outlining the way the court handles the automatic death-sentence appeals. She also broke down into percentages the number of appeals affirmed and denied during the past fifteen years, and summarized the lengths of time in each case between the date of the appeal and the actual execution. She did all that research the day she got my letter and sent the material back the very next day."

"Well," Cloud said, impressed, "it sounds like you've found yourself a valuable pen pal."

"Yeah. She issued me a state library card too, and sent me a catalog of all the books in the legal section. She said she'd send me whatever books I wanted for further research." He smiled crookedly. "I'm getting ready to take her up on it, now. I've got a list of a dozen law books I'm going to ask for. I plan to read up on all I can find about incomplete transcripts in civil cases. As soon as my automatic appeal is turned down, I plan to file a separate appeal on the incomplete trial transcript left by the old court reporter's death." Whit's smile faded into seriousness. "That's why I asked you to come see me," he said. "I need help."

Cloud shrugged. "I'm a newspaperman, Whit, not a lawyer."

"I'm not looking for a lawyer," he told Cloud. "I'm looking for a writer."

"A writer?"

"Yeah." He leaned forward, his eagerness returning. "Look, the legal end of it I think I can handle myself, at least until I can hire a lawyer to do it for me. I've got the help of the lady at the state law library, and I already found out that filing an appeal isn't all that involved. But there are two other problems that I *can't* handle. One is publicity, the other is money—" Whitman, seeing the skepticism cross the reporter's face, quickly held up both hands to intercept Cloud's words. "Now, wait a minute, please—just hear me out. Please. I'm not talking about the kind of publicity you've probably got in mind. I'm not going to ask you to write newspaper stories about me, or anything like that. And I didn't get you up here to borrow money from you, either. Okay?"

"Go ahead."

"All right." He took a quick, deep breath and put out his cigarette. "I'm writing a book." He watched to see if Cloud's expression changed. It did not, and he continued. "It's my own story, my own life, but I'm writing it like a novel. I think it's a good story and I think I'll be able to get it published. As far as I know, no one's ever written a book from the death house before, so that's a big plus in my favor right there. It's my intention to hit hard at capital punishment and to show the public just how easy it is in this day and age for an innocent man to be executed by the state." He sat back, his eyes riveted to Cloud's face. "What do you think?"

"I think it's a commendable idea," Cloud answered. "Provided you *are* innocent."

Whitman's eyes narrowed and he pursed his lips thoughtfully. For a moment he said nothing, merely staring at Cloud in the face of what both men recognized to be a potential obstacle in their association.

"Do *you* think I'm guilty?" Whitman asked at last.

"I don't know."

"If you *did* think I was guilty, do you think I deserve the gas chamber?"

It took Cloud a long, difficult moment to answer him. He had thought about it often since he first heard of the Whitman case. It was not an easy principle to resolve.

But Weldon Whitman had asked the question, and no one in the world had more right to ask it. Or more right to expect an answer.

"No," Cloud said at last, "I don't think you deserve the gas chamber."

"Then does it make any difference whether I'm guilty or not?"

Cloud shook his head. "How do you want me to help you?"

"I need someone to edit my book. I know what I want to say and how I want to say it, but I need a professional writer to take off the rough edges, to make it readable, you know?" He folded his hands before him. "If you'll do it, I'll split with you fifty-fifty on whatever money it makes."

Cloud pursed his lips and drummed his fingertips silently on the surface between them as he considered the offer.

Fifty-fifty. It was just possible that Whitman's story could have commercial value. This might well resolve the money question that sprang up between Laurel and him every time they tried to talk about the future.

"How much have you written so far?" he asked Whitman.

"A hundred and nineteen pages."

Cloud raised his eyebrows, impressed. "Typed?"

Whitman shook his head. "Handwritten, in pencil."

Cloud nodded, remembering Whitman's letter. His writing was legible, which was a point in favor of the project. He tugged thoughtfully on one ear as he watched Whitman finger another cigarette from his pocket and dig a thumbnail into the head of a stick match to light it.

"I thought you gave up smoking back in the county jail."

"I fell into the habit again," Whitman admitted casually. "We get them free on Death Row so it's no problem."

Cloud nodded and glanced at his watch. "How long are we allowed to visit?"

"Two hours. But we'd better cut it short if you want to take the pages I've finished. They have to be checked out through the deputy warden's office." Whitman paused tentatively, then asked, "Have we got a deal?"

"We've got a deal," Cloud said, deciding at that moment.

"How do I go about getting the pages?"

"You go back to the administration building and fill out an inmate-property-transfer form. They'll send the form over here and the guard commander downstairs will have me sign it and send it back with the pages." Whitman looked up at a clock on the wall behind him. "It might take an hour or so, for the approval and all. Can you wait that long?"

"I think so. What about the rest of it?"

"I'll just mail it to you, eight or ten pages at a time as I write them. I'm allowed twelve letters a month; I'll only use three or four writing to the state library."

"Don't you have any family at all to write to?"

Whitman shook his head. "Nope. No brothers, no sisters, and my parents are dead."

"At the L.A. jail, you said you'd been married once. I take it you don't keep in touch with your ex-wife."

"No, I don't." Whitman forced a smile. "I'd appreciate it if you'd just forget about that. I never should have mentioned her. I wouldn't want to get her involved in all this, you know?"

"Sure, I understand," Cloud said. "I just didn't want you using up your personal mail privileges. Incidentally, speaking of mail, how did you manage to get *my* address? I'm not even listed in the phone book."

Whitman grinned. "I have my ways." He leaned forward again, lowering his voice. "I'm no first-timer in here, you know. I still know a lot of guys over in the main part of the prison, and I've got good connections with the prison grapevine. I could probably find out what you had for breakfast this morning if I wanted to bad enough."

Cloud sat back and looked at him. "I'll give you credit for one thing: you're resourceful as hell."

"I have to be, Mr. Cloud," he answered quietly. "My life depends on it."

Cloud nodded soberly. "Listen, why don't you drop the formality and call me Rob? I have a feeling we might get to know one another pretty well before this thing is over." Cloud stood up and Whitman did too. "I'll go on back to the administration building now. You'll get a letter from me in a couple of days, after I've read what you've done so far."

"Good deal," Whitman replied.

They said goodbye and Cloud started over to the elevator. He was halfway there when Whitman spoke again.

"Hey—"

Cloud paused and turned back.

"Thanks," Whitman said.

Cloud nodded. "Okay."

Captain Dukes was waiting for Weldon Whitman when the elevator door opened.

"Step over there against the wall, Twenty-two." Whitman did as he was told. "Strip," Dukes said.

"What the fuck for?" Whitman demanded.

"For security," the big Death Row guard commander said. "Come on now, Twenty-two, you're a four-time loser; you know that even an ordinary convict has to stand a strip search anytime an officer orders it. And we're all aware that you're not just an ordinary convict: you're the famous Spotlight Bandit, the only man on the Row who's been sentenced to the gas chamber twice." Dukes folded his thick, gray-haired arms and his square face turned mean. "Now you strip out of those fucking clothes or I'll isolate your ass."

Whitman glared at him, openly hostile. Slowly, deliberately, he began to undress.

When Whitman was naked, Dukes took a penlight from his pocket. "All right, lift your arms." He directed the bright, tiny beam into the curly hair under Whitman's arms. "Get your feet apart and lift your cock; okay, now your balls. That's good. All right, turn around, bend over, and spread your cheeks. Okay, run your fingers through your hair. Faster, come on. Okay—" Dukes checked his toes, his ears, the inside of his mouth, and each article of clothing. "Pick up the clothes," he ordered. "Don't bother putting them on; just carry them and I'll escort you back to your cage."

They walked to the middle of the elevator corridor and through the barred door into the cell corridor. Along the way, Dukes stopped to visit some of the other condemned men. The first cell he stopped at was Twenty-nine. Its occupant was leaning indolently against the bars.

"Hello, Milo," said Dukes. "How's our cop-killer today?"

"Fine, Captain. Just fine," Milo answered. He was a bushy-haired, bushy-browed armed robber who had shot down a motorcycle policeman in a gunfight following a supermarket holdup.

"You know Milo, don't you, Twenty-two? He's a cop-killer."

Dukes resumed walking; he stopped again in front of Number Twenty-seven. A tall, rail-thin black man with a Fu Manchu mustache glared through the bars at him.

"Hello, Henry," Dukes said. He turned to Whitman. "Henry's one of our rapists, as I'm sure you already know? Used to rape a lot of white women. Really liked that white pussy. Liked one so well he went back and raped her a second time. Then he beat her to death."

They stopped next in front of Cell Twenty-five. A short, balding man of forty looked out at them.

"Hello, Franklin," Dukes said in a friendlier tone.

"Hello, Captain Dukes."

Dukes turned to Whitman. "Franklin's the only man on the Row who doesn't belong here. He came home early one day and caught his wife in bed with their insurance man. If he'd been smart he would have killed them both right then and there; he would have got twenty years and been out in six. But instead he beat the shit out of the insurance man and waited until bedtime to strangle his wife. That made it premeditated, and Franklin got maxed. Personally, I hope his sentence is commuted."

Dukes escorted the naked Whitman down to his own locked cell. Death Row cells were always locked except during recreation, when they were open in sections of ten. Dukes motioned to the control-room guard to release the safety bar at the top of the cell door. Then he nodded and Whitman entered the cell. As soon as the door was closed and safety-locked behind him, the condemned man began to put his clothes back on. Dukes stood and watched.

"You know, I've seen all kinds up here on the Row," the captain said, standing up close to the bars and speaking in a soft, conversational voice. "Cop-killers, wife-killers, rapists like Henry, psychos of every imaginable kind; but I have to admit that you're a new experience for me, Twenty-two. You're the first real pervert I've ever had up here."

Whitman, stepping into his coveralls, flushed an angry red but said nothing.

"I'm used to being around the cold-blooded killers and the guys who blow their tops and do something violent to a wife or a girlfriend or somebody like that. But I just don't know about a man who takes an innocent little teenage girl and makes her suck his dick at the point of a gun—"

"Did it ever occur to you, Captain, that I might just be innocent of that?" Whitman asked tightly. Dukes shook his head solemnly.

"Not for a minute," he said. "I've been a correctional officer for twenty-nine years; I've seen guys like you by the hundreds. Not as smart as you, maybe, but just as rotten. Just as evil. And you *are* evil, Twenty-two; I know it as well as I know my own face in the mirror. Guys like you, you can fool a lot of people; you can fool lawyers and judges and juries and social workers. But you can't fool me, Twenty-two. I *know* evil—and you're it. You're going to deserve exactly what you get when your time comes."

"Don't be too sure it's going to come," the condemned man said grimly.

"Oh, it will," Dukes assured him confidently. "It will."

The big guard captain walked away. Weldon Whitman walked up to the bars and leaned his face against the cold, hard steel. With one blue-gray bar dividing his face into uneven halves, he stared at his keeper's back.

Seven

"Do you mean," Laurel said rather coolly, "that you just got on a plane and went to San Francisco today? Without telling anyone?"

"What's wrong with that?" Cloud asked with a genuinely innocent shrug.

"Oh, nothing," she said, piqued. "Nothing at all. Except that if the plane had crashed, no one would have had the faintest idea that you were even on it."

They were sitting at a tiny corner table in Rosa's Pizzeria, a cozy, pungent-smelling, inexpensive place not far from Laurel's apartment. Between them were two glasses of very dark Bardolino and a flickering candle burning in a chipped saucer.

"I guess I should have called you this morning," Cloud admitted. "It was pretty much a last-minute decision; I don't think I realized I was really going until I was on my way to the airport."

"What ever possessed you to go?" She was still peeved.

"Whitman wrote me a letter. He asked me to come." Cloud took a sip of wine, then for a moment held the glass in front of the dancing candle flame and stared thoughtfully at it. "He's scared, Laurel. He's been sentenced to die and he's scared. He's starting a fight for his life from a prison cell, without a friend in the world to help him."

"I see. So he's picked you for his friend."

Cloud put down his glass. "In a way I guess we kind of picked each other. He's writing a book about himself, hoping to bring his case before the public and to make some money to fight his conviction. He asked me to edit the book for him. For a half interest in whatever it makes."

"What did you tell him?"

"I said I would."

Laurel's eyes narrowed the tiniest bit. "Do you think it's a profitable venture?"

"It could be. Especially if he turns out to be innocent."

"Do you think he's innocent?"

Before Cloud could answer, the waitress arrived with a large, steaming pizza. Cloud helped Laurel separate several of the cut slices to cool, taking his time because he knew she was waiting for his answer—he had none.

"Well, do you or don't you?"

"Think he's innocent?" Cloud shrugged, as if to relegate the matter to unimportance. "I don't really know. But innocent or guilty, I don't think he deserves to go to the gas chamber."

"Why not?"

"Because I don't think a death sentence is justified when no life has been taken. I'm not even sure it's justified in *any* case. I've been kind of researching it in my spare time; you'd be surprised at some of the arguments—really *lucid* arguments—against it."

"Such as?" Laurel said.

"Well, aside from the fact that statistics have proven that it isn't a deterrent to capital crimes—"

"Is that true?" she interrupted skeptically. "The death penalty doesn't prevent murders?"

"Not according to the figures," he assured her. "The murder rate is just as high per capita—sometimes even higher—in states where there's a death penalty as it is in states that have abolished capital punishment." Cloud balanced a slice of pizza on his thumb and index finger and took a bite. It was hot and he swallowed it quickly. "But one of the very *best* arguments for outlawing death penalties is by a man named Donald MacNamara, dean of the Institute of Criminology in New York. MacNamara says that the death penalty actually stands in the way of penal reform and that as long as it is a part of our system of justice, a truly rehabilitative approach to penology will never be fully attained." He glanced down at the pizza. "Why aren't you eating?"

"I am." She picked up her first slice of pizza. Her expression was disapproving.

"You don't think I should have agreed to help Whitman with his book."

"I think you were probably hasty, yes," she admitted. "If you were interested in making extra money, I'm sure you could find a much better way of doing it. How long will it take to finish it, do you think?"

"I'm not sure. Six months, maybe."

"At the end of which you might very well end up with fifty percent of nothing."

"On the other hand, I *could* come out of it with a lot of money and maybe even a name. Aren't you the one who wants me to be rich and successful so you won't have to marry beneath yourself?"

"That's not even close to funny."

"No, I guess not," he agreed.

Laurel was silent for a moment, then took a new tack. "Don't you think this is going to affect your regular job? It'll be on your mind, you'll be thinking about it when you're not working on it; it's bound to tap what little interest you have in your work on the paper. You don't really care for your job at the *Ledger;* you just go on working there because there's nothing different that you *do* care for. And when you finally decide to apply yourself to something, it's this . . . this Whitman thing—something that has no permanent direction to it and no definite reward." She bit her lip briefly. "Do you understand what I'm talking about, Rob?"

"Yes." He let it go at that. It was an old, familiar subject by now, one they had debated several times before. Their disagreement narrowed down to a difference in personal values.

They ate their pizza and drank their wine in uncomfortable silence, concentrating with elaborate, seemingly undivided attention to the task, as if every move, every bite, were being recorded for posterity. The longer the silence endured, the more self-conscious they became. The food grew tasteless in their mouths, and the wine, usually so mellow and perfectly suited to the particular cheese Rosa used in her pizzas, tonight seemed tart and vinegary. Finally the meal became such an ordeal that it simply was not worth the effort. By silent mutual agreement they decided to give up on it completely.

"Not very good tonight," Cloud commented, putting his napkin on the table.

"No," Laurel said quietly. She folded her own napkin and sat back in the chair, fingers toying with the stem of her glass. Cloud lighted a cigarette and studied her as she stared down at the red circle of wine shifting in the glass. Sitting as she was, turned slightly away, accentuated the round fullness of her breasts under the snugly fit crewneck sweater. He could not help thinking again how much he had come to want this woman. He felt helpless in the face of the seemingly impossible differences between them. As he sat there studying her, from somewhere deep inside him a sigh inadvertently but audibly slipped past his lips.

"You're tired," Laurel said. "I am too, a little. Why don't we forget the movie and both get home early?"

"All right," Cloud said. He *did* feel tired.

Walking back up the hill toward her apartment, they turned their coat collars up against a crisp, cool night breeze. They walked close together, but not holding hands as they usually did. When they entered the tiny lobby of her building, Laurel turned to him and said, "Let's say goodnight here, Rob. Do you mind? I'm really very tired."

"Sure," Cloud said. He touched her shoulder and leaned forward to kiss her lightly on the lips. "Want me to call you tomorrow?"

"You know I do."

"Then I will." He rubbed his fingertips over her cheek. "Goodnight."

Before he was out the door, she spoke to him again. "Rob—"

"Yes?"

"Have you definitely made up your mind to help this Whitman with his book?"

"Yes, I have."

"All right then," she said, and she turned and went up the stairs.

Cloud stood there frowning. Had her words meant an acceptance of his decision? Or were they a veiled implication that he was going to be sorry?

For the next six weeks, Cloud concentrated on the book that he and Weldon Whitman were writing—for that was the way it quickly turned out to be.

The manuscript, he found upon his first close reading, was badly in need of work—a lot of work. There was definitely a story in what Whitman had written, but it had to be dragged from the pages. The organization of his material was terrible, the writing itself atrocious. The script had no continuity, no real form, and was totally without style of any kind. But there *was* a story.

The title Weldon Whitman had selected for his book, in his dark humor, was *Room 22, Hotel Death.* Cloud thought it a good title—very good, in fact. But the rest of the book . . .

He wrote Whitman about it, candidly putting forth his opinion:

You do have a story here, Whit, and I think it's a good one, a story worth telling. However, I'm afraid that your narrative, your dialogue, the entire way you've attempted to tell the story, is pretty poorly done.

I am being very frank with you because I do not want any misunderstanding between us. Together we can probably come up with a book that will have a good chance of being published—but before we begin the project, I want you to understand two things: first, the finished product will more likely be quite different from the picture of it you now have in mind; and second, it's going to take a lot of compromise on your part because it's going to take a lot of rewriting before we finally get that finished product.

I'm ready to give it a try if you are—but I wanted to let you know that the script needs more than simply editing. I'll undoubtedly be changing a great deal of what you write. Let me know how you feel about that.

At the end of the letter, he put a postscript.

Incidentally, I like the title you chose. That's the one thing I won't change.

Three days later, Cloud received his reply:

Glad you liked the title. I thought it very appropriate. Enclosed are the next eight pages.

Cloud read the note and shook his head in irritation. Not a mention of the extensive rewriting he had proposed; not a word of agreement or disagreement with anything he had said in his letter.

Cloud shot a quick note back to him:

Did you read my letter??? I asked how you felt about my approach. I feel it is essential that we reach a definite understanding. Are you in agreement or aren't you?

To which Whitman calmly replied:

If I were not in agreement with your proposal I would not have sent you the next eight pages.

Please keep in mind that in addition to writing this book I am studying law books and preparing an appeal.

There is nothing I would like better than to enter into lengthy correspondence with you—but unfortunately my time is limited. Very limited.

This time Cloud read Whitman's reply with chagrin rather than irritation. Whitman was right, or course. The man was facing death in the gas chamber, and he, Cloud, was making an issue of his not answering letters in the proper manner.

Late one morning, nearly three months after starting on *Room 22, Hotel Death*, Cloud was called into Hoskins's office.

"I want you to go down to the Hall of Justice right after lunch," he said, speaking as usual around a fat black cigar. He thumbed through the top pages of a scratch pad and tore one of them off. He tossed it to the edge of the desk. "Go to Department Six of Superior Court. There's a jury trial about to begin there: five punks from some motorcycle gang, up for battery, rape, and sex perversion. The jury was picked this morning, so the opening statements by the prosecution and defense are first on the agenda for this afternoon. Go see the court clerk; he'll give you a transcript of the preliminary hearing, plus the Superior Court proceedings so far: names of the jurors and so on. Slip him five bucks and fill out a voucher for it when you get back."

Hoskins leaned precariously far back in his chair; he removed the cigar from his mouth and looked up at the ceiling.

"Stay in the courtroom for the afternoon session. Look around, observe: especially the five punks. I want a story with some drama in it, some social comment, something to hook the readers for a possible series on motorcycle gangs and how their existence affects society as a whole. Give me something with a point of view, something *creative.*"

The day editor jammed the cigar back into his mouth and suddenly sat upright again. His eyes narrowed at Cloud.

"You got all that?"

"Got it," Cloud assured him.

Cloud went back to his desk, quickly finished a story he was doing, and walked the page over to the city desk. Lew Lach was working the desk.

"I'm checking out for the afternoon," he told Lach. "On assignment for Hoskins."

"Anything interesting?"

"Yeah, big bus wreck out on Interstate 15," Cloud said straightfaced. "Bus was carrying a girls' wiffle-ball team from some junior college. At least a dozen dead."

"Listen, I'll take it for you if you want me to—"

"I'd better not, Lew. The old man wants a story with some social comment in it."

"Social comment? In a story about a bus wreck? I think he's been playing with himself again. Listen, get a lot of pictures, will you?"

"Sure, sure." Cloud walked away, vaguely wondering why he had put Lach on like that. Maybe it was the job; maybe he was getting tired of this one too. Damned if he knew why, but after he had been around a paper for ninety days or so, he just couldn't seem to maintain any job interest at all. Three months: that was about the extent of his interest span. After that he went from boredom to apathy to lethargy. Then he quit and moved on.

Except that in this case he probably wouldn't quit. He'd already stuck it out six months. Because of Laurel.

With his coat over his shoulder, he rode the elevator downstairs and walked out onto the street. There was a northbound bus waiting at the corner, and by hurrying he was able to board it. He found a seat by the window and slumped into it. Almost at once, he began thinking about *Room 22, Hotel Death*.

In the weeks since he had begun work on Whitman's book, Cloud had given little thought to anything else. At the paper, he went through the motions of doing his job. When he was with Laurel, he did pretty much the same, giving to their dates whatever he felt was required of him, but contributing nothing extra. His sex drive had decelerated considerably. He made no more intercourse demands of her, and in fact engaged in sex at all now more as a result of her initiative than his.

The book had become the whole thing with him; it was something that *did* hold his interest, something that challenged him, something he felt good doing. He worked and reworked the pages, feeling his writing technique honing down to a fine edge. He watched the manuscript metamorphose from Whitman's handwritten white sheets to his own handwritten yellow sheets to a typed yellow copy to a final typed white copy on the best-grade bond paper he could afford. He watched the manuscript grow and he was proud of it; he was proud of it somewhat the way a father is proud of a child whom he has created and is watching grow.

Getting off the bus in the Los Angeles Civic Center, he continued to think of Weldon Whitman—now not as much in terms of the book, as in actual memory of the times they had met: the first two times right in this very Hall of Justice, then on Death Row. It was odd to realize that all the things Whitman was writing about now, times and events which came before him, would eventually progress to a point where he himself would be included. In helping Whitman to tell his story, he had in fact become *part* of the story. Whether Whitman was guilty or innocent, whether he lived or died, whether he was remembered or forgotten, Robert Cloud now shared part of the responsibility for it.

Cloud entered the Hall of Justice and took the elevator up to Department Six. The court clerk was eating a sandwich at his desk. Cloud got the transcript from him and paid him five dollars as Hoskins had instructed. Going back downstairs to the lobby, he bought a packaged sandwich and an orange drink at the snack counter, and found a vacant bench where he could sit and read the transcript.

The defendants were five men between the ages of twenty-two and twenty-five, and all members of a motorcycle club known as the Black Jacks. Some two months earlier, the five had attended a Saturday-night party in Long Beach, fifteen miles south of Los Angeles. The party was held in a municipal housing project containing apartments for both low-income civilian families and dependents of Navy enlisted personnel stationed at Long Beach Navy Yard. The party was in a basement room of a twelve-unit building tenanted by both civilian and Navy families.

The party was an informal affair; the participants furnished their own beer and other refreshments. The host, also a member of the Black Jacks, lived in the building. There were five or six other Black Jacks present, and about two dozen more persons who drifted in and out during the evening.

Shortly before midnight, a young Navy wife who lived in the building entered the basement laundry room to retrieve a bundle of clothes she had put into the coin-operated dryer several hours earlier. Another young woman, a neighbor who was attending the party, invited the sailor's wife to join them. At first she declined: her husband was out on a practice cruise, and their year-old infant was alone in the apartment. After much urging, however, the sailor's wife did agree to join the party just long enough to have one glass of beer.

She stayed for approximately fifteen minutes and then excused herself. One of the defendants followed her into the laundry room and offered to carry the basket of clothes upstairs for her. She attempted to decline, but the defendant insisted; she finally consented to let him carry the basket as far as her apartment door and led the way to the second-floor apartment. Unknown to her, the man's four friends followed a short distance behind.

At the door to her apartment, the defendant asked if she would invite him inside. She declined, saying her baby was asleep. The defendant persisted; when the woman continued to refuse, he forced his way past the door and grabbed her by the throat with both hands, threatening to choke her if she screamed for help. The four co-defendants, who had been watching from the stairwell, hurried into the apartment and locked the door behind them.

At this point the young woman extricated herself from the defendant's hold and screamed loudly. She was slapped heavily across the face by the defendant and one of the co-defendants; she fell to the floor, dazed. The defendant and one of the co-defendants then carried her into the small bedroom.

The victim was stripped and forcibly raped, by each of the five in turn. Later she was forced to commit what the state termed an unnatural sex act by copulating with her mouth the penis of the defendant and one of the co-defendants, as well as being subjected to various other sexual indignities. The five defendants remained in the apartment for approximately two hours, helping themselves freely to the victim's food, drink, and cigarettes.

After warning the victim not to mention what had happened, the defendants returned to the party. The victim took her baby and ran to a friend's apartment in another section of the housing project. The friend called the police, and the victim furnished them with full details of the attack. Three police units were called and the victim accompanied the officers back to the party. Three of the five defendants were seized then; the other two were arrested the following day.

The victim was hospitalized about three hours after the attack. She was treated for superficial bruises, minor internal abrasions of the vagina, and mild shock; she was released the following morning. Her husband, granted emergency leave, returned from his cruise by helicopter.

The five defendants were held to answer the charges at a preliminary hearing and were bound over to the Superior Court for trial. Two of them had private attorneys; the other three were represented by the public defender's office.

Robert Cloud's eyes swept the last line of the transcript, and he shook his head. Thoughts flashed through his mind: how terrified the sailor's wife must have been; how her husband must have felt when he found out what had happened; how their future together, their very lives, would be marked by the memory of that one awful night. He could not help thinking briefly of Weldon Whitman. Frowning thoughtfully, he finished the last of his sandwich and went back upstairs to Department Six.

As he sat down in the press section, Cloud saw a familiar figure enter from the judge's chambers and walk over to the prosecutor's table. It was G. Foster Klein, the district attorney's chief prosecutor, the man who had convicted Weldon Whitman.

"Hello, Mr. Klein. I'm Robert Cloud of the *Ledger*—"

The dapper little lawyer turned, smiling. "Of course. How are you, Cloud? Nice to see you again."

"No hard feelings?" Cloud asked.

"Certainly not. Not a bit." His smiled widened. "Scrutiny like that keeps us on our toes. You covering this trial?"

"Yes."

"Well, you're just in time."

"I've just been reading the report of the preliminary hearing," Cloud remarked. "Looks like you've got five more candidates for the death house."

"Well, it isn't quite as bad as that," Klein said casually. "I expect they'll get nice long sentences, though."

"You're not asking for the death penalty?"

"Oh, no. Not on rape and sex-perversion charges. The

death sentence is reserved for murder and kidnapping offenses."

Cloud frowned and pursed his lips for a moment. "I thought the crimes in this case were very similar to those in the Whitman case. How is it that these five didn't get charged with kidnapping?"

"The best we could have done would have been technical kidnapping charges," Klein explained. "Moving the victim from one room to another. I don't think the charge would have held up—not for a death sentence, anyway. Even in the Whitman case, we asked for one of our death sentences on that technical charge of moving the store owner and his clerk into a back room, and the jury denied it."

"Yes," said Cloud, "but on the kidnapping charge based on the crime against Doris Calder, he *did* receive the death penalty, for moving her from one car to another car twenty feet away. And she wasn't subjected to near what this woman went through."

"Granted, she wasn't," Klein admitted, "but there's a very important difference between the two incidents: The law calls for the death penalty only if the victim suffers bodily harm after being kidnapped for the purpose of robbery. Whitman looted Doris Calder's purse while he had her in his car, so we were able to prove robbery as the motive for the kidnapping. Even on his other death sentence, we proved that same motive because he *attempted* to rob the Luza girl; she didn't have any money on her person, however." The prosecutor paused to nod at one of the defense attorneys who had just arrived. "Now, in the case of this sailor's wife," he went on, "the motive was obviously rape and not robbery—"

"But they *did* commit robbery," Cloud pointed out. "Not money, of course, but they stole her cigarettes and food. That's still robbery, isn't it?"

"Very definitely. The point is, did they invade the victim's apartment primarily to assault her or to rob her? I believe they did it to assault her. They had sex on their minds, not a few cans of beer and a couple of packs of cigarettes."

"Couldn't the same thing be said of Whitman?" Cloud argued. "In the case of Doris Calder, he robbed—or was convicted of robbing—her companion while they were both in the man's car, and then he forced Mrs. Calder to accompany him back to his own car. When he got her there, he took what money she had in her purse, then made her go down on him. If his primary intent had been merely to rob her, wouldn't he have done it when he robbed her companion? The only reason for taking her back to his car was for the head job. How can you justify a death penalty in Whitman's case and then not even *ask* for it in the case of these five defendants?"

"Well, first of all, Mr. Cloud," Klein said, stiffening, "I'm not attempting to justify anything; I don't have to. The policy of the district attorney's office is to ask the court for the maximum sentence which it feels a judge or jury will allow—"

"Who decides when to go for the limit and when not to? Who makes the decision to send Weldon Whitman to the Death House and then says that five rapist punks will only go to jail?"

"The facts decide that for us, Mr. Cloud." Klein's voice had now turned very cool and his face had lost its amiable expression. "The facts of the crime tell us what we have to prove. The facts of the evidence tell us what we *can* prove."

"Well, I'm no lawyer, Mr. Klein," Cloud said flatly, "but I do deal in facts. And from the facts I've read in this case, it seems to me that it would be just as proper for you to ask for death sentences for these five as it was to ask for death sentences for Weldon Whitman. That naturally makes me wonder why you aren't doing it, Mr. Klein. It makes me wonder if perhaps there might not be some truth in a statement Whitman made just before he was convicted."

"What statement was that?" Klein asked crisply.

"A statement to the effect that he was being persecuted by your office, the county sheriff's office, and the city police department, because he had spit in your faces so many times."

"That's absurd."

"Is it, Mr. Klein?" Cloud could feel anger building up inside him—anger at a system of justice that had such a flexible code of selectivity.

Cloud stared relentlessly at the man who had put Weldon Whitman on Death Row. Whatever Whitman had done, he had not committed murder. But this man Klein and the office he represented *would* have committed murder if the state executed Whitman in the gas chamber. Legal murder, to be sure. But murder all the same, if only because they had *arbitrarily* selected him for the gas chamber.

And that, he decided, was how he would write the story.

"You'll have to excuse me now, Mr. Cloud," the prosecutor said, not bothering to conceal his hostility. "Court is about to convene."

Yes, Cloud thought, it is.

That night, in Laurel's apartment, Cloud let her read a carbon of the story he had filed for the morning editions. Comparing the Whitman and Black Jacks cases, the story was a scathing denouncement of the ethics of the district attorney's office.

"What do you think?" he asked when she had finished.

Laurel shook her head. "I don't know, Rob. It's very well written, of course, like everything you do, but . . ."

"But what?"

"Well, it—it doesn't really read like what you ordinarily find in a newspaper. It's more like—well, like an *argument* rather than a newspaper story."

"That's what Hoskins asked for; I told you that. He said he wanted something creative, something with a point of view—"

"Yes, but you also said he was interested in a possible series of articles on motorcycle gangs. Most of what you've written is about your friend Weldon Whitman and why he's been sentenced to the gas chamber and these five men won't be."

"Exactly. That's the whole point of it." Cloud rose from the couch and paced the room. "Here we have five guys who have committed crimes almost identical to the crimes for which Whitman was convicted and sentenced to death. Sure, there are slight legal difference in the particular acts, but basically they're the same crimes: robbery, kidnapping, and what the state calls sex perversion. Now, Whitman is convicted and gets the death sentence—*two* death sentences, to be exact. But with these five punks, for the same crimes, the state doesn't even *ask* for the death penalty. The state puts them on trial for sex perversion and for rape. They don't even charge them with robbery, much less kidnapping. Why? What's the big difference?"

Laurel shrugged.

"I'll tell you," said Cloud. "There are five defendants in this trial instead of one. One man getting the death penalty on this kind of kidnapping charge the public might let slide past; but five—never. There'd be more committees and organizations and movements to save them than this town ever saw before. There'd be petitions and letters to the editor and pickets around the Hall of Justice and everything else. And at the next election there'd be a new district attorney, and the present district attorney—*and* his chief prosecutor—would be out of jobs. So the first reason is that the people in the district attorney's office are afraid they couldn't get away with it!

"The second reason," Cloud's voice rose slightly, "is even worse than the first. And it's so damned obvious! They aren't trying to put these Black Jacks in the gas chamber because they've got no *reason* to. These five guys are clean; except for a few traffic violations. So the law isn't out to get them like it was out to get Whitman. The city police and the county sheriff—neither one gives a damn that the Black Jacks will get ten years each and be out on parole in four. With Whitman though—he was an habitual criminal, a *defiant* habitual criminal. You should read some of the things in that manuscript of his. He'd tell the police to go fuck themselves and spit in their faces every time they arrested him. He was a complete rebel; he never confessed, never informed, never pled guilty to anything, never let the public defender handle his cases. He was strictly an outlaw, confirmed all the way; he was against all police officers and wasn't about to be rehabilitated out of the idea. Since he was fifteen he's been laughing at everybody in this county with a badge. *Laughing* at them. *That's* why they put Weldon Whitman in the death house."

"It sounds like he's some kind of criminal psychopath," Laurel said. "Maybe the court was right; maybe he *should* be permanently removed from society."

"Maybe he should," Cloud agreed. "I don't deny that he's probably criminally unstable. But he could be locked up permanently if all the law wants to do is protect society. He sure as hell doesn't have to be sent to the gas chamber, particularly for the same thing that those five punks from Long Beach are only going to serve a few years in prison for."

Laurel sighed heavily. "I still don't see how your story fits what Hoskins asked for. I just don't think it's what he had in mind."

"Maybe not," Cloud replied, "but that's what he's getting."

"Which," she said pointedly, "is not the most desirable attitude for one to have toward one's employer."

"Let's not get into a discussion of my attitude," Cloud said caustically.

"Have it your way," Laurel said, her voice growing distinctly cool. She drummed her fingers on the arm of the chair. "Would you like more coffee before you go?"

"Go? I wasn't going anyplace. Or is that your subtle way of asking me to leave?"

"You don't appear to be in a very good mood tonight. I thought maybe you'd prefer to be alone. That way there'd be no occasion for you to have to listen to anything critical about yourself."

Cloud looked thoughtfully at her for a moment. He got up, got his coat from the hall closet and left the apartment without either of them saying goodnight.

"Hoskins wants you."

Surprise, surprise, thought Cloud. He already knew that his story, as he had written it, had not appeared in the home edition that morning. Instead, on page five, had been a rewritten account covering only the basic facts of the Black Jacks trial. So Laurel had been right: the story *hadn't* been what Hoskins had wanted.

"You wanted to see me?" Cloud said pausing at the day editor's open door.

"Yes," Hoskins said. "Come in. Close the door."

Hoskins's voice, Cloud thought, seemed mellower, less threatening than usual. Maybe, it occurred to Cloud, he was about to be fired.

"Sit down, sit down." Hoskins waved his cigar at a chair and proceeded to rummage through the clutter on his desk. In a moment he found the original of Cloud's story.

"I suppose you know by now that we didn't run this piece of yours as you wrote it," Hoskins said. "And I suppose you're wondering why."

Cloud shrugged. "I guess you didn't run it because you didn't like it."

"On the contrary, I did like it. Liked it very much." Hoskins puffed several times on his cigar, then delicately balanced it on the edge of an ashtray. "It's well written, well organized, and makes a good, hard point. Unfortunately, it doesn't adequately cover the subject that was assigned to you. I wanted some in-depth coverage on the trial of the five Black Jack members—something interesting about the five punks themselves. I wanted the interest to spring not only from the fact that they are defendants in a rape trial, but also that they are members of an organized motorcycle gang. Instead"—Hoskins tossed the typed article back into the debris of his desk—"you give me a hearts-and-flowers thing about this guy Whitman, who's not even news anymore."

"He *could* be news," Cloud said. "He would be, too, if you'd printed the story the way I wrote it." Now, he thought defiantly, go ahead and fire me.

"If I had run that story the way you wrote it, son, we'd both be out of a job this morning. Did you ever hear of a little thing called editorial policy?"

"What's that got to do with it? I didn't write an editorial, I wrote a news story."

"Like hell you did." Hoskins retrieved the typed story and shoved it across the desk at him. "That's no more a news story than Orphan Annie is a news story. There isn't a single fact that you didn't elaborate on with a personal comment or opinion of your own." Hoskins picked up his cigar and slowly shook his head. "You wrote an editorial, my boy, pure and simple."

"All right, suppose I did," Cloud countered. "You said it was good, didn't you? You said it made a good, hard point. Why didn't you use it on the editorial page?"

"Because," Hoskins said tonelessly, "you are not the publisher of this newspaper. And neither am I. As a consequence of which it is neither your function nor mine to make editorial policy. The editorial page on this newspaper comes from the office of the publisher. He's the one who pays our salaries, and he's the one who establishes editorial policy."

"What do you think the publisher's editorial policy would be in this particular case?" Cloud asked.

"I don't even *have* to think," Hoskins answered confidently. "I *know* what it would be. Because of past and present political affiliations, and because this paper strongly backed the district attorney in the last election, the publisher would need just two short words to express his editorial policy to both of us: *Hands Off.*"

"Are you saying that this newspaper would avoid exposing a scandal in one of our highest county offices just because it supported the successful candidate for that office?"

"No," Hoskins replied coolly, "I am not saying that and you goddamn well know it. If you came up with a story in which you had clearly established some sort of conspiracy or some pattern of incompetence within the district attorney's office, then the story would be printed—editorial policy or not—because then it would be news. *News,* Cloud; not speculation, not conjecture, not supposition, assumption, theory, or even divine hypothesis—but *news:* factual, verifiable news."

Hoskins leaned far back in his chair. He sucked in on his cigar and exhaled a great burst of dirty gray smoke. For several long moments he studied Cloud. His eyes grew thoughtful as he recalled another eager young reporter from out of the long ago, another young writer filled with energy and enthusiasm, another young man seeking truth above all and placing his heart and soul at the altar of the press. Hoskins wondered briefly if this young man too would age eventually into a cantankerous old day editor. He sighed wistfully.

"Well," he said at last, "have I now made absolutely clear in your mind my position regarding editorial policy on this newspaper?"

"You have." Cloud stood up. "Is that all?"

"For now," Hoskins told him.

Cloud started out of the office. At the door he paused and turned back.

"What you said a few minutes ago, about Weldon Whitman not being news anymore; you're wrong about that. Someday I'll prove it to you."

He walked out of the office and across the big newsroom, winding his way around crowded desks, passing through the noise of two dozen typewriters, moving past the many faces of people who, like himself, were part of the putting together of a daily metropolitan newspaper. But as he walked he heard none of the noise and noticed none of the faces, because his mind was enclosed within the vacuum of the single thought he had just spoken to Hoskins.

Someday I'll prove it to you.

Eight

A month later, Cloud was on his couch, hunched over the coffee table, pages of *Room 22, Hotel Death* spread all around him, when the telephone rang. Goddammit, he thought immediately. He wondered if it was the paper, calling him in on some emergency assignment. It rang again. It wouldn't be Laurel; this was Monday, her counseling day. The phone rang a third time. Goddammit, he thought again, and snatched up the receiver.

"Hello—"

"Hello, is this Mr. Robert Cloud? Of the *Ledger?*" It was a woman's voice.

"Yes, this is Robert Cloud—"

"Mr. Cloud, you don't know me. My name is Genevieve Neller. We have a mutual friend who asked me to call you: Weldon Whitman."

For a moment Cloud was too surprised to speak.

"I don't know if Weldon has mentioned me to you or not, Mr. Cloud," she continued. "I'm director of the state law library up at Sacramento. I've been sending Weldon law books—"

"Oh, yes," Cloud said. "Yes, as a matter of fact, Weldon did tell me about you. He said you had been kind enough to do some legal research for him."

"It wasn't much, really."

"It was to him, Miss Neller. I'm sorry; is it Miss or Mrs.?"

"It's Miss, but please call me Genevieve. When I told Weldon in my last letter that I was coming down here, he wrote back and said to be sure and give you a call—"

"You're in Los Angeles?"

"Yes. There was a library-science convention here. It just ended today." She paused. "When did you hear from Weldon last?"

"Friday," Cloud said. "He sent me some more pages of the book we're—"

"Yes, he told me he was writing a book. I really don't see how he does it all: studying law, preparing an appeal, writing a book."

They fell silent for a moment.

"When are you going back to Sacramento?" Cloud asked.

"Tomorrow," Genevieve Neller said. "I drove down; I'll be starting back early in the morning."

"Are you free this evening?" Cloud had a sudden urge to meet this woman who, like himself, was trying to help Weldon Whitman stay alive.

"Why, yes, I am," she answered.

Cloud glanced at his watch: seven-thirty. "Have you had dinner yet?"

"No, I was just about to when I thought of calling you."

"Why don't we have dinner?" Cloud suggested.

"All right. But nothing fancy," she said. "There's a nice restaurant right here at the motel—the Warren, on Olympic Boulevard."

"I can be there in twenty minutes," Cloud said.

"Good. Why don't we just meet there? That way we can be informal and relax."

"Fine with me," Cloud said.

"This is very nice, our being able to get together like this," Genevieve Neller said.

They were sitting in a small booth; the waitress had brought them coffee and they had ordered steaks and fries.

"We're really members of a pretty exclusive club, you and I," said Cloud. "I don't think Weldon has any friends at all besides us."

"I *know*," she said enthusiastically. "That's why I'm so glad we were able to meet."

Genevieve Neller was a slightly overweight woman in her early thirties. She had lustrous brownish hair above a face that, because of its plumpness, was an accentuated heart-shape with a pert, pointed chin. Her smile was radiant but a little hesitant—perhaps, Cloud thought, due to shyness or self-consciousness because of her weight. Cloud liked her immediately.

"Tell me about Weldon," she said eagerly. "I have my own impressions from his letters, of course, but I'd like to know what he's really like, in person."

Cloud smiled. "Why don't you tell me first what your impressions are?"

"All right." She leaned forward with her elbows on the table, and put both hands around her coffee cup. "I think first of all that he's an extremely intelligent man."

"He is that," Cloud assured her.

"I think he's probably hardheaded and stubborn."

"Definitely."

"And," she said very slowly, "I also get the distinct impression that he is a very frightened person."

"I think you're right." Cloud smiled. "He'd probably disown both of us if he could hear us right now."

"I'm sure he would," Genevieve agreed. "He sounds in his letters as if he has a great deal of pride and self-confidence, and yet—I don't quite know how to put it—but I seem to sense from some of the things he writes that all he's really looking for is someone to give him a *chance*."

Cloud stared at her. There it was, he thought. There was the elusive attraction that had drawn him to Weldon Whitman. Suddenly Genevieve Neller's words made it all so very clear, made it so obvious that it was hard to believe he had not understood it all along. The *something* about Weldon Whitman that had pulled Cloud to him like a magnet—and apparently Genevieve also—was that he *did* need a chance. And no one had been willing to give him one.

No one except Robert Cloud. And now Genevieve Neller.

"I'd like to ask you a question," Genevieve said, "and I hope you'll give me an honest answer. Do you think he's guilty?"

"Of some of the crimes, yes," Cloud said. "But I don't think he committed the sex crimes, the so-called Spotlight Bandit crimes. I don't believe he's a sex pervert. And I don't believe he deserves to be sent to the gas chamber."

"I certainly don't either," she said emphatically. "I've researched the kidnapping-with-bodily-harm law all the way back to its inception, and the clear intent of it was to provide the death penalty in cases where a person was kidnapped for ransom, and was subsequently either killed or seriously injured in some way. The extortion of the ransom is technically a robbery; that's how the phrase 'kidnapping for the purpose of robbery' came to be used. And that's what has given prosecutors the loophole to file capital charges when ordinarily they wouldn't be able to. If that section of the Criminal Code had used the proper phraseology—'kidnapping for the purpose of *ransom*'—then the law couldn't be applied as promiscuously as it is today."

They mometarily suspended their conversation as the waitress served their dinner and replenished their coffee.

"These French fries are the last thing in the world I need,"

Genevieve said when the waitress was gone. "I wish I had thought to ask for cottage cheese instead."

"Let me order you some—"

"No, I'll eat the fries. I mean, I *like* French fries; with my weight I just don't need them."

As they began eating, Genevieve asked Cloud to tell her what Weldon Whitman looked like.

"He's an average-looking sort of guy, I guess," said Cloud. "Tall, dark-haired, dark-eyed. His nose is kind of crooked; I think it's been broken. But on the whole, he's not bad looking."

"I've tried to visualize him a dozen times," Genevieve said. "He's told me a little about himself in his letters; personal things, you know. And every time he tells me something new, my picture of him changes. At first, I thought of him as being very handsome; I'm an incurable romantic—" She patted Cloud's hand as she said that and gave him another of her brilliant smiles. "But then," she quickly went on, "I changed that concept of him when he told me he'd always felt awkward with girls, which was one of the reasons he'd never married—"

Cloud almost interrupted her at that point, to say that she was mistaken, that Weldon Whitman *had* been married at one time. But he quickly checked himself. He wondered why Weldon had lied to the woman. Perhaps it was simply Whitman's way of protecting his ex-wife.

"You know," Genevieve continued, "it's a very strange feeling for a woman to know that she's literally the only woman in a man's life. I mean, if you stop to think of it, Weldon has no contact at all with any other woman on the face of the earth. Does he?"

"No, I don't suppose he does," Cloud said, although he really was not sure at all. For all he knew, Whitman could be writing to a dozen women—or at least as many as his writing privileges permitted.

"Do you realize," she said speculatively, "that there may not be another woman in the entire world who can say that about herself?"

"It's a unique position, all right," Cloud agreed. He saw that she had finished her dinner, but still appeared to be hungry. "Would you like something else?" he offered.

"Heavens, no! Listen, I want to get your opinion on something." She reached over and helped herself to several of his French fries. "I belong to several clubs in Sacramento, mostly ladies' clubs: library groups, literary groups, that sort of thing. I was wondering what Weldon would think if I brought up his case as a topic for discussion at some of the various meetings?"

"For what purpose?" Cloud asked.

"I'm not really sure," she said. She reached for more French fries. Cloud pushed the plate toward her. "Thank you. I think I have it in the back of my mind to see if I can't enlist some additional help for him. Perhaps in the form of financial assistance, perhaps political or legal support; a lot of the ladies have very influential husbands. Do you think Weldon would mind?"

Does a fish mind water? Cloud thought. "I don't think he would mind at all," he said.

"I thought I might even try to form some kind of separate club, sort of a 'Help Weldon Whitman' sodality."

Cloud nodded. "Why don't you call it 'Save Whitman'?" he suggested.

"That's an excellent idea!" Genevieve said, beaming. "It has much more of a dramatic ring to it, much more urgency."

She ate the last of Cloud's French fries. They lingered over their third cups of coffee for a while, and then Genevieve decided she had better return to her room.

"I haven't even started packing, and I do want to get an early start tomorrow. I'm going to try to be on the road by six."

Cloud paid the check and walked to her room with her.

"It's nice that we were able to get acquainted," Genevieve said. They walked down a long, lighted sidewalk in front of an evenly spaced row of room doors. "Let's agree to keep in touch."

"Okay. Good idea," said Cloud.

"Let's write each other once a month. I'll tell you how the 'Save Whitman' club is doing, and you tell me how the book is coming along."

"It's a deal."

At her room, Genevieve unlocked the door and turned to

say goodbye. "I'm awfully glad you're Weldon's other friend," she said quietly. She reached up and kissed him on the cheek. "Goodbye, Robert."

"Goodbye, Genevieve."

When she was safely inside, he started back up the long, lighted sidewalk.

Cloud was halfway back to the front of the motel when one of the room doors opened in front of him and Laurel stepped out. She was followed immediately by a tall, well-groomed man of about forty. The man pulled the door closed behind him. He slipped his arm around Laurel's waist and they turned toward a late-model Cadillac parked facing the room. As they turned, Laurel saw Cloud standing there staring at them.

"Rob—"

She spoke only the one word, then her breath seemed to catch. Her eyes, which had widened, filled with a bewildered hurt. Cloud continued to stare at her, saying nothing. After a moment, Laurel swallowed and forced an awkward introduction.

"Uh, Rob, this is Ralph Blevins, a friend of mine. Ralph, this is Robert Cloud, a—a friend of mine too—"

Blevins, who had noted the incredulous expression on Cloud's face, as well as Laurel's discomposure, nodded, but had the good sense not to offer his hand.

"We were—just leaving, Rob," she said nervously. "Can we—can we drop you somewhere?"

Cloud forced words past his lips. "No. No, thank you."

"Well, we'll be running along then—" She pulled on Blevins's hand.

"Nice meeting you, Cloud," said Blevins, his manner strained.

"Goodnight," Cloud managed to say. He resumed walking past the row of doors. When he heard the Cadillac's engine turn over, he stopped and looked back to watch them drive off. He stood there for several minutes after they were gone, his expression blank. His mind quickly consumed the disbelief of the incredible seconds that has just passed, and he accepted the fact that what had happened was real. In its wake, he was stunned.

He started walking again, out to the street and down to the

corner bus stop. The bus came and he got on. It was a late-night bus: starkly lighted, nearly empty. He sat near the middle by a window that was open.

The lies, he thought: all the lies. School counseling on Monday and Thursday nights. Because she needed the extra money. And the part about being a virgin—

Why, he wondered, had she done it? Not why had she gone to a motel with Nevins or whatever his name was; but why had she bothered with him, Cloud? He obviously was not what she was looking for in a man: he was not stable enough for her, did not have enough ambition to suit her, did not dress exactly right, never seemed to have his hair properly trimmed, chewed his fingernails—he was biting them now, as a matter of fact—and on top of everything else he was now mixed up in this Weldon Whitman matter. Why in the hell did she take up with him in the first place? Why, when someone like Nevins was interested in her? He certainly looked like the kind of man Laurel would like; he looked successful, tailored, poised.

He sighed heavily and looked out the open window at the quiet night passing by. Fuck this town, he thought. He had had it with Los Angeles. Had it with the *Ledger.* Had it with Hoskins. Had it even with Lew Lach and his sick thing about young dead girls.

And now he had had it with Laurel too.

Time to hang it up and hit the road. Again.

When the bus came to his stop, Cloud got off and walked the three blocks to his apartment building. In the foyer, he picked up his mail: a couple of advertisements and an envelope from Whitman. Fairly thick: about five or six sheets of paper, he guessed. More pages for *Room 22, Hotel Death*.

Cloud went up to his apartment, let himself in, and tossed the Whitman envelope onto his coffee table. That was where he had his typewriter set up, where he worked on the book. The typewriter was in the center of the long table. To the left of the typewriter were two neat stacks of paper: the handwritten sheets of lined prison tablet on which Whitman was writing his story and Cloud's blue-lined yellow sheets. To the right, on the arm of the couch, were an ashtray, his cigarettes, and a small box containing typewriter erasers, black and red ballpoints, typewriter correction paper, and a scratchpad.

It was an ideal work area for him, and as he stood looking at it now, it became the only part of the little apartment that suddenly did not take on a depressing quality. Everything else was too quickly and easily associated with Laurel: the kitchenette where they had often cooked together; the bedroom where they lounged on the bed to watch Sunday-afternoon movies; the big recliner in the living room where he would lie naked while she ministered to him in whatever way she decided to—

Cloud shook his head. The apartment, like the job and the girl and everything else, had gone stale. He decided to pull the pin, right then and there. He rolled a sheet of paper into the typewriter and typed a quick note to his landlady: he was moving out of town; she could dispose of the groceries he was leaving behind. He folded the note and put it in his inside coat pocket.

In the bedroom, he took his two-suiter from the closet and packed his meager wardrobe into one side of it. In the bathroom, he put all his shaving gear and accessories in a zippered case and tossed it into the suitcase too. Then he took the bag into the living room and laid it open on the couch. He locked his typewriter in its case and neatly boxed up the various stacks of paper; everything fit neatly into three single-ream boxes. He packed them into the other side of the suitcase. He was about to close it when his apartment buzzer sounded.

Cloud frowned and looked at his watch. Twenty past midnight. He walked over and opened the door.

"Rob, can I come in, please?" Laurel's voice sounded hoarse; her eyes were red and slightly swollen.

Cloud let her in and closed the door behind her. He followed her into the living room. She saw his suitcase and typewriter. She turned to him, anguish etched in her face.

"That isn't necessary, Rob."

"I think it is." His voice was quiet, without rancor.

Laurel bit her lip. "Let me tell you about Ralph—"

"I'm not interested in Ralph." He really was not.

"Well then let me tell you about *me*," she pleaded. "Let me at least explain how I got caught up in the damned situation—"

"Laurel, it won't do either of us any good for you to go into a long involved explanation of your personal life—"

"It might," she said. "It might make you reconsider this . . ."

"It wouldn't," he assured her. "I've made up my mind to go."

"Rob, listen," she said, but then her hoarse voice broke. She turned away, biting her knuckle. "Damn, damn, damn! I knew it would be like this!" She snatched a crumpled tissue from her coat pocket and dabbed at her nose. "Would you mind if I made some coffee? My throat feels like sandpaper."

"Go ahead."

She left the room. Cloud straightened the things in his suitcase, then sat down in the space remaining on the couch and lighted a cigarette. Laurel returned in several minutes with two mugs of instant coffee.

"I didn't know if you wanted any or not—"

"I do," he said, taking one of the mugs. "Thanks."

Laurel sat in a chair opposite him. She took several brief, steaming sips of her coffee. "God, that feels good." Looking over at Cloud, she found him staring at her. "Do you feel that I've cheated you, Rob?"

"I'm not sure," he said. "I know I'm depressed because you lied to me."

"About being a virgin?"

Cloud nodded. "That, and the lies about your doing counseling work on Monday and Thursday nights."

"Rob, I don't know why I told you that lie about me being a virgin. It was just crazy, it was—I don't know—*dumb.* I did it because I liked you and I didn't want you to think I was just *ordinary.* I wanted you to think I was special in some way, and that was the first thing that came to mind. Can you understand that?"

"Sure," Cloud said. "I can understand anyone telling a lie. What I can't understand is a person *living* a lie."

"I didn't intend to, Rob, believe me I didn't." She sat forward in the chair, as if putting herself a few inches closer to him would make her story more credible. "I wanted to tell you so many times; God, Rob, you'll never know how many migraines I gave myself worrying about it. But the longer I put it off, well, finally I reached the point where I just *couldn't.*" She was looking at him with frank, wide eyes. "I couldn't *make* myself tell you, even when I wanted you to fuck me so badly that I actually ached for it."

"I did a little aching myself," Cloud reminded her.

"I know. I know." She put her coffee aside and knelt in front of him, tears starting down her cheeks. "Rob, I'm so mixed up, I can't even think straight. I've never had anything; my life, the people I came from, everything I can remember, was always drab and dull. We were on welfare half the time, moving from one place to the next the other half. You wouldn't believe what I was like at fifteen, Rob—" She shuddered involuntarily. "It wasn't until I left, until I was able to work my way through college and get my teaching certificate, that I finally got to see a little sunlight in all that goddamn gloom. Later, when I met Ralph, I was just so taken with him that he literally overwhelmed me. For the first time I was being paid attention to by a man who was *clean*. I mean clean all over: fingernails, breath, no dandruff, no body odor, just clean. He wasn't dirt poor, he wasn't a little kid college boy, he wasn't an insecure young teacher just starting out; he was *some*body, he had substance, he had—had—"

"Money," Cloud said. "That's what it all comes down to, isn't it? Money. Success. The ability to *buy*."

"Maybe it is, Rob—"

"Sure it is. That's the reason you let him ball you, because he had it all: the money, the clothes, the big car. I didn't have those things, so I got played with a little; but you couldn't quite bring yourself to let me have it all, because I didn't meet your standards."

She shook her head, tears streaming. "If I didn't care for you, do you think I would have bothered at all?"

"You cared for me, sure. Enough to try and make me over. But not enough to give me the same thing you were giving Ralph."

"Only because I didn't know *how*, Rob," she pled tearfully. "After telling you I was a virgin, I didn't know how to tell you I *wasn't*." She gripped his knees desperately. "Rob, do you believe that I care for you?"

Cloud stared at her anguished face for a moment. He wanted to say no, but he could not. "Yes," he answered simply.

She quickly got up and took his hands. "Prove you believe me. Come to bed with me now."

"After he's just been in you? You can go to hell, Laurel."

She looked away from him. "He wasn't," she told him. "I blew him tonight."

Cloud stood up. His jaw clenched. He slapped her hard across the face, knocking her six feet away from him. For an instant it appeared that she was going to fall, but she did not. She raised her hand and touched her cheek; it was fiery red from his blow. She did not utter a sound; and, oddly, her tears suddenly stopped. Looking directly into his eyes, locking them with hers, she calmly began taking off her clothes.

Cloud did not take his eyes from hers, but in his peripheral vision he watched her gradually become naked. The sweater was discarded first. The skirt, shoes, pantyhose, satin panties, all fell away, leaving her nude except for the low-cut bra that barely covered her nipples.

"He hasn't been in me tonight, Rob." She turned and walked into the bedroom.

Cloud followed her. He stood at the foot of the bed looking down at her as he took off his clothes. She spread her legs for him to see, and folded her arms under her breasts, making them nearly burst from their bra.

"I want it in me so bad, Rob. I've wanted it in me for so long—"

"I know," he said. He climbed onto the bed between her legs. "I want to put it in you just as bad—" He pulled her bra straps down on each arm and uncovered her breasts. They were tight and hard-nippled. Bending over her, he sucked first the left nipple, then the right, as he began working himself into her.

Cloud started his intercourse with her with his arms braced stiffly on each side of her, holding his upper body above her so that he could look down at her beautiful, oddly unmoving tits, or lower his head and see down between their bodies where they joined; then he let himself down on top of her, turning his lips to her neck while he changed from a thrusting motion to a back-and-forth countermotion that caused him to rub around inside her; and finally when he was ready to come, he pulled her legs up and slid back and up, spreading his knees on each side and just under her buttocks to raise her just enough to allow him maximum leverage into her body. He worked slowly, very slowly, toward the end, and when he came, he came slowly and deliciously and for what seemed like a long time.

They rested side by side when it was over, Cloud on his back looking up at the ceiling, Laurel on her side facing him, one cheek against his shoulder, one breast against his elbow.

"Was it good, Rob?" she asked.

"Yes."

"It's yours from now on, Rob. You can have it any time you want it."

Cloud said nothing.

"Can we start over, Rob?" she asked after a moment. Her eyes were closed and she was beginning to sound sleepy.

"I don't know, Laurel," he answered. "I don't know if we can or not."

She said nothing more for a little while. Then she said, very sleepily, "I hope we can, Rob. I hope we can start over."

Cloud waited. When he was sure she was asleep, he carefully slipped his arm away from her cheek and breast and got out of bed. He spread the covers over her, gathered up his clothes, and went back into the living room. It was nearly three o'clock. He smoked a cigarette while he sat naked and thought about what Laurel had asked him. By the time he finished the cigarette, he had made up his mind.

When he was dressed, he left the note for his landlady, picked up his suitcase and the portable typewriter, and quietly left the apartment.

Three hours later, when Genevieve Neller came out of her motel room, Cloud was leaning up against her car with his luggage at his feet.

Nine

Less than a week after he arrived in Sacramento, Cloud borrowed Genevieve Neller's car and drove up to San Quentin to see Weldon Whitman again. In the visiting room, he sat in the same middle chair. When Whitman stepped out of the elevator, he looked paler to Cloud, though he did not appear unhealthy.

Whitman smiled his familiar smile and sat down. "Hello, Rob. I got a letter from Genevieve Saturday saying you were living up in Sacramento now. What'd you do, quit the paper down in L.A.?"

Cloud nodded. "I had some differences with the management."

Whitman smiled, amused. "Tried to buck the establishment, huh?" He lighted a cigarette. "What are you going to do now? Work for one of the papers at the capital?"

"What would you think about me working for you full time?"

Whitman grunted. "Are you independently wealthy? Or did you want me to teach you how to stick up liquor stores?"

"I'm serious," Cloud said. "What I want to do, Whit, is write about you." He leaned forward. "Look, *Hotel Death* is at least six months away from being ready to show to a publisher. The rewriting takes a couple of hours' work a day. With my surplus time, I thought I'd start a series of magazine articles on you. If I get a magazine—maybe even several magazines—interested in your case, it might go a long way toward helping you. The articles would get you in the public eye outside of California, and that would build up some interest in the book—and give me some money to finish the book."

Whitman nodded. "What do you need from me?"

"Permission to do the articles, and cooperation in obtaining information about your case."

"You've got it," Whitman said without hesitation. "The permission and the cooperation."

"Great." Cloud nodded and sat back. "The first thing I want to do is decide on the approach. Do we take the approach that you *may* be guilty, but even if you are you don't deserve the death penalty? Or do we go strictly on the basis that you're innocent?"

"Which way would do me the most good?" Whitman asked.

"In the long run, Whit, the way that's going to work best for you is telling the truth. You can't sell a lie indefinitely; the public always catches up with somebody who tries to hustle them. If you want the public to come onto your side and help you, you're going to have to level with them."

"So you want me to tell you whether I'm guilty or not, right?"

"That's about what it comes down to."

The condemned man stared long and hard at Cloud, weighing his total evaluation of him back to the day they first met. Whitman's expression never changed, but his pupils dilated slightly as he seemed to try to decide what, and just how much, to tell Cloud. Cloud did not squirm under Whitman's cold appraisal; he merely sat and watched the condemned man's eyes unblinkingly. But all the time he was silently imploring: *Come on, Whit. Trust somebody. Just once.*

"All right," Whitman said at last, his voice habitually lowering. "I'll level with you. I'll lay it out for you, and you can handle it whatever way you want. But there are a couple of things that will have to be on *my* terms. Agreed?"

"Agreed."

Weldon Whitman swallowed hard and leaned forward with both elbows on the divided counter. He put his hands on each side of his mouth to cup his words. "I pulled the burglary and all the robberies except the Calder and Luza jobs. And the stolen car; I didn't do that either. The car was grabbed by the guy who was the lookout for me when I hit that menswear store. That was the last job before I was busted. I had just dropped this guy off and was on my way to put the car and the hot merchandise in a garage we had rented when the radio car spotted me."

"This guy was somebody you pulled jobs with?"

"Yeah, sometimes. We weren't full-time partners or anything like that. We usually worked alone, but sometimes we threw in together."

"Is he the Spotlight Bandit, Whit?" Cloud asked quietly.

"He could be," Whitman said. "I learned the spotlight gimmick from him. And he's just the kind of asshole who would mix business with sex—dumb stunts like the Calder and Luza jobs."

"Will you tell me who he is, Whit? Let me go after him to clear you?"

The condemned man shook his head emphatically. "Definitely not. That's one thing that will have to be my way. I won't blow the whistle on another guy. If I had wanted to go that route, I could have done it with the cops or the D.A.'s office." Whitman jabbed a stiff forefinger into the palm of his hand. "If I beat the Calder and Luza crimes, it will be because we proved that I was innocent, not that somebody else was guilty. And if you can't go along with that, Rob, we'll have to stop the streetcar right here. I don't fink—period."

"Okay, okay," Cloud said, raising a placating hand. "It's your—" He stopped, realizing what he was about to say.

"You're right," Whitman finished the sentence for him. "It *is* my life. And I've got to live it my way. Besides, if I copped out on this guy, he'd get back at me—hard."

"How? You're better guarded right now than the president."

"There are other ways to get back at a man besides hurting him personally," Whitman said darkly.

Cloud frowned. "Your ex-wife?"

"Let's just say there are ways he could do it, and leave it at that, okay?" Whitman's tone became more irritable. "I thought you promised to forget about my ex-wife. I don't want her involved in this fucking mess, okay?"

Cloud's placating hand came up again. "Sorry I mentioned her."

Both men fell silent for a moment, avoiding each other's eyes. Whitman busied himself putting out his cigarette. Cloud lighted one.

"What's the first article going to be about?" Whitman asked finally, his tone calmer.

"I want to shoot for something dramatic," Cloud said. "Do you remember what I wrote you about Doris Calder and Klein? We could do an article saying that while Klein's relationship with Doris Calder may not have influenced his prosecution, it could well influence the D.A.'s office to oppose any appeals you might file."

Whitman leaned forward, smiling. "How would you like to convince yourself that I didn't pull those particular spotlight jobs?"

Cloud's eyebrows raised in interest. "How?"

"The guy I was telling you about: we did time together in Folsom, used to shower in the same group. Naturally when you shower with a guy often enough, you're bound to notice how he's hung. Well, this ex-partner of mine has never been circumcised, see? He's got enough foreskin to hold a couple of marbles."

Cloud shrugged. "So?"

"So I *have* been clipped, man. And clipped good. Now, I don't know about that Luza kid, she's kind of young so she might not know about things like that; but the Calder broad has been around. She would defintely know a circumcised dick from an *un*circumcised dick—even in the dark. If you could interview her and get her to tell you whether she had to skin that guy's joint back before she sucked him—"

"That wouldn't be easy," Cloud said skeptically. But the idea immediately intrigued him. "Still, she doesn't know me. Klein may have mentioned my name, of course—"

"It's worth a try," Whitman said, "even if it's a long chance. If you could get that broad to make a positive statement—"

"Suppose I do?" Cloud said. "How do we establish that you *have* been circumcised?"

"I'll petition the Marin County Superior Court to order the San Quentin medical officer to conduct an examination of my dick and attest that I have no foreskin. It's a simple legal move."

Cloud thought about it a moment, then nodded enthusiastically. "Okay. Let's give it a shot."

Before Cloud left that day, Whitman, as casually as possible, said, "Incidentally, we're working against a deadline now. The state Supreme Court affirmed all my sentences. My date has been set for June first."

Cloud nodded slowly. June first. Less than four months away.

Robert Cloud returned to Los Angeles two weeks after he had left. He flew down from Sacramento on a morning commuter flight and checked into the International Hotel across the street from the airport. After quickly unpacking his overnight bag, he dialed the telephone number of Alicia's Style Shoppe, a beauty salon in the South Bay area where Doris Calder worked.

"May I speak to Doris Calder, please?"

A moment later, Doris Calder came on the line.

"Mrs. Calder, I'm a freelance magazine writer in town to collect material for an article on capital punishment," Cloud told her. "I'd very much like to interview you about the Weldon Whitman case. It would only take an hour or so, and I'd be happy to pay you for your time."

"Well, I don't know." Doris Calder's voice was at once scratchy and sensuous. "I haven't given any interviews about what happened, you know. It's not something I like talking about."

"I realize that, Mrs. Calder. That's why I'm offering to pay."

She was silent for a moment. Then: "How much were you thinking of paying?"

"For a short interview, an hour or so, I'd pay a hundred dollars. I'm at the International Hotel, if you could come by after work—"

"Could we do it on my lunch hour?" she asked. "There's a cocktail lounge near here called Bruno's; they don't exactly serve lunch, but you can get a sandwich, and they have cheese bits and such to munch on."

"Sounds fine to me," Cloud said at once. "Why don't you give me the address and I'll meet you there?"

Bruno's was on the edge of the South Bay shopping center. Cloud arrived a few minutes early and got a back booth, away from the jukebox. He sipped a glass of beer slowly as the noon crowd started trickling in. Doris Calder came in at five of twelve, wearing a green nylon beautician's uniform that outlined her excellent figure very nicely. Her blonde hair was styled rather conservatively and she was wearing only a trace of makeup. Cloud got up and went over to her.

"Hello, Mrs. Calder. I'm Robert Cloud."

"Oh, hello. How'd you know it was me?"

"I figured you'd be wearing a beautician's uniform."

As they sat down in the booth, Doris Calder said, "How did you know where to find me anyway?"

"It's in the trial record," Cloud replied truthfully. "Would you like a drink and a sandwich?"

"I shouldn't have a drink at lunchtime, I don't suppose—"

"One won't hurt. What would you like?"

"A vodka martini."

Cloud ordered her drink, their sandwiches, and another beer for himself.

"Which magazine do you work for?" she wanted to know.

"I don't work for one particular magazine," he said. "I'm a freelance writer. I'll do the article and then sell it to whichever magazine wants it."

"Does that mean I don't get the hundred dollars until you sell the story?"

"Not at all. You get the hundred as soon as I get the interview."

"I was hoping you'd say that. For a second I thought maybe you'd got me here under false pretenses."

The waitress brought their sandwiches and drinks. Doris drank half her martini and began to eat. "So interview," she said.

"Okay." Cloud took out a pocket notebook and ballpoint. "You said on the phone that this was not something you liked to talk about. Did you mean that it upsets you emotionally to talk about it, or is it just distasteful to you?"

"Both, I guess. But more distasteful than emotional." She took a sip of her drink. "Aren't you going to eat?"

"Sure." Cloud took a bite of his sandwich. "Now that some time has passed since the incident occurred, do you think the memory of it is fading any? Or is it still constantly on your mind, as you testified at the trial?"

"Well, I wouldn't say it's *constantly* on my mind anymore. I still think about it; just not as much, I guess."

"Do you think you're going to have any permanent psychological problems as a result of what happened?"

She sipped at the martini again and frowned. "I'm not sure I know what kind of problems you mean."

"May I be rather personal with you?"

"Why not?" she said, shrugging. She finished her drink and Cloud signaled for another one.

"What I mean is, do you think you'll be able—or have you already been able—to resume a normal sex life?"

Doris Calder did not answer at once. Cloud waited, sipping at his beer. The cocktail waitress brought Doris Calder's fresh drink.

"Am I being *too* personal?" Cloud asked. "I don't intend to be. I mean, you're obviously a very sophisticated, very attractive woman—"

"You're not getting too personal," she assured him, patting his hand. She sipped at her fresh drink. "I haven't had any problem at all with my sex life, either before *or* after," she said candidly.

Cloud made some illegible marks in his notebook. "Do you still remember Whitman? I mean what he looked like, the sound of his voice, things like that?"

"Sure," she said nonchalantly. "I can even remember how he *smelled*. He smelled kind of woolly, you know what I mean? Did you ever smell wet wool? Well, that's how he smelled, or at least how his clothes smelled. I thought afterward that he might have been wearing a wool shirt; it was kind of cool that evening, and it had been raining earlier. But when I told the police about it, they didn't seem too interested."

"Was there ever any doubt in your mind that it was Weldon Whitman who kidnapped you?" Cloud asked quietly.

Her eyes narrowed suspiciously. "Why would you ask a question like that?"

"No reason," Cloud told her, shrugging it off. "I just want to be able to quote you, that's all."

Doris Calder finished her second drink. "The guy's going to the gas chamber, isn't he? How could it *not* be him?"

"You're right," he said placatingly. He noticed she had finished eating. "Listen, how about another sandwich?" She shook her head. "Okay, just one more drink then and that's all." He signaled the waitress again before she could protest.

"You know what would really help me sell this story?" he said when she was working on her third martini. "If you could give me some little something to put in it that nobody's used before."

"What kind of some little something?" she asked. "You mean like the woolly smell?"

"Yeah, that's it. Only something that you haven't even told the police. Something that might have occurred to you since then."

"I sure as hell don't know what it would be," she said.

"Think about it," Cloud prompted. "You were in the car with him for about twenty minutes, if I remember your testimony right. There must be something that we can use to really personalize this interview—"

Doris Calder drank some more and shook her head. "*You* might be able to think of something, but I sure as hell can't—"

Cloud leaned a little closer to her. "Listen, do you mind if I get personal again?"

"Go ahead. It's your money."

"Suppose I could think of something? Something, well—a little intimate, but something I'm sure no one else has ever asked you—"

"How intimate?" she asked curiously.

"Very intimate," he said, "but not difficult to answer, not if you remember that night as well as you say you do."

"I remember it," she assured him.

"Then tell me something—"

"What?" Doris Calder leaned as close to him as she could. Cloud's next words were a whisper.

"Did you have to skin his penis back before you put it in your mouth?"

For a moment she frowned; then she sat back from Cloud and nodded with sudden, surprising emphasis. "Did I! I'll say I did! That guy had enough foreskin for *two* pricks—oops, excuse my French." She pushed her glass away. "I think I've had a little too much too quick. I've got a color rinse this afternoon that's liable to come out red, white, and blue if I take another single sip." She looked at her watch. "Jesus, it's one already. Time sure flies when you're having fun. Did you get your hundred dollars' worth?"

"Yes, I think so," Cloud said quietly. He gave her an envelope containing a hundred dollars that he and Genevieve Neller had chipped in together.

"Listen, be sure and let me know which magazine the story's going to be in—"

"I will," Cloud promised.

Doris Calder got out of the booth, took a second to steady herself, and headed for the door, turning and saying, " 'Bye," as she left. Cloud nodded and watched her leave.

That settled it: *Weldon Whitman was innocent*.

Cloud began work on his first Whitman article that afternoon, working on his portable typewriter in the hotel room.

The title he gave it was "Is Jealousy Sending This Man to the Gas Chamber?" He set forth all he knew about the relationship between Doris Calder and G. Foster Klein, including Klein's role in her son's case. The implication of the story was clear: it was not impossible that Klein had overzealously prosecuted Weldon Whitman after becoming emotionally involved with one of the leading witnesses against him.

The story further implied that Klein, as an officer of the court obligated to introduce evidence *favorable* as well as damaging to a defendant in a criminal case, would be derelict in his duty if he failed to pursue the irrefutable information obtained from Doris Calder: namely, that Mrs. Calder's assailant was uncircumcised, while Weldon Whitman had been certified as circumcised.

It was a good story; the writing went well. Cloud did ten pages before going downstairs for dinner at six. He was back by seven and was on page sixteen when he heard a knock at the door. He stopped typing. Who in the hell could that be? No one knew he was staying there except Doris Calder—

The knock sounded again. Cloud went to the door. "Yes?"

"Police. Open the door, please."

Cloud opened the door and found G. Foster Klein and two other men in the hall.

"Hello, Cloud," said the dapper little prosecutor. He walked right in, followed by the two men. "Lieutenant Kretz and Sergeant Lowe of the Sheriff's Department. We don't need a warrant to enter, since we have permission of the hotel manager." He turned in the center of the room and faced Cloud. "Understand you're now a freelance magazine writer."

"That's right," Cloud said coolly.

Klein walked over to the desk, looked at the stack of finished pages, and read the title aloud: " 'Is Jealousy Sending This Man to the Gas Chamber?' " His eyebrows went up. He started skimming rapidly—a few lines here, a paragraph there: enough to get the general idea of the piece. Twice he grunted softly, twice he shook his head in amusement, once he paused to look at Cloud in utter disgust. "What a lot of unadulterated bullshit," he said when he finished reading. "You're not seriously thinking of having this printed in a magazine?"

"You bet I am."

Klein snorted. "Why, I could sue for libel eighteen different ways on the basis of this."

"That would be between you and the magazine."

"Which magazine is it?"

Cloud shrugged. "Whichever one will give Weldon Whitman's story the broadest coverage."

"Then you really *are* going through with this insanity?"

"You bet I am."

"Well, we'll see just how far you get," Klein bristled. He began gathering up all the typed pages.

"What the hell do you think you're doing?" Cloud snapped. He started to move toward Klein, but as he did so the two sheriff's detectives stepped in to intercept him. Cloud stopped. "You have no right to take those pages," he said angrily.

"I'm confiscating this story on the ground that I have reasonable cause to suspect that its contents may constitute criminal libel—"

"Talk about unadulterated bullshit!" Cloud snapped. He stepped back and folded his arms defiantly. "Okay, go ahead and take the pages. I can't stop you, not with your two Gestapo men here. But you're not really taking anything, you know. The story's not just on those pages; it's in my head. How do you plan to take that?"

G. Foster Klein looked intently at Cloud. His indignation, so dominant just seconds before, wavered now and dissolved. Despite the bluster, Cloud thought he detected a troubled look in the little prosecutor's eyes.

Klein finally sighed wearily and put the typed pages back down in a neat stack. He turned to the detectives.

"Gentlemen, I wonder if you'd mind waiting for me in the lobby." When they were gone, Klein clasped his hands behind his back and squared his shoulders. "Cloud, I'd like to discuss this matter with you on a man-to-man basis. May I sit down?"

"Go ahead," Cloud said. Klein moved Cloud's typing chair away from the writing desk and sat down. Cloud sat on the edge of the bed.

"Would you mind telling me," Klein said, "why you're so interested in this Whitman matter?"

"Not at all. I think Weldon Whitman is innocent. As a

matter of fact, after talking with your Mrs. Calder this afternoon, I *know* he's innocent."

"Cloud," the lawyer said tolerantly, "let me assure you that Weldon Whitman *is* guilty. There is absolutely no question in my mind that he was properly convicted and that he deserves to go to the gas chamber."

"Mr. Klein, are you aware of what Doris Calder told me today?"

"You mean the circumcision thing? Yes, I know about that. It might interest you to know that she has already repudiated that statement by admitting to me that she might have been, ah—well, remembering someone else's, ah—anatomy."

Cloud got up and walked to the window. "Whether she's repudiated it or not," he told Klein, "it's still going to be a part of my story."

"I wish you'd reconsider that, Cloud." Klein turned in his chair and talked to the younger man's back. "Let me tell you a little about Doris Calder. She's basically an exceptionally *good* person, and by that I mean that she's very kind, very considerate, very generous when it comes to helping people who need help. All this in spite of having had some very bad times, times that have left their mark on her and may often make her seem, well, less sensitive than she really is. She was married to an alcoholic, a man who used to beat her severely; she had a daughter who died in her preteens of leukemia; her son Billy has been a constant problem to her—incidentally, you may be interested in knowing that my office was proved right in not opposing probation for the young man: he has since enlisted in the Marine Corps and distinguished himself in combat in Vietnam. Doris Calder is not some cheap floozy undeserving of your consideration. She has her weak moments; this afternoon you succeeded in encouraging her to drink too much. But on the whole she is a good woman making a genuine effort to improve herself and her position in the community. I hope I can convince you not to do anything to cause her to regress."

Cloud turned and sat back on the windowsill. "I can appreciate your interest in Mrs. Calder," he said quietly, "and I can understand your wanting to help her and protect her. But by the same token, you should appreciate my interest in Weldon Whitman."

"I would, if it were not so grossly misplaced."

"That's a judgment you have no right to make. Klein, you've got to admit that some doubt has been cast on her identification of Weldon Whitman."

"There's always *some* doubt in most criminal cases, Cloud. But by law there must be *reasonable* doubt."

"Don't you think this qualifies?" Cloud challenged.

"That isn't for me to say. Only a judge or a duly impaneled jury can decide something like that."

"It may come to that," Cloud warned. "If there's any way to impeach Doris Calder's testimony, Weldon Whitman will see that it gets done. And I'll help him do it, all the way."

"If that's where your conscience leads you, Cloud, by all means do so. But in the name of decency, man, do it in the courts, through the proper judicial processes, not in some sensationalistic magazine that will distort the thing all out of proportion and cause additional grief to a woman who's already had far more than her share."

"As I said earlier, Mr. Klein, I appreciate your concern for Mrs. Calder. But you keep forgetting the *other* person who's involved in this matter. Weldon Whitman is going through a lot of grief too. And his grief involves life and death."

"Whitman brought all of his grief on himself," Klein said adamantly. "He went out looking for it with a gun in his hand. Look at his record, for god's sake: he's a burglar, an armed robber, a car thief—"

"He admits to being all that," Cloud said. "But the fact remains that he has *not* killed anyone and he does *not* deserve to go to the goddamned gas chamber."

"I will never agree with you on the latter point," Klein said resolutely.

"Then I'm afraid I'll never be able to agree with you on anything," Cloud told him.

The two adversaries stared at each other. Each felt he had conceded to the very limits of compromise. But both realized they were at a standoff.

"It doesn't appear that we're getting anywhere." Klein stood up and straightened his coat. "I'll wait until your story is published; then I'll file a civil action against the magazine and you. In the meantime," he said, removing a folded document from his inside pocket and laying it on the desk, "this is a restraining order prohibiting you from contacting Doris

Calder again for any purpose. The order was requested by Mrs. Calder and has been signed by a judge. If you violate it, you'll be subject to arrest."

"There's no reason for me to violate it," Cloud said. "I got everything I wanted from Doris Calder this afternoon."

G. Foster Klein sighed a weary sigh and shook his head. "Goodnight, Mr. Cloud."

At ten-thirty the next morning, Cloud was in the West Coast editorial offices of *Argus* magazine. The West Coast editor, a tall, hawkfaced man named Ben Droller, had just read Cloud's article for the second time.

"I like it," he said without preliminary. "I'll buy it. Give you five hundred for it."

"I think I should warn you," Cloud said, "that Klein has threatened to sue me and whoever publishes the story."

"Big deal," Droller said. "We've been sued before, will be again. Got two lawsuits pending against us right now. But we didn't name our magazine *Argus* for nothing. Argus was the Greek god with a hundred eyes, who could see in all directions at once. They called him the watchful guardian. That's how we like to think of ourselves: a watchful guardian. If there's even a chance that Whitman is innocent, we'll go with him all the way. How about it? Five hundred dollars."

"There is a condition I have to ask for," Cloud said. "Because of the nearness of Whitman's execution date, it's vital that we get this story before the public as soon as possible. We'd like a guarantee that it'll be used in the next issue."

"Can't be done," said Droller. "The next issue is already printed and waiting for distribution next Tuesday. But I'll tell you what I will do. I'll make it the lead story in the next issue, which comes out in four weeks. Not only that, but I'll use a picture of your condemned man on the cover, and banner the story title right across the front. How's that?"

Cloud smiled. "You've got yourself a deal, Mr. Droller."

"Now I have a condition. I want an option on any follow-up stories you do on Whitman—first look and a chance to outbid any other offers."

"Agreed," Cloud said.

Droller took the manuscript and left the office for a minute. While he was gone, Cloud allowed himself a moment of exhilaration. Wait until Whit and Genevieve hear about this!

Then his smile faded, and a serious, determined expression replaced it. This is the beginning, he thought. This is where it all starts. And it won't stop until Weldon Whitman is free.

Ten

Robert Cloud settled permanently in Sacramento. He rented a small apartment near the state law library so that he could meet with Genevieve as conveniently as possible. It turned out to be a good move, because as they became more and more involved in the Whitman case, they needed to see each other for advice, moral support, and a wealth of other reasons. Before long they were meeting daily.

"Here's a copy of Weldon's appeal on the erroneous transcript issue," Genevieve said one day shortly after Cloud's return from Los Angeles. "I made an extra copy in case you needed it for reference."

"Thanks, I'm glad you did," he said. He thumbed through the lengthy document. "You type it?"

"Yes."

"Nice job." They were in the law library's employee lounge having coffee and rolls on Genevieve's morning break.

"I need this doughnut like Mt. Everest needs more snow," she said, eating away. "Listen, I wanted to tell you that the ladies' auxiliary of the Businessmen's Club has asked me to speak at their Thursday-afternoon meeting."

"That's great! That'll get us some good word-of-mouth publicity."

Genevieve, pleased with herself, flashed her splendid smile. "I expect we'll make a little money out of it too. Normally after I speak, the president indicates that the chair will entertain a motion that a collection be taken for the Save Whitman cause. Then the president starts the ball rolling by contributing five dollars. After that, *everybody* contributes five dollars. Do you know that I've got nearly a thousand dollars in the Save Whitman account already?"

Once a week Genevieve came to his apartment for lunch. They usually ate cheese sandwiches, which both were crazy about, and drank Cokes. While they ate, they talked about *Room 22, Hotel Death;* Genevieve was now proofreading the pages for Cloud.

"What did you think of that part where Whit describes the working over the police gave him after his capture?" Cloud asked. "Does it seem a little strong to you?"

"I'm not sure what you mean by strong," she said. "I think it's well described, particularly the way he tells about the pain he felt. Weldon certainly has a way with words."

Cloud did not bother to tell her that it was *he*, not Whitman, who had the way with words. He was continuing to work enthusiastically on the book, editing, rewriting, editing again, as fast as the handwritten pages arrived from Whitman. And he started a second article for *Argus.* He wanted badly to do a piece on Whitman's unnamed partner; but Whitman still refused to bring him into the case—and Cloud, even if he wanted to, had no way of finding the man without Whitman's help. All Cloud knew about him was that he had done time with Whitman in Folsom—which, without any additional facts, was an impossible lead for him, alone, to follow. Reluctantly, Cloud went on to another subject: the condemned man researching and preparing his own appeal without professional legal advice. Cloud titled the story "The Lawyer of Death Row."

The first *Argus* story caused a sensation when it came out—particularly the part about the obvious difference in penises. *Argus* sold out the issue in five days. People began to discuss Weldon Whitman. A few columnists did pieces on him. Some editorials were written. A lawsuit was filed—by G. Foster Klein, alleging libel. Ben Droller immediately contacted Cloud for a follow-up article, and Cloud sent him "The Lawyer of Death Row." Through all of this, one thing remained unchanged: Weldon Whitman still had a date with the executioner, and that date was only forty-one days away.

"Shouldn't he have heard on the transcript appeal by now?" Cloud asked Genevieve on one of their rare nights out, when they were walking home from a movie.

"Not necessarily," Genevieve explained. "It's getting close, but there's still plenty of time for a stay of execution. You see, besides filing the appeal with the Supreme Court, we've also filed a motion with the district court for a stay of execution. They usually wait a month or so to see if the high court will review the appeal right away; but if it looks like the high court is going to take awhile—as it does in this instance—then the district court will stay the execution until after a ruling on the appeal has been made."

"When do you think he'll hear?" Cloud asked.

"Another week, ten days maybe. I don't think the district court will let it get to within a month of the execution date."

When Cloud saw Genevieve for lunch the following day, he had some news. "I got a call this morning from the editor of the Sacramento *Independent News.* They want an article on you and your Save Whitman efforts for next week's Sunday supplement, and they want me to write it. What do you think?"

Genevieve was unimpressed. "I'd much rather see something on Weldon. He's the one who needs the publicity."

"We can work in quite a bit about Weldon; don't worry about that," he assured her. "What I want you to decide is whether you want to connect yourself that openly with the Whitman cause. Up until now, you've had exposure only to select groups in certain social and educational circles. With an article like this, you'll be opening up to the public at large."

"I don't care about that," Genevieve said. "I am totally committed to this cause. All I want to know is whether it will be good for Weldon."

"Every time we get his name in print our way, it's good for him," Cloud told her.

"Then do the article," she said.

He did, calling it "The Condemned Man and the Librarian." It was the cover story and lead piece in the following week's Sunday supplement. By noon on the day the paper came out, half of Sacramento was talking about the unmarried head librarian at the state law library who was working against the state trying to save a convicted sex-crimes kidnapper from the gas chamber. The newspaper story, like the article in *Argus*, caused a minor sensation.

The next day, Monday, was quiet. But on Tuesday Genevieve Neller received an unexpected visit from the assistant state director of public education.

"That article in Sunday's paper caused quite a stir over at the State House," he said. His name was Lenz and Genevieve had always considered him a decent sort. Pleasant, always helpful with budgets and other matters, he was a career civil servant who always seemed to try to do the right thing. At the moment, however, he appeared distinctly uncomfortable.

"What kind of stir?" Genevieve asked.

"Apparently there have been a number of complaints about your—ah—activities with this Whitman fellow—"

"Complaints from whom?" Genevieve asked, bristling slightly.

"People," Lenz shrugged. "Taxpayers."

"What I do on my own time is not the taxpayers' business unless I break a law of some kind, or violate the moral standards established for state employees. I don't believe I've done either, Mr. Lenz."

"I'm sure you haven't," Lenz said at once. "But Mr. Hardy, in his position as state director of public education, feels that it may *look* as if you had. I wonder if I might ask—strictly for Mr. Hardy's information, of course—how you became involved with this Whitman?"

"I was asked by Mr. Whitman to send him some law books. He explained that he was a condemned man, without funds, attempting to prepare his own legal appeals. Knowing how difficult it was going to be for him, I decided to help by doing some of his legal research here at the library."

"You volunteered then?"

"I suppose so, yes," Genevieve said.

"I don't suppose you're related to Whitman in any way? Eighth cousins or something?"

She shook her head. "As the article pointed out, Mr. Lenz, we've never met. When Mr. Whitman first wrote me, he didn't even know my name; he simply directed his letter to the head librarian. Besides, what difference would it make if we *were* related?"

Lenz cleared his throat and tried not to look embarrassed. "I think that Mr. Hardy is looking for a way to—ah—somehow justify to the public your activities—"

"*Justify!*" The word coursed through Genevieve Neller's mind like a charge of electricity. "Mr. Lenz," she said icily, "please tell Mr. Hardy that what I am doing needs no justification. I am not involved in a Communist plot, or advocating pornography and heroin for teenagers, or even criticizing the operation of state government. All I'm doing is trying to help a fellow human being who has been forsaken by everyone else on the face of the earth except one other person and myself."

"I'm sure Mr. Hardy realizes that," Lenz said quickly. "As I said before, what he is mainly concerned with is appearances."

"Well, I'm very sorry," Genevieve said with pronounced

impatience, "but I have no time for appearances. I have time only for realities."

"Of course. I understand." Lenz stood up. "I—ah—don't suppose you have any immediate plans for terminating your activities with regard to this Save Whitman movement."

"No, Mr. Lenz," Genevieve said firmly, "I do not."

Lenz nodded as if he had expected that answer, and left.

Genevieve told Cloud about it that night. She was incensed that after eleven years of faithful service to the state, the director of public education would attempt to pressure her into abandoning a cause she believed in so wholeheartedly.

"You may have misunderstood this fellow Lenz," Cloud said. "He might not have been suggesting that at all."

"Oh yes he was," she said angrily. "That's *exactly* what he was hinting at. Can you imagine!" She paced across Cloud's living room several times, until he finally took her arm and made her sit down on the couch.

"Even if that was his motive, you shouldn't let yourself get upset like this. Try to calm down."

"I *can't* calm down!" she stormed. "The *nerve* of them to even *try* it!"

Cloud warmed some coffee and brought two cups over to the couch. "Here, drink this and try to relax. Everything will look a lot better tomorrow. A week from now, you won't believe that you got this mad over it."

Cloud was right about the next day: Genevieve was *almost* as mad—but not quite. Thursday was even better, and by Friday she had calmed back down to normal again.

Cloud was at his typewriter at ten on Monday morning when the telephone rang. It was the city editor of the *Independent News.*

"Just got a call from our man at the district court," the city editor said. "Thought you'd like to know. They've granted Whitman's stay to allow the Supreme Court time to review the transcript appeal."

Cloud threw on a jacket and ran the two blocks to the library to tell Genevieve. He found her at her desk, staring vacantly at a single typed sheet of paper on her desk.

"Hey!" Cloud said exuberantly. "Good news! The district court granted the stay—" He stopped and looked closely at her. There was no color in her normally rosy cheeks, and her lips were parted slightly in an expression of incredulity. "Gen, what's the matter?" Cloud asked. Genevieve picked up the sheet of paper.

"The state director of education has formally charged me with dereliction of duty, and the civil service commission has ordered me before its board on Wednesday to answer the charges."

Cloud dropped into a chair facing her. "Dereliction of duty—?" He took the letter from her hand and read it. "What's the purpose of it?" Cloud asked.

"To force me to resign or to have the commission discharge me."

"I thought civil servants couldn't be fired."

"They can't, normally. But the civil service commission can dismiss anyone for certain causes. And dereliction of duty is one."

"Do you think they can prove it?"

Genevieve shrugged. "I don't know, Rob. I won't know until Wednesday." She smiled, but it was not her usual glowing smile. "It's wonderful about Weldon's stay."

"Yes," Cloud said absently. At the moment he was more concerned about Genevieve Neller. Whitman's future was temporarily secure; Genevieve's was in immediate jeopardy.

As he thought about what was being done to the dedicated, sincere woman behind the desk, a cold, vengeful anger began to build up in him. *Dirty bastards,* he thought. *Dirty bastards, all of them.*

On Wednesday at the appointed time, Genevieve Neller was shown into the civil-service commission hearing room. The three commissioners, along with Director of Education Hardy, his assistant Lenz, and a stenographer, were already present.

"Ah, Miss Neller, good morning," said the chairman of the commission, a completely bald man whose head reflected the ceiling fluorescents. He introduced her to his colleagues and then had her sit across the conference table from Hardy and Lenz. The three commissioners sat at a separate table perpendicular to the conference table.

"Please show the hearing called to order at this time," the

chairman said to the stenographer, "and add Miss Neller's name to the list of those present." He faced Genevieve and smiled. "Now then, Miss Neller, you've received our letter and are aware that a charge of dereliction of duty has been filed against you with this commission by your superior, Mr. Hardy. The commission at this time would like to advise you of the procedures that we are required to take, and of your statutory rights during those procedures." The chairman leaned forward and folded his hands judicially. "First of all, you are of course permitted to have an attorney represent you at any and all stages of the proceedings. You may even have an attorney present at this advisory hearing, and if you so desire, we will postpone this hearing and give you time to retain counsel of your choice." He paused and looked at Genevieve. When she did not speak, he said, "Would you like to get an attorney, Miss Neller?"

She shook her head. "No, thank you, I wouldn't."

"Very well then. The next step is to have Mr. Hardy present to this commission and to you a detailed statement of his charge, along with a statement as to exactly how he proposes to prove the charge. After being presented with these statements and after having read them, you may request and we will grant a recess to allow you time to consult with an attorney on the specifics of Mr. Hardy's accusation. Do you understand that?"

"Yes, I do, thank you," Genevieve said.

"All right. If you choose not to recess for the purpose of obtaining counsel at that point, the commission will then ask you if you desire to request a civil-service trial at which Mr. Hardy will be required to prove the allegation he has given against you. If you desire such a trial, you are again permitted to have legal counsel represent you. If you do not request a civil-service trial, then this commission is empowered to render a decision based solely on Mr. Hardy's statements plus any testimony or evidence you wish to present to the contrary. Is all that clear, Miss Neller?"

"Yes," Genevieve answered again.

"Finally," the chairman said, "if we do render a decision adverse to your position, you may retain an attorney at that time and appeal our decision to the Superior Court."

"I understand," Genevieve said. She had the odd feeling

that everyone in the room was staring at her as if she were the corpse at a funeral. "May I see Mr. Hardy's charges, please?" she asked.

"Certainly." Mr. Lenz rose and passed sets of stapled papers to each of the commissioners and to Genevieve.

Her hands trembling slightly, Genevieve read her copy. The allegation was simple and to the point. During a two-month period, Genevieve Neller was known to have addressed eleven separate gatherings of people in support of the Save Whitman Movement. Each of the eleven occasions was known to have taken place during normal work hours on a normal workday. On each occasion, Miss Neller was known to have been away from her job between two and three hours. Inquiry had been made of Miss Neller as to whether it was her intention to continue her activities in behalf of the Save Whitman Movement, and Miss Neller had indicated that such was her intention. In view of her past absenteeism in favor of the Save Whitman Movement, and her apparent decision to continue such conduct, the state director of education felt that Miss Neller was neglecting her duties as state law librarian and would continue to neglect those duties, and therefore recommended her dismissal from that position.

Genevieve finished reading the allegation, swallowed dryly, and glanced briefly at the statement of proposal of proof submitted with the charge. In it, Hardy indicated that he would subpoena the chairwomen of each of the eleven groups before which Genevieve had spoken, to prove the dates and times as well as the lengths of the meetings, and would offer the sworn testimony of his assistant, Harold Lenz, as to Miss Neller's statement that she intended to continue her activities in the same pattern.

How neat and tidy, Genevieve thought. How very neat and tidy.

"Have you finished reading the allegations, Miss Neller?" the chairman asked.

"Yes," Genevieve said quietly, placing the set of papers on the table before her.

"Do you desire to request a postponement of further proceedings to allow you to confer with an attorney?"

She shook her head. "No."

"Do you desire to formally request a civil-service trial and require Mr. Hardy to prove the allegations?"

"Of course not," Genevieve said, raising her chin in slight defiance. "There is no point in subjecting those ladies to such inconvenience. I do not deny being at any of those gatherings."

"Do you admit to the dates and times alleged?"

"I can't remember all the dates. I'm sure they're accurate, however." She gave Mr. Hardy a withering look.

"You admit to pursuing this activity on state time?" one of the other commission members asked.

"Yes, certainly. It's common practice at the administrative level; nearly all members of state management take time off to participate in various outside activities."

"Various *recognized* activities, Miss Neller," the commissioner pointed out. "State government allows its management certain latitude in participating in activities such as fund-raising for legitimate charities, community affairs, cultural activities, youth programs, even social and fraternal groups. But this Save Whitman Movement is certainly not to be put in the same category as those activities."

"And why not?" Genevieve challenged, shedding her nervousness. "Is it because instead of helping promote our symphony season, I'm trying to keep a possibly innocent man out of the gas chamber? Because instead of sipping tea and talking about how to get new exercise equipment for the YWCA, I'm trying to help one single human being fight for his life? Is Weldon Whitman's cause not recognized, as you say, because if he ever manages to prove his innocence, the State of California, which sentenced him to death twice, will be made to look utterly ridiculous in the eyes of the rest of the country? Is that what you're afraid of, gentlemen?"

"We aren't afraid of anything, Miss Neller," the chairman said tolerantly. "And as far as this commission is concerned, the particular type of activity in which you choose to participate is your own concern, so long as it is not illegal and does not in any way infringe upon your responsibilities as a state employee. However, when an activity *does* infringe on your time to the point where you find it necessary to be absent from your post on a more or less regular basis, then you yourself have put your superiors in a position of having to challenge that activity."

"With all due respect to your authority, sir, I simply do not believe that," Genevieve said firmly. "My participation in the Save Whitman Movement is being challenged because it *is* the Save Whitman Movement. If it were any other cause, none of us would be here right now."

"I'm sorry you feel that way, Miss Neller," the chairman said in a neutral voice. "I'm sure that nothing I could say would convince you to the contrary; therefore, perhaps it's best if we proceed in a businesslike manner. Your decision is *not* to ask for a formal civil-service trial, is that correct?"

"Yes," Genevieve said. Her tone lost all semblance of respect and proper demeanor. She now recognized her position: she was facing enemies. Very polite enemies, to be sure, but enemies nevertheless.

"In that case, this board of commissioners will hereby exercise its legislated authority and decide the issue based on Mr. Hardy's submitted statement and any evidence you wish to present in defense of his allegation." Again the chairman paused; again Genevieve remained silent, forcing him to frame a direct question. "Do you wish to make a statement in your own defense?" he asked.

"There is no defense to this kind of hypocrisy," Genevieve replied. For just an instant she saw a spark of anger in the chairman's eyes. It was to be her only victory of the hearing.

"You leave us no alternative, Miss Neller, but to decide in favor of Mr. Hardy." He turned briefly to each of his colleagues. "Is there any dissent from that opinion, gentlemen?" Neither commissioner replied in the affirmative, and the chairman said, "Let the record show that the board has voted unanimously to support the state director of education's petition to discharge Miss Neller, and that she is, by order of the state civil service commission, removed from her position as head librarian of the state law library as of this date . . ."

Genevieve chose not to even dignify the decision with attentiveness. As the chairman was talking, she was gathering up her copy of the charges, pushing her chair back, and rising to leave.

"As to the matter of severance pay," the chairman continued mechanically, "because of Miss Neller's eleven-year tenure, she is by statute entitled to severance pay in the amount of sixty days' salary—" He looked up and saw that Genevieve was preparing to leave the room. "Miss Neller," he called, "aren't you interested in your severance pay?"

Genevieve turned at the door. Her face was pale, her

usually pretty mouth tensed into a severe line. She wanted very badly to tell him what he could do with the severance pay; she wanted to say something crude and filthy, something to put just a tint of true, ugly color on the surface politeness of the proceedings. But she had been too genteel and too proper for too long; she lacked the capacity for crassness. Besides, she had a special use for the money.

"Yes, I'm interested, and I accept the severance pay," she said in a flat, deliberate voice. "As soon as I receive the check, I intend to donate it to the Save Whitman Movement. It will be put to very good use—to help save Weldon Whitman from the gas chamber!"

She walked out of the hearing room. But, out of habit, she closed the door quietly behind her.

Two days later, Genevieve Neller went to see Weldon Whitman for the first time.

The visit was widely covered by the California press. Through Cloud and the editor of the Sacramento *Independent News*, the story of Genevieve's dismissal had made state wire services. The preliminary news stories broke first:

LIBRARIAN FIRED FOR
AIDING DOOMED CONVICT

STATE FIRES WOMAN
WHO RAISED MONEY
FOR DEATH ROW INMATE

FRIEND OF SPOTLIGHT BANDIT
DISMISSED BY STATE BOARD

They were followed the next day by interviews at Genevieve's apartment.

"Miss Neller, are you angry about losing your job? Do you feel you've been treated unfairly?"

"I'm more disappointed than angry," she answered. "For eleven years I felt proud to be a part of the state government. Now that pride has been destroyed."

"Miss Neller, a spokesman for the civil service commission has stated that it would be inconsistent with good government to pay prosecutors to put Whitman on Death Row, and then allow you, on state time, to try to get him out. How do you feel about that?"

"I should think," Genevieve said firmly, "that the state's first interest would be justice, however it came about."

"Is it true that you've never met Whitman?"

"Yes, it's true. I will meet Mr. Whitman in person for the first time at two o'clock tomorrow afternoon."

"Would you have any objection to the press being there?"

"I have no objections if Mr. Whitman has none. There are authorities involved who might object, however."

"We'll handle the authorities, Miss Neller," one veteran newsman commented. A few of the reporters laughed briefly.

"Do you intend to appeal your dismissal to a court of law, Miss Neller?"

Genevieve thought about it for a moment, then shook her head determinedly. "I don't believe that I am mentally or psychologically capable of carrying on campaigns against two separate injustices at once. And since the injustice being perpetrated against Mr. Whitman is far more serious, I will concentrate on his situation instead of my own."

Accompanied by Cloud, Genevieve arrived at San Quentin the following afternoon and was escorted by the deputy warden to the Condemned Building. When she stepped out of the elevator into the Death Row visiting room, she found that she was again facing a battery of newsmen and photographers. Strobe lights began to flash immediately.

"If you have any objection to the press being here," the deputy warden said almost hopefully, "we can clear the room. You have the right to a private visit."

"That's perfectly all right," Genevieve said, "I have nothing to hide from the press, and I'm certain Mr. Whitman doesn't." Her voice was cool. She had already begun to develop a feeling of resentment toward the keepers of authority.

More strobes flashed. There were a few obvious questions calling for obvious answers.

"Is this your first visit to a prison, Miss Neller?"

"Yes. But I don't imagine it will be my last."

"What's your impression of San Quentin, Miss Neller?"

"I feel that it must be very lonely," she said quietly. "Despite the hundreds of people it contains, I'm sure that it's a terribly lonely place." She turned to Cloud and whispered, "Where is he?"

"He'll be here in a minute," Cloud whispered back. "They

have to bring him down from upstairs. Let's sit down," he said, guiding her to the midway point of the long visitors' table.

"My dress didn't get wrinkled in the car, did it?"

"You look great," Cloud assured her.

Genevieve *hoped* she looked all right. God knows she had tried hard enough. The neckline of her A-style navy dress was square-cut with a very narrow white trim; it showed her bustline to the best advantage possible without accentuating her plumpness. The sleeves of the dress were long, the white trim repeated at the cuffs; her upper arms were slightly constricted, but she did not care because the sleeves made them look thinner. Nervously she patted at her upper lip.

She looked up, startled, when the prisoner elevator opened and Weldon Whitman came into the room. He looked almost sporty in clean, starched denim, his shirt open an extra button at the throat, sleeve cuffs turned under, military fashion. Smiling, he walked directly toward Genevieve. She and Cloud rose to meet him.

Strobe lights began flashing as the cameramen moved in on them. Genevieve smiled back at the condemned man across the table.

"Hello, Weldon. It's nice to meet you at last."

"Hello," Whitman said awkwardly. "I'm sorry about your job."

Genevieve shrugged. "There are worse things in life than losing a job. I was happy to hear about your stay."

He nodded and grinned. "That makes two of us."

"Three," Robert Cloud interjected.

Whitman's grin widened. "Yeah, that's right. We're getting to be a regular army, aren't we?" He hooked his thumbs in the beltless loops of his trousers and looked at Genevieve again. At the first lull in their conversation, the reporters began firing questions.

"How do you feel meeting Miss Neller for the first time, Whitman?"

"Terrific," the condemned man answered. "She's much prettier than the pictures you guys had in the papers yesterday." He looked at Genevieve and she blushed slightly.

"Will you comment on Miss Neller's decision to forgo appealing her own case in order to continue working in your cause?"

"Yes, I'll comment on that," Whitman said. His expression became serious. "I am very grateful to Miss Neller for her support, but it is not my desire that she continue to help me at the expense of her career. One of the main things I intend to do today, when we talk privately, is try and convince her to fight what the government of this state has done to her—"

"No, I won't change my mind on that," Genevieve said when the newsmen instinctively turned to her. "I'm going to dedicate my full time for as long as possible to the fight to save Weldon Whitman from the gas chamber."

"Are you doing it because you think he's innocent, Miss Neller? Or because you think his sentence is too severe even if he's guilty?"

Genevieve looked deeply into Weldon Whitman's eyes. "Because I think he's innocent," she said quietly.

"This is a very courageous lady, gentlemen," said Weldon Whitman. "I hope your stories will do her justice. Now I wonder if we could go over here by ourselves for a few minutes—"

"Sure, how about it, boys?" said Cloud, putting his arms out to corral the group as Whitman walked away down his side of the partitioned table, and Genevieve followed down the visitors' side. A few more flashes went off as they moved far enough to be out of hearing range. They sat down, pulling their chairs as close to the table as possible.

"This is about the best we'll be able to do in the way of privacy, I guess," Whitman said. "It'll be better next time."

"Next time?"

"Yeah. You are coming to see me again, aren't you?"

"If you want me to, of course—"

"Listen," he said urgently, "the only thing I want more than you visiting me, is for me to get out of this joint and be able to visit *you.*"

Genevieve blushed again. Whitman leaned as close to the partition as the tabletop would allow.

"I've got to know something," he said tensely. "I've got to know if there's—I mean, if you've got—you know, a man—"

"No," she replied quickly, swallowing dryly. "No, there's no one."

His face seemed to relax. "It was important to me to know. If there was anybody, if you had somebody, then I was going to force myself to stop thinking the things I've been thinking about you."

Genevieve felt an odd sensation as he spoke, as if someone were touching the insides of her thighs with something feathery. Perspiration rose on her upper lip again and she dabbed at it with a handkerchief. "What—what things?" She *had* to ask.

Whitman stared frankly at her. "Are you sure you want me to tell you?"

"Yes."

"All right. Things like me putting my mouth down between your legs and kissing you there—"

Genevieve's breath caught in her breast for a second. She glanced furtively at the men standing at the other end of the room. They were talking to Cloud and the deputy warden now, paying little attention to her and Whitman.

"Things like taking off your blouse and your bra and pushing your breasts together and sucking both your nipples at the same time—"

Genevieve's lips parted and her nostrils flared one quick time. She suddenly felt moist in the thick hair of her womanhood. She pressed her thighs together harder.

"Things like pushing it up into you and pumping and pumping and pumping, and finally firing it into you like white-hot lava—"

"Oh—" The soft, ecstatic moan burst quietly from her mouth like the sigh of relief it was, as she achieved an orgasm through the sheer force and will of his words. She lowered her head while it passed.

They talked until the visiting period was over, and then Whitman was taken back to the prisoner elevator. Genevieve remained where she was until he was gone. Then she patted the moisture from her upper lip and went back to where Cloud and the newsmen stood.

"Are you still unequivocally committed to him, Miss Neller?" one of the reporters asked.

Genevieve smiled slightly.

"Yes," she said. "Unequivocally."

Eleven

Four months after her first meeting with Weldon Whitman, Genevieve Neller was sitting in a small storefront office talking long-distance to Robert Cloud, who was in New York.

"How does it look for Weldon's book?" she asked.

"Very good," Cloud replied, overlooking Genevieve's persistent reference to *Weldon's* book. "Grayson Hamilton, the head of Hamilton House, has promised me a decision in the morning. I'm almost certain he'll make an offer to publish it. I just wonder how much of an advance he'll offer."

"However much it is, don't quibble," Genevieve said. "We've got nearly five thousand dollars in the bank, and I booked three more speaking engagements yesterday at two-fifty each. The important thing is to get the book published as soon as possible."

"Did you see Whit today?" Cloud asked.

"Yes. I spent an hour with him early this afternoon."

"Has he come up with another appeal idea in case he gets turned down on the one the Supreme Court has now?"

"Not yet. He's still poring over the law books. I told him we had enough money to retain a legal-research firm to help us, but he wants to see if he can do it himself first. He gave me a long list of cases he wants looked up. I'll probably be in the law library all day tomorrow, in case you try to call. Which reminds me, I've got to get ready for tonight."

"What's happening tonight?"

"I'm speaking at a dinner meeting of the Sertoca Clubs of Northern California."

"Who are they?"

"Sertoca," Genevieve said. "It's a contraction of Service to California. They're a statewide service club that's been showing some interest lately in the abolition of capital punishment."

"Sounds promising," Cloud said.

"It's worth the effort," Genevieve said clinically. "They're bound to take up a collection if nothing else. I *thought* I'd be able to distribute our new pamphlet, *Is This Justice?*, but the damn printer didn't deliver them like he promised to."

"Did I hear you say damn?" Cloud asked in mock shock.

"Oh shut up! I'll be saying a lot more than that if those pamphlets aren't here in the morning. I'm addressing the League of Women Voters at lunch tomorrow and I *definitely* want those gals to have them."

After they hung up, Genevieve kept her hand on the receiver for a moment and sighed quietly. She hoped Cloud would hurry and come back. She did not like working alone. Besides, she missed him.

She straightened a few things on her desk and got up to leave. The Save Whitman Movement had its office in a vacant shop in a small corner shopping center. They had bought two second-hand desks and one three-drawer file cabinet; Genevieve had made inexpensive drapes for the storefront windows; Cloud had registered them as a fund-raising, nonprofit organization; and they had opened for business.

Genevieve turned off the lights in the little office and, at the door, paused for a moment and thought of Whitman, of earlier that afternoon when she had sat across from him in the visiting room. For the first few minutes they had talked business: she had told him of the various speaking engagements; he had suggested points she might emphasize with this group or that. Then, as always, their talk had become personal. Genevieve had sat watching his sensuously mismatched lips form words that she never thought she would have sat and listened to, much less desired and enjoyed. Their vulgar obscenity assaulted her hearing without resistance, and became crass caresses to her whole being. Once more the wetness came and gave her tightly pressed thighs a slick warmth. Once more her nipples swelled and her ample breasts tightened with yearning, and she could feel the bra straps cutting into her shoulders. Next time, she had thought, I won't even wear a bra. Or panties either . . .

Thinking about it now, Genevieve felt the longing return, the desire begin. She wet her lips, let herself out and locked the door behind her, and hurried home to get in the shower.

Genevieve's address that night received a standing ovation from the predominantly WASP, anti-capital-punishment audience. Afterward, the chairman closed the meeting with a resolution to propose at their next convention that the Save Whitman Movement be adopted as one of Sertoca's officially supported organizations. In addition, he hinted that contributions from the floor would certainly be in order. When it was all over, Genevieve had nearly three hundred dollars stuffed in her purse.

After the business meeting, refreshments were served in

an adjoining social hall. Genevieve, who hardly drank at all, nursed a rum-and-Coke until it became warm in her hand. She held it through conversations with Sertoca's Northern California chairman, his wife, the other Northern California chapter officers, their wives, the group's state delegates and *their* wives, the chaplain, and numerous other members and more wives who came and went as the evening progressed.

It was nearly ten when she finally managed to extricate herself for a moment of privacy. She quickly disposed of the now sad-looking drink, and visited the ladies' room, where she adjusted a girdle that she wished by then she had not even worn, and never mind how she looked from the rear. Unobtrusively returning to the gathering, she ordered a plain ginger ale at the bar and had just taken a long, cold sip of it when a strikingly handsome man came up and spoke to her.

"Miss Neller," he said easily, "my name is Borden White. I wanted to tell you how much I enjoyed your talk tonight."

Genevieve gave him one of her stock answers. "Thank you so much. It was really my pleasure. I think your organization does such marvelous work—"

"That isn't necessary, Miss Neller," Borden White interrupted, smiling. "I'm not a Sertoca member, nor am I particularly interested in their good deeds. I came here tonight for the sole purpose of hearing you speak, and to meet you. Can you spare me a few minutes? In the interest of the Save Whitman Movement?"

"Of course," Genevieve said, looking at him curiously. "That's my purpose in being here."

"And mine," White said. "Suppose we go back into the dining room where we can talk in private."

The dining room was deserted now except for two busboys mechanically cleaning off tables. White led Genevieve to a table that had already been stripped. As he held a chair for her, she detected a hint of what was probably some very good after-shave lotion. He sat opposite her and she had a moment to look at him more closely. He was perhaps forty, graying slightly at the temples, with a long face, eyes a little too close together, but a ready, charming smile.

"Miss Neller," White said without further preliminary, "I am an attorney with the firm of Niebold and White. Mr. Morris Niebold, the senior partner in the firm, and I have been following with great interest the progress of Mr. Whitman's difficulties with the state. Our firm's specialty is constitutional law, and frankly we feel that there might be strong grounds for constitutional appeals in his case. We would like to offer him the legal assistance of our firm. Without fee, of course."

Two months earlier, Genevieve Neller would have fallen all over herself accepting Borden White's offer. But the State of California and Weldon Whitman had worked subtle changes in her personality, and now she was more cautious. "How very generous of you, Mr. White. Constitutional appeals, you say. What are those, exactly?"

"Come now, Miss Neller," White said tolerantly, "I'm sure you couldn't have been head librarian at the state law library for eleven years without becoming familiar with constitutional appeals. They're appeals based on the premise that a given verdict may not stand if it violated a defendant's state or U.S. constitutional rights." His smile was now gone. "I hope you're not going to be coy about this, Miss Neller. It *is* a serious offer."

"All right," Genevieve said, discarding the pretense. "Let's be candid then. Exactly why are you offering us your services?"

"As I said, our field is constitutional law. We think Whitman's case might provide some very interesting areas of constitutional appeal."

"What you're saying is that you want to use Weldon as a legal guinea pig," Genevieve commented.

"In a manner of speaking, yes," White admitted. "With one notable exception, of course: most guinea pigs have to take their chances with fate; but in this case, our legal experiments can only further the cause of Mr. Whitman. Our appeals in Whitman's behalf will serve as delaying tactics which could keep him alive indefinitely."

Genevieve silently studied Borden White. His charming first impression had not lasted long. She decided quickly that this Borden White was a little too *smooth.* If it were up to her, she thought, she would send him packing. But he might be helpful to Weldon, so it wouldn't be smart to alienate him. Weldon was the important one.

"Would you like me to arrange for you to see Mr. Whitman?" she said. "So that you can make the offer directly to him?"

"If you think he might be receptive to it, please do. Let me give you my card," he said, taking a thin leather case from his inside coat pocket. "I'll make myself available to visit Mr. Whitman whenever it can be arranged. Just give me a call." He pushed his chair back and stood up. "May I take you back to your host?"

Genevieve walked back into the social hall with him, feeling oddly cold and ill at ease with his hand lightly on her elbow. Why, she wondered, was he having such a *peculiar* affect on her? Several months ago she would have been flattered, even charmed by the company of someone so urbane. But now, after knowing Weldon—

It crossed her mind that perhaps it was not Borden White *per se*, or even his type, that she had reservations about; rather it might be the fact that he was entering, or at least attempting to enter, what she and Cloud referred to as the most exclusive club in the world: the Weldon Whitman Fan Club; membership, two. Could that possibly be it? she asked herself. Did she feel threatened? She smiled inwardly. Not really. How could she, after the things Weldon had said to her today, things that by his own admission he had *never* been able to say to another woman?

No, she concluded, it was not that. It was not her. It had to be Borden White; something about *him*. Maybe it was the fact that she was uncertain whether to trust him. If it was that, she reassured herself, then there was nothing to worry about. Weldon would decide whether to let him join them or not.

Weldon always knew whom to trust.

Borden White met Weldon Whitman two days later. They faced each other across the partitioned visitors' table: the hooked-nosed, denim-clad condemned man, and the clean-featured, Italian-suited attorney. Before they even sat down, Whitman put his hands on his hips and challenged the very purpose of the meeting.

"My reason for meeting you is that the state is trying to kill me and I want to stay alive, Mr. White. What's your reason for meeting me?"

"My reason for meeting you," Borden White said without hesitation, "is that I want to become governor of the state that's trying to kill you."

Whitman nodded a slow, understanding nod. "Have a seat, Mr. White."

Borden White unbuttoned his precisely tailored gray coat and sat down, carefully crossing his legs. "I would like to make it clear, Mr. Whitman, that if you and I reach some kind of agreement, it will have to preclude the use of Miss Neller as an intermediary. A lawyer and his client cannot subject their relationship to the interpretation of a third party. Particularly if the lawyer and the client are going to use each other, as we both intend doing."

"You sure don't bullshit around, do you?" said Whitman. Borden White shrugged.

"Why should I? Why should either of us? It's much easier to be realistic. You want to live. I want to become governor. To accomplish our goals, we both need as much help as we can get."

Whitman fingered a cigarette from his shirt pocket and lighted it. "How do you know that supporting me won't hurt you instead of helping you?"

"I don't," White said. "You'd be a political risk, just like any other cause is a political risk. But I'm counting on your eventually having more supporters throughout the state than you have opponents. Those supporters will help elect me after I help you beat the gas chamber."

"Assuming that I'm innocent," Weldon Whitman said, testing his visitor. Again Borden White shrugged.

"Guilt or innocence makes no difference to me," he said candidly. "Our approach will be that even *if* guilty, you were not properly convicted; and even *if* properly convicted, you are not being properly punished. Constitutional deficiencies in a case are often much easier to find than evidence of innocence." White removed a handkerchief from his breast pocket and touched it to his nose. "I wonder if you'd mind holding your cigarette back a little? I have a dreadful sinus condition."

What a fucking pity, Whitman thought. I do hope it isn't terminal. "What kind of deal do you want to make, Mr. White?" he asked, putting the cigarette out.

"I want two things, basically," the attorney said. "One, the firm of Niebold and White is to be given the exclusive right to file all appeals in your case, beginning when your next execution date is set; and two, we shall be allowed to publicize what we are doing for you in any way we see fit: writing legal articles, giving interviews, whatever."

"How would that agreement affect the publicity already being handled by the Save Whitman Movement?"

"I shouldn't think it would affect it at all. We'll be happy to coordinate our publicity with Miss Neller if she wishes, so long as it is made clear to her that she has no approval authority."

"She's picking up a lot of newspaper space—*and* money—with this speaking bit she's been doing," Whitman said. "And there's a guy named Cloud—used to be a reporter on the *Ledger* down in L.A.—who's been helping me a little on a book I just finished writing. Both of them may be useful to me in the future. I don't want to alienate either one of them if I can help it."

"I'm sure we can work something out without bruising anyone's feelings," White said.

Whitman pursed his lips and nodded thoughtfully. "Okay, we've got a deal then."

"Good." The attorney put the tips of his fingers together. "Incidentally, I'm going to want a formal agreement between us, just in case some hick with a correspondence-school law degree comes along and claims to represent you. It's happened before. I want to make sure we're the attorneys of record."

"Whatever's fair," Weldon Whitman said.

"Suppose I come back tomorrow with the papers. I'll bring my legal assistant along to witness my signature for the firm, and you can have Miss Neller come up to witness yours. That way we can make her feel a part of things, and at the same time make it clear that the legal end of it will remain separate from the Save Whitman Movement. Agreed?"

"Agreed," Whitman said. "Would you mind calling Genevieve? Tell her I said to be here tomorrow at one."

"Tell her?" Borden White said, his eyebrows raising.

"That's right," Weldon Whitman replied with assurance. "Tell her."

So that was how it stood, White thought. How interesting.

When Genevieve Neller entered the visiting room the next afternoon, the first person she saw was a thin, angular woman with hair like ink. It was combed straight back from her forehead and fell like a nun's cowl to the middle of her shoulder blades, where it ended abruptly in a razor cut as perfect as a draftsman's edge. Her thin body lacked as many pounds as Genevieve carried as surplus. But she was a woman who obviously knew how to use what she had. The way she stood, the way she turned to look at something, the way she used her hands and arms, were all to the very best advantage. She was dressed in a bright summer print, the type Genevieve could never wear because of her weight. Her face was pretty: *gauntly* pretty, though not unhealthily so, because she had a nice even suntan. If only she were very pale, Genevieve thought, she would be a complete catastrophe. Then Weldon probably wouldn't look twice at her—

"Ah, Miss Neller," Borden White said as Genevieve walked over to them. "I'd like you to meet Carla Volt, my legal assistant. Carla, this is Genevieve Neller, the lady who's been so instrumental in keeping Weldon Whitman in the public eye."

The two women exchanged greetings and the briefest of handshakes.

"I hope coming up on such short notice didn't inconvenience you," Borden White said. He was wearing an exquisite blue suit today, perfectly tailored, accessories perfectly coordinated, as though he had just materialized from *Gentlemen's Quarterly*.

"I am always available when Weldon needs me," Genevieve replied. "You mentioned something on the phone yesterday about a contract, witnessing a signature?"

"Yes. Here, let me show you—" The attorney took several copies of a three-page agreement from his briefcase and gave one to Genevieve. As she read it, White briefly touched on its content. "It's more or less the standard contingency-fee contract, except that the fee portions have been omitted, leaving only the representation agreement."

"What is this paragraph regarding publicity?" Genevieve asked. "I don't recall ever seeing anything like that in a lawyer-client contract before."

"Yes, well, that was put in at Weldon's suggestion," White said. "He wanted to make sure the press knew that releases were authorized to come from our law firm as well as the Save Whitman Movement." Smiling, he turned to Carla

Volt. "Answer any further questions Miss Neller has, will you, Carla? I want to speak to the guard about giving these copies to Weldon to sign."

He was gone immediately, leaving the two women alone.

"Was there anything else you wanted to know?" Carla Volt asked. Her voice had a slight, natural huskiness to it. Before Genevieve had time to reply, both women heard the prisoner elevator open.

The condemned man appeared serious as he approached them; he was looking at Carla Volt, whom he had not seen before. Then his eyes shifted quickly to Genevieve and he grinned his engaging grin at her and she smiled brilliantly back at him. Genevieve introduced him to Carla.

"Oh, yeah," Whitman said. "You're the legal assistant. Hello."

"Hello," Carla said. "Yes, I'm Mr. White's legal assistant. He just stepped over there to see the guard."

"While we're waiting for him, I wonder if you'd excuse Genevieve and me for a minute? A little personal matter—"

Whitman motioned Genevieve to a spot farther along the table and they sat down with their faces again as close as the divider between them would permit.

"Hello, baby," he said to her, still grinning. "Wonder where White got that bag of bones?"

"Don't you think she's attractive?" Genevieve asked innocently.

"Not me, honey. I like a woman with something to hold onto, with some hot flesh to get next to. That broad there is probably like an icicle in bed." He could see that Genevieve was pleased by his words. "Listen," he said, changing the subject, "I'm sorry to have you rush up here on such short notice—"

"I don't mind."

"—but I wanted you to be here because I don't feel right dealing with these people by myself. I mean, I want this guy's help, his legal help, because I need it, you know? But it isn't like he's going to be one of *us:* you and me and Rob. We're the real *people* in this thing. Maybe this Borden White and his law firm can do us some good, maybe not. Personally I think it's worth taking a chance on. That's why I agreed to sign an attorney-client contract with him—but that's also why I wanted you here. If we find out later that White and his partner are looking out for their own interests at the expense of *our* interests, then I want to be able to get out of the agreement as quickly as possible."

"How could I help you do that?"

"If it came down to it, I'd want to petition the court to discharge White and his firm as my counsel, and the reason I'd use is that I didn't fully understand the agreement. I'd want you to back me up on that; to say that in your opinion I didn't really know what I was signing. Would you do that for me, Gen?"

"Why, I—yes, I suppose so." She put the palm of one hand on her cheek. "I'm sure I'd feel very odd lying like that, but—"

"I know," Whitman said quietly. "I'd feel very odd going to the gas chamber, too."

The color drained from Genevieve Neller's face. She stared starkly at him for a long, terrible moment, then said, "Of course. I'll say whatever you want me to, whenever you want me to."

"That's my girl," Whitman said proudly. "Listen, let's get this signature business over with and send Borden White and his skinny helper out of here so we can have our private visit."

"Yes, let's," Genevieve said eagerly.

When Genevieve arrived back home early that evening, she found Robert Cloud, to whom she had given a key to her apartment, having a sandwich and glass of milk in front of her television.

"Well, hello," she said, surprised. "When'd you get back?"

"Couple of hours ago," Cloud said around a bite of the sandwich. He got up, turned off the television, and stepped over to a chair where he had draped his coat. From his pocket he took a folded document and waved it before her. "One publishing contract," he announced. "Five thousand dollars advance against royalties and a guarantee to have *Room 22, Hotel Death* in the bookstores within ninety days."

"Oh, Rob, that's wonderful!" Genevieve shrieked. She threw her arms around him and kissed him wetly on the lips. "You're a genius! A genius who tastes like mayonnaise, but a genius nevertheless. Publication so soon; that's marvelous! And five thousand dollars!"

"There's more," Cloud said. "Grayson Hamilton, the head of Hamilton House, is personally going to handle the sale of paperback reprint rights and movie rights."

"Movie rights! You mean Weldon's book might be made into a movie?"

"Maybe," Cloud said. *Weldon's* book, he thought. He went back to the couch, sat down, and drank some more milk. "Hamilton is even talking about a sequel. Wants to know if Whit and—well, if Whit would like to do a second book, with you and me in it. Picking up the story where he leaves off in *Room 22*."

"What did you tell him?" she asked eagerly.

"I said yes, I thought so. It could probably be done in six months, maybe less. And it would mean another advance that we could use for legal fees that are sure to be—" He noticed her expression change. "What's the matter?"

"We won't have to worry about legal fees," she said with an obvious lack of enthusiasm. She slumped down in a armchair facing him. "Weldon is now being represented, free of charge, by the law firm of Niebold and White."

"Did you say *free of charge?*"

"I did. But I'm not so sure it won't cost us something in the long run. And I don't mean money."

Twelve

"There's someone I haven't mentioned yet," Genevieve said the following Monday evening. They were in her car on their way to an after-dinner meeting at the home of Morris Niebold, Borden White's senior partner. "A woman," she continued. "Her name is Carla Volt."

"Who is she?" Cloud asked.

"She's a legal assistant to Borden White; at least, that's what she *calls* herself."

"You don't like her," Cloud observed.

"I don't," she replied almost impatiently, "and don't ask me why. Maybe it's just intuition. Or something in her eyes. Her close association with Borden White. The fact that she's *thinner* than I am. I don't know. Anyway, I'm sure you'll be meeting Carla tonight," Genevieve said. "You can draw your own conclusions about her. I just wanted you to know how I felt."

Genevieve guided the car off the freeway onto a four-lane boulevard with a divider of cypress trees down its center. She followed the boulevard north into the plush Madre Grande district, an area of wide, walkless streets fronted by the grounds, mostly fenced, of large estates.

"I think this is it," she said, as she turned into a long, straight drive. The extensive manicured grounds on both sides of the drive were subtly lighted. In the distance stood what Cloud supposed must be the closest thing to an English manor that northern California could boast, complete with ringed hitching posts on one side as they approached the house. Genevieve drove onto a cobblestoned area off the front entry and parked next to a gunmetal gray Continental. Cloud rang and they heard the faint sound of chimes inside. The door was opened immediately by a black butler who greeted them pleasantly and showed them into the library, where their host awaited them with Borden White and Carla Volt.

"Ah, Genevieve. And this must be Mr. Cloud." White extended his hand. "Good of you to come."

White led them to a massive fireplace set between two walls of solid books. Carla Volt was standing next to the hearth. Sitting near her, in a shining chrome wheelchair, was their host.

"I'd like you both to meet Morris Niebold," White said, leading Genevieve and Cloud up to him. He was a dark-eyed, bushy-browed man with thick, almost pouting lips, and cheeks slightly too plump for the rest of his face. There was about him such an aura of confidence that one might easily have wondered why he did not simply get out of the wheelchair and walk if it pleased him to do so.

"I am delighted to meet you both," Morris Niebold said. He squeezed Genevieve's hand and smiled. "Times like these I regret more than ever being unable to stand and bow."

"Why, thank you, that's very kind," Genevieve said. Niebold turned to Cloud.

"I'll call you Robert, if you'll permit me the familiarity of age," he said, shaking hands. "In fact, nothing would please me more than for all of us to be on a first-name basis."

"Fine," Cloud said. He glanced past Niebold at Carla Volt. She was staring frankly at him.

The man in the wheelchair noticed Cloud and Carla Volt with their eyes locked. "I'm afraid we've been remiss in the introductions. There are still two of us who haven't met." Niebold deftly spun his chair around. "Carla Volt, Robert Cloud."

Cloud stepped over to where she stood and took the hand she offered. For a moment neither of them spoke, then Cloud said quietly, "Hello, Carla."

"Hello, Robert," she replied. Her touch and the huskiness of her voice affected him instantly; the back of his neck warmed and he suddenly felt very good.

They all sat near the fireplace, sipping Niebold's fine old brandy from handcut lead-crystal glasses, talking quietly about Weldon Whitman and capital punishment in California. Cloud and Genevieve sat together, as did Borden White and Carla; Niebold had wheeled himself to a point between the two settees so he could attend them all conversationally, although he obviously concentrated on the two newcomers.

As they talked, Cloud observed Carla Volt. She was wearing a bright flowered jersey in two pieces: a longsleeved blouse open at the throat, and a long skirt. It was impossible to tell much about her figure, except that there was not a great deal to it: barely any bustline interrupted the flatness of the jersey top, and all that could be distinguished of her hips was that they were extremely angular. Cloud was fascinated by her hair—the sheer pitch of it—and by her too-wide mouth with corners that turned down, so her smile had to go a little farther to reach the surface. Cloud kept his eyes on her as much as he dared throughout the evening, and several times she caught him watching her. And then several times when he looked away from her and then brought his eyes back, he caught her watching him. It became an obsessive game with them all evening.

"I'm sure you're all waiting to hear my ulterior motive for our little get-together this evening," Niebold said after almost an hour of generalities. "Being cognizant of the fact that I am an attorney—and one whose specialty is constitutional law, at that—I am sure you must have suspected something underhanded." He paused to allow his guests time to chuckle respectfully, then said, "As a matter of fact, I do want to propose something, and I'd like to get the opinions of all of you on the merits of that proposal. Our main purpose, as we all know, is to save from California's gas chamber a young man whom we all feel is being punished unjustly. Guilty or innocent, it matters not: Weldon Whitman should not have been condemned to death." He leaned over and patted Genevieve's hand. "And I'm sure we all know that but for the gallantry of this young lady in determining to help a fellow human being, none of us would even be aware of the injustice being done Weldon Whitman."

Not *quite* true, Cloud thought. But he let it pass. Like *Weldon's* book, he decided, it really didn't make that much difference. Besides, his mind was busy with Carla Volt.

"What I want to propose here tonight is that we incorporate and formally establish an organization to be called the Weldon Whitman Foundation—"

Genevieve started to object. "But we—"

"Wait, please," Morris Niebold stopped her with a slight but commanding movement of his hand. "Hear an old man out first," he said, with a smile, "and then I'll listen to objections all around." He sipped the last bit of his brandy and put the glass aside. "I realize that you, Genevieve, and you, Robert, already have what you call the Save Whitman Movement, and I think that is splendid; I wouldn't suggest changing that in the slightest. After all, it is fairly well known by now and already established in some circles as *the* Whitman organization. What I'm proposing in the foundation, however, is not merely a movement to save Weldon Whitman, not merely a movement to remedy the injustice being done to one person, but an organization which will attack the very principle of that injustice, an organization that will ultimately benefit *all* Weldon Whitmans. Do you begin to see what I'm driving at? Robert, do you?"

"Yes, I think so," Cloud replied. He was already thinking of the publicity and feature-article possibilities.

"Good. Let me touch on a few advantages I think will interest all of us. First, of course, the foundation would at once remove the suggestion of our fight being *personal*, being a battle strictly to save one man from the gas chamber. Instead, it would immediately become a drive to combat *general* judicial injustice; it would become something that—superficially, at least—could be identified with by many, many more people than would ever cast their lot with one condemned man." Niebold smiled and spread his hands before him as if pleading. "Now, I don't advocate that we actually attempt to help anyone except Weldon Whitman; certainly, he is to remain our primary interest. But in the mind and eye of the public, he will gradually become the symbol of something far bigger." He paused and looked intently at Genevieve. "Am I beginning to make any sense to you, my dear?"

"I'm not sure yet," Genevieve said. Her caution had been increasing daily since she met Borden White.

"Exactly how would you go about establishing this foundation?" Cloud asked.

"You tell him, please, Borden," the older man said.

"Certainly," said White. "There's not much to it really. We would first draw up a statement of intent and purpose, much the same as for any nonprofit corporation. We would have to elect officers, of course—"

"That would be no problem at all," Niebold interjected. "The only logical, the only *acceptable*, president of the foundation would be Genevieve."

"Oh my, I don't know," Genevieve said uncertainly.

"And Robert here for her next-in-command, her vice-president," Niebold continued unabashed. "One of the other of us could serve as treasurer, or we could elect an outside member from some accounting firm. Carla could serve as secretary." He turned to Cloud, whom he sensed to be on his side—or at any rate not against him. "Tell me, Robert, do you think Weldon would like having a foundation named after him?"

Is the Pope Catholic? Cloud thought. "I think he would probably agree to it if we all decided it was the right way to go."

"And how about you, Genevieve?" he asked, patting her hand again. "Do you still have reservations?"

"I'm afraid so," she said, although not as adamantly as Cloud expected. "I would have to have time to really give it some thought—"

"Well, of course," Niebold said patronizingly. "It isn't as though we have to make a decision tonight. I think that's enough business for one evening anyway. Suppose I have some chocolate mousse and coffee brought in—" He quickly wheeled himself to the desk where he had an intercom.

"None for me, thanks," Carla Volt said. "I have to run." She went over to a side table where she had left her purse. Cloud put down his brandy glass and followed her.

"It's still early," he said. "Do you have to leave?"

"I want to leave," she said simply.

"I was hoping we might have a few minutes together—"

"We still can."

"How?"

"You leave, too."

Just like that. *You leave, too.*

And just like that he said he would. "Give me a minute—"

He went over to where Genevieve was sitting. She was momentarily alone, Niebold on the intercom and Borden White pouring more brandy. Cloud sat down beside her.

"Gen," he said quietly, "I'm going to leave with Carla, if you don't mind."

Her face clouded at once. "Oh that's *great.*"

"Look, I know you don't like her—"

"*You* apparently do."

"I don't know if I do or not. I'll probably find out tonight."

"I'm sure you will. Meanwhile you walk out and leave me with young Kildare and old Dr. Gillespie there."

"I'm surprised at you, Gen," he said, taken aback. "A few months ago you wouldn't have dreamed of saying a thing like that."

"A few months ago I didn't know the things I know today," she countered. "Look, just run along if you want to."

"Not if it's going to upset you."

"It isn't going to upset me."

"You sound like it is."

"Will you just go," she said through gritted teeth.

Borden White walked back over to them, smiling, and Cloud rose and said goodnight.

"Glad you and Carla are hitting it off so quickly," the lawyer said. "She's a fine girl."

Cloud exchanged amenities with his host, who also uttered high praise for Carla Volt, and they all promised to meet later in the week for further discussion of the Weldon Whitman Foundation.

Once they were in her car, everything happened very quickly. She put the key in the ignition but did not turn it on. She merely sat behind the wheel, looking straight ahead at the windshield, waiting for him to touch her.

Cloud turned partway toward her, resting his elbow on the seat back. Her profile was etched as clearly in the gray night as if it were on a coin, and Cloud studied her with growing desire. His hand, when it finally moved to her, stroked the straight fall of her hair where it covered her neck.

"Your hair is incredible," he said. "It's like the wing of a big, shiny blackbird."

"Poetic," she said, turning toward him for the first time.

Cloud's fingers parted the thick drape of hair and found her neck. He slid his hand lightly around and gently pulled her forward until their mouths touched. Their lips parted and their tongues slipped together.

"We mustn't stay here," she said when their kiss was over. She started the car and drove away from the house, down the long drive toward the boulevard. "Where do you live?" she asked. He told her. "That's too far," she said. "I live closer than that and *my* place is even too far for the way I feel right now. I'm a strong believer in seizing special feelings, special moments, when and where you *can* seize them."

They came to the gate, she slowed, then turned into the wide boulevard and drove toward the lights of the business district that preceded the freeway.

"Too often a special feeling comes and goes without being taken advantage of," she said. "Then it's gone forever."

Like a hard-on, Cloud thought. He decided that he could wait no longer. He had to know if she had *any* tits at all. He slid over next to her and put his right hand on her right breast. It was small, barely filling his palm, but firm and coned, like the breasts, he remembered, of teenaged girls, but the nipple, he could tell, was large, the areola large. He massaged the breast; there was nothing between it and his hand except the jersey blouse.

Carla pulled into the first motel that had its vacancy sign on. She drove past the office, parked next to the pool area, and turned off the headlights.

"Walk back and register," she said. "Try to get one of the back rooms."

Cloud got out of the car and went back to the office. He used the old Los Angeles address on his driver's license, and signed them in as Mr. and Mrs.

They drove down to Room 128 and parked in front of the door. Cloud opened the motel room door and she went in ahead of him. She turned on the lights and looked around.

"This isn't bad," she said. She walked back to the closet, unbuttoning her shirt blouse as she walked, and took it off. With her naked back to him, her inky hair streaking it in black, she calmly put her blouse neatly on a hanger and hung it up. Then she slipped out of her long skirt, folded it with equal care, and draped it over a trousers hanger. Finished, she turned to face him. He was still fully dressed, standing by the door.

"You're not shy, are you?" she asked.

"No," Cloud said, shaking his head. He looked at her tall, thin body, clad at that moment in shoes and pantyhose. "You don't wear much, do you?"

"Only what's necessary." She sat down on a corner of the bed and smiled at him. "You *are* shy."

Cloud smiled back at her. "No, I'm not, really. I'm just fascinated by you."

"I'm not moving too fast for you, am I?" she asked in her throaty voice. "I wouldn't want to frighten you away."

"You won't," Cloud said.

He tossed the room key onto the bureau and began undressing.

One week later, the Weldon Whitman Foundation was formally established in Morris Niebold's richly appointed law office near the capitol.

"Here is the original document incorporating us as a legal nonprofit foundation," Niebold said from his chrome wheelchair behind his specially built U-shaped desk. "Essentially what it says is that we will use whatever funds are at our disposal to press a perpetual fight against capital punishment for crimes in which no life was taken. Naturally, our primary efforts in that direction will be in behalf of Weldon Whitman, who has graciously consented to the use of his name as founder." Niebold handed the bound document to Carla Volt, who stood near his side. "My dear, pass this to Genevieve, please."

Carla came around the desk and gave the document to Genevieve Neller who, along with Robert Cloud and Borden White, sat facing the big desk. As she stepped over to hand the papers to Genevieve, Carla's leg brushed lightly against Cloud's knee, and they exchanged quick glances.

"Genevieve, as we all agreed, is unanimously elected president of the foundation, and is also employed as a general fund-raiser and speaker at a salary of twelve thousand dollars per annum. Genevieve, if you will sign in the appropriate place there on the front page and then pass the document to Robert—"

After Genevieve had signed and given the papers to Cloud, Niebold asked that he put his signature beneath hers. "Robert is elected vice-president of the foundation and is hired as an investigative reporter and publicity writer, also at a salary of twelve thousand dollars per annum."

The last person to sign before notarization of the document was Borden White.

"Borden will serve as treasurer of the foundation and chief legal counsel, at a retainer of one dollar per year. The three of you, along with myself, will constitute the board of directors of the foundation, and I will serve as chairman of that board, if there's no objection, with a vote, but not as an officer. Carla here, who will now witness and notarize the signatures, will serve as the foundation's official secretary, also at a salary of one dollar per year."

When all the formalities were over, Niebold leaned as far back as he could in his wheelchair and smiled a wide smile that spread thin his naturally pouting lips and puffed up his round cheeks slightly.

"Thank you all," he said in a pleased tone. "I think we

have taken a very important step here today, one that will well serve both Mr. Whitman *and* the cause of true justice in California."

"I'll second that remark," Borden White said cheerfully.

"So will I," said Cloud.

The three men looked at Genevieve Neller. She pursed her lips slightly, then said, "Forgive my pessimism, gentlemen. I prefer to reserve my enthusiasm until the foundation has done something positive for its namesake."

Morris Niebold pounded his desk exuberantly. "Well said, young lady!" He chuckled loudly. "Every board needs a stabilizing influence, and it looks like you're going to be ours. You'll keep us in line, all right! And you'll see something positive being done for your Mr. Whitman too, I'll guarantee that!"

When they were ready to leave, Cloud and Genevieve walked out to the reception area and Cloud asked her to wait a moment for him. He stepped to an office just down the hall and stuck his head in the door. Carla was back at her desk.

"Hello, Miss Volt."

"Hello, Mr. Cloud."

"You going to be home tonight?"

"You coming over?"

"Like to."

"Then I'll be home."

"Okay. See you."

She smiled. "I imagine you will."

He hurried back down the hall where Genevieve waited. They walked out to the parking lot.

"I don't think you'll be sorry about the foundation, Gen," he told her. "I think you made a wise decision to give your approval."

"A reluctant decision," she said. "And one in which I really had no choice. After you decided to join with Niebold and White, it was three to one in favor of the foundation."

"I didn't exactly *join* with them, Gen—"

"It amounted to the same thing," she said firmly, stopping and facing him. "I know you have to do what you think is right, Rob, but I want you to remember one thing: Weldon is my main concern; as a matter of fact, he is my *only* concern. I don't intend to let anything or anybody—or any *foundation*, for that matter—jeopardize any chance he may have for freedom. I'm going to see him out of that place, Rob, do you understand me?—*out!*"

"Gen, relax, will you, please?" Cloud said urgently. "We all want Whit out; and nothing we do is going to jeopardize him in any way. The foundation is a *good* idea, Gen. Please try to believe that."

"I want to believe it, Rob. Very much so. But I can't help feeling that the foundation might survive and Weldon might not. It's like naming the thing after him because he's already dead, or because they know he's going to die. I just have a cold, creepy fear that this foundation is looking for a built-in martyr and that it's picked Weldon for the honors."

"That's not so, Gen," Cloud said. "You're mistaken—and as soon as we all begin to function as a team, you'll realize that you're mistaken."

"I hope so," she said.

Thirteen

The occupants of cells twenty through twenty-nine were in the corridor for recreation.

Franklin, the mild-mannered wife-killer, was playing chess with Rimm, an Imperial Valley farmer who had shot and killed his neighbor and the neighbor's two brothers over a property dispute.

Milo, the bushy-browed stickup man and cop-killer, was sitting on the tiled floor, reading that morning's San Francisco *Chronicle.* The paper belonged to Clayton, a former University of California student who had unaccountably murdered a family of five on whose ranch he had been living and working during summer vacation.

Near the far end of the barred corridor, Henry, the black rapist-killer who lived in Cell Twenty-seven, and Stiles, another black, who had stabbed to death his ex-wife, her new husband, and his own seven-year-old son, were exercising, using the steel bars for tension. They had been exercising together on the bars for forty months. Henry remained rail-thin while Stiles had a magnificent physique, but oddly enough they were of equal strength and proved it often in dead-heat arm wrestling. Each of them was easily stronger than any two other men on the Row.

At the opposite end of the corridor were two rap partners: they had killed and been convicted together. Caldwell was a psychopathic white man with a long and varied criminal record. Jones was an illiterate mulatto who had been a petty thief all his adolescent and adult life. They were homosexuals; once each month, just for the record, Captain Dukes would catch Jones in the act of orally copulating Caldwell, for which both would be written up and lose three days of privileges. The rest of the time Jones sucked off his partner and sweetheart anytime he wanted to, as he was doing this morning in Cell Twenty-three, Caldwell's cell. Their crime had been the kidnapping off the street and cold-blooded execution-murder of a uniformed policeman in southern California.

The ninth and last occupant of the Twenty Section was Weldon Whitman, and as usual he quietly walked the length of the corridor studying one of the growing stack of law books that was now occupying a corner of his hole, as the inmates called their cells.

Whitman had been on Death Row for seventeen months.

He had gained eleven pounds, most of it around his middle, and his thick black hair had receded a little at the temples, emphasizing his already severe widow's peak. He was beginning to suffer periodic headaches—the result of eye-strain from the many months of poring over the seemingly endless columns of copy in a seemingly endless procession of thick law books; he was to see an ophthalmologist from the California Health Department early the following month.

Fifteen minutes before the Twenty Section was to be locked back up, Captain Dukes came with the daily announcements.

"Somebody holler into Twenty-three and tell Jones to get up off his knees," the captain ordered easily. "Caldwell, too. Tell him to button up his pants and join us on the patio."

Moments later, looking not in the least disturbed, the two cop-killers stepped into the corridor and sat side by side against the bars of Caldwell's hole.

"All right, boys and girls," Dukes said when he had their attention, "the movie for Sunday night is *Last Train from Gun Hill.* It stars Kirk Douglas and it's the story of a fellow who thinks he can get away with rape and murder in the Old West. Naturally the sheriff can't put up with that kind of thing, so he blows the criminal's head off with a shotgun. I'm sure you boys and girls will all enjoy it. Might even teach some of you a lesson."

Dukes flipped a page in his pocket notebook and studied it briefly.

"Franklin, that book you requested from the prison library is no longer available. Seems that someone stole it." Henry and Stiles, the two black exercisers, cheered and applauded this news. Dukes ignored them. "Since you're one of the better inmates on the Row, Franklin, I'm having my wife pick the book up for you at the public library. I'll bring it in for you in a couple of days."

"Thank you, Captain," Franklin replied.

"What a fuckin' teacher's pet," said Jones, the less intelligent of the two cop-executioners.

"At least he's not a cocksucker," Captain Dukes said dryly. He checked his notebook again. "There's a new magazine on the approved list. It's called the *Evergreen Review.* I understand it has pictures of naked women in it, so I imagine at least a couple of you will want to subscribe to it."

"It has more than naked women in it, Captain," said Clayton, the former student. "The magazine also has some very thought-provoking articles and stories. And it is very *anti*-capital-punishment." Once again, Henry and Stiles cheered and applauded. And once again the captain ignored them.

"Thank you for the added comments, Twenty-one," Dukes said. "It certainly is nice to have an intellectual among us." Referring to his notes again, he said, "Rimm, the warden has granted you a special visit next Tuesday with your aunt and uncle who have come from Germany to see you. You'll be allowed three hours with them beginning at ten A.M."

Rimm looked up from his chess game and nodded. "Thank the warden for me, please, Captain. They're old folks and they'll have come a long way. It was nice of the warden to accommodate them."

Dukes acknowledged Rimm's gratitude with a nod. "All right, that's it for now," he said. The big captain walked back to the electronically controlled door that separated the Row corridor from the elevator corridor. He nodded to the guard in the control room at the end of the double corridor. The barred door slid back almost silently. As Dukes started to step through the opening, he paused and looked back. "Oh, I almost forgot. There *is* one more item." He turned cold eyes toward Weldon Whitman. "Twenty-two, your appeal has been denied and a new date set for your execution. You go to the chamber now on October fourteenth."

Whitman, standing near the middle of the Row, holding his heavy lawbook, turned pale. He stared at Dukes for a moment as the full impact of the keeper's words settled in his mind. Then he closed the book, tried unsuccessfully to wet his lips with a dry tongue, and walked silently back to his hole.

Following the denial of the appeal, the wheels of the Whitman Foundation began to turn in synchronization for the first time in its five months of existence. The officers of the foundation met in Morris Niebold's office to plot strategy.

"The first step from the legal point of view, of course, is to file another appeal as quickly as effectively possible," the invalid attorney told them. "And I say *effectively* possible because I want our appeal to have some meaning, some *sub-*

stance: something for the high court to have to ponder. I want them to know that we mean business, that we aren't simply going through the motions with routine delaying tactics. We must show them from the outset that we intend striking to the very heart of capital punishment in California, and that for our first victory we will accept no less payment than the restoration of Weldon Whitman's right to live."

"Exactly what is to be the substance, as you call it, of the appeal?" Genevieve asked. For her, this was the initial test of Niebold and White, Attorneys at Law. Weldon needed them now. So now she would find out whether they were going to contribute or just try to ride along for the publicity.

"Will you outline our plan, please, Borden?"

"Certainly." Borden White rose, resplendent in a brown Italian knit suit, Countess Mara tie knotted perfectly at the collar of his Oleg Cassini shirt. "Our basis for this first appeal," he said, speaking primarily to Genevieve and Cloud, "is that it was a reversible error for the trial judge not to have appointed a private attorney to act as an advisor to Whitman in his original trial. Since he was facing *capital charges* at the time he elected to conduct his own defense, our position will be that even though it was Whitman's *right* to act in his own defense, it was the trial judge's *obligation* to appoint a practicing attorney as advisor and observer. Only with an attorney acting in such capacity would there be even a tacit guarantee that the defendant's constitutional and trial rights would be protected."

White carefully pushed his coat back and put his hands in his pockets. He paced slowly across the big, book-lined office, as if he were addressing a jury.

"What we're going to be saying," he continued, "is that in a jury trial of criminal charges, the presiding judge is a protector of rights more than an arbiter of justice. The *jury* is there to decide guilt or innocence. Thus, the judge should devote himself even more earnestly to the protection of the rights of the defendant—particularly if that defendant is facing capital charges."

White reached up to lightly grasp each lapel of his coat and raised his chin slightly. "When a defendant in a criminal case elects to conduct his own defense, that defendant is, in actuality, throwing himself on the mercy of the court. He is saying, 'Here I am, Your Honor. I'm innocent and I don't think

I need a lawyer to prove it. I'm simply going to tell the truth, on the assumption that right will triumph.' The defendant is entrusting to the trial judge a very grave responsibility: the responsibility of seeing to it that none of the defendant's *inherent* rights as an accused citizen are abused in any way—not by the prosecution, not by the jury, not by the judicial system itself. There will, of course, be no question in our appeal that a trial judge must accept this trust and deal with it in the most exact and equitable manner possible. The trust must not be compromised even slightly; if it is, then the rights of the defendant have been compromised completely."

White let go of his lapels and clasped his hands behind his back, pacing slowly across the office again. By now he had totally captured his listeners. His presentation was faultless.

"The only way a trial judge can assure that an accused's rights are fully protected is by appointing a qualified person to guard those rights. As precedents for this position, we will offer California cases in which judges, *against the wishes of defendants*, appointed lawyers to represent or advise them in cases involving such diverse crimes as cattle-rustling, arson, sodomy, and mayhem. We will also cite cases from other states involving crimes against the person as well as crimes against property, and federal district-court cases involving crimes against the United States, ranging from bootlegging and other tax-stamp violations to the killing of a federal correctional officer, all of which had in common the fact that in each case the judge saw fit to assure himself the defendant's rights would not be put in jeopardy through his ignorance of the law or the misjudgment to defend himself—and so appointed an attorney to either represent or to advise that defendant." White paused and studied his audience briefly, then quickly concluded. "That, in essence, is going to be our position: that Judge Lukey was morally obligated to assign an attorney of record to act as a court-paid guardian of Weldon Whitman's rights; and that his failure to do so was an error of sufficient significance to warrant a reversal of the verdict and a new trial."

Morris Niebold nodded approval of his younger partner's performance. "Thank you, Borden, that was excellent. I want to remember to incorporate into the actual appeal that phrasc about a slight compromise of the judge's trust amounting to a total compromise of the defendant's rights.

That's good, very good." Niebold sat back in his wheelchair. "Well," he said, mostly to Genevieve, "any comments, any questions?"

"Just one," said Genevieve. "Why the goal of a new trial rather than a reduction of the death sentence?"

"First of all, my dear," Niebold said, smiling, "the goal really isn't a new trial; the goal is to keep your Mr. Whitman alive—and that's precisely what a new trial will do. At the minimum, it will guarantee him an additional thirty months of life from the time the appeal is granted. That's a good deal more than he has now. Secondly, a new trial will give us a far greater chance of a reduction in sentence; in a retrial there would probably be only a fifty-fifty chance of a death sentence being rendered."

Genevieve nodded. "I understand."

"We'd like your opinion of our approach, Genevieve," said Borden White.

Genevieve Neller looked at him for a moment; then at Niebold, and at Carla Volt. As reserved as she was in her personal association with all of them, and as reluctant as she was to admit it, the appeal approach was, at least on the surface, not only judicially sound but strategically superior.

"I think it's a fine ground for appeal," she said to all of them. "Very fine."

"Good!" said Niebold with his usual enthusiasm. "Now, as long as we're showing off today, why don't you take a few bows yourself, Genevieve? Our Miss Neller," he said to the rest of them, "has drawn up a splendid proposal to add our own printshop to the Weldon Whitman Foundation. Tell them about it, my dear."

"Why don't you just read my proposal—"

"Come now, we want no modesty from the president of our foundation," Borden White said.

Genevieve cleared her throat and sat forward slightly. For some reason she was acutely aware of Carla Volt's slim presence. "My thought," she said, "was that if we—that is, the foundation—were to install a small printing facility, we could begin telling Weldon's story on a broader scale. We could print our own brochures, pamphlets, mailers, anything of that nature that we needed. All it would require really would be a reproduction camera, a plate-maker, and an eleven-by-seventeen press. I've already checked about the press: we can pick up a rebuilt A. B. Dick model that would be more than adequate for our needs. I've also checked with the printer's union about getting help to run the shop. They have a man who's been out on sick leave for a year from his regular job. He can't work full-time yet, but the union steward was sure he would be interested in an on-call arrangement with us. If we could get him, and Rob would do the writing, I could take care of the mailing end of it—"

"I could help with that," Carla Volt volunteered.

"Hell, we all could!" Niebold said. "I'm not above sealing an envelope and licking a stamp. Frankly, I think it's an excellent idea."

"And I," said Borden White. "I move we consider it a formal motion and vote on it."

A moment later Genevieve was formally endowed with the responsibility for setting up a Weldon Whitman Foundation printshop.

Carla Volt brought up the subject of a letter from Weldon Whitman; he had requested that the law firm attempt to get a court order allowing him to have a typewriter in his cell. "I've done a little research on the subject," she said. "Non-condemned prisoners have been allowed typewriters for quite some time. But as far as I know, no convict on Death Row has ever asked for one. At least not through the courts."

"It's an interesting idea," Niebold said thoughtfully. "What do you think, Borden?"

"Sounds like it might have excellent potential. We might even combine several areas of relief in one appeal. The typewriter, unlimited letter writing privileges, longer visiting periods: in general, a wider latitude of communications for condemned men."

"Genevieve," said Niebold, "have you ever heard of such an appeal being attempted before?"

"Not that I recall."

The invalid drummed his fingers on the padded leather arm of his chair for a moment. "All right, let's shoot the works on a second appeal too—more for nuisance value than anything else. We'll ask for everything but the warden's refrigerator, just to see how much we can get."

They talked on, covering a number of generalities, including the recent publication of *Room 22, Hotel Death,* which had attracted national attention as well as becoming an immediate best-seller in California bookstores. A respectable segment of the public had become instantly taken with the story of a supposedly lone man fighting the establishment from a death cell. Contributions had increased significantly, and letters were even coming in inquiring about forming separate chapters of the Save Whitman Movement.

In the meantime, Cloud had been rewriting the second book Whitman was trying to scribble out. Whitman had titled it *Judgment in Anguish.* This one too had an interesting story buried deep within the morass of amateurish prose and generally sloppy storytelling. Cloud's job, as with the first book, was to take this roughest of rough material and mold something commercially readable out of it. It had become tedious, irritating work for him, but thankfully it came only in short bursts and was quickly done. Whitman's pace kept Cloud busy only about three days a week; the rest of the time he helped Genevieve at the foundation office. But lately he had begun to feel his investigative juices flowing again.

"I have a project of my own in mind," he said now. "It might not be a bad idea to go back down to L.A. and see if I could dig up something on Glory Ann Luza. We got a lot of mileage out of the Doris Calder story; it's possible that something on the Luza girl might go just as far."

"What approach would you take on the story?" Borden White asked.

"I'm not sure," said Cloud. "I'd have to wait and see what I turned up. I'd be looking for some way to impugn her original identification of Whit as her assailant."

"It's probably worth a try," Morris Niebold said. "I recall very well your article on the Calder woman. It was one of the things that first interested Borden and me in the Whitman case. Yes, Robert, by all means make your trip to Los Angeles. By God, if we can discredit enough witnesses, we'll petition the governor for a full pardon!"

"When would you be leaving?" Carla Volt asked. Genevieve looked knowingly at her, and Carla quickly added, "You'll be wanting expense money, I'm sure."

"I'll finish up my current work over the weekend and fly down Monday," he told her. The brief wicked look in her eyes told him she understood that they would spend the weekend together.

When Cloud and Genevieve were driving back to the foundation office, Genevieve said, "I was surprised at your volunteering to leave town like that. I didn't think you and your friend could bear to be apart for even a night."

"Gen," Cloud said patiently, "what is it that you dislike about Carla?"

"I'm not sure I really *dis*like anything about her. I simply can't find anything to *like*. Obviously you have, though."

"Yes, I have. You see, Gen," he said quietly, "I can't give all my affection to Whit, as you have. My needs are a little different from yours."

They rode the rest of the way in awkward silence.

Fourteen

On Monday morning, Robert Cloud was again in Los Angeles, driving a rented car to the east side of town.

His open briefcase contained transcripts of Weldon Whitman's preliminary hearing and Superior Court trial, at both of which Glory Ann Luza had testified. The first transcript gave an address on Carmelita Avenue in the Chicano district on the east side of town; the trial transcript gave Chico Avenue in El Monte. The family had moved after the hearing—very likely, Cloud mused, because of the attendant publicity; so they might well have moved again after the trial. Sighing, he pulled off the San Bernardino Freeway at El Monte.

The house on Chico was a duplex of cheap stucco, painted in mismatched shades of green. The landlady was a heavy-set woman named Burney who had a stale odor about her.

"Sure, I know the Luzas," she said. "I had them for tenants for seven months. Pretty good tenants too. Clean for Mexicans."

"How long have they been gone?" Cloud asked.

"Oh, Christ, better than a year. They moved out right after that kid of theirs testified against that sex fiend that raped her. You remember that case?"

"Yes, I remember it."

"Well, that little Luza girl was one of the victims that he committed all them perversions on."

Cloud nodded. "You say they moved away right after the trial?"

"Yep. Very next day. Her picture was in the paper and all, you know. Whole neighborhood was talking about her. And you know how some of them Mexicans are. Proud as princes even when they ain't got a pot *or* a window."

"Do you have any idea where they moved to, Mrs. Burney?"

"Couldn't even guess. The girl's brother just backed a rental truck up to the door the day after the trial, and him and the old man loaded everything on it, and they was gone."

"What was the brother's name, do you remember?"

"They called him Ray, but I think it was short for something. Ramón, probably. Don't ask me the parents' names 'cause I couldn't begin to pronounce *them*."

"Did the girl go to school while the family lived here?"

"I think so. I think she went to the high school over on Concert Street."

In the El Monte Union High School office, Cloud was refused information by a series of clerks until finally, after much insistence, he ended up in the principal's office. The principal was an attractive woman of fifty, whose manner was pleasant but firm.

"Mr. Cloud, it is absolutely against school policy to release personal information on any student except to law-enforcement agencies."

"I thought perhaps you could make an exception since she's a former student," Cloud said.

"I'm sorry," the principal said, "I'm afraid not."

"Do you know about the trial the girl was involved in?"

"Of course. The whole school knew about it. It was the reason the family moved."

"Let me ask you a question," Cloud said. "How would you feel about helping me locate this girl if I told you there was a very strong possibility that she had identified the wrong man? And that an innocent man was on Death Row."

"Why, I suppose I'd feel pretty much like anyone else would," the principal replied. "I'd feel that it was an injustice that should be corrected. But I'm still bound by certain policies set down by the school authorities. If this man is innocent, as you say, I'm sure you should have no difficulty in getting proper authorization to obtain the information."

"My problem is time," Cloud explained. "This man is due to go to the gas chamber in a very short time."

The principal thought about it a moment. "What makes you so certain that the man Glory Ann identified is innocent?"

"We've already proved that the other major witness against him was mistaken. That's why it's so urgent that we find the Luza girl. If we can show the same discrepancy in her identification, then we can get the death sentences reversed."

"Mr. Cloud," she said, "I would like to help you. Really. But you see, when the Luzas moved away, they gave the school no forwarding address. They didn't even obtain a school transfer for Glory Ann; nor have we received a request for her records from any other school."

Cloud pressed forward. "Would you be able to give me some information about Glory Ann's family? Her father's name, where he worked—anything at all to help me keep looking."

The principal studied Cloud thoughtfully for a moment. Then she sighed quietly. "Wait here, please," she said finally. She left the office and returned a moment later with a manila folder.

"Father: Emiliano," she said. "Employed as a meat packer for Rancher Bob's Sausage Company in Vernon. Mother: Josefa. Housewife." She closed the folder and looked steadily at him. "I've just put my job on the line telling you that."

Cloud shook his head. "No you haven't." He held out his hand. "It's nice to meet someone like you."

"I wish you luck," she said, shaking his hand.

Rancher Bob's Sausage Company was on a narrow industrial side street. Next to a scarred and rusted loading dock, Cloud found a door with a sign that read: GENERAL OFFICES—UPSTAIRS. He went up the narrow wooden stairway and entered a large, drab room of desks and file cabinets crowded together on an ancient tile floor. After a preliminary inquiry, Cloud found himself back down on the loading dock talking to the firm's production foreman.

"Hell yes, I know 'Miliano Luza," the man said. "One of the best meat packers I ever had."

"Had?"

"Yeah. He left a year ago last August. With me eleven years."

"Do you know where he went?" Cloud asked.

"Wait a minute. Before I do too much talking, what do you want him for, anyway?" The production foreman's eyes had narrowed to a suspicious squint.

"It's a legal matter," Cloud said, "involving his daughter."

"Legal matter, huh? Wouldn't have anything to do with that son of a bitch that raped the girl, would it?"

"Well, first of all, the girl wasn't raped—"

"She wasn't, huh? That's all you know, mister. Let me ask you one question: are you working for the guy that's waitin' to be gassed for what he did to that little girl?"

"I work for a foundation that represents him, yes."

"Well, ain't that nice!" He looked back over his shoulder. "Hey, Manuel, Dutch, Gerardo, all you guys come here!"

Half a dozen meat packers wearing heavy canvas aprons and thick canvas gloves left their packing tables and came up to the foreman.

"This here guy works for the son of a bitch that raped 'Miliano's little girl," the foreman said belligerently.

"Look, I told you the girl wasn't raped," Cloud said. "The man who was convicted wasn't even charged with rape—"

"Let me tell you something, mister," the foreman said, his tone growing bolder with reinforcements behind him. "You better get the fuck out of here, you understand me? Don't come sucking around here with your lousy questions trying to get us to help save that cocksucker from the gas chamber. We all liked 'Miliano, see? He was one of us, you understand me? Now you get your ass out of here and you do it quick!"

He took a menacing step forward and Cloud held up a hand in submission.

"Okay, pal, take it easy—"

"I'm not your fucking pal either!"

"Whatever you say." Cloud backed down the concrete steps to the street. When he got far enough back from his threatening adversary, he turned and started walking away.

"For your information," the foreman yelled after him, " 'Miliano didn't tell nobody where he was going. We just want you to know we wouldn't tell you nothin' even if we *did* know!"

An hour later, Cloud was in downtown Los Angeles, in a bar on Hill Street, nursing his second martini. It was two o'clock; he had been in town barely five hours and already he had come to a complete dead end. The Luza family had disappeared. And it was obvious why. Everywhere Cloud had looked for them, he had found the stigma of what had happened to the girl. Everyone had instantly identified the family with the daughter's tragedy. The shadow of their shame was long and dark.

Cloud leaned his forearm on the bar and sipped at his drink. The second martini, on a stomach that had long since digested breakfast, was beginning to make him feel warm. And he was tired. It had been a long day, even if it was still early afternoon.

He tried to think of other ways to trace the Luzas. The father, and probably the son Ramón, were more than likely employed somewhere in the vast, sprawling megalopolis of Los Angeles county. There was a good chance that the elder Luza still worked in the meat-packing business. Maybe there was a meat-packers' union that had records he could check.

The son, Cloud reasoned, would have had to register for the draft too; but whether draft records were available for scrutiny or not was something Cloud did not know. The only records he knew were open to public examination were marriage licenses, business licenses, and voter registrations. Business licenses would probably be a long shot, but the other two might be definite possibilities. The father, mother, and brother might have registered to vote in their new precinct, and brother Ramón might have taken out a marriage license. For that matter, Glory Ann herself could have married; she was past twenty now.

He checked the Registrar of Voters first, in a building just north of the Civic Center. A large ground-floor room contained thick, heavy volumes stored row upon row above long, slanted reference ledges. The room, as Cloud had learned when he worked for the *Ledger*, was open to the public. When he got there, he went directly to the L section. Pulling the very last L volume down, he thumbed through to the back of it and began going down the list. Another dead end. Emiliano Luza had not registered to vote, nor had Josefa Luza, nor Glory Ann Luza. He did find three Ramón Luzas registered, but none of them was the right age.

Cloud drove next to the Hall of Records in the Civic Center. Because the business-license section was closest, he checked there first. Eighteen county business licenses had been issued to people named Luza—but none of them had the given names Cloud sought.

He went next to the marriage-license section. During the preceding two years, eight Luzas had been parties to marriage licenses issued in Los Angeles county. None of them had given names of Ramón or Glory Ann. Cloud even checked for the names Emiliano and Josefa, in case the parents might have divorced and remarried. Still nothing.

He was about to leave the marriage-license section when a thought suddenly came to the surface of his mind—a thought that had emerged from time to time ever since the day he and Lew Lach had interviewed Whitman in the county-jail visiting room.

"Married?"

"Not any more."

"Where's your ex?"

Whitman had shaken his head. "*Forget it.*"

Forget it. Cloud suspected Whitman wanted her kept under such deep cover because he was afraid that his former partner would threaten her in some way to keep Whitman from naming him. Perhaps had *already* threatened her; maybe that was why Whitman would not let Cloud look for him. Cloud fervently wished there was some way he could trace that former partner without Whitman knowing about it . . .

Maybe there *was* a way. If he could find Whitman's ex-wife—talk to her quietly, without publicity, without revealing her whereabouts to anyone—perhaps he could learn the identity of the man Whitman himself so adamantly refused to name. It was an outside chance—but so was nearly everything else they had done. Cloud felt his enthusiasm returning. He went back to the marriage-license bureau's master card index and found a card dated nearly six years earlier, indicating that a marriage license had been issued to Weldon Carpenter Whitman and Carol Ann Carter. Cloud felt a slight surge of excitement at the sight of the card; locating it was the first thing he had accomplished that day. He copied down the date and number of the license, and took the information up to the records counter.

"May I see the application for this license, please?"

The clerk looked at the date. "That'll be on microfilm," she said, handing Cloud a records-request form. "Fill this out, please, and then have a seat in the microfilm room right through that door."

After five minutes, the counter clerk handed Cloud a reel of microfilm. "Take any available machine," she said. "Instructions are on the card in each booth."

Cloud sat down in one of the viewing booths, threaded the film through the viewer, turned on the light, and adjusted the image on the screen. He moved the film forward until he reached the number he had copied down. And there it was: an application for a marriage license, one half of it filled out in a neat, feminine hand, the other in Weldon Whitman's now-familiar writing.

Cloud stared at the half of the form which had been filled out by Carol Ann Carter. He read it and re-read it, as if obligated to commit to memory its details: date of birth, place of birth, sex, race, religion, other now-inane facts. His eyes traced the neat, precise script of her handwriting: the penmanship was practiced, determined, exact. He knew without further thought that he was going to search for her.

Cloud left the Civic Center and drove east on the San Bernardino Freeway toward Alhambra, a suburb seven miles northeast of Los Angeles, where Carol Carter had lived when she and Whitman applied for their license. As he drove, he lighted another cigarette and immediately felt acid begin to churn in his stomach. He promised himself that he would at least stop for a hamburger as soon as he had found out what leads the Alhambra address would produce.

It was an old stucco house, long neglected. But to Robert Cloud, it might have been a palace, so buoyantly did it lift his spirits; for on a rusty, lidless mailbox, scribbled on a carelessly torn piece of paper held in place by an aged, yellowed strip of transparent tape, was the name Carter.

There was no sound from within when he pushed the doorbell, so Cloud knocked gently on the glass pane in the door. When there was no answer he knocked again, a little louder. After his second knock, a curtain on the inside of the door was pulled back and a scowling middle-aged female face peered suspiciously at him.

"Yeah, what do you want?"

"Is Carol Carter in?" Cloud asked. The woman's mouth dropped open in as much surprise as if Cloud had cursed at her. Almost angrily she let go of the curtain and snatched open the door.

"Who are you?" she demanded with unconcealed suspicion.

"My name is Robert Cloud," he told her. "I'm a writer. I'm looking for Carol Carter in connection with a story I'm doing."

The woman's eyes narrowed, showing dark lids and lower circles in a face that Cloud now saw was puffy and dough-colored. She clutched a soiled terrycloth robe together in front. "A story? On who?" she snorted. "That sex pervert she married?"

"Partly on Weldon Whitman, yes. Are you Carol's mother?"

"I used to be," the woman said loftily, "before I disowned her."

"Mrs. Carter, do you suppose I could come in and talk to you for a few minutes?"

"Not about Carol," she said flatly. "I'm not going to talk about Carol. I already told you that I disowned her."

"About Weldon Whitman then. Will you talk about him?"

"Sure. If I don't have to say nothing good about him."

She let Cloud in. The living room of the house looked as if it had come out of the mind of Tennessee Williams: ancient lace doilies, a green frieze sofa and matching club chair, a round table with a tall lamp built into it, a lampshade with tassels hanging from its rim.

Cloud sat in the club chair; he was at once engulfed by a musty, sour odor. "Mrs. Carter," he began, "you sound like you really dislike Weldon Whitman. Would you mind telling me why?"

Lowering her heavy body into a half-sprawl on the couch facing him, she gathered the terrycloth robe between her knees. "He's a sex pervert and he stole my daughter from me."

"How did he steal her from you?"

"He made her run away. He encouraged her to leave her own mother, her own flesh and blood. That's why I disowned her. That's why I won't talk about her."

"Do you know where Carol is now, Mrs. Carter?"

She shook her head wearily. "No. I couldn't find her if my life depended on it."

"She doesn't keep in touch with you at all?"

Again the weary shake of the head. "No. Why should she? I told you I've disowned her. She knows it too."

"When was the last time you saw her?" Cloud asked.

"Three years ago," the woman said. Cloud noticed her lip tremble slightly when she said it.

"Was she living with Weldon then?" he asked. He kept his voice controlled, but his mind was racing. Three years ago was a few months before the Spotlight Bandit crimes.

"She couldn't have been living with him," Mrs. Carter said. "He was in prison."

Or just ready to get out, Cloud thought. "Do you have any idea where she might be working?"

"Probably in some hamburger joint somewheres," the old woman said. "All she's ever done is wait tables or carhop.

She don't know nothing else. Didn't finish her last year of high school even. Last time I heard, she was working as a counter girl in the Donald's Drive-in up in South Pasadena. A lady friend of mind was visiting her sister up there one afternoon and they stopped in for a bite to eat. Carol was the one who waited on them. She was probably working to support that pervert she was married to."

"Why do you keep calling Whitman a pervert, Mrs. Carter? Is it because of what you've read about the Spotlight Bandit?"

The old woman snorted. "I don't have to read no newspaper to be able to call him a pervert. I've heard about things he done to girls right here in Alhambra, things he never got caught for because them and their families was too ashamed to file charges."

"What kind of things, Mrs. Carter?"

"Just things," she said indignantly. "I don't want to talk about them. They happened after him and Carol had split up, though, so it's no reflection on her, you hear?"

"Sure." Cloud nodded and rose to leave. "Do you know of any other place I can start looking for her besides Donald's Drive-in?"

"No. I wouldn't even know that if it hadn't been for my lady friend. Carol, she quit telling me things years ago. That's another reason why I disowned her."

Cloud went to the door to let himself out. As he was about to go, the woman spoke to him again.

"Mister—?"

He paused and turned back.

"If you do find her will your tell her something for me?"

"Sure."

"Tell her that her mother is all alone," she said in as agonized a voice as Cloud had ever heard. "Tell her she ought to come see me some time and not leave me to just—just . . ." Her voice trailed off to nothing. Across the room, Cloud could see wetness starting in her eyes.

"I'll tell her," he said quietly.

At Donald's Drive-in in South Pasadena, the first thing Cloud did was to wolf down two big Donaldburgers and a chocolate shake, eating so fast that for a moment he felt slightly nauseated. It was now nearly five o'clock. When

Cloud finished eating, he smoked a cigarette and then asked to see the manager. A cheerful little man with a cherubic face came over to the booth.

"I'm the manager," he said. "Barry Woodbury. What can I do for you?"

"I'm looking for a girl that worked here about three years ago," Cloud said. "Were you here then?"

"Sure was." The manager slid into the seat facing him.

"The girl I'm trying to locate is Carol Carter. Do you remember her?"

"Sure do. Great little gal. Real hustler when the counter got busy."

"She's not still with you by any chance, is she?"

"She may still be with the chain," Woodbury said. "She transferred to another branch so she could be close to school."

"What school was that?"

"I'm not real sure. It was one of those adult-education programs where you go nights to get a high-school diploma."

Cloud nodded. "Is there a main office you can call to find out if she's still working for the chain?"

"Yeah, I guess so," the manager said, a little hesitantly now. "What are you trying to find her for, anyway?"

"It's kind of personal," Cloud said, "but I'll tell you since you're going to all this trouble to help me. Carol used to be married, before she came to work here. The man she was married to may be dying. I want to get in touch with her about it."

"That's too bad," Woodbury said. "He must be a pretty young guy, too."

"Too young to die," Cloud replied.

"Yeah." Woodbury stood up, looking slightly uncomfortable. "I'll go make that call."

While he waited, Cloud looked out the window at the night's slow traffic. It was dark now and cars were backed up at all four traffic signals. Cloud still had no place to stay for the night. He had picked up the rental car at the airport and started right out looking for Glory Ann Luza. His suitcase was still in the trunk. Wondering idly where he was going to sleep that night made him think, for some reason, of Laurel. Actually, Whitman's mother-in-law reminded him of Laurel, he realized. He thought of the home Whitman's wife had come from, the same kind of home Laurel had worked so hard to get away from. Now Laurel had a good job and apartment . . . He wondered if she still lived at the same place. Then he thought that it really made no difference whether she did or not, because it was Monday, and on Mondays and Thursdays she did counseling in the evening. For extra money. He grunted softly.

Barry Woodbury returned to interrupt his thoughts. "I found out a couple of things for you," he said. "First off, Carol's not with the company anymore. When she left here, she transferred to our downtown L.A. location, on Olive near Eighth—"

Cloud sighed softly. That was a block from the bar he had been sitting in at two o'clock that afternoon.

"Like I said, she was going to night school somewhere down in that area to get her high-school diploma. When she finally got it, about six months later, she quit hustling hamburgers to get a better job."

"Did they know where?" Cloud asked.

"Not for sure," Woodbury said. "She didn't tell anybody where she was going, but her personnel record shows that about a week later there was an inquiry from General Telephone out in Santa Monica. She was applying for a job in the accounting department there. And I guess she must've got it, because that was the only place that ever called for a reference."

"Sounds like a good lead," Cloud said. "I appreciate the help."

Woodbury smiled a good-natured smile as Cloud got up to leave. "Well, if you find her, tell her Barry Woodbury said hello."

"I'll do that," Cloud said.

Cloud went outside and took several breaths of the cooling South Pasadena air. He lighted another cigarette, curled his lips in distaste at the staleness of it, but chose not to throw it away. He got into the car and waited patiently to pull into the freeway-bound traffic. There was no sense in rushing; it was a good twenty miles to Santa Monica, and there was nothing he could do there except find a motel for the night and check out his lead in the morning.

The General Telephone Company, he thought as he drove

along in the crawling traffic. The accounting department yet. That made Carol Carter's mother wrong about one thing: there apparently was something Carol could do besides wait tables or carhop.

Fifteen

Shortly after nine the following morning, Cloud walked into the main office building of General Telephone Company and spoke to the receptionist.

"I'd like to see Miss Carol Carter, please," he said, adopting a straightforward, businesslike attitude. "I believe she's in accounting."

"May I have your name, please?" the girl asked. Cloud gave her his name. "And who are you with, sir?"

"Donald's Hamburger Drive-ins," Cloud lied. He could think of nothing else to say in the face of the unexpected question.

"Would you have a seat, please, Mr. Cloud, and I'll call Miss Carter."

Cloud sat down on one end of a modern couch next to a large potted plant. He opened a fresh pack of cigarettes and lighted one. He was smoking far too much lately, and it was beginning to bother him. He invariably had a dry, stuffy taste in his mouth; his sinuses seemed to be enlarged to the point of difficult breathing half the time; and he was developing a periodic hacking cough. Nevertheless he sat there smoking until he heard a voice next to him.

"Mr. Cloud?"

He looked up at a young woman who had approached without his noticing. She was a small woman but not slight, with shoulders wider than a woman's should be, and a waist too narrow for the shoulders. A soft slide of blonde hair, parted slightly off-center, fell to each side of her face. She had a broad, solemn mouth that should have been her least attractive feature, but somehow was not. There was about her an instantly recognizable reserve.

"I'm Carol Carter," she said. "The receptionist said you were from Donald's Hamburgers—"

Cloud stood up. "I'm not," he said. "I found you through the Donald's chain. The name just came out when she asked who I was with."

Carol Carter frowned. "I'm afraid I don't understand—"

"I work for the Weldon Whitman Foundation, Miss Carter," he said quietly.

"Oh, my God—" The color vanished from her face.

"It's a group that's trying to help Weldon. I suppose you know he's in San Quentin condemned to die?"

"Why have you come here?" she said. "My job—" Cloud noticed that even her full, wide lips had paled. "No one knows who I am—"

"No one has to," Cloud said quickly. "Let's walk over here," he said, leading her across the lobby.

"What do you want with me?" she asked almost fearfully. "Did Weldon send you?"

"He doesn't even know I'm here," Cloud assured her. "I wanted to find you for my own reasons."

"If the people who know me here find out I was married to Weldon, I'll have to leave. I couldn't bear to be looked at and talked about the way they'd look at me and talk about me—"

"Please try to calm down," Cloud said. "I promise you no one is going to find out. I'm not here to do anything that will jeopardize your job. All I want to do is talk to you."

"About what?"

"About Weldon. I want to talk to someone who's been close to him, who knows him—"

"There *is* no such person," she said bluntly. "No one knows Weldon except Weldon. And no one ever will."

"You must have come close," Cloud ventured. "Closer than anyone else."

"Why? Because I was married to him? That didn't mean anything." She wrung her hands briefly. "Look, I've got to get back upstairs—"

"Let me meet you after work," Cloud urged. "Just for a little while. Anywhere you say; someplace public, anywhere. It's really important—"

"To who? You? Weldon?"

"Maybe both of us," Cloud said. "Maybe you, too."

"Me? How could it possibly be important to me?"

"Because you'll know you helped. Or tried to."

Carol Carter sighed and shook her head in exasperation. "All right," she said firmly. "I'll let you come to my apartment tonight for one hour. *One hour.* You can come over at six and you have to leave at seven sharp. That's because my boyfriend is coming over at seven-thirty, and he usually gets there a little early."

"Six to seven," Cloud agreed. "One hour."

She gave him an address on Montana Street there in Santa Monica, then hurried back to her job.

At the stroke of six he rang her doorbell. She lived on the second floor of an L-shaped two-story building that occupied a deep, narrow lot in a neighborhood of apartment houses. There were eight apartments in the building: four up, four down. Hers was the last, number eight, upstairs in the back. Cloud was about to ring a second time when she opened the door.

"Hello. Come in. I'm just finishing dinner. Would you like some coffee?"

"Sure. Thanks."

She seemed more relaxed now. Cloud followed her to a tiny kitchen separated from the living room by a counter and stools. She was wearing snug-fitting pants and as she walked in front of him, Cloud could not help admiring her ass.

He sat down while she poured his coffee. "You seem to feel a lot better about this tonight," he commented.

Carol Carter shrugged. "I've had a few hours to get over the surprise." She sat down across the counter from him and tilted her head slightly. "I think I knew all along that I wasn't completely free of Weldon. I don't suppose I'll ever be, not until he's dead. Maybe not even then." She toyed with what was left of her meal. "How did you find me anyway? How did you know I used to work at Donald's?"

"Your mother," said Cloud.

Carol Carter stiffened very slightly. "When did you see my mother?"

"Yesterday. In Alhambra."

The young woman nodded. "So she still lives in the same old dump. Did she have a man in the house?"

"I didn't see anyone but her."

Carol shrugged. "Maybe you caught her between men. Do you know she's been married six times since my father left? Six times. And the funny thing of it is, I think she's only been divorced by two of them." She smiled sardonically. "You wouldn't believe the assortment of stepfathers I've had. Everything from boozers to lechers to one guy I'm *positive* was gay."

Cloud looked around at what he could see of the little apartment. It was sparsely but smartly furnished, immaculately kept. "You seem to have done all right for yourself."

"I've earned it too," she said almost fiercely. "Every bit of it. All by myself."

"I heard that you went to night school," he said.

"I still do," she told him. "Only now I go to the university. I'm an accounting major. I'll get my degree in just seven and a half short years. I may even become a CPA."

"That's a long way from Alhambra," Cloud said.

"The farther the better," she said with grim seriousness. She got up and cleared off the counter with an expert style no doubt left over from her waitress days. "Look, you've wasted ten minutes of your time already, just talking about me."

"It hasn't been wasted," Cloud said. "Knowing what kind of person you are will help me to understand better how you feel about Weldon. How do you feel about him, anyway?"

She poured him some more coffee and sat back down. Her wide, solemn mouth became sad. "I'm not sure. I feel sorry for him, a little. I used to feel sorry for him a *lot.* I used to feel so sorry for him that I hurt and I cried. Mostly it was because he was such a failure at life. It's odd, you know, but Weldon had so much going for him: he had ambition, intelligence, initiative, drive. But he just could not succeed at anything honest. That's what I felt sorry for him the most about: he couldn't make an honest living. No matter how hard he tried. It simply wasn't in him."

"Did you know when you married him that he was a criminal?"

"I knew he'd been in reform school," she said. "And I knew he had some pretty rough friends. But I thought that he was just like me, that he needed somebody to care, and that if he had that somebody, he'd straighten out. All he seemed to need was a chance."

There it was again, Cloud thought. The Whitman mystique. The same one that had touched Genevieve, touched him. *He just seemed to need a chance.*

"I was very young, very naïve, when Weldon and I met," Carol said. "Like a lot of very young, very immature women, I thought it was possible to make a man out of a guy by marrying him and giving him a home and responsibilities and all that supposedly good stuff."

"So you got married."

She nodded. "It seemed like a good idea at the time."

"Have any children?"

"No!" she said almost in horror. "Thank God for that, too!"

"What finally caused you to break up?"

"Something came between us," she said wryly. "A five-to-eight-year sentence in Folsom for armed robbery." She sighed wistfully. "Like I said, Weldon just didn't know how to be honest. He was a confirmed criminal." Her expression turned bitter. "If the state of California had taken a good long look at him, they would have known it too. They had him in prison three times, and they turned him loose every time. Now they're going to have to kill him."

Cloud leaned forward on the counter in order to be closer to her. "Let me ask you a couple of specifics," he said. "You've read about his case in the papers, right?"

"Of course."

"Are you familiar with the crimes he's been convicted of? The kidnapping and sex-perversion crimes?"

"Yes."

"Tell me honestly, do you think he could have committed those crimes?"

She hesitated for just a split instant, then said, "No, I don't think so."

"Tell me why."

"I just don't think he would have gone that route, that's all."

"Your mother seems to think he would have," Cloud said. "She mentioned some similar incidents that happened in Alhambra that Whit was never arrested for. Do you know anything about those?"

She shook her head. "No."

"May I get personal with you?" Cloud said.

"That depends. You can try."

"I'm interested in the sex life you and Whit had together."

"What about it?"

"What kind of relationship was it? Mutually satisfactory? One way? Conventional? Any extremes?"

Carol Carter looked slightly uncomfortable. "It wasn't spectacular," she admitted, "but it was pretty good. Weldon satisfied me about half the time." She looked at him very directly again. "I satisfied him all the time."

"Was he demanding about sex?"

"Not really. Eager at times. But always gentle. Never rough."

"I see." Cloud chewed one fingernail briefly. "You know the nature of the sex-perversion crimes he was convicted of. I was just wondering if he showed any preference or inclination toward, ah—"

"The answer is yes, Mr. Cloud. Weldon liked an occasional head job. What man doesn't?"

"Sure," Cloud said. He was feeling a little embarrassed and was immediately irritated with himself for it. If she didn't mind talking about it, there was certainly no reason for him to mind listening to it.

"Actually," Carol continued, "if Weldon had been an honest working man instead of a criminal, we would have had a pretty good marriage. This may sound odd to you, but aside from his stealing, Weldon was almost an ideal husband. He drank very little. He liked to fix things around the house. He was there most evenings when I got home from work; sometimes he even had dinner ready. There were no other women. I think he really *liked* marriage."

"Why did he let you divorce him then?"

Carol shrugged. "He had no choice. He was a convicted felon, serving time. That's grounds for divorce in California. When I found out that he was a three-time loser, I was pretty shook up. I went to Folsom to visit him and I asked him to tell me honestly if he thought he'd ever change and straighten out. He thought about it for quite a while before he answered. Then he finally said no, he honestly didn't think so. He said he wished he could, because he really did care for me. But he said he'd just been a crook too long and he didn't think he had the will power and character it would take to become anything else. Those were the exact words he used: will power and character. Would you like more coffee?"

"No, I've had plenty, thanks. Whose idea was the divorce?"

"Mine," she said. "I told him on that one visit I made up there to that horrible place—have you ever been to Folsom?"

Cloud shook his head. "No."

"It's like the kind of prison they used to show in the movies," she said. "Cold, ugly granite. And dirty; everything about the place looked dirty. And the guards—God, they looked as bad as the convicts. I told Weldon that first visit that I would never come to that place again. And I told him that I thought it would be best if I divorced him. I said I wanted to try and make something of my life. He agreed without any kind of argument. He said he thought I was right, that it would be best for both of us. Best for me because I could go ahead and *try* to make a better life for myself; and best for him because it would be easier for him to do his time if he didn't have to feel guilty about ruining my life. He said he was sorry he had married me, not because he didn't care for me, but because it hadn't been fair to me. He said he hoped I wouldn't hold it against him. I told him of course I wouldn't. And then I left."

"Was that the last time you saw him?"

"No. I saw him once more after that. When he was paroled from Folsom, he found out where I was living through some friends that I was still in touch with at that time. He came over one evening to see me. Just to say hello and chat a few minutes, nothing intimate. He seemed glad to see that I was getting along fairly well. We had a nice little visit. He even gave me a present, a little silver cross and chain; not expensive but very thoughtful, very nice of him."

"Did you see him any more after that?"

"No. That was the last time. The next I heard of him was a short time later when I read in the papers about his capture and identification as the Spotlight Bandit."

"What did you think when you read that?" Cloud asked. "Did you believe it?"

Carol Carter hesitated again, then seemed to take hold of herself and answer. "No. I didn't believe it."

"That's twice you've had to make yourself answer," Cloud said quietly. "You do have doubts, don't you?"

"I—I'm not sure," she admitted. "Sometimes I remember Weldon as he was when we first met, and I tell myself that he *couldn't* have done those things, particularly to that teenage girl. Then—then I think of how he became worse and worse during the time I knew him; how each crime he committed was a worse crime than the one before it. I can't help recalling how Weldon seemed to be turning into—I don't know, a *harder* person. Understand, he still wasn't the monster the newspapers have made him out to be; but he *was* getting worse. When I force myself to be completely honest about it, I have to admit that if he kept on as he was going at that time, maybe he *could* have become what they say he is now—a criminal sex pervert. He used to rob just for money. Maybe he got to the point where that wasn't enough; maybe he had to get something more out of it. Maybe he turned into the kind that does it just out of meanness or for kicks. Or maybe he just plain turned cruel because of all that's happened to him. I don't know, I really don't." She fell silent for a long moment, staring vacantly at some distant memory; then she sighed a quiet sigh and looked at her kitchen clock. "It's almost seven."

"Right," Cloud said, getting up. He smiled. "Is your boyfriend always on time?"

"Always," Carol Carter said in mock exasperation. "He's an accountant. Very prompt."

"And very proper?"

"Yes. Very." She too smiled a little then. At the door she gave him her hand, though still with a certain reserve. "I'm glad Weldon has you for a friend," she said. "I hope you'll be able to help him."

"I hope so too. Incidentally, there was one other thing I wanted to ask you. Did you ever know any partner that Weldon had? Someone he pulled jobs with after he got out of Folsom?"

Carol shook her head. "No. As I told you, I only saw him that one time after Folsom: when he came over to visit and gave me the cross and chain."

"So you've never met or had any communication with anyone who served time with him in Folsom?"

"No, never. As a matter of fact, I never see anybody we knew *before* he went to Folsom. I don't even go back to see my own mother, and I never will. I've worked very hard to get away from the ugly side of life. If people found out about my having been married to Weldon, it would ruin everything. I'd have to start all over again—"

"No one is going to find out," Cloud assured her. "I don't intend even to tell Weldon about seeing you."

She looked at him penetratingly, her broad mouth solemn and anxious. It was obvious that she was becoming nervous again.

"Please don't worry," he said. She nodded the briefest of nods.

"All right, I won't. I'll trust you. I don't have any choice, anyway."

"You won't be hurt," Cloud promised. "You'll see."

"All right. Goodbye, Mr. Cloud."

"Goodbye."

Cloud went back downstairs and walked past the other apartments to the front of the building. As he crossed to where he had parked, he noticed a tall, rather smug-looking man get out of a car at the curb and walk toward the building. The prompt accountant, he thought.

He got into the rented sedan and lighted a cigarette. For a few minutes he sat there in the dark, smoking, thinking. He reached no new conclusions as a result of finding Weldon Whitman's ex-wife—except possibly that she was not in any danger from Whitman's former Folsom partner. He *definitely* would not tell Whitman he had found Carol Carter; it would only incense the condemned man and would serve no useful purpose.

Finishing his cigarette, Cloud decided to go back to the motel, pack his things, and take one of the night commuters back up north. There was no sense spending an idle night in Los Angeles when he could just as easily get back to where the work was. *Judgment in Anguish* was waiting for him. Weldon's second book, as Genevieve persisted in calling it. Cloud grunted. He supposed it made no difference. The important thing was the life of Weldon Whitman.

Cloud started the car and drove away in the darkness, leaving Carol Carter and her new, better life behind.

Sixteen

Four months later, the California Supreme Court denied Weldon Whitman's appeal. It ruled against him by a vote of four to one, with the dissenting justice writing his own minority opinion. The decision was handed down on a Wednesday, and almost within the hour, the principals in the Weldon Whitman Foundation were gathered again in the office of Morris Niebold.

"A temporary setback," the older attorney said from his gleaming wheelchair. "That's how I want all of you to think of this. Not as a defeat, but only as a temporary setback."

Genevieve, fire in her eyes, was in no mood for platitudes. "What do we do next?" she asked without preliminary. Borden White almost winced at her tone.

"Before we attempt to chart our future course," Niebold said, "I suggest we take the time to examine the position taken by the court in denying us relief. Borden, would you mind summing up the decision?"

White took a blue-covered copy of the court's majority opinion and folded back the top sheet. "Essentially what the court ruled is that it cannot be construed reversible error for a trial judge to fail to appoint an attorney as advisor to a criminally charged defendant who insists upon exercising his right to conduct his own defense." White sat back on the edge of Niebold's reference table. "The basis for the opinion primarily was that if a trial judge *did* overrule the defendant's desire to represent himself, if the court *did* appoint an attorney to, in effect, force-feed advice to the defendant, and the defendant were found guilty, at that point it *would* be reversible error because the defendant could make an appeal case of the fact that an attorney forced upon him against his desire by the court had persuaded him to follow a course of trial strategy contrary to his own plans, and the result had been a judgment against him. That, says the court majority, would establish a precedent under which every defendant could plead the right to self-defense, resist for the record the court's offer of legal help, then tacitly accept the court-appointed attorney's guidance, and, if subsequently found guilty, turn around and reject that same guidance as having been forced upon him—thus establishing his right to a retrial. Such a precedent, the court felt, would result in trial courts throughout the state having to try defendants twice instead of once. Therefore, the majority denied Whitman's appeal on the ground that to do contrary would create an untenable position for the trial courts."

"It's sound reasoning," Morris Niebold commented. "Even though it rejects our argument, I think we have to admit that the court's logic is faultless."

"I don't admit it," Genevieve said firmly. "If it were faultless, the opinion would be unanimous. We did have one dissenting justice, I believe."

"Quite true, my dear," Niebold conceded. Genevieve clenched her jaw. How she *wished* he would stop calling her that. "Borden," said Niebold, "why don't you go over the minority opinion for our colleagues?"

"Surely." White thumbed to the back of the opinion. "The dissent was from Mr. Justice Tanaka, the court's newest and only non-Caucasian member. His position is pretty much in line with our own: he feels that a trial judge *must* appoint *someone* to act as guardian of the defendant's rights. He feels that such an appointment is doubly essential in cases involving defendants from disadvantaged ethnic backgrounds—" Borden White smiled. "This doesn't surprise me in the least, coming from a Jap," he said smugly. "At any rate what Tanaka does *not* agree with is our position that this guardian of the defendant's rights must also be an advisor to the defendant in trial strategy. He feels that these are separate and distinct functions and should be treated as such. He even goes so far as to say that in some instances, such as in controversial cases of national interest or notoriety, two individuals be appointed: one to advise, one to monitor. In that way, he states, there can be no question as to the concern of the court in protecting the individual's rights. Justice Tanaka concludes his opinion by observing that the placing of trial courts in what the majority refers to as an untenable position is a weak excuse for failing to take positive steps to buttress the foundation of individual rights."

"I must say," Morris Niebold intoned, "that Tanaka has guts, Jap or no Jap."

"May we get on with a discussion of future plans?" Genevieve asked.

"Of course, my dear," said Niebold. His round, shiny cheeks gleamed almost as brightly as the chrome of his wheelchair. "Which would you care to take up first, the legal or nonlegal plans?"

"The legal."

"Very well, that's simple enough. Borden and I have already discussed that point and we've decided that we will take the appeal that was denied by the state and file on the same grounds in the federal court."

"The same appeal?"

"Yes. The fact that we had one California justice on our side I think indicates that our position has some definite judicial merit. And whereas the California court was disinclined to place any undue burden on the trial judges in its own state, the federal court may not be so reluctant. Borden and I both feel, from a constitutional point of view, that we will have a very good chance in the federal court of appeals."

"Fine," Genevieve said. "That will amount to a nice delaying tactic, nothing more, because I don't think a federal court is going to overrule a state supreme court on the matter of a trial judge's jurisdiction within its own state. What I'm primarily interested in is what we're going to do at the *state* level. If we're going to get Weldon off Death Row, it'll be through our own state courts, not the federal court system. I'm convinced of that. So while this delaying appeal is being studied in the federal courts, what do we intend to do at the state level?"

"Well, I'm afraid we'll have to do a little research before we decide that," Niebold said with a smile. "After all, the denial of our appeal has just been sent down; we need a little time to regroup and decide how best to next attack the state court. That sort of thing takes quite a bit of digging." He turned his smile on Carla Volt. "We'll put our expert legal assistant on it right away. In the meantime, I wonder if now wouldn't be an appropriate time to discuss the nonlegal aspects of the case. Robert," he said, turning to Cloud, "would you be agreeable to Weldon himself taking a somewhat harder stand with regard to his situation?"

"A harder stand in what way?" Cloud asked.

Morris Niebold hunched slightly in his chair and put the tips of his fingers together tent-fashion. "Up until now," he said in an academic voice, "Weldon's profile to the public has been one of innocence, wrongful conviction, and lawful but irresponsible condemnation to death in the gas chamber. His image has been one of a quiet, thoughtful person laboring under a miscarriage of justice, but being aided by a small, dedicated group of people—"

"That is precisely the image that Rob and I have worked very hard to convey to the public," Genevieve interrupted evenly.

"We realize that, Genevieve," said Borden White, "and the two of you have done a splendid job of it. It's just that Morris and I now wonder if it might not be time for a reevaluation of that image."

"Exactly," said Niebold. "The soft sell, as they call it, has served its purpose by getting people interested in Weldon's plight. I wonder now if a somewhat more—ah—active role on his part might not benefit our cause even more."

"Would you mind defining what you mean by active?" Genevieve said.

"All right. Let me give you an example. Until now, practically the only quote the public has heard from Weldon is that he's innocent. The people who are interested in him don't know, for instance, how he feels about G. Foster Klein, or the members of the jury who found him guilty, or old Judge Lukey, who could have overruled the jury and given him life in prison instead of death. And then there's the Calder woman and that little Mexican girl who both had to have made mistaken identifications for him to be innocent. Incidentally, we never have come up with that Mexican girl's whereabouts, have we?"

"No," Cloud said, "we haven't."

"Carla, make a note for the agenda of our next meeting to discuss the feasibility of hiring a private detective agency to track her down." Niebold turned back to Cloud. "The point I was making is that now might be the time to encourage Weldon to become somewhat more positive in the outward image that the public sees—"

"You want him to begin attacking people like Klein and Lukey, is that it?" Genevieve asked bluntly.

"Not *attacking*," Borden White said quickly. "We don't want anything vehement—"

"Not at the outset, at any rate," Niebold put in.

"But we do feel that some retaliation on his part is in order—"

"I am against it," Genevieve said unequivocally.

"Come now, Genevieve," said White. "Without even discussing it?"

"We've *been* discussing it," she replied imperviously. "What you're suggesting will change Weldon from a victim to an aggressor. It will lose him ninety percent of the public support he has gained."

"It *could* have the opposite affect," argued Niebold. "It could whip his present supporters into a fine frenzy *and* gain him a legion of new followers. People love a scrapper, you know, dear. Always have." Before Genevieve could comment, Niebold had turned to Cloud. "Robert, what do you think?"

"I don't know," Cloud said hesitantly. "The thought of undoing all we've done to make Whit a sympathetic person doesn't instantly appeal to me. Even a slight change would involve a lot of careful planning. The tone of this second book we're doing would have to be completely changed—"

"I'm sure that could be accomplished with some editing," Borden White observed. He paced around the desk until he was standing near Morris Niebold. "Please understand that we're not asking for anything drastic," he said with growing agitation. "What we basically want is to reach agreement among ourselves to explore the feasibility of having Whitman *project* a little more strongly. We think it will be good for the foundation, good for the next appeal we file, and good for our cause in general. We don't have to resolve exactly what degree of change we want or how we intend to accomplish it—but for the minutes of this meeting we would like to record a definite commitment from each director to pursue the matter. Therefore I am putting the matter in the form of a motion."

"I will second it," Morris Niebold announced, as solemnly as if he were naming a new Pope.

"All in favor?" Carla Volt, recording the minutes, asked.

Niebold and White both voted aye.

"All opposed?" Carla asked.

"Opposed," Genevieve said.

Carla turned to her lover. "Mr. Cloud?"

Cloud remained silent.

"You may abstain if you like, Robert," advised Niebold.

Cloud looked over at Genevieve. She met his stare but neither spoke nor allowed her expression to speak for her. Only deep in her eyes did Cloud see—or imagine that he saw—a plea.

"I'm opposed," he said finally. "I'm sorry, gentlemen, but I have to go along with Genevieve."

There was a second of silence in the office. Then Morris Niebold brought it back to life again.

"Sorry! Don't be, Robert! That's why we each have a vote, so we can express ourselves in complete good faith. This is a matter on which we happen to be equally divided in opinion. So be it! Carla, let the minutes show that the motion was neither carried nor defeated but was tabled for further discussion at a later date. Is that satisfactory with everyone?"

"Fine," said Cloud as Genevieve and Borden White mumbled their assent.

"Done," Niebold said, "and let's have no more talk of anyone being sorry." He smiled like an aging cherub. "Now, I move that we adjourn this meeting."

So concerned had Cloud and Genevieve been with the denial of Weldon Whitman's main appeal that they had forgotten the far less important, secondary appeal which had been suggested by Carla Volt and subsequently filed along with the primary papers. That appeal had put forth the theory that to limit the number of letters a condemned man was allowed to send and receive was, in essence, placing a limitation on the latitude given him by the law to appeal his case. Since the law had created so many avenues of appeal for the convicted criminal, it seemed inconsistent that at the same time it would permit a penitentiary regulation to so restrict those avenues as to actually dilute the right of appeal. It was true, Whitman's plea admitted, that exceptions were made for correspondence with attorneys and the courts—there being no restrictions at all on those classifications of mail—but by limiting other forms of correspondence, the regulation was in fact circumventing the prisoners' right to appeal by curtailing correspondence which might be contingent or supplemental to unrestricted mail. As an example, the appeal set forth a theoretical case wherein an incarcerated man might be allowed to write as many letters as he desired in an attempt to retain an appellate lawyer, but be strictly limited in the number of letters he might write to relatives and friends in an attempt to raise funds to *pay* that lawyer. The situation—so claimed the first part of Whitman's sub-appeal—was definitely an anomaly of the law and worth the Supreme Court's attention to correct it.

The second part of the sub-appeal was that the arbitrary San Quentin regulation prohibiting the possession of typewriters by condemned men was essentially a violation of the same right of appeal by virtue of the fact that it placed an unfair burden on prisoners such as Weldon Whitman who were playing active roles in their appeals. A typewriter, the appeal argued, could help the prisoners' correspondence create a neat, favorable, businesslike impression, quite the contrary to that created by a penciled letter written on lined prison stationery. Such an impression might well make the difference whether a person or organization decided to aid the condemned man in his quest for freedom. Regarding the prison's security reasons for prohibiting typewriters on Death Row, it was pointed out that such reasons were nothing more than token excuses, because typewriters were allowed in all other cellblocks, except Isolation and similar punishment units, and those other cellblocks were not nearly as secure as the Condemned cellblock. The argument narrowed down to the fact that Death Row was the most secure block in the prison, therefore it was the block where the permitting of typewriters would pose the least potential danger.

The California Supreme Court, after considering both arguments, agreed with the appeal and granted the requested relief.

"Can you believe this?" Genevieve asked incredulously the next day. "Can you believe a court that in one breath says a man has to die, and in the next lets him have a typewriter? It's absurd."

They were in her apartment; she had invited Cloud over for breakfast before they went to the printshop to look at the first run of a new anti-capital-punishment pamphlet.

"At least the court is giving us *something* for our efforts," Cloud rationalized.

"They're giving us crumbs."

"Maybe so, but we still might be able to get some publicity out of it. In a way, it's really a major decision as far as California prisons are concerned. It conceivably could affect every convict in California; certainly it will affect the future rights of every *condemned* convict."

"I suppose you can look at it that way," Genevieve conceded.

"We *have* to look at it that way," he told her. "We have to take advantage of everything they give us. I think we can get some good newspaper coverage on the first man on Death Row to get a typewriter. And I've got an idea for a magazine article that might do us some good. As soon as we get to the office, I think I'll call Ben Droller at *Argus* and see what he thinks of it."

Three weeks later, when Genevieve was visiting Whitman at the prison, he told her he had received the typewriter. She was delighted to see that he was pleased with it.

"It's really great," the condemned man said enthusiastically. "The store sent me a ream of paper and a typing manual. I've already started teaching myself."

"I'm so glad you like it, Weldon," she said. "It's the very best manual I could find. I just wish it could be an electric model."

Whitman grinned. "I can just see them letting us have electrical outlets in each cell. Somebody, somehow, would find a way to blow the fuse on the whole block at least once a day."

Genevieve smiled and sat back to study him. He was wearing the new glasses that the state had recently issued to him.

"I know," he said, grinning. "With this beak of mine they make me look like the wise old owl."

Presently they got down to the serious talk.

"Did Niebold and White get that appeal filed in federal court yet?" Whitman asked.

Genevieve nodded. "Yes, it's been filed. But they still haven't come up with any grounds on which to base a new appeal in the state court. And I'm worried about it, Weldon. You've got an—" she had to force the words out—"an execution date that's less than four months away. If the federal court turns you down before then, and no new appeal has been filed in the state court—"

"No chance," he said confidently. "In the first place, the federal court won't act that fast; they've got too many appeals to decide, so they'll have to grant me a stay before they even get to my case. I figure that'll come about a week before my date. Secondly, Niebold and White have got to come up with something by then; hell, I could write an appeal myself in that length of time."

Maybe you should, Genevieve felt like saying. But she curbed her tongue because she had faith in Weldon's judgment and she did not want to influence him unduly by voicing a prejudicial opinion of her own. "Perhaps I'm worrying over nothing," she said in quiet retreat.

"I think so," Whitman said reassuringly. He smiled affectionately at her. "But I'd be a liar if I said it didn't make me feel good to know that you worry about me."

"I know," she told him softly. "I *like* to worry about you. It's awful in a way, but I don't really know what I'd do without it."

"You're very important to me, honey," he said in a gradually lowering voice.

"And you to me, darling," she whispered.

They leaned toward each other as much as the partition between them would permit, and began their sex talk.

The story Robert Cloud wrote for *Argus* magazine was called "The Hero of Death Row." Weldon Whitman was depicted once again as the quiet, unassuming, wrongfully convicted condemned man who, besides filing an appeal to reverse his own conviction, had also taken some of his valuable time to improve the rights of his fellow convicts on Death Row by asking the court to allow the use of typewriters in the Condemned block and to let prisoners have broader correspondence privileges. Whitman had lost his plea for life, but had been granted the other relief he sought—not only for himself, but for all the incarcerated men who wanted to send and receive more letters while appealing their sentences, or who wanted typewriters in their Condemned Row cells.

The article blatantly fictionalized Weldon Whitman—a man respected and admired by the men with whom he shared Death Row, a father confessor who listened to their troubles and consoled them, a wise scholar who counseled them in their personal problems, a self-taught lawyer who pointed out to them the weaknesses in the state's case against them and suggested avenues of appeal—in short, an almost infallible, near-holy being who occupied a sort of death cell throne on the row of the condemned. The article was received with mixed response among Weldon Whitman's block partners.

"Hey, Whit!" yelled Stiles. "It say in this here story that you our hero and we can always 'pend on you to he'p us out from our problems. Well, I gots this here problem, babe, an' I wanna know if you can he'p me out from it."

Whitman, sitting on the floor outside his cell, looked up from the book he was reading. "What's your problem, Stiles?"

"Well," the muscle-bound black replied with a straight face, "see, there's some motherfuckers around here who tryin' to put me in the fuckin' gas chamber." The others in the corridor, listening to the put-on, laughed. "You got any advice for me, babe?" Stiles asked above the laughter.

"Yeah, daddy," Whitman replied. "Learn to hold your breath. For a long time."

Stiles broke up and joined the others laughing.

Milo, the stickup man and cop-killer, did not take the article as lightly. "Hey, Whitman, who is this guy Cloud who wrote this bullshit?"

"Why do you want to know?" Whitman asked.

"I'm thinking about having some friends of mine lace him a little. The son of a bitch called me a cold-eyed, psychopathic killer."

"Well, let's face it, Milo," Whitman said almost absently, "That's just about what you are."

"Why, you fucking pervert," Milo growled, "I'll tear your fucking balls off—" He pushed himself up from the floor and started for Whitman.

"Don't start anything, Milo," warned the deputy guard patrolling the corridor outside the bars.

"Fuck you!" Milo snarled, continuing toward Whitman.

Whitman laid down his book and got quickly to his feet. From his shirt pocket he took an ordinary wooden pencil with its lead sharpened to a fine point. "Which eye do you want this in, Milo?" he asked tensely.

Milo stopped and fell into a crouch like a cornered animal. The corridor guard blew his whistle to signal trouble on the Row. The control-room guard at the end of the corridor turned to a console and immediately began pressing buttons. All cell doors closed. Two backup guards hurried from a nearby dayroom with riot sticks. Within forty seconds, the elevator door opened and six more guards poured out and lined up at preassigned spots along the bars.

"I'll get you, Whitman," Milo threatened. But he did not move.

"You'll lose an eye doing it," Weldon Whitman warned.

"What the fuck is going on here?" stormed another voice. Captain Dukes strode through the guards and signaled for the separating door to be opened. The barred door slid back to admit the big guard captain into the prisoners' area. "Well, what have we here now?" he said with an open sneer. "A little disagreement of some kind? You both must be having your period at the same time."

"I'll rip your balls off, Whitman," the coiled cop-killer said. "I'll get you good—"

"The only thing you're going to get is your ass in an isolation unit," Captain Dukes said. "Now you back up to your cell and face the door."

Milo did not move. His eyes were riveted to Whitman.

"Do it now!" Dukes shouted, advancing a step. Milo backed away, his eyes shifting now from Whitman to Dukes to the backup guards. "Move!" Dukes ordered when he saw the first indication of a retreat. "Move! Move! Move!"

Milo moved.

"Open the cells," Dukes instructed. The cell doors slid open. "Get in," he told Milo. The cop-killer stepped into the cell. "Close and lock twenty-nine," the captain said. He turned to the patrol corridor. "Duty officer?"

"Yessir," the patrol guard said, stepping forward.

"Who started it?" the captain asked.

"Milo, sir."

"All right." Dukes nodded to the backup guards. "Secure," he said. He stepped over to Milo's cell. "You start any more trouble in this section, cop-killer, and I'll have your ass in an isolation cell until the day they gas you." He stalked away from the cell and over to Whitman. "What were you going to go for, an eye or the throat?" he asked, nodding at the pencil.

"I don't know what you mean, Captain," Whitman lied easily. "I just happened to have the pencil in my hand when I got up."

Dukes smiled his steel-hard smile. "You're a lying son of a bitch, Whitman. You know, I would have *let* Milo tear off your balls except for one thing: I don't think you've got any."

Dukes left the cell corridor. The duty guard began patrolling again. The Row inmates gradually went back to what they had been doing. With a weary sigh, Weldon Whitman took his law book and pencil-weapon and returned to his cell, where he might find at least a modicum of privacy.

A month passed. Clayton, the college student who had killed the ranch family, was granted a stay of execution pending an insanity appeal. His lawyers claimed that he had become demented since arriving at San Quentin and could not legally be executed because he would not be fully aware of why he was being punished.

Following Clayton's stay, the next man with a date was Franklin, the short, balding, ordinarily rather mild wife-slayer.

"You'll beat it, don't worry yourself," Captain Dukes told the little man. "I've been on this block a long time. I can pick 'em, believe me I can. I can *smell* the ones who are dead already and I can tell you the ones who'll beat it. You're one of those who'll cheat the old gas house, Franklin. Wait and see."

Dukes was right. Ten days before he was to go, the governor commuted Franklin's sentence to life imprisonment without possibility of parole. Franklin was transferred to the general inmate population.

The next man up was Whitman. His date was five weeks away.

"You'll go," Dukes delighted in telling him every day. "You'll definitely go. There's no way you're going to beat the gas pill, pervert."

Whitman had been practicing day and night on his new typewriter and was up to nearly forty words a minute. He fired off several letters to Niebold and White, inquiring about the new state appeal. To each letter he received a carefully worded reply from Carla Volt to the effect that the firm was still researching the matter. When Cloud visited him, Whitman raised hell about the situation.

"What is that bitch giving me with this research bullshit?" he demanded. "I'm down to less than a month and they're researching."

"They claim they're doing the best they can," Cloud said. "Anyway, I thought you told Genevieve that you were sure of getting a stay from the federal court because it wouldn't have time to rule on an old appeal before your date."

"That's not really the point," Whitman practically snapped at his friend. "I get the impression that things have bogged down, that the whole movement is in some kind of a rut. I don't like the feeling."

"I think it's a mistaken impression, Whit. Everybody's working for you just as we always have. Niebold and White are handling the legal end; Genevieve is grinding out mailing pieces in that printshop of hers every day, and still making three or four speaking engagements every week; and I'm right down to the wire on *Judgment in Anguish:* it should be ready to go to New York in another couple of weeks. On top of all that, donations are still rolling in and we've got a nice healthy bank balance—"

"Okay, okay," the condemned man said restlessly. "But I want some pressure put on those goddamned lawyers, Rob. I want you to bug those people, every day. Especially that little researcher who keeps sending me form letter number twelve or whatever in hell it is. If she can't find anything in all her research, tell her to come up here and talk to me. If we start kicking the thing around we're bound to come up with something."

"I'll work on them," Cloud promised.

A week passed. Niebold and White failed to come up with grounds for a new state appeal. At Cloud's insistence, and much to Genevieve's chagrin, Carla Volt visited Whitman at San Quentin. They talked for two hours, with Carla making copious notes on all the ideas Whitman had. She returned to Sacramento and began researching the ideas. Another week passed. Nothing came of any of Whitman's ideas. Then the bomb fell. The federal court, instead of granting a stay, handed down a unanimous opinion based on virtually the same grounds stated by the California supreme court majority.

Whitman's appeal was denied. The previously scheduled execution date remained in effect. Weldon Whitman had eight days to live.

Seventeen

Cloud and Genevieve descended on the offices of Niebold and White like avenging angels. But the only person they found there, besides clerical help, was Carla Volt.

"They're in Washington," she said. "Arguing a constitutional-law case they've had pending before the U.S. Supreme Court for four years. It involves the question of police authority over juvenile offenders—"

"I don't give a *damn* what it involves!" Genevieve Neller stormed at her. "What do they intend to do about Weldon? He's due to go to the gas chamber a week from tomorrow!"

"There's no need to shout, Genevieve," Carla snapped at her.

The two women faced each other across the desk with open hostility: Carla, lean, angular, her too-wide mouth drawn down at the corners, her long, glossy hair almost sepulchrally black; and Genevieve, her once-radiant features now looking slightly haggard from the pressure and worry.

Cloud stepped to the side of the desk so that he was at least technically between the two women. "Now look," he said sternly, "I want both of you to calm down." He looked at Carla. "When did Morris and Borden go to Washington?"

"This morning."

"Do they know yet about Whit's federal appeal being denied?"

"No. Not unless they've heard about it in Washington."

Cloud tapped the edge of the desk soundlessly with his fingertips, thinking. "When are they due back?"

"They weren't sure. This juvenile-offenders matter is a somewhat complicated issue."

Genevieve grunted contemptuously. "I hope they do a better job with it than they have in developing a new appeal for Weldon."

"Listen, you," Carla said angrily, "putting together a legal appeal is a little more complicated than running a printshop and speaking to a lot of old ladies at luncheons."

"Don't you tell *me* about that," Genevieve retorted instinctively. "I know more about the law and legal research than you ever will—"

"Why in the hell don't *you* write the appeal then!" Carla challenged.

Cloud slammed his open palm down loudly on the desktop. "All right! That's enough, goddammit! Both of you knock it off!" They fell silent at once, both gritting their teeth. "Jesus," Cloud murmured. He directed himself to Carla again. "Did either Morris or Borden give you any instructions about Whit's case before they left?"

"No special instructions, no. Just to keep going over old cases, the statutes, the trial transcript—anything that might give us a solid foundation for an appeal."

Cloud sighed. "How soon do you think you can contact either or both of them?"

"I can call their hotel right now," she said. "They won't be in, but I can leave a message."

"Make the call," Cloud said. "Tell the hotel that it is urgent that Mr. Niebold or Mr. White contact his office at once."

"All right."

"Do it now," Cloud said. "While we're here."

"Well," Carla said caustically. "One would think you didn't trust me or something."

"Just make the call," Cloud said. He took Genevieve by the arm and sat her down in a chair facing the desk, then sat in a chair next to her. Carla glowered at them for a moment, then snatched up the telephone.

"I'd like to call the Mayflower Hotel in Washington, D.C.," she told the operator. When the hotel answered, she said, "Yes, I'd like to leave messages for two of your guests, please. Mr. Morris Niebold and Mr. Borden White. Please tell them that it is urgent that they contact their office as soon as possible. My name is Miss Volt. Thank you."

She hung up and looked coldly at Cloud and Genevieve. "Satisfied?" she asked.

Cloud nodded. He and Genevieve stood up. "When one of them calls," Cloud said, "inform them of the situation and tell them that I feel it's essential that we discuss it at once. I'll either be at my apartment, Gen's apartment, or the foundation office. You have all the numbers."

"Yes, Mr. Cloud," Carla said icily. Her eyes, as they met his, were as devoid of warmth as steel chisels. Cloud turned away from their coldness.

"Come on, Gen," he said.

They waited two days, but no word came from Morris Niebold or Borden White. Cloud called Carla Volt a dozen times. Each time he called, she told him the same thing: neither attorney had responded to her messages. Cloud himself tried calling four times; he got no answer in either room on any of the calls. The last call he made, he placed at midnight, which would have made it three A.M. in Washington.

"Goddammit!" he said, slamming the phone down furiously. "Where the hell could they be?"

"Probably staying at another hotel and using these rooms as decoys to avoid us," Genevieve said. They were in her apartment, where they had been waiting impatiently since dinner.

"Come on, Gen," Cloud said irritably. "Why would they do a thing like that?"

"I don't know, Rob. I don't know why. All I know is that it's being done. And we've used up two precious days finding out that it's being done."

"We'll hear from them tomorrow," he said. "We've *got* to."

Thursday came. By noon they still had heard nothing. They ate a miserable lunch, saying little. The early afternoon mail brought a frantic note from Weldon Whitman:

What in the hell is going on!!! Will both of you please come down here at once! I am scheduled to go to the gas chamber on Tuesday!

Genevieve almost cried. "God," she said in an anguished voice. "Rob, what are we going to do?"

"Why don't you hop in the car and drive down to see him? Try to reassure him—"

"I can't even reassure myself, much less Weldon. No, I couldn't face him. Anyway, that's not what I meant. I meant what are we going to *do?* I think we should retain another lawyer. Today."

"Can we do that? I mean legally?"

"Of course. We have the money to do it—" She paused to briefly bite on a knuckle. "No, we don't. We don't even have that. Borden White is the foundation's treasurer. He has to sign all checks."

"Goddamn," Cloud said quietly.

They were sitting silently, caught up in the dull gloom of the situation, when the telephone rang like a fire alarm. Cloud got to the phone first.

"Mr. White just called," he heard Carla Volt say. "He and Mr. Niebold will be returning late tonight. They will see you and Miss Neller in Mr. Niebold's office at nine tomorrow morning."

"Did he say anything about what we're going to do?" Cloud asked eagerly.

"He said exactly what I told you he said," she replied icily. "Nothing more, nothing less. Goodbye."

She hung up, leaving Cloud with a dead receiver in his hand. He turned to Genevieve.

"Morris and Borden are coming back tonight. We'll meet with them first thing in the morning."

Genevieve finally let herself go and cried.

In Morris Niebold's office the following morning, the two factions gathered like enemies. Genevieve Neller, by then fully cried out, resumed her former posture with the foundation board and was again the most belligerent among them.

"Today is Friday," she said as soon as the meeting was called to order. "On Tuesday morning at ten o'clock Weldon Whitman is scheduled to die. I would like to know for the record why nothing is being done about it."

She was looking at Morris Niebold, but it was Borden White who answered. "Nothing is being done because at this point nothing *can* be done," he replied in a crisp, businesslike voice. "Our firm is continuing diligent legal research in an effort to find grounds for an appeal strong enough to merit being filed. And since we're speaking for the record, let it also show that this firm is of the opinion that were it not for the contrary attitude of the president of this foundation—you, Miss Neller—we might already have found such grounds."

Genevieve felt as if she had been slapped. Her lips parted and she sat stunned by the lawyer's words. Robert Cloud, however, was not so stupefied.

"What the hell is that supposed to mean, Borden?" he asked harshly.

"Just this," Borden White said, whirling to face him. "We asked months ago to have Whitman assume a stronger, more forceful position in this matter. We asked to show the public—*and* the courts—a bolder, more vociferous Weldon

Whitman: a Whitman who was determined to wade in and fight with both hands. It is the opinion of this firm that if we had begun building a dynamic Weldon Whitman who was going to have to be *dragged* into that gas chamber, today we would not be faced with the problem confronting us. We have to find today an extremely *strong* appellate position, because we have a very *weak* appellant. If we had created a very strong appellant, as this firm suggested, then today we could very easily go into court with a much weaker appeal, because we would have a great deal more public sentiment on our side and we would have a certain amount of psychological leverage with the court." White was standing very straight, very proper, like a New England missionary of another time. "So, *for the record*," he concluded, "let me remind you that it was Miss Neller who voted against our proposal, and it was you, Mr. Cloud, who supported that vote, and by doing so deadlocked the proposal."

"That is the most preposterous goddamned excuse for failure I have ever heard," Cloud said in a tightly controlled voice. "You are actually trying to blame Genevieve and me for the great constitutional law firm of Niebold and White not being able to come up with an appeal that will keep an *innocent* man, *not* convicted of a killing, out of the gas chamber. What unadulterated bullshit!"

White's lip curled. "Let the record accurately reflect Mr. Cloud's crude and gross language."

Cloud started out of his chair. "White, how would you like the record to reflect a few of your teeth—"

"Rob, don't!" Genevieve said, grabbing his arm. "That won't settle anything!"

"It'll settle him," Cloud said threateningly. He continued to move, Genevieve clinging to him tenaciously.

"Rob, no! It won't help! Can't you see they've got us right where they want us?"

Cloud stopped and turned to her. "What?"

"They don't have to do anything," Genevieve told him bluntly. "Not anything at all. And they've covered themselves perfectly against any accusation of malfeasance. It's all very clear now." She fixed her eyes on Morris Niebold. "Why so quiet today, *dear* Mr. Niebold?" she asked pointedly. "Why no words of wisdom, no battle cries, no morale-building slogans?"

"The time for all that is past," the invalid replied flatly. For the first time his walnut-cheeked face did not smile or even soften. "You have grasped the situation much more quickly than your friend Robert, my dear." He glanced at Carla Volt. "You can stop taking the minutes; this isn't by any stretch of the imagination going into the record."

"What is it you want?" Genevieve asked without further preliminary.

"Control of the foundation," Niebold said. "And through it, control of Weldon Whitman."

"Why?"

"So that we can conduct his campaign as we see fit."

"So you can manipulate him, you mean."

Niebold shrugged. "Call it that if you like, my dear—"

"Goddamn it, stop calling me your dear!" Genevieve stormed, shocking all of them, including Cloud. "Suppose Rob and I refuse to relinquish control of the foundation to you, then what?"

"Then you may have it back," Niebold said simply. "The firm of Niebold and White will disassociate itself from it entirely. As a matter of fact, let me tell you—strictly *off* the record—that we are not prepared to file any further appeals of any kind in Weldon Whitman's behalf unless and until this firm has a majority vote in the future conduct of the foundation. And if you desire to seek other counsel, we're prepared to make it as easy for you as possible." He removed two pieces of paper from a drawer and placed them on the edge of the desk in front of Genevieve. "A blank check drawn on the foundation's account and duly signed by Borden; and a certified statement of how much money the account contained as of the end of the business day yesterday."

Silence came over the office as if someone had touched a switch. Genevieve and Cloud looked at the check and certified statement lying on the desk. Niebold, White, and Carla Volt watched them closely. It was clearly time to choose.

"What'll it be, Gen?" Robert Cloud said.

Genevieve thought for a moment, then snatched up the two pieces of paper and put them in her purse.

"We'll find another law firm."

She strode from the office, Cloud only a step behind her. Morris Niebold's voice followed them out the door.

"If you have no success by Monday noon, come back. There still might be time—"

The two departing people ignored him.

At ten A.M. on Monday the execution squad came for Weldon Whitman. It was twenty-four hours to his execution time; he would spend the remainder of the time in a holding cell a dozen feet from the gas chamber. The execution squad—five guards selected by rotation—each received fifty dollars extra pay for the duty. They were led by an execution-squad commander who received one hundred dollars: Captain Dukes.

"Open Twenty-two," Dukes instructed the guard in the control room. The cell door slid open. Dukes stepped into the cell. The execution squad waited outside, two on each side of the door, one facing it. They would enter only if they had to; if there was no trouble with the condemned man, the five guards would serve only as an escort and death-watch squad until the next morning, when they would assist in the execution itself.

"Time to go downstairs, Twenty-two," Dukes said tonelessly. "Get up and strip."

Weldon Whitman sat up on his bunk and took a final drag on a cigarette. He dropped the butt in the toilet and silently started undressing. Dukes looked around the cluttered cell, at the books, the papers, the pamphlets.

"You can dispose of your personal belongings in one or more ways," he advised the prisoner mechanically. "You can give the items to other inmates on the Row; you can instruct that they be boxed for pickup by anyone you name; or you can instruct that they be burned or otherwise destroyed."

"Burn them," Whitman said listlessly. He peeled off the last of his clothes and let them drop to the floor. Fuck it, he thought. Let somebody else pick them up. Dukes ignored the gesture. He nodded to one of the guards.

"Buckle him up."

The guard entered the cell and strapped a six-inch leather belt around Whitman's bare waist, buckling it in the back. Strapped to the front of the belt were a pair of steel handcuffs. The guard pulled Whitman's hands in front of him and locked the cuffs on his wrists.

"Let's go," Dukes said.

Whitman, naked except for the restraining belt, stepped into the exercise corridor. The execution squad formed a loose circle around him and Dukes led the way to the door leading into the guard corridor. As he walked naked past the others with whom he had shared the Row for so long, Whitman was acutely aware that all of them were watching him go, but he knew that none of them would say goodbye or otherwise speak. That was an unwritten law on the Row. Over the years, farewells had more often than not proved to be a waste of time and emotion: because of the number of avenues of appeal open to condemned men, the average Death Row resident usually made two or three trips to the holding cell before he was finally executed. Sometimes he was there an hour or so, sometimes longer—dangerously longer—but more often than not, a last-minute stay of execution was telephoned in to grant him a few more weeks or months of life. Since Whitman had been there, he had seen eleven trips to the holding cell: Milo, Stiles, and Franklin had gone once, Henry had gone twice, Clayton and Rimm had gone three times. But there had been no executions.

But they always watched the man with the date as he left. They watched Weldon Whitman now as he walked by, his pale white body uncovered for all to see, his dick shrunken in coldness and fear almost to total concealment in his pubic hair. He walked in his phalanx of guards through the separating bars into the adjacent corridor and back its length to the Death House elevator. There was no wait at the elevator; the car was already there. The condemned man stepped aboard with his execution squad. Captain Dukes followed, and the door closed.

When the elevator door opened again, the condemned man and his escort stepped into a short passageway which led to a small room containing two holding cells. This was the Ready Room. The guards took him quickly into it and guided him into the first of the cells. They unlocked his wrists and removed the leather restraining belt. Stuck between two bars of the holding cell door, rolled together in a bundle, were a pair of new blue denim trousers, a new blue denim shirt, and a pair of the inevitably ugly felt slippers.

"Put those on," Dukes instructed. Whitman unrolled the clothing.

"No underwear?" he asked. "No socks?"

"Just what's there," the guard captain said flatly. He locked the cell door and, with three of the five death-watch guards, left the Ready Room. Whitman shook out the wrinkled clothes and got dressed.

The holding cell was claustrophobically small: three feet wide, eight feet long, seven feet high. At the back was a lidless toilet. There was not even room for a cot; a bare twin mattress had been placed on the floor; Whitman had to walk on the mattress to get to the toilet. From the cell nothing could be seen except the door through which they had entered the room, the bare cement walls of the room itself, an upholstered two-seat bench on which at least one of the two death-watch guards on duty would sit and watch the condemned man at all times, and a very short corridor and a right-angle doorway which led to the gas chamber itself.

As Whitman was dressing, one of the guards disappeared for several moments in the direction of the gas chamber, then returned with a two-burner hotplate and a coffeepot. He set the hotplate on the floor and plugged it in.

"This is fresh coffee from the dining room, Whitman," the guard said. "We'll be keeping it hot around the clock."

Whitman nodded. "I'll take a cup now," he said.

The guard asked Whitman how he took his coffee, prepared it for him in a styrofoam cup, and passed it through the bars to him.

Whitman took the coffee and sat down on the mattress on the floor, leaning back against the bars and drawing his knees up in front of him. Silently he blew on the coffee to cool it. He thought about Genevieve and Cloud and the others.

What in the fuck are they *doing?* he wondered.

He shivered with a sudden chill.

Two hours after Weldon Whitman was moved to the holding cell, Genevieve Neller and Robert Cloud returned to the offices of Niebold and White. Genevieve was pale, her eyes swollen from crying. Cloud's eyes were bloodshot and dark-circled, his face gray and pinched-looking. Neither of them had slept for more than sixty hours; they had existed on quickly consumed sandwiches, black coffee, and sheer determination. In three cities—Sacramento, San Francisco, and

Oakland—they had seen in person seventeen lawyers. On the telephone they had spoken with an additional eighteen. A total of nearly three dozen attorneys and they had failed to enlist even one willing to represent Weldon Whitman in his last-ditch, final-hour effort to avoid the gas chamber.

The first attorney they talked to had given them the general answer that all the others would eventually give: "It's too near his execution time. We aren't familiar with the legal background of the case. We wouldn't have time to prepare an adequate appeal. It wouldn't be fair to the condemned man." Several were honest enough to comment on the adverse publicity they would receive if a quickly prepared appeal failed. But even those who avoided that aspect of it, or denied that it made any difference to them, still refused to negotiate. So Genevieve and Cloud had come back. And the invalid received them benevolently.

"Sit down, my dear, please. Robert, do sit down. You both look exhausted. I really, *sincerely* regret that you had to go through this ordeal." He folded his pudgy hands on the desk and hunched forward. "Are you ready now to cooperate in reorganizing the Whitman Foundation board of directors?"

"Can you stop the execution?" Genevieve asked in a hoarse, haunted voice.

"I can't guarantee it," Niebold said frankly, "but I will say this: if we can't stop it, no one can."

Genevieve nodded and looked down, away from the lawyer's face. "Then we'll do whatever you want," she said.

"Carla," said Niebold, "bring in the papers."

Within five minutes, the necessary legal documents had been signed and witnessed making Morris Niebold president as well as chairman of the board of directors of the Weldon Whitman Foundation. The other board members were Borden White, vice-president; Carla Volt, treasurer; Genevieve Neller, secretary; and Robert Cloud, assistant secretary. The reorganization assured the law firm a three-to-two majority in any vote.

Morris Niebold looked at his watch and said, "Borden, you're all set with the appeal, I presume?"

"Yes," White said. "The brief is all prepared. The Supreme Court justices usually return from lunch between one-thirty and two. I'll have a copy on one of their desks before then."

"Fine," Niebold nodded approvingly.

"What—what are you going to do?" Genevieve asked.

"We've drafted an unusual appeal, my dear," Niebold said with a crafty smile. "One which we feel the Supreme Court of California is ripe to have presented to it. In it we are contending that the death penalty is cruel and unusual punishment and violates the constitutions of both the state and the nation. In effect, we are attacking a judicial tradition which has been practiced in this state since it adopted the English common-law system. *We are questioning the state's right to kill.*" Niebold sat back in his mechanical chair and hooked both thumbs in his vest pockets. "It is a challenge the court will have to face. There is no way it can be avoided."

Genevieve looked puzzled. "But—I don't understand—you haven't time to file such an appeal—"

"We're not going to file it," Borden White told her. "Not through ordinary channels. I am going to deliver a copy personally to one of the justices in his chambers, along with a note pleading the urgency of his reading it. He won't be inclined to read it right then, of course, but he will certainly glance at the front page. And when he reads the opening contention he will find himself caught in an ethical trap. He won't be able to put the appeal aside because on it will hinge the life of a man who is to be executed within some twenty hours. And he won't be able to pass judgment on its merits, even if he does read it, because it is a gauntlet flung at the entire court, not just him. As I said, he'll be in a trap. He will have no choice but to issue a stay of execution for Whitman in order to allow the court as a body to determine whether taking a man's life, by today's standards, constitutes cruel and unusual punishment."

Robert Cloud, sitting next to Genevieve, turned to her, and said, "Does it sound to you like it'll work, Gen? Does it make sense?"

She nodded slowly, and Cloud could detect visible signs of relief slowly softening her features. "Yes," she said. "Yes, it makes sense. It—it's a brilliant legal move." She shifted her glance back to Niebold. "I'm not happy that you have control of the foundation," she said simply, "but I can't say that you haven't earned it with this."

"No words could give me greater pleasure than that morsel of praise from you, Genevieve," the invalid said.

"Have you decided which justice you're going to give it to?" she asked Borden White.

"I thought I'd give it to Tanaka," he said.

Niebold smiled. "The little Jap, yes. Youngest man on the court, racially inferior, a born rebel and troublemaker. An excellent choice, Borden." Niebold turned his attention to Genevieve and Cloud. "You're both very tired, I'm sure. I want you to take the week off and rest. Come in on Monday and we'll talk about realigning duties and getting started on future projects. Robert, in the meantime I wonder if you'd send over the final draft of *Judgment in Anguish;* I'd like to read it before it goes to New York."

"All right," Cloud said. He glanced at Genevieve; they both knew he now had no choice.

"See you Monday then," Niebold said, smiling. "And Genevieve, please give my best to your Mr. Whitman; I'm sure you'll be going down to see him. Tell him we're all sorry things got so close to the wire."

He turned his attention to some papers in front of him; Cloud and Genevieve knew they had been dismissed.

They went to Genevieve's apartment, got out what food was in the refrigerator, and halfheartedly ate a weary lunch. For the rest of the afternoon they sat around the living room, alternately dozing and fighting sleep, keeping both the television and the radio on to listen to the periodic news announcements for some word on the appeal. They waited all afternoon. Finally, on the six o'clock news, there was a bulletin:

"Weldon Whitman, the convicted Spotlight Bandit, has been granted a stay of execution by State Supreme Court Justice Jesse Tanaka. Just seventeen hours before the condemned man was scheduled to be put to death in San Quentin's gas chamber, the recently appointed Tanaka, serving his first term on the Supreme Court, issued an order to the state department of corrections instructing that the execution proceedings be halted. Although Tanaka did not state specifically why he had stayed the proceedings, he did indicate that a question of constitutional rights had arisen which conceivably could affect the condemned man's sentence. Whitman, convicted more than two years ago of sex and kidnapping charges, is the only condemned man on San Quentin's Death Row who has not been convicted of taking a life. Justice

Tanaka, the first non-Caucasian appointed to the state's highest court, said that his order would delay Whitman's execution indefinitely until the entire Supreme Court could rule on the constitutional point in question. . . ."

When the announcement was over, Cloud laid his head on the arm of the couch and closed his eyes. Genevieve rose from her chair, turned off the television and radio, and went over to him.

"That's no way to sleep, Rob," she said. She took his hand. "Come on."

Cloud let her lead him into the bedroom and lay him down on her bed. She untied his shoes and took them off. Then she took off her own and lay down beside him. She drew a satin comforter over them. Then she took his hand in hers and instantly went to sleep.

They slept like that, under the comforter, fully clothed, holding hands, for thirteen hours.

Eighteen

When Cloud and Genevieve returned to see Morris Niebold the following Monday, it very quickly became apparent exactly what the future thrust of the Whitman Foundation was to be.

"The first thing we're going to do," Niebold said in his most benevolent tone, "is relieve Genevieve of some of the responsibility we've let her take on. She has much too heavy a load to carry, and I'm afraid we're all to blame for not recognizing it sooner."

"I don't feel that my responsibility is that great a burden," Genevieve told him quietly.

"Of course you don't, my dear. The rare person as dedicated as you never realizes it. But the fact remains that we've been letting you do far too much, and we must put a stop to it immediately. To begin with we'll give you a respite from those public-speaking engagements that take up so many of your evenings."

"But I've made commitments—"

"Yes, yes," Niebold said. "I had Carla bring me the foundation appointment calendar. I've made arrangements to honor all the engagements you had already made."

"But how?"

"Professional speakers, my dear, professional speakers," he said almost proudly. "We have hired four people who are experts in the field to go out on the lecture circuit and really promote our cause for us. They'll do wonders, take my word for it. They work together as a crew, you see, and they tailor their presentation to fit the particular audience and to determine which of them will handle the assignment. There are two men and two women: one man and one woman are in their early thirties, the other two are in their early fifties. They can work singly or in pairs—"

"Sort of like an animal act in a circus," Robert Cloud commented.

"That's very good, Robert," the older man said, without a trace of a smile. "Incidentally, I'm going to turn over the *Judgment in Anguish* manuscript to someone else to re-edit for us, but I have another assignment for you which I'll get to in a moment." He turned away from Cloud and resumed talking to Genevieve. "What we had in mind for you, my dear, was the full-time supervision of the foundation's printshop. We're going to begin regularly scheduled mailings all over the state: pamphlets, brochures, questionnaires, possibly even a monthly foundation newsletter. The material will deal specifically with the courts, certain judges and district attorneys, the state's prosecution system—"

"That kind of material will only hurt Weldon, not help him," Genevieve stated in a controlled voice.

"Well, of course, I'm only speaking in generalities," Niebold said. "The board of directors will have the final approval of specific material. The point I'm making right now is that with an increased production schedule, we will need someone reliable to keep our printshop at its most efficient level. We'd like to be able to depend on you for that."

"Naturally, I'll do whatever I can to help, but—"

"I knew you wouldn't let us down, my dear," Niebold fairly gushed. "You'll be your own supervisor, of course. And I insist that you take whatever time you need to visit your Mr. Whitman as often as you like. Now then, Robert," he said, turning back to Cloud.

"Are you going to tell me I've been working too hard also?" Cloud challenged at once.

"Not at all," the lawyer said in a slightly cooling voice. "As a matter of fact, perhaps you haven't been working hard enough. Borden, Carla, and I have gone over the final draft of *Judgment in Anguish*, and frankly none of us were overly impressed by it."

"That's just too goddamned bad," Cloud said evenly. "When did you three become literary critics?"

"We don't profess to be literary critics," Niebold said. His tone hardened ever so slightly more. "Nor are we being critical of your writing *per se*. However, we do know exactly what tone we want the book to take—and unfortunately you have not generated that tone."

"Which is?"

"Aggressiveness. We think that it was all right for *Room 22, Hotel Death* to project a soft image of Whitman as a victim—of circumstance, of law-enforcement overzealousness, of illogical California justice, whatever. But for this second book we feel that a sharper focus is needed. We want the victim to begin struggling. Where he once inspired pity, we now want him to command admiration. To accomplish this we have employed another writer to re-edit the book for us. A young man named Eugene Terrier. Ever heard of him?"

"Who hasn't?" Cloud said with a grunt. "Former Black Panther, former just about anything radical that you can name."

"You left out that he's also a very capable writer," Niebold said pointedly.

"So am I," Cloud reminded him. "How do you intend to use me?"

"Doing news releases," said Niebold. "Writing newspaper stories that the press wouldn't have its own reporters cover. As a matter of fact, we already have your first assignment ready for you: a story on a special fund-raising dinner being given by a wealthy Los Angeles accountant who is taking a very active interest in us. We would hope, by doing such a story, to stimulate more activity of this nature, both for the money and the favorable publicity it can bring us."

Niebold turned his wheelchair slightly so that he could rest one arm on his desk. He drummed his plump fingertips on the shiny, smooth surface for a moment. Then he spoke again, slowly and deliberately.

"I think I might mention at this point that it has already been decided by a majority of the board that we will accept the resignation of anyone who does not feel that he or she wishes to comply with the decisions of the board."

"You mean comply with *your* decisions, don't you, Morris?" said Cloud.

Niebold shrugged. "The point is, Robert, that if you don't care for the new posture which the foundation is going to assume, you needn't force yourself to remain in the group."

"Let me tell you something, Morris," Cloud said with unconcealed hostility. "I got on this bandwagon at the very first stop—back in L.A. on the day the jury brought in those two death sentences. I was with Weldon Whitman the day Judge Lukey sentenced him to die. I declared a personal war against G. Foster Klein and the L.A. County district attorney's office over Whitman. I alienated myself from the newspaper that employed me because I believed that Whitman had been shafted. In other words, Morris, I am a charter member of the effort to keep Weldon Whitman out of the goddamned gas chamber. And being that, I am not about to resign what little authority I have left in this organization and give you a *completely* free hand. I'd much rather stick around and see that you get an argument once in a while."

"I presume by that little speech that you are agreeable to covering the fund-raising dinner I mentioned a moment ago."

"That and anything else you give me to do, Mr. Foundation President. I'm on for the whole ride."

"Good for you, Rob," Genevieve said with an enthusiasm long absent from her voice.

"Yes, good for you, I'm sure," Niebold said. He took a folder from his desk and passed it over to Cloud. "Here is all the correspondence on the dinner. It's being held Saturday night. The address is on the letterhead."

When they left Niebold's office, Cloud let Genevieve go ahead without him while he went in to see Carla. He found her in her office with a tall, handsome young mulatto wearing a turtleneck sweater and white leather jacket. They were talking intimately when Cloud entered.

"Excuse me. Carla, may I see you privately for a moment?"

"I'm sorry," she said coolly, "I'm busy at the moment. Incidentally, I don't believe you've met our newest member. This is Eugene Terrier. Gene, this is Robert Cloud, the gentlemen Borden was telling you about."

"Oh yes," Terrier said, nodding. "How are you, Cloud? I've read some of your stuff. It's not bad."

"Thanks. I've read some of yours too." Cloud turned back to Carla. "I really would like to speak with you for a moment."

"I'm really *very* busy right now," Carla said. She rose from her desk and took Eugene Terrier's arm. "Let me show you the rest of our offices, Gene. Excuse us, won't you?" she said to Cloud.

The following Saturday night, Cloud was in a taxi wending its way along Sunset Boulevard. On the plane to Los Angeles he had studied the correspondence file Niebold had given him. The fund-raising affair was being held at the Jerome Traynor residence in Brentwood. Traynor had been reached by an early Whitman Foundation pamphlet and had sent a check for twenty-five dollars, so his name went onto a contributors list. He had been sent two more mailings *not* asking for a donation, then was asked in a fourth letter again to help the foundation financially. He responded with another check. After that he received periodic letters asking him to refer to the foundation others who might be interested in joining the Weldon Whitman Movement. He referred several names. Subsequently, he participated in a capital-punishment survey the foundation conducted, and twice more sent personal donations. Recently he had written to the foundation proposing that he and his wife host a dinner party for some two dozen or so of their friends. At the affair they would distribute foundation literature about Whitman, and both during and after dinner they would keep a discussion going about the Whitman case in particular and capital punishment in general. They were certain they could convince most of their friends to contribute. Jerome Traynor, in his letter, estimated that they expected to collect in excess of two thousand dollars for the foundation.

The Traynor home was a two-story Moorish structure on a rounded corner lot with a circular drive. There were several Cadillacs and Continentals parked in the drive. When Cloud rang the bell, he heard chimes inside play several notes of a Spanish tune.

In a moment the door was opened by a tall, very thin man. Cloud said good evening and introduced himself.

"Yes, of course," the thin man said, "we've been expecting you. Come in. I'm Jerry Traynor." They shook hands and Traynor led him at once away from the entry foyer to a small study nearby. "I wanted to have a word with you in private before I introduce you around, do you mind?"

"Not at all," said Cloud. "It's your party."

Traynor mixed them each a drink and brought the glasses to a pair of matched leather couches, where the two men sat down facing each other.

"There's something I wanted to clarify with you before the evening gets too far underway." Traynor said, taking a quick sip of his drink. "You see, this whole thing—the dinner, the contributions, the referrals, everything—is really my wife's idea. I suppose you could call it her crusade or something."

"I thought the correspondence came from you," Cloud said.

"It did. You see, my wife insists that we share our roles in life. The point is, I'm in this thing more or less to support my wife's interest. I don't mean that without her I'd be *against* your cause, you understand; it's just that I probably wouldn't be actively for it."

"I see," Cloud said, nodding.

Traynor shifted his thin body on the couch. "I'm telling you this because I don't want to cause any embarrassment to my wife or myself this evening. I don't really know that much about the pros or cons of this capital-punishment issue, and I'll have to admit that I'm not that familiar with the background of the Whitman case. I'm afraid I just haven't kept up with my homework." He wet his lips and took another sip of his drink.

Cloud suspected that Traynor's conscience might be bothering him because he had treated his wife's chosen cause so lightly. "How can I help you?" Cloud asked.

"I wonder if you could keep me out of the discussions as much as possible tonight. I don't want to be put on the spot."

"I think I can manage that all right," Cloud said. "I presume Mrs. Traynor can discuss the case knowledgeably?"

"Can she! She goes on about it through a whole meal, at times."

"Well, why don't we just agree that her viewpoint is in all respects shared by you," Cloud said. "And you take the position that because the dinner party was her idea, you're letting her do the talking for both of you tonight. How does that sound to you?"

"Like music," Traynor said with a smile of relief. "I really do appreciate it."

Cloud shrugged off his thanks. "We appreciate the effort you and Mrs. Traynor are making."

"What do you think Whitman's chances are of beating the gas chamber?" Traynor asked. "That last one was a pretty close call, wasn't it?"

"Pretty close," Cloud agreed. He decided not to go into detail about it. "Naturally, we think Weldon will eventually be pardoned. We're all convinced that he's innocent."

"Well, you're certainly going to have the support of my wife and me," Traynor said with sudden overtones of loyalty. "I may never know enough about the cause to argue for it, but I do know how to sign a check. Come on, let me introduce you around."

They left the small study. Traynor led him through a door and down two steps into a large, elegantly appointed living room. A dozen or so people were spread throughout the room, and a woman with richly red, deeply dark, upswept hair was just turning around in time to meet them as they entered.

"Mr. Cloud, I'd like you to meet my wife, Laurel," Traynor said. "Dear, this is Robert Cloud from the Whitman Foundation—"

"So nice of you to come, Mr. Cloud," she said, holding her hand out to him and looking straight into his eyes without the barest hint that she had ever seen him before, or masturbated him or fellated him or had been caught by him coming out of a motel room with another man when she was supposed to have been his virgin girlfriend. Not the barest hint.

Cloud managed to check the surprise that laced his body. "My pleasure, Mrs. Traynor," he said. His palm was moist when he took her hand. But so was hers. "The foundation appreciates your interest."

"Thank you." She turned to her husband. "Jerry, dear, will you see to the guests for five minutes? I have simply got to get Mr. Cloud to tell me some things about Weldon Whitman before we turn him loose. I'll just take him into the playroom for a bit." She took Cloud's arm. "Right around this way, Mr. Cloud."

Laurel led him into a nicely designed recreation room complete with a bar, pool table, movie projector and screen, pinball machine, dartboard, and other accouterments of indoor play. She closed the door behind them and leaned back against it.

"You look well, Rob," she said.

"Thank you. So do you."

"It's been a long time."

"Yes. But I'd never know it to look at you." She still looked the twenty-three or twenty-four that she had always looked. Her face was still girlish; her attractiveness still derived from the velvety red hair above it, and the superbly sculptured breasts below it.

Cloud walked around the pool table, dragging his fingertips over the brushed green felt. He looked admiringly around the room—he thought that was probably what she wanted him to do. "This is very nice, Laurel. You've done very well for yourself."

"I've married well, you mean. Yes, I have."

"Obviously a very successful man. How did you meet him?"

"By accident more than anything else. I broke up with Ralph after that night you saw us together. The night I came to your place and you fucked me and then walked out on me. You remember that, I'm sure."

Cloud folded his arms and leaned back against the pool table. He did not reply.

"I was in a pretty bad way after that," she continued. "Mentally, physically, psychologically, every which way. Ralph kept calling, of course, but I wouldn't see him. Wouldn't even talk to him. All the telephone-answering for a long time was done by Nancy. You remember Nancy, don't you?"

"Yes, I remember her."

"She'll be here tonight. With her new husband, who is even skinnier than mine. Anyway, as I was saying, she helped me to keep Ralph at bay long enough for me to get him out of my system. I never went out with him again. I've got you to thank for that. Your walking out on me was what did it."

Cloud nodded, but said nothing.

"Nancy and I started going back to the tennis club in Beverly Hills where I had first met Ralph. I ran into him one weekend; he asked if I'd start seeing him again and I said no. I kept saying no. I enjoyed saying no." She walked away from the door she had been leaning against and sat on one of the barstools. "About two months went by, then one afternoon at the club I met Jerry Traynor. Jerry was quite taken with me right from the start. He asked if I had a tennis date for the following Saturday, I told him I didn't, and we made a date right then and there."

"How long was it before you and Traynor were married?" Cloud asked.

"Less than three months. We started going out on a regular basis and one night he asked me to marry him and I just accepted. I don't *think* I did it to spite Ralph or to forget you—but I don't know. People do peculiar things sometimes."

"Well, everything seems to have turned out for the best, as

they say," Cloud commented. "This is the kind of life you seem to have wanted—security, nice things, not having to count every dollar. You should be very happy."

"I am," she said, raising her chin with just a trace of defiance. "I am very happy."

At that moment, Jerome Traynor stuck his head in the room. "Everyone is here now, honey. Are you about ready to bring Mr. Cloud in for a cocktail?"

"Be right there," Laurel called cheerily. Her husband pulled his head back and closed the door. "I guess we'd better get out there," she said. "Incidentally, Jerry doesn't know about Ralph and me, so naturally I don't care to have him know about you and me."

"Naturally," Cloud said.

They joined the others in the living room. There were about thirty guests, most of them congregating in small groups in the room and outside in a patio-and-pool area. Japanese lanterns lighted the outside; two waiters in white jackets served drinks from a temporary bar just inside a pair of open glass doors.

Laurel introduced Cloud to half a dozen people at one end of the room as they entered. The guests immediately began asking Cloud questions about Weldon Whitman. For the most part the queries were very trite, and his answers were standard. But Cloud found he could lie quite glibly: Yes, Weldon Whitman played a significant role in the conduct of the foundation's campaign against capital punishment; yes, he really wrote *Room 22, Hotel Death* all by himself. Of course, there had been the usual editorial polishing done by the publisher, but for the most part it was Weldon's book all the way.

Occasionally, as the evening progressed, someone in a group would ask a question that bespoke genuine interest: How many hours per day were the condemned men let out of their cells? What kind of sanitation facilities did Death Row provide? Was there any kind of accurate figure as to how many Californians supported abolition of the death penalty? Had any of the state Supreme Court justices, who were to rule on the issue, ever attended an actual execution? These questions were to Robert Cloud refreshing oases in a desert of clichés.

At one point during the evening, a pert, bouncy young woman with a familiar freckled face and a Texas accent came up and slipped her arm through Cloud's, saying, "Hello there, stranger. Where you been keeping yourself?"

"Hello, Nancy," Cloud said, genuinely happy to see Laurel's former roommate.

"How've you been, old buddy? You're looking good."

"Been fine," he said. "Pretty busy and all that. Hey, I hear you're an old married broad now."

"Lord, *am* I!" She pointed out a rather frail man in a group across the room. "See that skinny feller over there? That's my guy." At that moment Laurel looked across the room at them. Nancy waved jovially and Cloud nodded cordially. "Have you and Laur had a chance to be alone?" Nancy asked.

"Very briefly," Cloud said.

Nancy sighed heavily. "Life's sure funny, Rob."

Cloud nodded without answering.

He sat with strangers during dinner, answering more cliché questions, helping Jerome Traynor out of a couple of corners he got himself backed into, and in general trying to get through the evening as painlessly as possible.

Before the evening was over, Cloud had an opportunity to spend another few minutes alone with Laurel. They shared a drink at a small table at the edge of the patio.

"May I ask you something?" Cloud said.

"Of course."

"How did you happen to become interested in the Weldon Whitman Movement? Back then you resented *my* involvement; now you're involved yourself. Why?"

"I'll be honest with you, Rob: I don't know why," she said. "I thought I might be doing it in order to establish some kind of contact with you again. In the hope there might still be some feeling left. Incidentally, I found out tonight that there's none on my part. Any on yours?"

"No. But no bad memories, either."

She patted his hand fondly. "Good. I'm glad." She took a sip of the drink they were sharing. "Another reason I came up with was that subconsciously I might be trying to make it up to you for the way I treated you. Of course, I've known of your involvement all along: I've seen your magazine articles and news stories—"

"But you don't think that's the reason either, do you?" Cloud said. Laurel shook her head.

"No, not really." She met his eyes directly. "I think the simple fact of the matter is that I've just been hooked. Call it the Whitman mystique, call it social conscience, call it moral rebellion against the taking of a human life by the state—whatever. I think I've joined forces with you and the others simply because I don't want him to be executed."

"Whether he's innocent or not?"

"Yes. I don't think guilt or innocence has anything to do with it, really. It's the taking of a human life by the state that is the crux of it. Do you know, Rob—of course, you probably do!—that experts in the field are against capital punishment because they feel it actually *contributes* to the crime rate. One man, Donald MacNamara, who is the dean of the Institute of Criminology, contends that as long as the death penalty is a part of our system of justice, a truly rehabilitative approach to penology will never be fully attained."

Cloud suppressed a smile. That was exactly the theory he had quoted to her over pizza that evening so long ago when he had just returned from his first trip to San Quentin.

"Confide in me, Rob," Laurel said. "Do *you* think he's innocent?"

"I do. Definitely."

"Well, for your sake, I'm glad." She reached for the glass again, took another sip, and sat back contentedly. "Just think, if I had followed my heart instead of those dollar signs, I might be with you now up in Sacramento. We might be working side by side to save Weldon Whitman. I might have done something useful for a change."

"What you're doing here *is* useful," Cloud told her. "The movement doesn't move without money."

"Yes, but it's *people* who make a cause," she said zealously. "Particularly people like you, Rob. If I had any reservations at all about supporting the Whitman Foundation, they would be alleviated at once by my knowledge that a person of your character was on the board. You're an ethical person, Rob, so it stands to reason that what the foundation does will also be ethical."

Cloud squirmed slightly and took back the glass she was holding. What would she think of him, he wondered, if she knew how many lies he had told just tonight in the interest of the Whitman mystique? And how would she feel if she knew that his ethics, such as they were, now amounted to no more than a minority vote on the foundation board, and that the direction of the Whitman movement was controlled completely by others? He grunted silently, derisively, at himself, and drained the rest of the gin from the glass.

He left the party a while later. Laurel and Jerome Traynor saw him to the door. A taxi he had summoned was waiting in the street.

"It was nice meeting you both," he said.

"We'll send you a check tomorrow for whatever this bunch kicks in," Jerome Traynor said. "It'll be better than two thousand, I'm sure."

"Wonderful," said Cloud. He turned to Laurel. "Mrs. Traynor, I'm sure Weldon will drop you a personal note of thanks."

"Oh no," she protested. "His time is much too valuable."

"Weldon will want to, I'm sure, when he learns of your interest," Cloud said. Your interest and the two thousand, that is.

They said their goodnights and Cloud walked out to get in the waiting taxi.

Argus turned down the article that Cloud halfheartedly wrote on the Traynor dinner, but through Eugene Terrier it was placed in a West Coast regional magazine. It stimulated mild interest and resulted in a few similar affairs to which Niebold again sent Cloud.

Another summer had ended and fall arrived. Cloud began to lead a drone existence. *Judgment in Anguish* was now completely out of his hands, and Niebold gave him no further writing assignments; Terrier now handled *all* the writing for the foundation: pamphlets, flyers, press releases, even form letters. Cloud, hanging around the foundation printshop trying to be of some help to Genevieve, saw a steady flow of material prepared by Terrier. Gritting his teeth, he helped Genevieve get it printed and distributed.

After Thanksgiving, a lot of what they were doing went into limbo. Things slowed down until just before Christmas—then stopped altogether. On his own, Cloud did a quick piece about what Christmas would be like on Death Row—but when he finished, he did not even bother to show it to anyone; to be used at Christmas, it should have been done three months earlier.

Cloud and Genevieve spent a dull, cheerless Christmas in her apartment; there was no visiting at San Quentin that day. Cloud drank too much and fell asleep in a chair. Genevieve, who had not bothered to decorate the apartment, had not even sent Christmas cards, ate alone; then she too drank enough to dull her mind so that she could sleep. It was a pathetic holiday all the way around.

The new year arrived and the foundation's activities slowly resumed. Terrier planted a few press releases and did a mailer on fund-raising affairs—and before January was over, the dinners began again. Niebold sent Cloud to all of them; he traveled to San Diego, Santa Ana, Claremont, Orange, Santa Barbara, and Los Angeles. Always Los Angeles, more frequently than anywhere else, as if the place where it all started was determined to stay in the forefront to the end.

It was in Los Angeles that Cloud's stint in purgatory finally ended. Arriving back at his hotel near the airport one night, after attending a dinner in Westwood, he found a message to call Borden White, no matter what the hour. It was past midnight, but he dialed the switchboard and had a call put through to White's home.

"Borden?" he said when White answered. "What's so urgent?"

"We've located Glory Ann Luza's family," the attorney said.

Cloud became instantly alert. "Where?"

"They're living in Reseda, out in the San Fernando Valley. Morris thought as long as you were down there, you could check out the possibility of a story."

Cloud wrote down the address White gave him. "How did you find them?" he asked.

"We put a private detective firm on the thing quite some time ago."

"No one mentioned it to me," Cloud said coolly.

"No matter," White said. "The important thing is that we've found them. The family anyway. We're not so sure about the girl."

"What do you mean?"

"The detective agency hasn't been able to place the girl in the house. The parents are seen coming and going, as is the girl's older brother. But so far there's been no sight of the girl herself. She could be ill or something, of course. Or she might have married and moved away. Anyway, check it out first thing tomorrow."

"Yessir, Mr. White. First thing in the morning, Mr. White."

"I'd cut out some of the sarcasm too, if I were you, Cloud," White told him. "Remember, the foundation *can* replace you."

"Fuck you, Borden," Cloud said flatly and hung up.

He stretched out on the bed and lighted a cigarette. He smoked for several minutes, trying to relax; but he could not: he was too keyed up. Finally he called room service and ordered a double martini. When it came, he set it on the window sill, put his cigarettes and an ashtray next to it, pulled a chair up to the window, and turned off the lights in the room.

Smoking, drinking, staring out at the planes landing and taking off in the night, he thought about Glory Ann Luza and wondered what tomorrow would bring.

Nineteen

Cloud made the drive to Reseda in less than an hour. Traffic, even for Sunday morning, was light. He found the street he was looking for, and drove several blocks until he came to the address Borden White had given him. It was a small tract house, modest in the extreme, but tidy and well maintained.

As Cloud parked at the curb, an older-model sedan pulled up and drove into the narrow driveway. Cloud walked up to the porch and waited there for the old sedan's three passengers: a middle-aged man and woman, and a young man in his mid twenties. The family was obviously returning from mass. The woman wore a scarf pinned to her severely combed hair, and carried rosary beads. Both men wore neckties over stiffly starched white shirts. The older man had on an out-of-style suit which he had probably owned for two decades; the younger man wore a sport coat. As they approached Cloud at the steps to the porch, their faces reflected their respective feelings: curiosity in the woman, suspicion in the older man, hostility in the younger man.

Cloud spoke to the older man. "Good morning, sir. Are you Mr. Luza?"

"I am Emiliano Luza," the older man answered simply.

"My name is Robert Cloud, Mr. Luza. I'm a magazine writer. I'm interested in doing a story on your daughter, Glory Ann. I wonder if I might see her—"

"My daughter is not here, Mr. Cloud," Emiliano Luza said, stiffening. "She does not live here and I do not expect her ever to live here." He took his wife's elbow. "Come, Josefa—"

They walked past Cloud, up the few steps to the porch, and went into the house. Cloud and the younger man were left facing each other. The younger man was handsome in an angry way.

"You're Ramón," Cloud said.

"I am Ramón." His tone was slightly challenging.

"Is there any way I can find out where your sister is?"

"Only if my father consents to tell you," Ramón said. "And apparently he will not do that."

"Can you tell me why?" Cloud asked.

Ramón's face darkened. "Perhaps he does not care to have his daughter further degraded just to entertain some magazine readers."

"Magazine articles aren't always written for entertainment," Cloud said. "Sometimes they are written to tell the truth."

"Would that be the purpose of your magazine story?" Ramón asked skeptically. "To tell the truth?"

"That would be my object, yes," Cloud replied.

The young Chicano studied Cloud, biting his lower lip thoughtfully as he did. "How much truth do you want to tell in this story of yours?"

"All of it," Cloud said. "All there is to tell."

"No matter what that truth is? And no matter who it hurts?"

Something inside Cloud activated a warning signal to remind him whose side he was on. But something else inside him—his conscience, perhaps, or his pride—*de*activated the warning and negated it. He did not have to play qualifying games about writing the truth. He was already on truth's side. "I'll write it, whatever it is," he told Ramón flatly. "And regardless of who it hurts."

Ramón thought about it a moment longer, then said, "Come into the house."

Cloud followed him through the front door. They entered a small, immaculate living room, crowded with furnishings as outdated as Emiliano Luza's suit, and heavily ornamented with religious decorations: crucifixes, pictures of Jesus and of the Sacred Heart, holy candles, a prominently placed Catholic bible with a binding of simulated white leather.

In a large overstuffed chair in one corner, Emiliano Luza sat: small, slightly hunched, his face etched with coarseness, his mustache graying and in need of a trim. But still he sat as the head of his household, and his wife, who had just served him his after-mass coffee, sat in a straightbacked chair nearby.

Ramón Luza did not invite Cloud to sit; instead the two men stood to face the elder Luza.

"Papa, I think we should listen to this man," Ramón said.

"Excuse me," Emiliano Luza said formally, "but I do not agree with you. The matter is closed." He handed his cup to his wife. "Josefa, more sugar," he said with a sour face.

"Yes, 'Miliano," his wife responded quickly, taking his cup and leaving the room. For nearly thirty years she had prepared his coffee exactly the same way, but always when he was irritated about something, he imagined that his coffee was not the same: it needed more sugar, a little water, it was too hot, it was not hot enough. Whenever it happened, Josefa Luza would take her husband's cup, leave the room for a moment, then bring the coffee back to him exactly as it was before.

When she returned his cup, he sipped its contents at once and nodded his approval. "Much better, Josefa, much better." Josefa Luza smiled slightly and sat down in the straight-backed chair again. Ramón and the magazine writer were also sitting now, so she assumed that the matter was not closed after all.

"I will tell you, Mr. Cloud," the elder Luza said, "why I keep my daughter's whereabouts a secret. She has suffered enough from the ordeal that this animal Whitman caused. Not only did she have to endure the attack, but she then had to describe it in detail for the police—not once, but several times; she had to face her attacker to identify him; she had to describe his violation of her again, in public, at his preliminary hearing, and at his trial. And at his trial, she was forced to talk to him, to answer his questions, as he tried to make a liar out of her about what he had done. No, Mr. Cloud, my child has suffered enough."

"I understand how you feel, Mr. Luza—"

"I do not think so, Mr. Cloud," the old Chicano said. "To understand how I feel, you must know what it is to live in poverty with a young wife and two little babies in Mazatlán. You must know how it is to dream of coming to the United States, to Los Angeles, to improve the life of your family. You must know how it is to wait years for a permit to enter this country. Know how it is to walk all the way to the border with your wife and little children, carrying on your shoulders all that belongs to you on this earth. Know how it feels to work as an immigrant, to slave day and night for your family until finally, after many years, you begin to see the results of your labor: you begin to see your family in a house instead of a shack, your children in clean, new clothes, your wife wearing a lace *mantilla* to the church on Sunday. And then, Mr. Cloud—" Emiliano Luza sat forward, a wild look in his eyes. "—then you must know how it feels to have your beautiful young daughter, whom you love with your whole heart, taken at gunpoint by a savage like this Whitman, have him strip the clothes from her virgin body, hold her captive for two hours while he violates her in the most foul ways that men know." Luza shook his head tragically. "And then you must know what happened *after* that, you must know what it caused. Only if you know *that*, Mr. Cloud, will you then understand how I feel."

"But, Papa, listen to me," Ramón Luza pleaded to his father. "It is because he *doesn't* know that he doesn't understand. That is one of the reasons that this Whitman has not gone to the gas chamber yet: too many people *don't* know; too many people are not aware of what his crime did to Glory Ann." Ramón fell to his knees before his father. "Listen to me, Papa. If we let Mr. Cloud tell Glory Ann's story the way it really is, then maybe the state will finally kill him next time. Maybe he won't keep getting off!" The young man turned imploring eyes to his mother. "Mamma, please, tell him it is right."

Josefa Luza, her severely combed black hair framing a face that still showed traces of early beauty, lifted her chin with delicate dignity and said, "He is your father. He will decide what is right."

At that, the elder Luza turned to his wife and studied her thoughtfully, fondly. "Tell me how you feel, Josefa," he said quietly. "I want to know."

Josefa Luza looked from her husband to her son, her son to her husband. "What I think may seem foolish," she said. "I only know that the three of us think of what happened to our baby in three different ways. 'Miliano, you blame yourself because it was you who brought us here. Better, you say, that we were still in a mud hut in Mazatlán, where Gloriana would not have been violated." She looked at her son. "And you, Ramón, you are consumed with vengeance against this person Whitman. You have become angry at the world because of it." She lowered her eyes and looked at a tiny handkerchief that she had been twisting in her hands. "As for myself, I believe that my child's suffering was ordained by God. For one so young and so innocent to suffer as she has must be a design of heaven. I do not pretend to know for what reason this has happened; I only know what is in my heart." She looked back up at her husband and her son. "It saddens me that our three hearts are so different. Perhaps if this man writes of our Gloriana and we all read his words, it will help us to understand why this terrible thing happened."

Emiliano Luza nodded slowly. "What you say may be right, Josefa. Perhaps we *have* looked upon this tragedy long enough with different eyes. The Lord God knows that I do not enjoy blaming myself for this thing; I do not enjoy seeing blood in the eyes of my only son. Maybe this is to be God's way of helping both of us to see as you see."

Emiliano Luza addressed Cloud again. "We will take you to see Glory Ann," he said gravely.

"If you are interested in the truth, Mr. Luza, you will not regret it," Cloud promised. "From what Glory Ann tells me, we may be able to learn many things about what happened."

"From what my sister tells you, you will learn nothing," Ramón Luza said evenly. "The truth you learn today, you will learn with your eyes."

"I don't understand," Cloud said.

"My sister is confined to an asylum. She has lost her mind."

Cloud's expression did not change. Only what he felt inside himself changed.

Cloud went with the Luzas that afternoon to visit the girl at the California State Mental Hospital in Camarillo, forty miles from Reseda. Cloud offered to take the family in the rental car, but Mr. Luza insisted on having Ramón drive their old sedan. He sat in front with his son, and Cloud shared the back seat with Mrs. Luza. Josefa Luza told Cloud how her daughter had reacted after her ordeal in the Hollywood Hills.

"She came home at nearly three o'clock in the morning. We already knew that she was kidnapped because the boy she was out with that evening—Thomas Glenn, an Anglo boy, very nice young boy—had already been to the house with the police and told us. So we were all up, all very nervous: 'Miliano, he pace the floor like the night she was born; and Ramón, he cry like a baby because he is so helpless to do anything. I pray. Always I pray. And I wait."

The car cruised at fifty in the slow lane of the Ventura Freeway. The day was bright; the sunlight spread like a warm yellow blanket over the sloped landscape of Woodland Hills and on to the flatlands of Calabasas.

"A little before three, Gloriana came home. She was pale and trembling. She walked past her father and her brother and came up to me and said, 'Mamma, I want to wash.' I took her into the bathroom and helped her wash. While we were in there, she told me what he had made her do. While she was telling me what he made her do with her mouth, she got sick and threw up all over herself. Then we had to wash her again.

"After we got her clean and dressed, we went back to the front room. The police asked to take Gloriana to the hospital to be examined. She was very nervous, so the police let us all go with her. The doctor who examined her said she was all right; the man had not penetrated her body, so Gloriana was still a virgin. She was very bruised down there and in the back, but he said she would be all right. We took her home and put her to bed just as the sun was coming up."

The once-pretty Chicano woman paused and looked out at the passing landscape. Her face was set, determined, yet deeply sad.

"Mamma, would you like me to finish telling it?" Ramón asked from the front seat.

"I am all right, my son," Josefa Luza replied. She took a deep, hollow breath and resumed the story. "That afternoon when Gloriana woke up, we knew there was something wrong with her. Her lips and cheeks were swollen to twice their size and she had a very bad rash all over her mouth. She began to scream and cry that she had caught some terrible disease from the man who had kidnapped her. She begged us to take her back to the doctor and we did. He examined her and told us it was a nervous reaction to what she had experienced. He gave Gloriana a shot and some salve to put on the rash." Josefa Luza put a brown, wrinkled hand on Cloud's arm as if to emphasize her next remarks. "From that day forward, Mr. Cloud, my baby was never the same. At first it was just the rash and the swelling; it came and went. Then, after she had to identify the man for the police, her nightmares began. Every night in her sleep she would cry and whimper and beg to be left alone. Sometimes her father and brother and I would stand by her bed and watch and listen. We knew what she was dreaming, but we were afraid to awaken her. When the nightmares first began, we took her to a psychiatrist, and he said to let them run their course; he did not think they would last long. But we should not wake her up. So all we could do was stand there and watch her suffer in her sleep. Cry and whimper and beg—and then finally plead not to be hurt and say she would do what he wanted. And then—then, my God in heaven, she would begin making that terrible—horrible—sound . . ."

"It was a sucking noise," Ramón said from the front seat, to save his mother the humiliation of even having to say the word.

"Yes, yes," Josefa Luza almost hissed. "It was an awful sound, the most awful I ever heard." The grieved mother buried her face in her wrinkled brown hands and sobbed pitifully.

Cloud, unable to look at her, turned his eyes to the car window.

The hospital lay behind a high fence, halfway between the freeway to the front of it and gently rising hills behind it. The car was stopped at the gate and each passenger required to sign a log; then they parked in a visitors' parking area and walked to a nearby registration center. At the center they filled out a visitors' slip and were directed to the office of a doctor who had to approve the visit. The Luzas and Cloud went to the office of Dr. Helen Jacobs, who had been treating Glory Ann at the hospital for nearly three years.

Dr. Jacobs was a big-boned, full-bodied woman of fifty who could still turn heads when she walked on the Point Mugu beach in a two-piece swimsuit. Her hair was blonde, clipped haphazardly short, as if she did it herself. She had an excellent figure and strikingly direct blue eyes. In her office, with the Luzas and Cloud sitting in front of her desk, she professionally appraised the stranger that Glory Ann's family had brought with them.

"Exactly what is it you intend to write about Glory Ann, Mr. Cloud?" she asked.

"I don't know, Doctor," Cloud replied. "I had no idea the young lady was in a mental institution. My original intent had been to interview her—"

"That, of course, is quite out of the question," Dr. Jacobs said. "You would be able to elicit no coherent response from her whatsoever." She continued to study him as she spoke. "Since you can't interview the girl, what do you propose to do?"

"I'm open to suggestions, Doctor."

Dr. Jacobs pursed her lips. "What, may I ask, was to be the purpose of your story?"

"If I had been able to interview her," Cloud said, "I would have concentrated primarily on her feelings about Weldon Whitman today, what she thinks of his repeated denials that he was the man who kidnapped her, things like that. But any story I do now will have to be more documentary: what her condition is, your prognosis of her condition, and so on."

"Please, Doctor," said Emiliano Luza, speaking in the office for the first time. "Before Mr. Cloud writes his story, we would like for him to see Glory Ann."

"Do you mean face to face?" Dr. Jacobs asked.

"If you will permit it, yes."

The doctor tapped an index finger pensively against her upper lip for a moment, then said, "Yes, I think so. It's almost time to measure her progress again anyway. Using a stranger like Mr. Cloud will give us a good gut reaction to go by."

"What are you talking about, Doctor?" Cloud asked. Dr. Jacobs rose and walked around the desk.

"Come along and find out," she said.

Helen Jacobs led the way through an enclosed walkway connecting the doctors' offices with the hospital buildings. "This is G Ward," she told Cloud as she used an electronic card key to open a controlled door. "It's a segregated female ward for borderline behavioral cases. Women who are normally nonviolent in nature, but who have emotional action levers which are easily tripped, causing the subject to undergo immediate and marked mental agitation and physical excitability."

They proceeded down a wide corridor between treatment, examination, and therapy rooms. They turned into a narrower hall containing small, private rooms where patients could be observed under controlled conditions. Each of the rooms was equipped with a frame of unbreakable one-way observation glass set in the front wall next to the door.

At Room G-8, Dr. Jacobs unlocked a control panel and turned an illumination switch; the frame of glass became diaphanous, allowing them to watch Glory Ann. A second switch opened a ceiling transmitter which allowed them also to listen to the patient. The Luza family stood to one side to allow Cloud to step up close to the window. Dr. Jacobs stood next to him.

"Glory Ann Luza," she said clinically. "Female, Mexican-American by naturalization; age, nearly twenty-two; height, five feet one inch; weight, one hundred and nine; I.Q., low average; education, three-and-a-half years of high school; present physical condition, excellent; bodily functions, normal; mental condition—" she paused, as if the word she were about to say simply did not fit. But she had no choice, it had to be said. "Mental condition, schizoid."

Cloud stared into the room. Glory Ann Luza was dark, pretty, with flawless skin and large eyes like plums. She was wearing a flowered cotton dress, white anklets, and sandals. She sat on the room's single bed, a sketchpad on her lap. Humming softly to herself, she worked at drawing a picture with colored pencils. Around her on the bed were sketches, completed drawings, and fully colored pictures that she had finished. They were of church steeples, chapels, altars, and other religious subjects.

Cloud turned to Helen Jacobs. "Schizoid. Doesn't that have something to do with split personality?"

"That's an oversimplification," Dr. Jacobs said. "In Glory Ann's case it amounts to a psychotic disorder that causes her to lose contact with her present environment."

"Lose contact how?" he asked.

"Why don't I show you?" Dr. Jacobs said. She quietly unlocked the door. "Go into the room and speak to her."

"Just like that?"

"Yes. Say anything you like, in just a normal voice."

Cloud glanced uneasily at the Luza family, who were still standing slightly back from the window. An odd feeling of apprehension slipped over him; his whole being warned him that he was not going to like what was to come. Nevertheless, he had come this far to learn the truth about Glory Ann Luza; he certainly was not going to stop on the threshold of that truth. Reluctant but determined, he entered the room.

The young woman sitting on the side of the bed had her back to Cloud. Humming softly, she went on with her sketching. Cloud stepped to the foot of the bed.

"Hello, Glory Ann," he said quietly.

The young woman leaped from the bed and whirled

around, dropping her sketchpad and spilling her pencils on the floor. Her eyes widened fearfully. Her lips began to twitch.

"Don't be afraid, I'm not going to hurt you," Cloud said as gently as he could.

Suddenly Glory Ann went berserk. She screamed a terrified, stricken scream and flung herself into the farthest corner of the little room. Cringing there like a trapped animal, she alternately clutched at her throat with both hands and then clawed at the wall as if trying to dig her way to escape from some pursuing demon. All the while she continued to scream at a frantic pitch—screams filled with such intense dread that they were like needles being pushed into Cloud's nerve ends.

Cloud looked pleadingly at the window panel, knowing that the Luzas and Helen Jacobs were watching him. He took a tentative step toward the possessed girl, saw her try to literally force her body into the wall, heard her screams grow more gruesome, and quickly retreated from her. He turned back to the door and hurried from the room.

Outside, he leaned against the door, pale and shaken. "Did you get enough gut reaction out of that?" he angrily asked Dr. Jacobs.

"Yes, I did," she replied matter-of-factly. "Such experiments are necessary from time to time to tell us whether we are making any progress with the patient. Ordinarily I would have used a male orderly for the guinea pig, but since you wanted a story, well—"

"Don't you have any *other* way of measuring your progress? That poor kid is probably butting her head against the wall by now!"

"Calm down, Mr. Cloud," said Helen Jacobs. "Come back over here."

Cloud stepped back to the observation window.

"Look," said the doctor.

Cloud looked into the room. Glory Ann Luza was back on the bed, sketching quietly, humming softly.

"It is called an Adam syndrome," Dr. Jacobs explained. "It is, in its simplest sense, a violent emotional reaction to any exposure to a man. *Any* man—even her own father, her brother."

Cloud was back in the doctor's office, sitting before her desk. The Luza men were waiting in the visitors' lounge; Josefa Luza was visiting her daughter in the little room.

"I believe her condition has grown out of some deep-seated guilt feelings which manifested themselves following her attack by the Spotlight Bandit. I don't think it was the attack itself, mind you, but rather what happened after the attack."

"I'm not sure I follow you, Doctor," Cloud said.

"All right, let me explain if this way. At the time of her kidnap experience, Glory Ann was eighteen. She was not overly mature for her age, almost totally inexperienced insofar as sex was concerned. She had been exposed to the usual health and hygiene classes in high school, had probably read a sex book or two out of curiosity, was familiar with the common four-letter words, and so on; but I don't believe she ever personally indulged in any sex play herself, and it is my personal opinion that she had never even masturbated. It appears that she was a very religious girl, very close to the sisters where she went to school, and even seriously considering becoming a nun herself."

Helen Jacobs rummaged in a large purse on her desk for a pack of cigarettes. She took one out and Cloud leaned across the desk to light it for her.

"Thanks," she said, smiling briefly and exhaling. "All right, that's the picture of Glory Ann Luza as she was the night she went to the dance and then parked in the hills to neck or whatever they call it these days. Now, along comes the Spotlight Bandit and kidnaps her. He drives her to an isolated place and holds her captive for two hours. During that time he forces her to take off all her clothes and submit to numerous sexual violations and indignities. This, naturally, was a terrible shock to her sensibilities—but *not* something she couldn't survive. The immediate results of the experience were the swelling and rash, and the subsequent nightmares. Both were temporary conditions; both, I believe, would have gradually and normally been alleviated by the passage of time—*if the matter had been let alone*."

"Let alone by whom?" Cloud asked.

"By *everyone*," the doctor said emphatically. "By her mother, her father, her brother, the family priest, all the nuns at her school, the police, the district attorney's office—everybody. If they had all let her alone, I believe she would have recovered completely, physically and emotionally, in two or three months." She paused to drag almost belligerently on her cigarette. "But they didn't leave her alone. They made her describe her ordeal over and over again to strangers and in front of strangers. They made her appear in open court not once but twice, and publicly admit what she had been a party to—an unwilling party, certainly; that was made very clear. But the fact that she didn't *want* to suck Weldon Whitman's penis didn't alter the fact that she did it; the fact that she didn't *want* to have anal intercourse with him didn't alter the fact that he did it to her. Neither his forcing of her nor her being forced changed the actuality of what happened between them—and it was that actuality that she was compelled time and again to admit, to relate, to describe. Then, finally, the ultimate humiliation: to actually have her story *questioned* as if she were lying about it; and not only questioned, but, because he was conducting his own defense, questioned by the very man who had subjected her to the abuse in the first place."

"What you're saying," Cloud suggested, "is that Glory Ann's present state is just as much the fault of the prosecution and the court as it is the fault of Weldon Whitman."

"Oh, no!" Dr. Jacobs said quickly. "No, no, definitely not. The prosecution and the courts, the family, the priest, anyone else involved with the girl, did what they did out of ignorance. None of those people would have deliberately harmed the girl. But the Spotlight Bandit *did* deliberately harm her. The contributory harm to her emotional condition may be divided, for the sake of discussion; but make no mistake about the guilt factor, Mr. Cloud: it is Weldon Whitman's—and his alone."

"But you do believe that the trial and all the rest were also harmful to her?"

"Definitely." The doctor finished her cigarette and tamped it out in an ashtray. "I believe she could easily have coped with what happened to her if she had not been required by our legal processes to display it in public. To her, what happened was a dreadful, shameful thing. When she had to participate in making a production, a public spectacle, of that shame, she began to protect herself by retreating back into her own mind. It was as natural a process as the clotting of blood. With each subsequent incident of exposure, she retreated a little farther. And as she retreated, she began to shut out associations with male figures. This was all done subconsciously, very subtly; it probably began with relatively insignificant acts: not staying in the same room with her father or brother, declining dates, refusing to sit next to a man on a bus or in a theater—that sort of thing. But as her condition became progressively worse, she actually devised ways to avoid men: hiding when her father called her, lying that she had no appetite in order to avoid sitting at the dinner table, going back and forth across streets to keep from passing a man on the sidewalk. The day finally came when the last thread holding her to reality was broken; after that the mere sight of a man triggered the extreme reaction you saw earlier, and the girl was committed."

"What's your prognosis for her, Doctor?" Cloud asked.

"Not good," Helen Jacobs said decisively. "For the moment her condition seems to have stabilized, but there is no guarantee that she will not become worse as she grows older. It is possible that she may regress to the point where even a picture or a drawing of a man will affect her as violently as a real person." She reached up and pinched her nose directly between the eyes, as if to relieve a headache. "It is my professional evaluation, Mr. Cloud, that barring some unforeseen, highly unusual eventuality, Glory Ann will probably have to live her life totally segregated from any form of man—because in her mind, every man she sees is the man who attacked her that terrible night in the Hollywood Hills."

Cloud stared soberly at the woman behind the desk, wondering what she would think if she knew that she had just materially altered his views on capital punishment. Cloud could no longer honestly advocate that the death penalty be applied only in cases where a life had been taken. There were, he had to admit now, psychological conditions horrible enough in tenor to be ranked with death. If the Spotlight Bandit had killed Glory Ann that fateful night, he would actually have saved her poor child's mind a vast amount of suffering and terror. Who knew what awful agony she had endured over the years, what ugly images, monstrous fears? Who knew what inward torture had driven her to a limbo where two of the three people who loved her most were forbidden? The state of California had measured the crime against her body—but who, Cloud wondered, could ever accurately measure the crime against her mind? At what point could it be said that a mind had been capitally abused—that it had, in effect, been killed? Did a person have to have the last tendrils of sanity utterly destroyed in order for the mind to be considered murdered? Or was it sufficient simply to do enough to terminate normality? If a person's eyesight were purposely impaired to the point where only light was distinguishable from dark, and nothing more, then that person had been rendered blind. So was it not equitable to also conclude that even though shreds of intelligence were left in the wake of a deliberate criminal attack, if the mind as a whole had lost its normality, its purpose, then it had been murdered?

Robert Cloud thought so. With Helen Jacobs's closing words, he rejected completely his former position on the death penalty; he now accepted the fact that there *were* crimes short of the taking of a human life that deserved to be punished by exactly that—the taking of a human life.

He was very thankful that he did not believe Weldon Whitman to be the Spotlight Bandit.

Twenty

It was late in the afternoon when Ramón Luza drove them back to Reseda. The sun was falling rapidly behind the rolling hills that lay like huge muscles in the land between the freeway and the ocean. The drive back was strangely quiet—a subdued stillness, like the calm after the storm.

"When she was a little girl," Josefa recalled, "Sunday was always her favorite day. She loved more than anything to put on her prettiest dress and *mantilla* and go to mass. When we were poor, you know, before we came here from Mexico, we didn't have pretty dresses for her to wear, but I always managed to find cloth to make a bright ribbon for her hair or a little hankie to pin to her dress. I always managed that, didn't I, 'Miliano?"

"Yes, Josefa, always," her husband quietly confirmed.

"I'll never forget the day I bought her her first American dress after we came here. We were living out in East L.A., you know, and 'Miliano had found a good job and Ramón got himself a paper route and I was taking in ironing, so we were getting along pretty well. We went to mass at a little church called Santo Tomás and Gloriana always just wore her regular school clothes on Sunday because that's all we had for her. But 'Miliano and I talked it over, about buying her a dress, you know, and we decided it would be our first luxury in this country. Even Ramón put in part of his paper-route money. Ramón, you remember that, don't you?"

"Yes, Mamma," her son answered softly.

"I took her on Saturday down to the May Company," Josefa continued, her eyes glowing with memory. "I told her we were going to just look, so that later when we could afford it, we would know what to buy. I let her try on three dresses: a blue, a green, and a yellow. She looked best in the yellow one—because of her coloring, you know. After the saleslady put the dresses back on the rack, I took Gloriana to the lunch counter and bought her a Coca-Cola. Then I made her wait there because I said I left something in the dress department. I went back and bought the little yellow dress and I hid it in with some other packages I had. The next morning when she had bathed for mass and came out to get dressed, the yellow dress was on the chair where she had put her other clothes. We all watched her when she found it. She held it up to her and she cried, and she was so happy. And then I cried. And then 'Miliano cried. You did cry, didn't you, 'Miliano?"

"Yes, Josefa, I cried."

"She was so proud to go to mass that day. Like a little angel. A little angel." Josefa Luza looked out the window at the passing landscape. Long, angular shadows stretched inward with the last rays of a disappearing sun. Some of the shadows looked like church steeples. "You know," she said solemnly, "it is really very strange how much Gloriana was drawn to the church. I honestly believe she would have become a nun someday. I mean, to her it was more than just something she played at; it was—it was like something she *felt.* Even as a very little girl she had shown a genuine closeness to the church. More than one of the sisters told me this. She loved the mass and she loved the holy altar. And particularly she loved the confessional. One time she said to me, 'Mamma, the confessional is so cool and dark; I feel so close to the Holy Mother when I am in there.' Always when she had a problem, she would go to the church to solve it. Even when she was just deep in thought about something, she reached out to the church in some way. She had a habit of always putting her hand up and touching a cross she wore around her neck. That is why now she clutches at her throat when she is excited. You saw how she did that; she has never stopped reaching up for her cross, even though it was lost the night she was attacked—"

Robert Cloud turned cold at the sound of Josefa Luza's words. For he suddenly remembered other words, words spoken to him by Carol Carter, the woman who had once been married to Weldon Whitman:

"*I saw him once more after that. When he was paroled from Folsom, he came over one evening to see me. Just to say hello and chat a few minutes, nothing intimate. We had a nice little visit. He even gave me a present, a little silver cross and chain; not expensive, but very thoughtful, very nice of him . . .*"

Cloud had turned now and was staring at Josefa Luza. "What kind of cross was it, Mrs. Luza?" he asked the woman in a controlled voice. Josefa Luza frowned.

"What kind?"

"Yes. Can you describe it for me?" Cloud saw Ramón's eyes flick suspiciously to the rearview mirror.

" 'Miliano can describe it better," Josefa said. "It once belonged to his mother, God rest her soul. 'Miliano, tell Mr. Cloud what Gloriana's cross looked like."

The elder Luza sighed quietly. "It was silver, originally made in Oaxaca around the turn of the century. It was smooth on the top and bottom, and had a Florentine scroll engraved completely around its outside edge."

"It was very beautiful, very delicate," Josefa said. "Gloriana loved it dearly. Since she has been at the hospital, we have given her several others to replace it. We even gave her one that looked like the one she had lost. But she will have none of them. She throws them away and begins feeling at her throat as if searching for the *real* one. It is a very strange thing."

Cloud said nothing. But when he glanced up, he caught Ramón's eyes on him in the rearview mirror again.

When they arrived back at the little house in Reseda, Cloud said goodbye to Emiliano and Josefa Luza on the sidewalk. Ramón waited until his parents were in the house, then turned to Cloud.

"Why did you want the cross described to you?" he asked directly.

"No particular reason—"

"You are lying," Ramón accused. His face was a mask of contempt. "You promised the truth, and already the lying begins."

Cloud looked down at the sidewalk. His mind was in a turmoil; he felt very indecisive.

"I do not think you are interested in the truth," the young Chicano said tightly. "I do not think you care about what has happened to my sister, or whether that bastard Whitman goes unpunished for it. I think I made a mistake taking you to see Glory Ann."

"You didn't, Ramón," Cloud said urgently; it was essential to him that he be believed.

"Then why won't you tell me what you know about Glory Ann's cross?" Ramon challenged. "You know something about that cross; I can *feel* it."

"I may know something," Cloud admitted, "but I'm not sure. And until I am sure, it would do no good to talk about it."

"Do no good for who, Mr. Cloud?" the young man asked

coldly. "For my sister? Or for Weldon Whitman?" Ramón tilted his head slightly and his eyes narrowed. "Which side are you on, Mr. Cloud? The side of truth or the side of Whitman?"

Cloud parted his lips to speak—but no words came. He had no answer for Ramón Luza, and he could not face the angry young man's accusing eyes any longer. Swallowing dryly, he turned away from him and walked back to his rented car.

It was fully nighttime as Cloud drove the Ventura Freeway back toward Los Angeles. His face was troubled; he drove hunched forward, gripping the wheel almost tensely. He followed the wide, fast freeway east to the interchange, then turned south on the San Diego Freeway. As that road wound and curved its way through the deep canyon that separated the San Fernando Valley from the West Los Angeles area, Cloud several times looked out to his left at the darkness as if straining to see into it. He knew that the darkness covered the high hills above Hollywood, the hills that overlooked the city's billion twinkling lights; the hills that had once been prowled by the Spotlight Bandit. He thought about the dreadful terror that had been implanted in Glory Ann Luza's mind during the hours of her captivity in those hills.

Cloud left the freeway at Wilshire and drove west into Santa Monica. He cruised along Montana Street until he found the address where Carol Carter lived. He parked and hurried across the street to the L-shaped building, to the last apartment on the second floor. As he rang her bell, he remembered that the last time he had visited her, she had been anxious about her boyfriend coming over at seven-thirty. It was almost that time now. He started to ring again, but before he could do so, the door was opened. In the four inches allowed by the safety chain, he saw Carol Carter's broad, solemn mouth.

"Miss Carter, I'm Robert Cloud," he said quickly, as if afraid she might close the door again. "I was here some time ago—"

"I remember you," she said. They stared at each other in silence for a moment, then she said, "Wait a second—" She closed the door, removed the chain, and opened it again.

"I'm sorry to show up unannounced like this," Cloud apologized. "I know your boyfriend comes over at seven-thirty, but if I could just have a couple of minutes—"

"Don't worry about the time," she said simply. "There is no boyfriend at the moment. Come in."

He followed her into the little living room, looking at her back and realizing that he had forgotten how boldly wide her shoulders were, how delicately thin her waist. She was wearing faded jeans and a body shirt with the sleeves pushed up. Her feet were bare. The soft slide of straight blond hair that fell on either side of her head was darker tonight and looked damp. He saw that she had a towel on the arm of the chair where she sat. She picked it up and started patting the ends of her hair.

"Excuse me," she said. "I've just washed my hair and I don't want to catch cold." She waited until he had sat on the couch opposite her, then said, "What was it you wanted?"

Cloud took a deep breath. "I came here to ask you to show me the cross and chain you said Whit gave you the last time you saw him."

"Why do you want to see it?"

"I visited Glory Ann Luza this afternoon. She's in the state asylum up at Camarillo." He described the girl's condition and the doctor's prognosis.

Carol winced and shook her head briefly. "How awful. But what does that have to do with the cross Whit gave me?"

"One thing that Glory Ann does during her hysterics is clutch at her throat for a cross that she used to wear. A cross that was lost when the Spotlight Bandit made her strip naked in his car up in the hills."

"Oh. I see." Carol Carter stopped drying her hair and put down the towel. She and Cloud stared meditatively at each other.

"The last time I was here," Cloud said, "you admitted that maybe Whit *could* have committed the sex crimes. You said that when you knew him he seemed to be getting worse and worse; you said that if he kept on as he was going at that time, maybe he *could* have eventually turned into a criminal sex pervert. But you didn't believe he had. Do you remember telling me that?"

"Yes," she said, "I remember."

"The cross and chain should tell us whether he turned out like that or not," Cloud said.

Carol Carter studied him. He was tired, tense, his knuckles white as he clasped his hands together. He was obviously fighting a battle inside himself.

"I could always say I don't have them any longer," she told him.

Cloud shook his head. "That wouldn't do either of us any good." He locked eyes with her. "Get it for me," he said.

She hesitated, finally nodded briefly. "All right."

Cloud did not move while she was gone. He did not unclasp his hands, did not sit back and relax, did not even look around the room.

Carol returned and stood in front of him. Her right hand was closed tightly. Cloud stared at it, wondering what answer it contained.

"Is it a silver cross?" he asked quietly. "With its top and bottom surfaces smooth? And a Florentine scroll around its sides?"

Carol said nothing. She simply opened her hand and held the cross and chain out to him. Cloud unclasped his hands and took it. It was exactly as Emiliano Luza had described it.

Cloud did not know how long he sat bent forward staring at the cross. His next conscious realization was that Carol was taking the cross from him and putting it on the coffee table; and she was gently forcing a glass into his hand and telling him to drink.

"It's gin with a little soda. It'll help you to unwind. Sit back now, relax—"

He allowed himself to be coaxed back until he was resting properly on the couch. "It all begins to make sense now," he said listlessly. "Whit encouraged me to try and prove that Doris Calder was lying—but he was never interested in me trying to do the same with Glory Ann." Cloud raised the glass to his lips and drank half of its contents. His face was etched with bitterness, his mouth drawn down cruelly. "It was the same whenever I mentioned you. He always had some reason to get me off the subject. But what he was really doing was trying to keep me away from *that*," he bobbed his chin at the cross and chain lying on the coffee table. "The only piece of hard evidence that could conclusively connect him to the Luza girl. Jesus, what a fool I've been!"

"No more so than a lot of other people," Carol said. "Myself included." Her fingers played nervously with the towel. "A moment ago you said I didn't believe it. You were right. I didn't want to. I kept wanting to give him that last benefit of the doubt in my mind; that last little bit of a chance. That's all he ever seemed to need, you know; just a chance."

"Sure," Cloud said wryly. "Just a chance. The Whitman mystique." He grunted softly and drank some more of the gin. Then, frowning, he stood up and began to pace. "What *doesn't* make any sense is the Calder thing," he said, perplexed. "I'm *convinced* that Doris Calder was mistaken when she said Whit made her blow him. I know she was lying. So if Whit did do the Luza crime, but he didn't do the Calder crime, then there would have to have been two Spotlight Bandits." He turned almost fiercely to Carol. "That ex-partner of his! You know, I've always suspected that the ex-partner Whit won't tell me anything about had a lot more to do with this case than—" He suddenly set the glass down and put both hands to his temple. "Christ, I feel like my head's going to explode—"

"Listen, you have *got* to relax," Carol Carter said firmly. She took his arm and dragged him from the room. "I want you to lie down and rest while I fix you something to eat." She led him to her tiny bedroom and sat him down on the side of the bed. As she bent to peel off his coat, her damp hair brushed his face. It smelled fresh and clean, and the touch of it was pleasantly cool.

"Look, this is my problem, not yours," he said. "Let me go back to my hotel—"

"Shut up and lie down." She pushed him sideways onto the bed and lifted his feet up. Quickly she removed his shoes. Then she sat down beside him and loosened his tie. The room was only partly lighted by a ceiling lamp in the short hallway outside the door. As Cloud looked up at her, the right side of her face was in shadow. He could only see half of her too-big, too-full mouth, but that was enough to tell him that it was even more solemn than usual.

"What happened to the boyfriend?" he asked. Carol pulled the unknotted tie from around his neck and held it, both hands resting on his chest. She looked intently at him without answering. Cloud reached up and touched her cheek with his knuckles. "Tell me, Carol," he said quietly, calling her by name for the first time.

"It just didn't work out," she said. Her fingers toyed with the necktie on his chest. "When we started talking marriage—I mean, really making plans—I felt that I had to tell him who I had been married to the first time. As soon as I did, he became a different person. He said he couldn't understand how I could have been married to a criminal pervert like Whit." She looked away, and in the dull light, Cloud saw a tear streak halfway down her cheek. "I tried to explain that the marriage was a long time ago," she said, "and that Whit had been a different person then; but when I said that, it just made matters worse. He accused me of sticking up for Whit and insinuated that maybe I still cared for him. He reminded me that he had a sister about the same age as the girl in the Spotlight Bandit case, and asked how I would feel if the victim had been his sister." She paused to shake her head, as if she could not believe her own words. "It was completely irrational, the whole thing. He kept making it seem very current and personal, instead of so far in the past. It was crazy."

"*He* was crazy," Cloud said.

She turned her face back to him. "The last thing he said was that he was sorry, but that—that he would have felt—dirty—every time he touched me . . ."

Ignorant fucking bastard, Cloud thought. He took the necktie from her hands and tossed it on the floor. He put his palms on her cheeks and drew her face down and kissed her gently on the mouth.

"There's nothing dirty about you," he whispered.

He held her face like that and kissed her again and again, feasting on the too-full lips that he found had suddenly become enormously attractive to him. Her damp hair slid down and made a cool, silky tent for their locked mouths.

Taking her by the shoulders, he rolled her slowly over his body onto the bed and quickly sat up so that their positions were reversed. "There's nothing dirty about you, Carol," he told her again. He deftly undid the front of her jeans and slipped them down and off her legs. His hand brushed one breast as he searched for the entry to her body shirt.

"Between my legs," she whispered eagerly. "It unsnaps—"

His fingers found the way: three snaps that opened at the crotch; he pulled them apart all at once and pushed the shirt up to expose her white naked hips. He pressed his face into her and began to kiss and lick softly and wetly, and she came almost at once.

He got up and quickly undressed. Waiting, she spread her legs for him. He climbed back onto the bed and thrust himself into her, feeling her climax again. Then he began a smooth, rhythmic fucking motion that made her draw her breath in sharply. He threw his head back as a throbbing, rushing ejaculation gushed out of him, and he fell forward to press his mouth against her wonderful big wide lips again.

"God, that was good," Carol said through labored breathing as he lay on top of her.

"It was," he said back.

And it had been too. Except for one thing. At the precise moment he climaxed, the thought came to his mind, from out of nowhere, that Weldon Whitman had once ejaculated into this very same woman.

She was gone when Cloud awoke the next morning, though not by long. She had slipped out of the apartment at eight-ten in order to be at work by eight-thirty; and he awoke at quarter of nine. He was famished, having not eaten since breakfast the previous day. Getting up, he prowled naked through the tiny apartment. On the breakfast bar he found her note: *Juice and milk in the fridge, powdered doughnuts in the breadbox. Be home at 5:20. Hope you're here.* It was unsigned.

Cloud sat down naked at the breakfast bar and ate nine doughnuts and drank a quart and a half of milk. While he was wolfing down the food, he thought about Glory Ann Luza and Doris Calder. He was now convinced that Whitman *might* have committed the crime against Glory Ann Luza; the cross and chain proved that. But Cloud still did *not* believe that Whitman was Doris Calder's attacker. Which meant that there *had* to be a second Spotlight Bandit. And if there *was* a second Spotlight Bandit—Whitman's ex-partner, probably—then it was possible that the other bandit, and *not* Whitman, might have committed the Luza crime.

Whitman's possession of the cross still had to be explained, Cloud knew; but first the matter of the second bandit had to be settled. And Robert Cloud knew just the person who could probably settle it.

Finished eating, walking back through the living room, Cloud noticed the silver cross and chain on the coffee table. He picked it up, took it into the bedroom with him, and put it in the pocket of his coat, which was still hanging on the doorknob where Carol had hung it the night before.

After he was dressed, Cloud went back to where Carol had left the note. He scribbled on the bottom of it: *I took the cross*, signed it *Rob*, and left it in the same place. He left the apartment at nine-thirty.

An hour and a half later, in his hotel room, Cloud had showered, shaved, and put on fresh clothes. He transferred the cross and chain to a pocket of the suit he had changed to, and put all his other clothes in his suitcase. Before leaving the room, he telephoned across the boulevard to the airport terminal and booked a seat on the three-thirty commuter back to Sacramento. Then he went downstairs and checked out.

Still driving the rented car, he got on the inbound Santa Monica Freeway and headed for downtown Los Angeles. It was nearly noon when he reached the Civic Center. He drove around for ten minutes trying to find a parking place, and finally said to hell with it and pulled onto a lot clearly marked *County Employees Only.* Let them tow it away if they want to, he thought as he walked across the street to the Hall of Justice. If it wasn't there when he got back, he'd tell the rental company it had been stolen. Only after he was in the building and on the elevator did he remember that his suitcase was in the car. He swore softly to himself.

He got off on the floor where the district attorney's offices were located and hurriedly made his way to the chief prosecutor's office. The secretary was just getting up to go to lunch when he entered.

"Excuse me, is Mr. Klein in?" he asked before she could get away from her desk. She looked at him curiously.

"Mr. Klein hasn't been the chief prosecutor for a year."

Cloud's mouth dropped open in surprise. "I'm from out of town," he explained. "I didn't know he wasn't here any longer. Did he go into private practice?"

"Oh, no. Mr. Klein was appointed to the bench. He's serving as municipal court judge in Huntington Park."

Cloud thanked her and left. In the lobby downstairs, he called the airport again; he changed his reservation from three-thirty to five o'clock. Then, remembering that he was illegally parked, he hurried back to the lot. He was relieved to see that his car was still there.

It took him forty minutes to drive to Huntington Park. When he got there, he realized that he was only a few blocks from Rancher Bob's Sausage Company, where he had tried to find Emiliano Luza during his first unsuccessful search more than a year ago. The Weldon Whitman web, he thought. It crossed and recrossed.

He parked in front of the Huntington Park municipal court, went into the low building, and found the courtroom that had Klein's name posted next to the double doors. Entering, he found a few people sitting in the spectator section outside the rails, and a uniformed bailiff reading a paperback novel at his duty desk. Cloud went over to the bailiff.

"Excuse me. My name is Robert Cloud. I'm a former reporter with the *Ledger*. Judge Klein and I were acquainted a few years back when he was the D.A.'s chief prosecutor. I'd like to see him if he has a few minutes."

"Have a seat, please, and I'll tell him you're here," the bailiff said. He put his paperback in a desk drawer and went through a door leading to the judge's chambers. In a moment, he was back. "This way, please."

Cloud followed him into a book-lined office where, in one corner, a black judge's robe hung from a coat tree, and behind a neat and orderly desk, sat G. Foster Klein. The bailiff left and closed the door.

"Well, well, the crusading magazine writer," Klein said deprecatingly. He had not changed much, Cloud thought: he still sat board-straight, his black hair was still slicked back unpretentiously, and there was still about him that very definite aura of crispness, sharpness, alertness. Someday, undoubtedly, he would become as much a legend on the bench as Carl Lukey had been when he sentenced Weldon Whitman to die twice. "To what do I owe this rather unpleasant surprise?" Klein asked.

"I'd like to talk to you about the Whitman case," Cloud said. "May I sit down?"

"By all means," the dapper little judge said elaborately. "Although I really can't see what there is to discuss about the

Whitman case. You and your associates seem to be doing a splendid job of subverting justice. You've managed to keep Whiman alive for—how many years?"

"Your Honor, I didn't come here to antagonize you or argue with you," Cloud said quietly. "I came here to discuss a case which you yourself prosecuted. Despite our differences, I do respect you, and I think you want justice in the Whitman case as much as I do."

"That's extremely flattering, Cloud, considering some of the things you've written about me," Klein said acidly. "Now, what is it you want?"

Cloud swallowed dryly. "I want to know how much, in your opinion, the outcome of the Whitman case would have been affected if evidence had been presented showing the existence of a second Spotlight Bandit?"

Klein's face registered sudden surprise. "Why do you ask that?" he demanded.

"Because I think such a person existed," Cloud said. He immediately noted the effect his words had on the little judge: Klein was almost stunned by what Cloud had said.

He knows! Cloud thought.

Cloud leaned forward urgently. "There *was* another bandit, wasn't there?"

"Suppose there had been?" Klein said, quickly composing himself. "It doesn't change anything. Whitman was rightfully convicted and he is rightfully on Death Row."

"How can you be so sure of that if there was another man involved?" Cloud challenged.

"Because I know who that other man is," Klein snapped impulsively. "And I know which crimes he committed."

Cloud sat back in his chair and stared at Klein. The little judge immediately looked distressed, obviously upset by the impulsiveness of his words. Both men seemed embarrassed by the secret that had just passed between them. It was Klein, almost self-consciously, who resumed the conversation.

"The other man was a former criminal associate of Whitman. They served time together in Folsom. We picked him up on other charges about a year after Whitman went to Death Row. It was while we were preparing for trial on the other charges that we learned of his implication in the Spotlight crimes. The man was eventually sent back to Folsom.

He's a three-time loser serving a fifty-year sentence. Chances are he'll never be released."

Cloud wet his lips. "Which of the Spotlight crimes did he do?"

"He committed the car theft in Pasadena. He was an accomplice of Whitman's in the Redondo Beach menswear store stickup." Klein paused for the briefest of instants. "And he did the Doris Calder crime."

"But not the Luza crime?"

"No," Klein said emphatically.

"How do you know?"

"The man confessed," Klein said. "We had him on a dozen other counts, including two technical kidnapping charges. We made a deal not to ask for a death penalty if he'd wipe the slate clean. There was no reason for him not to confess to the Luza crime if it was his."

"Why did Doris Calder lie and say it was Whitman who attacked her?" Cloud asked.

"She didn't lie," said Klein. "She mistakenly identified Whitman. He and this other man strongly resemble each other. It was an honest mistake."

"Well, tell me something, Judge," said Cloud, sitting forward again. "Why haven't you done anything about that honest mistake?"

"Such as?" Klein asked, his voice suddenly crisp again.

"Such as getting Whitman off Death Row! Such as getting him a new trial!"

"A new trial!" snorted Klein. "If he had been convicted of only one crime, I *would* get him a new trial. But he was convicted on *nineteen* separate counts. I don't believe he deserves to be tried again simply because he didn't commit the crimes in *two* of those counts."

"One of those crimes," Cloud said tensely, "happens to be one of the capital offenses that got him put on Death Row!"

"Which is exactly where he belongs," Klein said adamantly. "He was rightfully convicted of the Luza crime and sentenced to death for that."

"He might not have received the death penalty for the Luza crime if the jury hadn't had the Calder crime to back it up—"

"Nonsense," Klein said dogmatically. "That jury would have sent him to the gas chamber if the Luza crime had been the *only* one he was charged with. And even if they hadn't, he would have wound up there sooner or later anyway." Klein emphatically poked a finger in the air at Cloud. "No one has ever deserved a death sentence more than Weldon Whitman. In executing him—unlike most of them we gas—we will be *preventing* the taking of an innocent life."

"*That* is not justice," Cloud accused.

"Oh, yes, it is," Klein insisted. "Very much so. As a matter of fact, it's the best kind of justice. Preventive justice. Like preventive surgery. Cut out the cancer before it kills the body."

Cloud stood and faced Klein coldly across the desk. "I want a new trial for Weldon Whitman."

"You'll never get it," Judge Klein assured him.

"I'll expose you. I'll take this conversation to the papers."

"I'll deny it. The papers won't use it then and you know it."

Cloud's expression darkened in outrage. He whirled from the desk and stalked to the door. "I'll have the Whitman Foundation file a show-cause suit. I'll subpoena Doris Calder to court and *make* her admit it." He jerked open the door to leave.

"Just a moment, Cloud!"

Klein's voice was like a gunshot. It stopped Cloud as effectively as a bullet would have.

"Turn around and look at me," the judge ordered. "I want to see your face when I tell you why you won't get a new trial for Weldon Whitman."

Cloud turned, his hand still on the doorknob. His eyes met Klein's flat, unyielding stare.

"You won't be subpoenaing Doris Calder, and you won't be making her admit anything," Klein said tonelessly. "Doris Calder is dead, Cloud. She committed suicide six months after your magazine article about her was published."

Robert Cloud's face drained of color. His hand slipped away from the doorknob.

"She was conscience-stricken," Klein said. "She began to believe that she *had* mistakenly identified Whitman—and this was before we found out that she really had. I tried to convince her that even if it were true, Whitman still deserved to go to the gas chamber for what he did to that little Luza girl. But no matter what I said, she continued to brood about it.

She and her son Billy had been terribly humiliated by that magazine story of yours. When Billy came back from the Marines, he and Doris changed their names and moved to a neighborhood where they weren't known. That should have solved their problems, but it didn't. Doris just couldn't get it out of her head that she might be helping send an innocent man to the gas chamber. It gradually became an intolerable mental problem, one she finally couldn't cope with. One night she simply ended it with a lethal overdose of sleeping tablets."

Judge G. Foster Klein leaned forward and placed his small hands on the desktop. His face was at once aggrieved and accusing. He said nothing further to Cloud, merely reached over briefly to press a button on his desk. A moment later his bailiff entered.

"Show this person out of my chambers and out of my courtroom," Klein said.

"This way, please," the bailiff said to Cloud.

Cloud's shoulders sagged noticeably. He turned and mutely followed the bailiff.

He was escorted as far as the hall; the courtroom door was closed behind him. He stood there for a moment, staring vacantly, oblivious to the few people who walked past him. Finally he made his way slowly down the hall and out of the building. Instinctively he walked back to where he had parked the rented car. He unlocked it and got in. He started the car and put both hands on the steering wheel. But he made no effort to drive away. It suddenly occurred to him that he did not know where to go.

Twenty-one

Two weeks later, Genevieve Neller was pacing nervously back and forth in Morris Niebold's office. Her face was drawn, her eyes circled, and she looked much as she had looked the weekend Weldon Whitman had come so close to being executed.

Borden White entered the office and Genevieve whirled to face him. "Where's Morris?" she demanded. "I insist on seeing Morris."

"I'm afraid you'll have to go to Washington, then," White said. "He left on the morning plane."

"The receptionist didn't say he was out of town," she said suspiciously.

"The receptionist doesn't know." White sat at Niebold's desk and eyed her wearily. "What is it this time, Genevieve?"

"You know what it is," she snapped. "Rob has been missing for two weeks!"

"Cloud has been *gone* for two weeks," White corrected. "That does not necessarily mean that he's missing—"

"Just what in the goddamn hell does it mean then?" she challenged, standing in front of the desk and leaning over it threateningly.

"Vulgarity does not become you, Genevieve," White chastised mildly. "From a person of your nature, it carries no shock value at all. Only awkwardness. Besides, you know very well that you'll get nowhere at all with me unless you conduct yourself like a lady."

Genevieve stared at him for a moment, wanting passionately to reach across the desk and slap his smug, superior face. But that satisfaction, she knew, would cost her dearly, for then Borden White would probably also stop seeing her, as Morris Niebold already had done. Niebold was not in Washington; she was sure of it. He simply was not seeing her, just as he was no longer talking to her on the telephone. It had been that way since the morning in his office when he had sent Cloud to Los Angeles and ostracized her to the foundation's printshop. She had tried to call him, she had come in person to see him, all on matters of the production of certain foundation printed material to which she objected. Each time she called or tried to see him, he had been "out" or "in conference" or "on long distance." And now he was "in Washington."

Genevieve quickly capitulated now. She sat in a chair facing the desk and hung her head in despair. "Borden, *please*. We've got to do something to find him."

"We've tried to find him," White said easily. "We've had our private detective agency trying to locate him. We know that he spent an entire day with the Luza family; they all went somewhere together in the Luza car, but no one at the Luza residence will say where. Later that day, Robert drove away from the Luza home in a car he had rented at the hotel. We know he checked out of the hotel the following morning and returned the rental car two mornings after that. Further, we know that he has not been admitted to any hospitals in the L.A. area, nor has he been arrested, nor has he checked into any of the major hotels. Nor is he in the morgue. It seems to me, on the basis of all that information, that we really have no choice but to assume that Cloud has simply terminated his relationship with us of his own free will."

"Rob wouldn't do that," Genevieve said staunchly. "I know he wouldn't."

"Well, *I* think he would. And has. As a matter of fact, if he has not communicated with us by the time we hold our next board meeting, I intend to move that he be relieved of his responsibility as an officer of the foundation." White smiled and stood up. "I'm afraid you'll have to excuse me now. I have a client coming in. If you have any problems at the printshop and can't reach Morris or me, why don't you take them up with Carla? Any decisions that have to be made can be made by her. Morris and I will support whatever decisions she makes. Do you understand?"

"Yes," Genevieve said stiffly. "I understand perfectly."

Genevieve left the office. She managed to maintain her composure until she got into her car, and then she had to let the anguish out. She leaned her head against the steering wheel and allowed a great, hollow sob to escape from her breast. It's all gone wrong, she thought despondently. Everything's gone wrong.

Raising her head, she stared dismally out the windshield. She thought of the foundation. The literature it was now printing and distributing was no longer pro-humanitarian in its stand against capital punishment; now it was anti-government. It openly attacked the present state administration and the state Supreme Court; not only attacked but actually vilified. Instead of creating doubt in the minds of legislators regarding the propriety of capital punishment, the material was now generating anger; not only was it charging specific lawmakers with negligence in not presenting legislation to abolish the death penalty, but it actually accused some of them of dereliction of duty in failing to somehow organize a moratorium on further executions in the state. The literature still pretended to have as its purpose the gaining of public support against capital punishment, but now it had also become a vehicle for political propaganda.

And while the foundation press created animosity with the printed word, foundation speakers were doing likewise with the spoken word. The four professionals retained by Morris Niebold were traveling the length and breadth of the state, spreading political venom in the guise of arousing public sentiment for Weldon Whitman. Singly, in pairs, sometimes all four on the same podium, they spoke before groups large and small, social and religious, ethnic and integrated, male and female and mixed. And like the foundation literature, these speakers left in their wake three things: a suspicion that perhaps Weldon Whitman did not deserve to die in the gas chamber after all; a curiosity as to whether their present elected officials were competent; and, in the minds of those elected officials, a seething anger at having been so scathingly attacked. All over the state, more and more people were joining the ranks in support of the Save Whitman Movement, while more and more elected officials began to exert more and more pressure in more and more directions in an effort to end, once and for all, the controversy of Weldon Whitman.

Genevieve could see what was coming. She could see it clearly, without delusions. She was not sure *how* it would come, or *when*, but she knew it would come. There was no longer any doubt in her mind.

They were definitely going to kill Weldon.

Sucking her breath to keep from sobbing openly, she sat back and started the car. Swallowing, she glanced at the package on the seat beside her. Whatever reservations she had felt about that package and what it contained and what it was for, she now dismissed. The final admission to herself that Weldon would die had changed her thinking about many things. She reached over and touched the package, gently, as if she were touching Weldon himself; then she shifted gears and drove away.

When she arrived at her apartment, Genevieve took the package inside with her and put it carefully on the dresser in the bedroom. She undressed, hung her clothes neatly in her garment bag, and got into the tub. She decided to shower instead of bathe, so she drew the flowered plastic curtain closed. The water came out of the shower head in a fine spray, and Genevieve stepped into the wet tent it formed. She washed leisurely, soaping her body all over and rinsing longer than was necessary because the warmth of the water felt so good to her.

When she had finished, she stood drying herself and examining her plump body in a full-length mirror on the door. She had thought, with all the activity and tension of the past few years, that she would have lost some weight. But obviously she had not, and she looked at herself now far less satisfied than she would like to have been. Her body, she knew, was not badly put together; she was not *obese* or anything like that; she was simply too *big*, all over. Her thighs were such that they often rubbed together when she walked, and chapped; her calves were just plain exaggerated, there was no other word for them; her breasts were so fleshy that they bounced at the least provocation; her buttocks rolled with every step; her upper arms were beyond looking decent in short sleeves anymore; and in general she thought of herself, not necessarily as being fat, but certainly well into the *too heavy* category.

Feeling as she did about herself, she often had nagging doubts about the sincerity of Weldon Whitman's feelings toward her. She could not help but suspect that had he been a free man, he would not have given her a second look. Not that he himself was outstanding when it came to good looks; he wasn't; as a matter of fact, Genevieve considered herself prettier of face than Whitman was handsome; though certainly his body, which was trim and muscular, was much more attractive than her plump form. But even though he was not a handsome man, at least not handsome in the classic sense, there was about his face a rugged, even tough, attractiveness. She hoped, whenever her conscience forced her to think of it, that their respective shortcomings would have balanced each other out, and that if they had met under different circumstances they would have felt the same way about each other. She did not completely, totally believe it. But she hoped.

When she was dry, she opened a large bottle of body moisturizer and began applying it to herself. When she had covered herself with the lotion and rubbed it in well, she put on a robe and belted it around her. She went into the bedroom, took the package from the dresser, and sat on the bed, holding it in her lap. Thinking about the contents of the package, she remembered how opposed she had been to the idea when Weldon first suggested it. That had been a number of months earlier, when things had still been going well at the foundation and there had been high hopes, at least on her part, that Weldon's death sentence would be commuted. Now—well, now things were so much different; Niebold and White and that vile bitch Carla Volt were running the foundation, literally had *control* of it; and—something she never would have guessed would happen—Rob had deserted her. No, there was no other word for it, she might as well admit it—he must have deserted her. Her *and* Weldon.

So now everything was different, and *she* was different. She was different because she now believed that Weldon would die. And being different, she could no longer muster any opposition to anything Weldon wanted if it was in her power to grant it. So she unwrapped the package and removed the Polaroid camera from its box.

It was very simple to use; the salesman at the camera shop had demonstrated it for her several times and she had mastered it with no difficulty at all. Now she expertly put the film pack in, attached the flash, adjusted the exposure indicator, and set the camera on the dresser so that it pointed toward the bed. Then she set the automatic timer.

Taking off her robe, she stretched out on the bed in the eye of the lens.

Just before ten o'clock that night, Genevieve stood in the doorway of an all-night drugstore in downtown Sacramento. Tired and sated, she was oddly resigned to what she was doing. No longer did she even attempt to justify it to herself, to reconcile it with her new acceptance of Weldon Whitman's eventual execution. What did it matter? she had asked herself earlier, as she had carefully sealed the eight color Polaroid pictures and six ten-dollar bills in an ordinary letter envelope. What did any of it matter anymore?

Standing in the doorway, she had just glanced at her watch and seen that it was exactly ten o'clock, when a man turned in from the street and paused next to her.

"Do you have the time?" he asked.

"It's ten o'clock," she answered.

"I thought it was a lot later than that," the man said.

They both stood there for a moment, neither speaking again. Then Genevieve opened her purse and handed him the envelope containing the pictures and the money. He slipped it into his pocket and walked quickly away. Only after he was gone did Genevieve realize that she did not even know what he had looked like.

The next morning, the pictures and four of the ten-dollar bills, now in a stamped, addressed manila envelope, were dropped into a mailbox. The posted envelope was delivered the following afternoon to a man in San Francisco. That man removed two of the remaining bills and repackaged the rest of the contents in a plastic sandwich bag. He took the bag with him the next morning when he left his apartment before dawn and reported to his job as a milk delivery man. The delivery man's route included the Tiburon and San Quentin areas, and by six o'clock he was at the main outside gate of the San Quentin complex. Beyond the gate was that part of the prison compound that was outside the walls. The milk truck was passed without question through the gate, just as numerous other delivery vehicles were passed daily. Immediately beyond the gate, the truck made a sharp right turn into a narrow, tree-lined street on which were situated the residences of the warden, his deputies, medical personnel, the chaplain, senior guard captains, and other prison employees whose fringe benefits included living quarters. The street went straight for a block, then split and wound off in separate directions.

The delivery man made his deliveries along the street at a leisurely pace. Aside from the newspaper delivery boy, whom he could see half a block ahead of him, there was no one else in sight. Moving casually, he placed the tri-weekly orders of milk on the warden's porch, on two of the deputy wardens' porches, on Captain Dukes's porch, and so on down the street. As he worked, he hummed a quiet tune to himself. He did not interrupt either the pace of his work or his quiet humming when he made the delivery to the chaplain's house. Walking up to the porch, he stood next to the steps, put down his metal basket, and expertly removed the bottles of milk and lined them up neatly in the shade of the porch rail. Then, as he was picking up the basket, he quickly palmed the sandwich bag, and slipped the small package into a narrow space between the porch and the back of the top step.

Intentionally built by an inmate carpenter, the space was set back under the overhang of both the step and the porch, and could not be seen except by someone on hands and knees searching the underside of that particular step. Just beyond the opening, which served as a slot for the convict mailbox, was a single shelf of wood, put there by the same carpenter, onto which the smuggled packets fell when dropped by their mailman. The mailbox was used only for letters, photographs, money, and drugs. Soft contraband, the inmates called it. It was never used for hard contraband: guns, knives, razors, saw blades, or the like.

The packet dropped by the mailman lay on the dark shelf under the chaplain's porch for four hours, until shortly after ten A.M., when it was picked up by an inmate trusty who was a member of the garden squad. The garden squad was a group of trusty inmates who worked outside the walls but within the surrounding fenced compound; they mowed lawns, trimmed trees and shrubs, watered and fertilized, and in general took care of all landscape maintenance around the homes of prison personnel.

The garden squad trusty who picked up the milkman's drop was working on the chaplain's back lawn this particular morning, trimming and edging. He finished up at ten-thirty and sat down on the grass next to the back porch to clean the blade of the edger. Halfway through the job, when he was certain no one was around to see him, he moved backwards under the porch and scurried quickly beneath the house to the front steps. He saw the pickup waiting for him on the shelf, snatched it off, and hurried back to where he had been sitting.

Giving the appearance of again cleaning the edger blade,

he put the sandwich bag on the ground between his legs and deftly opened it. He took one of the two remaining ten-dollar bills, folded it in quarters, unlaced the high-top work shoe on his left foot, and put the bill neatly, flatly, under the tongue of the shoe. The sandwich bag and the rest of its contents he bundled together and stuffed into the top of one of the heavy, oatmeal-colored socks he wore. It barely made a bulge inside the sock, and did not show at all under his trouser leg.

The trusty finished cleaning the edger, placed it over his shoulder like a rifle, and went out to the front of the house. The garden-squad truck, a gray prison pickup, was parked a block down, in front of the residence of Captain Dukes. At the truck the trusty checked in his edger, then walked down past the last row of houses to the trusty gate.

All trusty inmates who worked in the outer compound were required to enter and leave the prison proper through the Trusty Room, built into the actual wall of the prison, one door inside the wall, the other door outside the wall. The room itself was divided by a waist-high railing, in the center of which were two red spots painted on the concrete floor. The first spot was in the middle of a metal detector, an apparatus resembling a telephone booth without door or back, in which an inmate returning to the walls had to stand while its invisible beams searched his person for metal. The second spot, six feet past the first, was the position for a strip search. If, after triggering the metal detector, or if the duty guard decided that an inmate should be strip-searched, it was on this spot that he stood and removed all his clothes and had his body and its orifices meticulously examined.

Other than for triggering the metal detector, there was no established routine for strip seaches; they were conducted strictly at the whim of the duty guard. The trusty inmates knew, as did the guards, that the odds against catching someone with soft contraband by the use of random strip searches were extremely high. That, plus the fact that the guards were primarily concerned with the smuggling of *hard* goods, gave inmate couriers a wide margin of safety. They knew that most of the correctional officers connected with the prison could not have cared less about uncensored correspondence, pornography, and drugs getting behind the walls. All of those items, the experienced guard knew, were harmless to the operation of the institution, and actually helped keep the place calmer than it might otherwise have been.

On the morning he was smuggling the sandwich bag inside, the garden squad trusty entered the Trusty Room, signed the log on the compound side of the rail, and dutifully stepped into the metal detector. He stood on the red spot while the detector scanned him, waiting for the hold light to go off, the pass light to go on. When the light did change, the trusty stepped forward to the next red spot. The duty guard, one of the older, experienced correctional officers, was sitting at the post desk, chewing on a toothpick. He looked up at the trusty, studying him, as he moved his toothpick from one side of his mouth to the other. After a moment, he nodded silently and passed the trusty back to prison-side.

The trusty walked around the prison chapel and cut across a corner of the big yard to the dining room. He entered the big warehouselike room and walked back to the kitchen. In a tiny partitioned cubicle back in one corner, an inmate storekeeper sat at a desk checking food bills of lading. The trusty went over to the cubicle and stood next to the desk. He waited while the storekeeper eyeballed the entire kitchen without moving his head. There were three guards on duty, none of them near or paying attention. In a minute, the storekeeper nodded toward the wastebasket next to the desk. The trusty knelt and retied his shoe, and as he stood up he dropped the sandwich bag into the storekeeper's half-filled wastebasket. Then he walked quickly away.

The storekeeper waited a full hour after the trusty had left before he fished the plastic bag out of the basket. Keeping a practiced eye on the three guards—again without raising his head—he opened the bag and removed the last ten-dollar bill, casually putting it in his trousers pocket. He knew without examining the rest of the contents who the delivery was for. At that particular time he was expecting some homosexual love letters for a fairy named Dewey in D Block, some sniffing-grade cocaine for a user named Partell who worked in the laundry, and some beaver pictures for Whitman up on the Row. This packet was obviously the one for Whitman.

The storekeeper shoved the bag of Polaroid shots in his pocket, picked up his clipboard, and walked back to the storeroom. He began to check his inventory of cooking utensils, cups, food trays, and other kitchenware. In one corner of the storeroom, on a reinforced shelf, were eight stacks of metal food trays which were used to feed inmates who did not go through the chow line: those in the prison hospital, those locked away in the Isolation Unit, and the condemned men on Death Row. The sixth tray down, in the third row over, had a specially constructed false bottom which had been fabricated for the storekeeper in the metal shop at a cost of eighty dollars. It was this tray that the storekeeper removed. He placed it on a crate, pressed with his thumbs on two of the corners, and lifted the top section away. Quickly he spread the photographs out in four rows of two inside the bottom tray; then he pressed the top tray back into place over them. He put three ordinary trays on top of the special one, two others under it, and carried all of them out of the storeroom and over to a cart which, two hours earlier, had come from the Deah Row kitchen laden with dirty trays, and which would shortly be returned there with clean trays. The storekeeper removed six trays from the cart, put them back in the scrubber to be washed and sterilized again, and replaced them with the six he had brought from the storeroom. The kitchen orderly who would push the cart back to the Row kitchen was standing nearby. The storekeeper walked over to him.

"Tray number four is for Whitman. Pass it along."

"Check," said the orderly.

At quarter of four, the steam table containing the evening meal was rolled off the Death Row elevator and taken into the Twenty Section.

"Come and get it," the Death Row kitchen helper said loudly as he put a tray of hot food on the tray shelf in the cell door of Twenty. "Hot roast beef tonight," he said as he passed a tray to Cell Twenty-one. "Got a good dessert tonight," he commented as he put a tray on the shelf of Cell Twenty-two.

In Cell Twenty-two, Weldon Whitman got off his bunk at once and pulled his dinner tray into the cell. He watched the kitchen helper push the table on, followed by the Row duty guard. When they had passed, he looked curiously at his tray. *A good dessert tonight* was the code phrase used to tell an inmate that he had the special tray.

Whitman, anxious to open the tray, was patient enough to know that he had to wait until he had eaten most of the food. He drew his chair over and used it as a table while he sat on the edge of his bunk to eat. He was wearing glasses all the time now, his hair had receded a little farther at each temple, and when he sat, a slightly thickening middle bulged under his blue cotton shirt. As he ate, he wondered if the tray contained some message of Robert Cloud's whereabouts. The ex-reporter had been missing for going on three weeks now and no one, not even Genevieve, seemed to know where he was. The cocksucker had probably run out on him, Whitman thought as he chewed a mouthful of roast beef. He should have known better than to ever trust a fucking newspaperman, anyway. Half of them were lushes and fuck-offs, and the other half were lowlife rabble-rousers with about as much style and intelligence as a Mongoloid idiot. The condemned man shrugged. What the fuck difference did it make, anyway? Cloud had come in handy when he was needed—but he really wasn't needed anymore. With Niebold and White in his corner, with the foundation flourishing like a whorehouse on Saturday night, with organizations all over the state starting to take a good hard look at the California Supreme Court—who needed a hack like Cloud?

Thinking of Cloud made him think of Eugene Terrier. The ex-Black Panther, whom Borden White had brought up to visit shortly after he had been retained by the foundation, was presently rewriting the draft of *Judgment in Anguish* that had been done by Cloud. Personally, Whitman had been satisfied with Cloud's version; but White—and Niebold, apparently—had wanted it to read more strongly, to take a more aggressive approach, to project its author, Weldon Whitman, less as a victim of society and more as a victim of the court system. They wanted, they said, to elevate Weldon Whitman to the status of a citizen demanding justice. And they felt that the smooth, urbane, well-educated Eugene Terrier was just the man to do that.

Whitman finished eating, putting the warm peach cobbler away in two huge bites. Then he shifted the chair ninety degrees so that its back was to the cell door and the dinner tray concealed. Pressing with his thumbs, he released the false bottom of the tray and quickly looked to see what had been delivered to him. There were eight Polaroid pictures, all turned face down. He flipped one over, stared at it, and his mouth dropped open incredulously. *Well, I'll be god-damned—!*

He slid the eight pictures into a deck, removed them from the bottom of the tray, and shoved them under his pillow. Snapping the top back in place, he took the tray over to the shelf and left it for the kitchen helper to take away. Propping himself up on his bunk, he opened a law book and slipped the pictures behind it. He studied them one by one, his incredulity gradually giving way to delighted amusement. Son of a bitch! Fat mamma actually *did* it for him!

He felt an erection coming on; he wanted badly to jack off. But there was still too much activity in the corridor, with the two duty guards and the kitchen helper. Even so—

He propped his feet up, bending his knees in front of the book. Unbuttoning his fly, he worked his erect penis out and let it stand free behind the book. He looked through the bars into the corridor. He could hear voices but there was no one in sight. He looked back at his throbbing hard-on saluting the pictures of Genevieve. He wanted to do it. But he hated the idea of anyone seeing him. He had a certain status to maintain. If someone should walk by—

Fuck it. He *wanted* it.

He closed his fist around his all-demanding dick.

When he was finished, he felt better. He always felt better after he masturbated. Even though it was only a halfway kind of satisfaction, a relief shadowed by the anxiety of being observed by someone, it was still a tension-relaxant of no little value in his present situation.

He washed his hands and sat back on the bunk again. Putting the open law book in front of him, he went through Genevieve's pictures a second time, uninspired now by the heat of passion, giving them a much more clinical, and critical, examination. Old fat mamma really did it up good for me, he thought. He shook his head, half chuckling. You are really something, fat mamma. I mean, really!

He got up and took a cigar box from the shelf above the table where his typewriter and typing supplies were kept. The box was one of three in which he kept newspaper clippings about himself; two of them were full, the third was used for current clippings. The box he took from the shelf was the first one, containing the oldest clippings. He set the box inside him on the bunk, spread a few yellowing clippings around to make it look good, then removed two-dozen-odd snapshots from the bottom of the box. He looked through them as a man might look through his stamp collection. Three of the dozen were of Carla Volt going down on an unidentified man whose face could not be seen. Carla had sent him a set of a dozen like that; he had traded nine of them for other pictures, and favors: six of them and a five-dollar bill had gone to Jones, the illiterate, homosexual cop-killer, for a blow job in his cell during one of the Row's weekly movies. The others, along with some more current shots of Carla, these showing her being fucked in different positions by a lean, handsome black man, Whitman kept for himself. He was certain that the man in the photographs was Eugene Terrier, even though the man's face was either turned partly away from the lens, or was buried in cunt. Not that it made any difference to Whitman; he just wanted the pictures and wanted Carla to keep visiting him every two weeks and telling him about all the sex things she had done with Cloud and was now doing with this spade Terrier.

He sorted through the rest of his pictures, those he had acquired through trade from other men on the Row. He had a good variety, and to his collection he now added one of the shots of Genevieve. He covered the pictures back up with his old newspaper clippings and returned the box to the shelf. Then he sat down at his table, spread the other seven pictures of Genevieve out next to the typewriter, and started analyzing their worth. They might bring him something in trade, he thought. But he rather doubted it. Poor old fat mamma was a real dog; she was really hurting. But maybe Henry, the black rapist-killer in Twenty-seven, would trade him one good one for all seven of them. Henry was a psycho who really freaked out over white pussy. He just might go for this poor fat cunt.

Weldon Whitman hoped so. It would be a shame for fat mamma's pictures to go to waste.

Twenty-two

Robert Cloud awoke just before noon, opening his eyes under a hand he had placed over one side of his face. He was glad he had the hand there; he could feel warm sunlight on it, and he knew if that sunlight had been on his face instead of his hand, he would have awakened with a rotten headache. Keeping his hand in place, he craftily moved his head over until he found a cool place on the pillow where the sunlight had not fallen; then he took his hand away. He saw that the room itself was dim and cool; the sunlight was a maverick beam that had found its way past a crooked slat in the blinds.

Cloud sat up and stretched. He was on Carol's side of the bed. She had left before eight; he usually moved onto her side, into her warmth, as soon as she got up. He stood, naked, and stretched again. Yawning, he went into the bathroom, lifted the toilet seat, and urinated. The odor of the urine reached his nostrils and made him sneeze. He put the toilet seat lid down and flushed it quickly, but not before he sneezed a second time.

At the sink he brushed his teeth and gums vigorously, taking pleasure in destroying the foul taste that was inevitably in his mouth every morning. He washed his face, lathered, and shaved; when he finished shaving, he examined his face critically in the mirror. His skin was pale, almost unhealthy-looking—the result of his not having left the apartment in more than six weeks. Shrugging off his whiteness, he rubbed some of Carol's hand lotion onto his freshly shaved cheeks and neck.

After showering, Cloud dressed in a new set of underwear, a pair of Levis, and a turtleneck sweater Carol had bought for him. "I'm tired of washing your underwear every other night," she had told him, referring to the two sets he had brought from Sacramento on the trip that was supposed to have lasted only two days. "Besides, I don't like those boxer shorts you wear. These are sexier," she had said, and handed him several packages of brightly designed men's bikini briefs with matching undershirts. He had not worn the boxers since.

When he was dressed, he picked up Glory Ann Luza's cross and chain from the dresser, slipped it into his trousers pocket, and went into the living room. As usual, Carol had opened the drapes and bathed the room in daylight. Cloud closed them at once and turned on the lights. The morning edition of his old alma mater, the *Ledger*, was laid neatly at a place set for him at the table. He dropped it in the trash container without even looking at the headline. He turned to the refrigerator; there was a note Scotch-taped to the door. *Eat something decent for breakfast*, it implored. *Decent* was underlined three times. Cloud opened the door, got out what he wanted, and sat down at the table. He ate four slices of cold, leftover pizza supreme, half a dozen chocolate marshmallow cookies, and drank a Coke.

Cloud had come back to Carol Carter like a wounded animal on that day which now seemed like an eternity ago when Judge G. Foster Klein had told him first of Weldon Whitman's partial innocence, then of Doris Calder's suicide. From that utterly shocking moment, Cloud's mind had absolutely refused to function for him in any matter relating to the Weldon Whitman case. The many complexities of the affair had compounded one time too many. His consciousness had been left reeling under the impact of Klein's disclosures; his thought processes refused to attempt any further evaluation of these latest numbing pieces of information. Defensively, his subconscious had sucked the whole awful mess down into its protective custody; and Robert Cloud had been left with only enough lethargic thought processes to care for himself in a calm, nonchallenging environment.

He found that environment for his mind, as well as a placid, comforting place for his body, in the apartment and the arms of Carol Carter. He had come back to her seeking shelter and solace—and she had taken him in eagerly, without hesitation or reservation. She had known instinctively that he was on the brink of something, that one more step would send him plunging into a psychological abyss. Having stood on that same kind of brink herself, Carol Carter understood both the threat and the challenge of it. She had backed away from the dangers of *her* abyss long ago—and she had needed no help from anyone to do it; and being a very intelligent woman, she was proud of herself but not vain about that accomplishment, and she had the good sense to realize that Robert Cloud's brink might be higher and more precipitous than hers had been, and the abyss below it deeper and darker. So she helped him—and at no time did she consider herself either stronger than he was, or superior to him.

After he told her what he had learned from G. Foster Klein, Carol was able to assemble a fairly accurate picture of Cloud's dilemma. He had originally thrown himself into the case with no preconceived notion of Whitman's guilt or innocence—merely a conviction that Whitman should not be executed for a crime in which no life had been taken. Subsequently, Cloud had become convinced that Whitman had not committed the Calder crime, and believed therefore that Whitman was innocent of both sex crimes. Then, two years later, came the meeting with Glory Ann Luza, and the evidence of the cross and chain proving that Whitman possibly *had* committed *that* crime. And the awful spectacle of the girl's Adam syndrome had forced him to admit that possibly the death penalty *was* justified for crimes less than murder: crimes such as the one committed against Glory Ann's mind. With that admission the quandary had begun. Problem: if Whitman committed the one crime but not the other, was it possible that the Luza crime alone would *not* have resulted in a death sentence? To find out, Cloud had turned to the one person who probably knew more about the legal aspects of the Whitman case than anyone else in the world: G. Foster Klein. But instead of Klein clarifying the equity of it, he had served only to further compound Cloud's confusion by first admitting to him that Whitman did *not* commit the Calder crime, by convincing him finally that Whitman *did* commit the Luza crime, then by blasting his conscience wide open by telling of Doris Calder's suicide and intimating that it had in part been Robert Cloud's fault.

Cloud had refused to talk about the Whitman case any longer. He had not talked about it since his return to Carol's apartment, except for a brief explanation of where he had gone, why, and what he had learned. Beyond that, he had become distant and remote on the subject, and was quickly perturbed if Carol brought up the matter.

"Shouldn't you at least call someone in Sacramento to let them know that you haven't been hurt or killed?" Carol asked early on in his stay.

Cloud had merely shaken his head. "It doesn't matter."

"I'm sure that isn't so," she argued. "I'm sure that—what's her name, Genevieve Neller—is probably very concerned about you. It wouldn't hurt to pick up the phone and call her—"

"No, Carol," he said simply, emphatically, with finality.

She let it go—but not before she classified his decision with the all-inclusive blanket comment she used for anything with which she disagreed. "I think that's pretty dumb."

On that first night when he returned, Carol had no idea that his plans for the future extended only as far as her front door. They ate together that night, sat and talked together, went to bed together, made love, and slept together. Carol got up the next morning and went to work, first making him promise to stay there all day and rest. He kept the promise and was there waiting for her when she got home. Their second evening was a repetition of the first: dinner, talk, bed, make love, sleep. They repeated the routine the following night, and the following, and the night after that. She asked twice that first week if he wanted to have dinner out, perhaps go to a show. He did not. After ten days of the same routine night after night, Cloud began to feel guilty about his presence in her apartment; he asked if she wanted him to leave. She put her arms around his neck and told him that of course she did not want him to leave; she wanted him to stay.

"It's just that I'm concerned about you. I worry about you being here by yourself all day with nothing to do."

"I keep occupied," he said.

"Would you mind telling me at what? I'm not being critical; I'm just curious."

Cloud had shrugged. "I watch television. I play solitaire. I read your magazines. I've even gone through your desk and read some of the notes and letters you got from that guy you were going with."

"Oh?" A cold, vindictive anger rose up in her at the admission of such a flagrant invasion of her privacy. It showed in her eyes, which lost every degree of their warmth, and in her lips, as they compressed tightly to contain a flow of profanity which gathered quickly in her mind for immediate use. But she was able to control herself, to hold back the initial impulse to call him a dirty lowlife son of a bitch and tell him to get the fuck out of her apartment. She was able to curb what she knew would be nothing but an emotional outburst, able to overcome it by coolly reminding herself that she did *care* for this man, that he needed her help and understanding, and that the letters no longer meant anything to her. "What did you think of the letters?" she finally asked in a beautifully controlled voice.

"They were no good at all," Cloud said professionally. "The composition was sloppy, some of the sentence structure was poor—"

He gave her a short oral critique on the basics of good writing, and then they dropped the subject.

The next evening, when she was ready to take the trash out, she took all of her letters with it.

Two things about him disturbed her. The most important was their sexual relationship. As was her nature, her drive, she completely abandoned herself to him. She quickly came to worship his body and she wanted it in every way possible. As often as possible. And, as was her preference, with the lights on. But Cloud, after undressing, invariably darkened the room.

"Why do you do that?" she asked one night.

"Do what?"

"Turn off the lights."

"I like it better with them out," he said. He slipped onto the bed and put his hand between her legs.

"Don't you like to look at my body?"

"I love to look at your body."

"Wouldn't you like to look at it while we're fucking?" He was rubbing her, working a finger into her, feeling her wetness begin. "Wouldn't you?" she persisted.

"Sure I would," he told her. "But right now I like you in the dark where it's cool and quiet and private. You like it in the dark, don't you?"

"Yes—God—yes—" she answered, because as he asked the question he rolled over her leg and entered her in a single slow, delicious stroke. "Oh, sweet Jesus—"

They were splendid together. But they were always splendid in the dark.

Cloud could not bring himself to tell her that he had to take her in the dark because every time he came, he thought the same thought that had come into his head the very first time they had made it together: that Weldon Whitman had once ejaculated into this same woman. No matter how hard he tried, he could not keep that persistent thought out of his mind. And he lived with an awful dread that if he left the lights on, she would be able to see it—see that thought—in his face, in his eyes.

So he kept putting her off about the lights. And finally she stopped asking.

The other thing that bothered her about him was that damned cross and chain. He *carried* it around with him. In the mornings when he dressed he apparently put the thing in one of his pockets and kept it there all day. Sometimes when they were sprawled close to each other on the couch watching television, she would notice him occasionally move his hand down and touch his trousers pocket, or reach up and touch his shirt pocket, as if to reassure himself that the damned thing was still there and had not somehow mysteriously disappeared. Later, when they would be undressing for bed, he would remove it from whichever pocket he had carried it in all day, and put it on the dresser with his handkerchief and lighter. It was there every morning during the week when she got up to get ready for work; it was there on weekend mornings when they got up together; but always it was gone as soon as Cloud was dressed. He made no effort to conceal the fact that he was carrying it around with him, but neither did he speak of it or offer any reason for what he was doing—and Carol did not ask him. She did not pretend to understand all the psychological implications of why he was doing it, but she was certain of one thing: Robert Cloud's physical possession of Glory Ann Luza's cross and chain was the single remining link he had with the Weldon Whitman case—and it was a link he obviously felt compelled to retain.

Toward the end of the second month with her, Cloud began to cultivate a mustache. He had insisted that she use the safety razor to blade cut his hair every eight or ten days to keep it from becoming too shaggy—then he had turned around and grown as bushy and shaggy a mustache as she had ever seen. Not that she didn't like it; she did; she particularly liked the feel of it when he sucked her nipples: she had never felt such a sensation before. But she did not think it needed to be quite so full and drooping. She was of the opinion—and in her completely open manner told him so—that a *neat, decently trimmed* mustache would probably be very becoming to him.

One of the primary reasons for Cloud's growing the mustache was that he knew it made him look different, and consequently it made him *feel* different. He was trying desperately to exorcise the influence of Weldon Whitman from his mind—particularly that element of it that intruded into his physical love for Carol at the precise instant when the result of that love was going from his body into hers. He simply *had* to drive away whatever it was. It did not bother him in the least to think of other men who probably had been intimate with her; and he knew there had been others; as a matter of fact, one of her letters that he had read specifically mentioned an incident of intercourse that had taken place on a picnic somewhere. But those thoughts did not bother him; only the persistently intruding thought of Weldon Whitman bothered him.

It was a problem he had to solve. He thought by changing the pattern of their lovemaking that he might also change the pattern of his thoughts. So he began making love to her as soon as she got home from work in the evenings. And not only in the bedroom, but in other places: the living room, the floor, the couch; and in places where it was lighter—though still not as light as Carol wanted it to be; and in different ways, in different stages of undress, with varying intensity. He did anything he could think of to make the intrusive thought vanish.

But it did not.

Changing their lovemaking habits of necessity changed all their other habits also. They ate dinner later because they usually dozed for half an hour after their lovemaking, then showered or entwined together in a hot tub. After dinner, they watched television or played Scrabble or Casino, or just lounged on the couch, his head in her lap or her head in his lap, one of them massaging the other's temple, until eleven o'clock or so when Carol would go sleepily off to bed. Cloud rarely if ever went to bed with her on weeknights; he preferred to stay up by himself, usually until three or so in the morning, watching talk shows or late movies, playing solitaire, reading books he had her pick up for him at the library—Steinbeck and Dos Passos and Faulkner—works he had read in college and earlier, but liked and wanted to read again. Several times, when Carol bought a *Cosmopolitan* or a *McCall's* for herself, she would also pick up a magazine or two for Cloud: a *Playboy* or *True* or *Argus*, whatever looked interesting. But she noticed that even though he accepted the magazines and thanked her, there was no indication that he ever actually read them. They lay on the end table, their covers as unwrinkled as when she had given them to him; she never saw him touch them again, and a week or so later they would be in the trash. It was the same with the morning newspaper. She would read it while she ate breakfast, then put it neatly back together and leave it at the place she set for him. At night, when she finally got into the kitchen after their lovemaking and bathing, she would see the newspaper in the trash, as neatly as she had left it, as if it had simply been picked up from the table, folded once, and discarded.

It was the same with television. He would watch anything and everything—except news shows. If she turned on the early news while she was preparing dinner, he would busy himself with something in the bedroom. If she left the TV on for the late news after the movie, he would get up and go into the bathroom. He simply refused to watch the news.

For a while, all of his idiosyncrasies seemed separate and distinct; but eventually Carol was able to link them all up: magazines, newspapers, television. Cloud was avoiding all current events, all present news. He had retreated into the word-picture world of Steinbeck, Dos Passos, Faulkner, where the problems were not of his making, and their solutions no obligation upon him.

And Carol Carter knew *why* Robert Cloud had chosen that refuge for himself. It was the only certain way he had of avoiding any and all word of the Weldon Whitman matter and its progress. Just as the Luza girl's cross and chain was the security link he needed to keep him from being completely severed from that same matter, that same progress.

So Robert Cloud, in effect, had gone into limbo. He had run away—though not *completely* away—from the Whitman case. He refused to speak of it, read of it, hear of it—yet he carried Glory Ann's lost cross and chain as if it were his lifeline back to the world outside the little apartment in which he hid. He lived and ate and slept with and made love to Weldon Whitman's ex-wife—yet he could not reach sexual climax with a free mind. He grew to hate the days, when Carol was gone and he was alone; so he forced himself to stay awake through the night and far into the morning while she was there with him; then he slept away as much of the empty day as he could. He watched television for endless hours, always careful never to let a newscast slip into his schedule. Special bulletins drove him instantly from his chair to turn off the set. In the mornings he would not look directly at the newspaper Carol left for him; he approached it obliquely, folded it upside down, discarded it quickly. He wanted to be, *tried* to be, a different Robert Cloud, one whose past went back no farther than the night he returned to Carol's doorstep.

He altered his appearance: wearing the exotic underwear Carol bought him, growing a mustache, letting his hair grow full but keeping it from being long by having Carol razor-cut it.

All these things he did in the blind expectation that they would somehow make a difference in his future, his fate. In the belief that what was to come for him was not already ordained, that he himself was not already predestined. Hoping, secretly against hope, that perhaps the things he did would matter.

Then Carol came home one night, bringing the outside world with her, and destroyed that hope.

It was the middle of his sixth month with her. Carol opened the door on her return from work and Cloud was waiting there for her as usual. It was raining out; she had on a loose rain cape and was dripping wet. Cloud kissed her briefly and took the cape and hung it in the bathroom. Then he returned to kiss her less briefly and to do other things that he had been thinking about all the rainy, thundering afternoon; but when he approached her, he saw that under the rain cape she had been holding a late edition of the *Ledger*.

"This is one you're going to have to read, Rob," she said simply.

He turned away from her and went to fix himself a drink. To hell with the sex. She followed him across the room.

"You've been hibernating long enough, Rob. Now it's time to stop. I want you to look at this paper."

"I don't want to look at the paper." He poured gin over two ice cubes, ignoring the vermouth.

"I want you to read this, Rob."

"I'm not interested." He lifted the glass.

"I *want* you to—"

Cloud slammed the glass down. "I'm not reading the fucking paper, so leave me alone!" He looked at the gin all over his hand and sleeve, amazed that the glass had not broken.

Carol glared at him. "All right then," she said in cold defiance, "if you won't read it, I'll read it *to* you. And if you don't want to listen, you'll have to turn around and get your ass the hell out of this apartment." She unfolded the damp newspaper and slammed it down on the breakfast bar. "Headline: 'Whitman Appeal Denied.' "

"Carol, I don't want to hear about it—"

"Sub-headline: 'Death Penalty Legal, Says Supreme Court.' "

"Save your breath, I'm not listening—"

"Sub-sub-headline: 'Whitman to Die in Three Days.' "

Cloud's head snapped around. "*What?*"

"That's right," Carol confirmed. "Three days."

Cloud snatched up the paper and quickly scanned the story. In an instant he knew it was true. The California Supreme Court, in a four-to-one decision, had ruled that the death sentence, as it had been applied in the Weldon Whitman conviction, did not constitute cruel and unusual punishment. Whitman's appeal was denied, the conviction in his case affirmed, and the matter returned to the Superior Court of Los Angeles County for imposition of sentence. That court, which under the criminal statutes could set the date of execution no earlier than seventy-two hours or later than ninety days, set it for ten o'clock the morning of the third day following its receipt of the Supreme Court ruling. The time set was exactly seventy-*three* hours later. A death warrant was immediately issued by the court to the warden at San Quentin.

Cloud left his glass and went over to the couch. He sat down heavily, holding the newspaper on his knees. The heavy odor of damp newsprint reached his nostrils. Outside, in the pouring rain, a crack of lightning split the dark sky. Carol came and sat in the club chair opposite him.

"Is that fair, what they're doing?" she asked.

"It's legal," Cloud said quietly.

"That's not what I asked."

Cloud sighed. "If he deserves to be executed, then it's fair."

Carol stared at him for a long, thoughtful moment. She

had already decided to make him admit his feelings, to force him to take a stand on Weldon Whitman once and for all; but now that the moment had arrived, she was less certain of her decision than of any she had previously made regarding him. Her love for him was now dominant in her emotional structure, and consequently was causing her to be more cautious than she had been earlier in their relationship. As deeply as she cared for him now, she would not have needlessly hurt him for anything in the world. But at the same time, she was determined to make him help himself.

"*Does* he deserve to be executed?" she asked flatly. The quickness of Cloud's response surprised her.

"I think he does," Cloud said with no hesitation at all.

"Then you don't intend to do anything to delay it again?"

"There's nothing I *can* do."

"I don't mean just you," she said. "I mean by helping the others at the foundation."

"I don't think there's any way I could help them," he told her. "The only people who can really do anything now are Niebold and White, the two lawyers."

"Will they?"

"I'm sure they will." Even as he said it, he felt a frown forming on the surface of his face. He did not know why. "They'll probably file an emergency writ of some kind," he said, much less positive now.

"Do you want to see Whit again?" she asked. "Before it happens, *if* it happens?"

Cloud shook his head. "I don't think so. There'd be no point in it." He tilted his head slightly and studied her. "You know I love you, don't you?"

Feeling very warm, she moved over to the couch next to him. "I know it now," she said, pleased.

Cloud let the newspaper fall to the floor. They sat quietly, close to each other, for several minutes, she thinking about him, he thinking about Weldon Whitman. Until his thoughts moved on to someone else.

"There's Genevieve, too," he said nebulously.

"What about her?"

"If this is really the end of the whole thing, she'll be all alone. You see, she's really in love with Whit."

Carol did not say anything to that; she remained silent and left the problem, if there was one, for him to decide.

"Genevieve is the one decent person in the whole fucking mess," he said after a while.

Again Carol did not reply.

"She's the only one who'll be hurt—really hurt, deep down inside—when they gas Whit."

Still Carol Carter maintained her silence.

"She doesn't really deserve being left all alone like that," Cloud said finally.

Carol got up from the couch and went into the bedroom.

Several minutes later Cloud got up and followed her. Carol had his suitcase open on the bed and was already packing for him.

Twenty-three

Cloud arrived in Sacramento on the noon commuter the following day. He took a taxi to the foundation and walked in unannounced, suitcase in hand. Genevieve was sitting alone in her cluttered little office, staring vacantly at the wall. The rest of the place was deserted. Cloud stood in the doorway of the office, holding his suitcase, until she looked up and noticed him.

She blinked twice when she saw him, and her lips parted in consternation more than surprise. "Oh, Rob," she said in an unusually toneless voice. "For a moment I wasn't sure it was you."

Only then did it occur to Cloud how different he probably looked to her, with his mustache and several months of amateur haircuts.

"If it weren't for your eyes, I wouldn't have recognized you," Genevieve said. "You look older. Shabbier too, if you don't mind me saying so."

"I don't mind," Cloud told her. He set his bag down and came in. "How are you, Gen?"

"I'm all right." She swallowed and struggled to hold back the tears. The tremble in her breast escaped and caught in her voice. "I've—just—resigned myself—to—"

She surrendered, burying her face in her hands, sobbing convulsively. Cloud went to her, knelt beside her chair, took her tenderly in his arms.

"Okay now," he said, squeezing her shoulders, patting her head. "Okay now, okay . . ."

She cried for five minutes, the sobs racking and wrenching her body as if it were being struck by heavy blows. All the while Cloud held her and stroked her head and spoke quietly to her. And when he sensed that it was nearly over, that she had cried herself out, he found her box of tissues in a desk drawer, gave her several of them, and went out in the printshop to the cooler and brought her a cup of water. She drank it, sniffing loudly, wiping at eyes that were puffy and red. She managed to half-smile miserably.

"I knew you'd come back, Rob," she said. "I knew you wouldn't just let them kill Weldon without making some kind of effort to save him."

Her words made him feel wretched. "Gen, I don't really know of anything I can do—"

"You can make Morris and Borden do something," she told him."

"Aren't they doing something already?"

"Nothing," she said bitterly. "At least I don't know of anything they're doing. Neither of them will even talk to me on the phone anymore. But I have a friend who clerks for the federal district court of appeals. She's promised to call me if they file anything at all on Weldon."

"Wait a minute, I don't understand what you just said," Cloud told her, frowning. "What do you mean, Morris and Borden won't even talk to you on the phone?"

"Just that I haven't spoken to either of them directly in more than five months. Any word I get from them comes through your friend Carla."

"Forget that business of 'your friend Carla,' " he said with a hint of irritation. "She's not my friend anymore. In fact, I'm not at all sure she ever was."

"Well, I'm glad you're finally seeing her in a true light," Genevieve said with almost maternal relief. "If you knew how she's been carrying on with that man Terrier who's been rewriting Weldon's book—"

Cloud grunted. He might have known. "Let's get off the subject of Carla," he said. "She's not important anymore. Tell me why Morris and Borden won't talk to you."

"That's pretty obvious, Rob. I don't agree with them on anything; I mean *anything*. It's much simpler to ignore me than to argue with me. Besides, the way the foundation is organized now, all I do is supervise the printshop. The professional speakers that Borden hired take care of all the speaking engagements, and that Terrier person does all the writing. Or *did* all the writing. As you can see, there's nothing at all going on around here. They stopped giving us printing to do a week ago. I suspect that they had advance information on the ruling."

Cloud shook his head. "It's hard for me to believe that Niebold and White aren't going to make *some* effort for a stay of execution."

"I could be wrong," Genevieve said quietly, "but I don't think I am. I truly believe that they will make no further effort to save Weldon."

Cloud could not help feeling a growing resentment over

the possibility that Morris Niebold and Borden White might have arbitrarily decided to terminate Whitman's legal help. Niebold and White did not *know*, as Cloud knew, that Whitman was guilty of the Luza crime. As far as they were concerned, he might very well be totally and completely innocent of *all* the charges against him. It galled Cloud to think that they might have decided between themselves that Weldon Whitman had lived long enough.

There was always the possibility, of course, that Genevieve was mistaken; she had admitted that herself. It had been barely a day since the court's ruling had been handed down and the new execution date set. Perhaps Niebold and White *were* planning some last-minute legal maneuver and had not made Genevieve aware of it because, as she had also admitted, she was prone to disagree with them on most matters. With a total of only three days to prepare and file an appeal for a stay of execution, they would certainly have no spare time for arguing.

"I'm going to talk to Morris or Borden or both of them," he said, sitting down and turning her phone around to face him. He dialed the number.

"Niebold and White Law Offices," a female voice answered.

"Morris Niebold, please," Cloud said.

"May I tell him who's calling, please?"

"Robert Cloud."

"One moment, please."

While he waited, Genevieve reached over and lightly touched his mustache. "You look so *different*," she said again. "So much older." Cloud snapped at her fingers as if trying to bite them, and she jerked her hand back. He grinned under his mustache as the female voice returned to the line.

"I'm sorry, sir, but Mr. Niebold is not available right now."

"Connect me with Borden White then," Cloud said.

"Mr. White is not available either, sir."

Irritation rose quickly in Cloud. "What about Carla Volt? I'll bet she isn't available either, is she?"

"No sir, she isn't." The female voice was beginning to sound slightly embarrassed.

"Well, if any of them should become available," he said

coldly, "please say I called. Robert Cloud. I'll be at the Whitman Foundation."

"I'll give them your message, Mr. Cloud."

"Thank you." Cloud hung up, silently fuming.

"Welcome to the club," Genevieve said.

Cloud looked at his watch. It was two o'clock. Genevieve put on a kettle of water back in the deserted printshop and made instant coffee. They sat in her office, drinking the coffee and talking. Their conversation flowed from generalities of the past to specifics of the present. Genevieve told him virtually everything of significance that had transpired while he had been gone—and not once did she ask where he had been, with whom, or why. He briefly considered fabricating some kind of story for her, leaving out any reference to the existence of Carol Carter; subsequently he considered telling her *about* Carol but not telling her who Carol *was;* but finally he decided to simply tell her nothing. Anything he told her would, for her sake, have to be a lie—and at that particular point he did not think he could stomach lying to her. Somehow to lie to her at such a time seemed almost obscene.

Three o'clock came. They talked some more. Genevieve showed him samples of all the printed material the foundation had done since he had been gone, as well as the newsclippings file of articles on Whitman done by Eugene Terrier. Cloud admired the design and layout of the brochures even though he did not agree with the aggressive approach taken by the copy. He even reluctantly admired the writing style of Eugene Terrier in the clippings, though he almost cringed at some of the quotations attributed to Whitman and accusations made by the foundation. The tone of all the writing, with its blatant indictment of the state government and state judiciary, left no doubt in Cloud's mind as to the motive for the swift setting of such an early execution date.

Four o'clock came. The minutes began to pass more slowly. Conversation between Cloud and Genevieve slowed, dragged, had to be forced. At four-thirty Cloud called the offices of Niebold and White again. He was handled in the same manner: Mr. Niebold, Mr. White, and Miss Volt were still not available. His earlier messages had been given to each of them. Cloud left another message. Stronger this time.

"This is an urgent matter," he said, with no further pretense at courtesy. "I expect one of them to return my call just as soon as possible!"

Five o'clock came. Five-thirty. Six. Genevieve set the telephone on an answering-recording device and she and Cloud drove to a nearby coffee shop and had a supper of hamburgers and French fries. It reminded them both of the first time they had met, in the restaurant of the motel where Genevieve had been staying in Los Angeles.

"God, we were innocent in those days, weren't we?" Genevieve said.

"Babes in the woods," said Cloud. And Genevieve would never know *how* innocent, he thought, because she would never know how guilty Whitman was.

"But we were right, weren't we Rob?" she asked. "We were right to become his friends when he didn't have anyone else."

Cloud nodded. "We were right," he assured her. And he meant it.

They reminisced throughout the meal, and when they were finished, when Genevieve had eaten the last of his French fries as she had done that first night and so many times since, they left the coffee shop and drove back to the foundation.

As soon as they got into Genevieve's office, she checked the answering device. The call recorder was still on zero; the telephone had not rung.

Cloud sat down in front of the desk and dialed Niebold and White again. He let the phone ring for a full minute. There was no answer; the offices were closed. He put the receiver back in its cradle.

"Let me borrow your car, Gen," he said.

"I want to go with you."

He shook his head. "No."

"Rob, I want to—"

"No." He was firm. He knew he might have to tell Niebold and White things he did not want her to know. "I might want to say I haven't talked to you yet," he improvised. "I might want to make them think I'm on their side, to see what they'll say." It was a ridiculous excuse and he knew it, but to his amazement she accepted it.

"All right," she said. "Drop me off at home, then you can take the car."

She's tired, Cloud thought. So tired she can't even think straight.

They locked up the foundation offices and Cloud drove Genevieve to her apartment. He let her out in front of the building.

"You'll let me know as soon as you can?" she said.

"As soon as I can," he promised.

He drove away. Genevieve remained where she was on the curb, watching as the car went down the street. Cloud saw her in the rearview mirror. She just stood there, looking after him. Each time he glanced into the mirror, she was still there; becoming a smaller image, but still there. It was as if she felt the longer she kept him in sight, the shorter the time until he would be back.

A maid opened the door at Morris Niebold's big house.

"Is Mr. Niebold expecting you, sir?" she asked.

"Probably," Cloud said, pushing past her. "Where is he?"

"In the library, sir. If you'd care to sit down—"

"Never mind." Cloud remembered where the library was. He strode down the hall to its big double doors and walked in unannounced. Niebold was sitting in his glistening chrome wheelchair before the fireplace, drinking brandy. The flames reflected like multiple torches on the curved rim of one wheel of the chair. The invalid's round, walnut-shaped cheeks were flushed from the combined warmth of the fire and the brandy. He looked up at Cloud, his expression completely neutral for the first time in Cloud's memory.

"Well, Robert," he said almost resignedly. It was by no means a greeting, any more than it was an expression of resentment at the intrusion. Looking past Cloud, he saw his maid, very nervous. "It's all right, Alma," he said reassuringly. "Mr. Cloud and I are old friends."

Cloud walked farther into the room, until he was standing on the other side of the fireplace, facing Niebold. He heard the maid close the library doors behind him.

"Brandy, Robert?" the attorney said, indicating a decanter and glasses nearby.

"I didn't come here to socialize," Cloud said flatly. "I came here to find out what you intend to do to stop Weldon Whitman's execution."

"Why, nothing," Niebold said unconcernedly. "There's

nothing *to* do; the Supreme Court has ruled." He took a bare sip of the fiery red brandy and rolled it over his tongue before swallowing it. "Poor Weldon," he said without a trace of pity. "I'm afraid he's going to be one more victim in the long line of innocent men unjustly punished by our state's warped system of justice."

Cloud's eyes narrowed slightly. "You're convinced that Whitman is innocent, yet you're going to make no effort to keep him from going to the gas chamber?"

"No *further* effort," Niebold corrected.

"Even though you've convinced he's innocent?" Cloud drove home the point again.

"*Particularly* because I'm convinced he's innocent," Niebold admitted.

"Why, Morris?" Cloud asked quietly. "Why have you done all this?"

The old invalid took another slight sip of his drink and stared into the small circle of crystal that formed the lip of the glass, at the larger circle of red that was the brandy below it. Slowly he rotated the glass, tilting the red circle this way and that, moving its position within the crystal but never disrupting its perfect symmetry. His lips pursed, he studied the circle of red as if deciding whether to answer Cloud's question. Finally he looked back up.

"I want to see Borden elected governor," he said simply.

"I don't see what it has to do with Whitman," Cloud lied. He *did* see by now; but he wanted to hear Niebold say it.

"Weldon Whitman is an innocent man," the invalid explained. "Day after tomorrow he's going to be gassed for crimes he did not commit. You yourself have already proved him innocent of the Calder crime, and when our detectives find the Luza girl we'll prove him innocent of that one too. By then, of course, it will be too late. It'll be too late to save him—but it won't be too late to make a martyr out of him. And the person who'll make that martyr will be Borden White. He'll use Weldon Whitman to indict every facet of this state's administration, from the chairman of the California department of corrections to the Supreme Court to the governor himself. He'll carry the bloody cross of Weldon Whitman from one end of this state to the other, preaching the inhumanity of capital punishment and the fallibility of the system that wrongfully executed this innocent man. Believe me, Robert, it will be a political campaign unequaled in the history of this state. And it will carry Borden White right into the governor's mansion."

Cloud stared at Morris Niebold. He said nothing, because he decided that nothing he could say would serve any useful purpose. Weldon Whitman was going to die in the gas chamber the day after tomorrow, and Morris Niebold was going to do nothing to prevent it. Because in Morris Niebold's scheme of things to come, the execution of Weldon Whitman was an essential ingredient.

"Robert," said Niebold, leaning forward, "you know I have always liked you, my boy. Despite our differences in philosophy and approach regarding Whitman, I am still of the opinion that you are a much better writer than—than—" Niebold's face wrinkled in a frown. "—whatever his name is. You know who I mean: the nigger that Borden found to pick up where you left off."

"Eugene Terrier," said Cloud.

"Yes, that's him. You're a much better writer than he is, Robert. He's got a little bit of that black radical approach to things, and sometimes it shows through. I'd much rather have you back with us. How would you like to be in charge of all the writing for Borden's campaign?"

"I don't think so," Cloud replied coldly.

"We could increase the money considerably," Niebold said.

"You couldn't increase it enough," Cloud assured him.

Niebold's face constricted until he resembled an angry rodent. "What you're saying, I take it, is that you are not prepared to work for us again at any price?"

"Exactly."

Cloud had had enough. He stepped away from the big fireplace and walked over to the double doors through which he had entered the room. At the doors he paused and turned back.

"You know, Morris," he said deliberately, "your legs aren't the only lame part of you. You may not realize it, but your mind is crippled too. Someday you'll have to be put away."

He pulled open the double doors and walked out. He left the doors open behind him, and he could hear Niebold's shouted curses all the way out of the mansion.

Genevieve's reaction was one of calm. It was a sad, sick calm, but it was a calm nevertheless.

"He's going to die, isn't he?" she asked in a resigned voice as soon as she had admitted Cloud to the apartment.

Cloud stared at her without answering.

"Isn't he, Rob?" she asked again. This time Cloud nodded. "Yes, Gen, he is."

She went into her living room and sat down. Cloud followed but remained standing.

"I suppose I knew it weeks ago," she said in a tone almost conversational. "I may even have known it all along."

"No, neither of us knew it all along," Cloud told her. "One thing we mustn't forget, Gen, and that's that we *believed* in Weldon Whitman. We believed in him totally: one hundred percent. And we may very well be the only two people on earth who did. That's something we mustn't lose. Either of us."

Even knowing all he knew, Cloud meant what he said. He believed in the importance of it to both of them. It was, after all, the only thing in the entire Whitman matter that separated them from people like Niebold and White and Carla Volt.

While Cloud was standing there in the middle of the room, Genevieve rose and walked over to her desk. She picked up a telegram and handed it to Cloud. If there had been any way he could have avoided reading it, he would have; the premonition he had when Genevieve handed it to him was totally grim. But he had to read it, so he did. It was addressed to Genevieve and it said:

LAST VISITING HOURS TOMORROW 7:00 TO 10:00 A.M. IMPERATIVE I SEE YOU. HAVE ONE LAST CHANCE FOR REPRIEVE. COUNTING ON YOU.

WELDON

"You'll have to go in my place, Rob," she said. Her words were like needles in his brain.

"It's you he wants to see, Gen," he said weakly.

"No, it'll have to be you," Genevieve said, as plainly and sensibly as if she were telling him what day or what time it was. "I can't go because I'm not strong enough to see him when I know he's this close to execution."

"If I weren't here, you'd *have* to see him," Cloud said.

"If you weren't here, I'd be stronger," she replied with a nervous half-smile.

"But what if he's *not* as close to execution as we think?" Cloud said. "What if he does have one last chance at a reprieve, as he says he does: shouldn't you be the one to pass on its merits? You know far more law than I do."

"Whatever it is Weldon's talking about has nothing to do with the law," Genevieve said confidently. "His legal cards have been played and replayed. I'm sure that whatever he's talking about is more a last-ditch gimmick than anything else." She saw that Cloud was staring at her in surprise. He obviously had not expected such a comment from her. "Oh, yes, I know Weldon pretty well by now," she said. "I may care for him very deeply, but I'm not completely blind to the kind of person he is. Nor does it lessen my feelings toward him. That's why you have to go to him in my place tomorrow." She bit her bottom lip tentatively. "Will you?"

Cloud nodded.

Twenty-four

At seven-fifteen the next morning, Cloud was escorted across one of the San Quentin yards by a service guard, on his way to the Condemned Row building where he had visited Weldon Whitman so many times in the past. It was gray and foggy out, but even in the damp, chilly air Cloud could feel perspiration moistening the underarms of his shirt. He had thought several times while living with Carol Carter that he would never again have to make this walk over to the grim, windowless red brick building which Weldon Whitman had so aptly named Hotel Death. He had told himself that he was through with everything having to do with the Whitman movement: the foundation, the lawyers, the appeals, the hustling—all of it. But he had omitted one factor: Genevieve Neller.

Genevieve, the only one in the entire affair with no ulterior motive of any kind. Everyone else had been in it for *something.* Everyone else had been looking to profit from it in some way. Even he himself, with all his lofty ideals, had been bought and paid for with half the royalties from *Room 22, Hotel Death.* But Genevieve had been in it for *principle.* Sure, by now she was emotionally hung up on Weldon Whitman, but that had not always been the case. In the beginning she had become Whitman's friend simply because he seemed to *need* a friend. Cloud shook his head bitterly. She was the one who cared the most—and would get the least out of it.

Cloud followed the service guard into the Condemned Row building, went through the usual security procedures, and was passed upstairs to the visiting room.

For some reason, he half expected the visiting room to be different this morning, although different in what way he had no idea; but sterile, windowless, it remained exactly the same.

As he stood, hands jammed into his raincoat pockets, watching the Death Row elevator close its doors and go upstairs for Whitman, Cloud remembered the sealed envelope in his inside coat pocket. Genevieve had handed it to him last thing before he left, with no instructions offered and none needed. It was her last letter to Whitman. On his way to the prison that morning, Cloud had considered destroying the letter, not even giving it to Whitman, because in his opinion Whitman was not deserving of the words Cloud knew the letter contained: the outpouring of Genevieve's heart. But then he asked himself who in hell he thought *he* was to be making such a judgment. He had no assurance that Genevieve would not feel the same way about Weldon Whitman even if she knew all that Cloud now knew; no guarantee that Genevieve would not have written exactly the same message to Whitman even if she had full knowledge of his crimes. So he stepped over to the guard at the near end of the long visiting table and handed him the sealed envelope.

"Personal correspondence for Weldon Whitman," he said.

He walked down to the middle of the partitioned visiting table and took the same chair in which he had sat the very first time he visited Whitman: the seat midway between the two observation guards, as Lew Lach had taught him so long ago. He unbuttoned his raincoat but did not bother to remove it; he did not plan to stay long.

The door of the prisoner elevator opened and Weldon Whitman stepped into the room. His eyes were narrowed and his lips curled into an *actual* sneer, not the unintentional one so often created by his features. He walked purposefully over to the table, and instead of sitting, remained standing to look down at Cloud.

"I asked Genevieve to come," he said curtly. "Where is she?"

"She's not coming," Cloud said in a quietly neutral voice.

"Why are you here?" Whitman demanded. "You're the one who walked out on me."

"I'm here because Genevieve asked me to come," Cloud said. "And because there's no one else left *to* come."

"What do you mean no one else left?" Whitman said contemptuously. "I have a *foundation* behind me. I have *thousands* of supporters all over the fucking state!"

"Then where are they?" Cloud asked.

Whitman ignored the question. "Where are Niebold and White?" he said irritably. "What are they doing for me?"

"Nothing."

Whitman chewed his bottom lip for a moment, then snatched back the chair on his side and quickly sat down. He leaned forward urgently. "I've got to get some information to the governor," he said tensely. "That's why I wanted Genevieve here."

"She sent me in her place," Cloud told him again.

"How can I depend on you?" the condemned man said. "You walked out on me once already. And besides, I need someone *impressive* to see the governor for me. Someone like Genevieve, who has some stature. I can't send you. Look at you: your hair needs cutting, you look like hell with that mustache, your clothes *never* look neat. You won't do at all."

"That's too bad," Cloud told him. "Because I'm the only one you've got."

Weldon Whitman thought about that. He looked up at the clock on the wall; it was almost eight. In two hours he would be removed from the Row and taken down to the holding cell where he was scheduled to spend the last twenty-four hours of his life. Once there, in that tiny cell behind the gas chamber, he would be totally out of touch with everyone on the outside except through prison officials.

"Nobody else is coming to see me this morning?" he asked suspiciously.

"I don't think so."

Whitman slammed a fist into the open palm of his other hand. "I have information that *must* get to the governor today!" he said again. "I'm certain he'll grant me a stay when he hears what I have to say."

"Tell me that it is then," said Cloud. "If it's the truth, I'll see that it gets to the governor."

Whitman's eyes flashed suspicion. "What do you mean by that?" he asked. "Who's to decide whether it's the truth or not?"

"I will," Cloud told him.

A little of Whitman's sneer returned. "How will you know?"

"I'll know," Cloud said.

Whitman studied him for a long moment, his lips parted in concentration, the sneer gone, wiped away by an overall expression of indecision. Again, as so many times in the past, he seemed at that moment to have about him an odd vulnerability, a suggestion of helplessness, a look that cried out for a friend. Robert Cloud remembered that look and his jaw tightened slightly.

"All right," Whitman said, "I'll trust you. It doesn't appear that I have a great deal of choice in the matter." He tried to lean closer across the divided table, his shoulders hunched, elbows planted firmly, fingers laced together. "You remember I told you a long time ago that I had committed all the crimes I was convicted of except the car theft and the Calder and Luza jobs? And I told you I thought an ex-partner of mine had pulled those? Well, I want to confess to the crimes I committed, and I want to make a deal to name the guy who did the other crimes."

"Are you saying you didn't commit the Calder and Luza crimes but you'll name the person who did?" Cloud asked, cutting directly to the core of it. Whitman nodded his head emphatically.

"Exactly. I told you I knew who the guy was, and I do. As a matter of fact, the car I used on that last job was the same car he used to pull the Calder and Luza jobs. I had been borrowing the goddamned car from him and using that spotlight gimmick to pull jobs by myself. In fact, I *got* the idea for the gimmick from him."

Cloud kept his eyes riveted on Whitman. "Now you're willing to give the governor the name of this man and accuse him of the Calder and Luza crimes?"

Whitman nodded. "Yes."

"Can this man be found? Can he be brought to trial?"

Whitman nodded. "He's right here in San Quentin. He took a fall for another rap and just got transferred up here from Folsom."

"If what you're saying is true, why didn't you name him before now?" Cloud asked bluntly. "Why didn't you do it the last time you were this close to execution, when Gen and I had to finally turn the foundation over to Niebold and White in order to get you a stay?"

"I couldn't do it then," the condemned man said. "I didn't know my ex-partner was back in at that time; I thought he was still on the street. I didn't know he was doing time again until a week ago when he came in on a Folsom transfer."

"What difference does that make?"

"While he was outside, he was a potential threat to someone I had to protect," Whitman explained. "I knew if I finked on him, he'd hurt that person before the law could get to him."

Cloud's expression did not change, but he suddenly felt peculiar in the pit of his stomach. *He's lying to me,* he thought. His mind gave him no clue as to why he thought it;

he knew only that the thought was clear and irrevocable. The Whitman mystique was gone.

"Who's the person you had to protect?" Cloud asked in as even a voice as he could muster.

"That's something I don't want to go into," Whitman told him.

An act, thought Cloud. *He's putting on an act.*

"You'll have to go into it with the governor," Cloud told him.

Whitman again was silent for a long, thoughtful moment. Then he nodded his head once, firmly, and looked Cloud squarely in the eye. "I've got a daughter, Rob. She's eight years old. I was protecting her and her mother."

"Who's her mother, Whit?"

"My ex-wife."

"You never did tell me her name," Cloud said.

"I still want her kept out of it."

"I'll keep her out of it," Cloud promised. "Just tell me her name. I'm curious."

"Carol," said Weldon Whitman. "Her name is Carol."

You lousy fucking liar.

"Do you believe me, Rob?" Whitman asked after a few moments.

Cloud nodded. "Yes, I believe you," he lied back.

"Will you help me?"

"I'll help you," he lied again.

"You'll go to the governor for me?"

"Yes. Either me or Genevieve. One of us will do it." Another lie. Cloud was beginning to enjoy it. Like sweet revenge. "There's a lot to do," he said, standing. "I'd better go. Incidentally, there's a letter from Gen waiting for you. It was supposed to be her last words to you. Do me a favor, will you: sit down and answer it, just like you were writing your last words to her. I don't know how you really feel about her, but she can still be very useful to us. A really sincere-sounding last letter from you would make all the difference in the world in how she thinks of you in the future. Will you do that for me?"

"Hell, yes," said Whitman. "Whatever you say, Rob." The condemned man was also standing now, smiling across the long table. "It'll be like old times, won't it, buddy? You and me again." Whitman rubbed his hands together jubilantly. "Hey, man, we'll beat this fucking place yet. Won't we, Rob?"

"We sure will, Whit," said Robert Cloud.

And that was the last lie he told him.

At nine-thirty the next morning, Whitman was vomiting.

He was on his knees in one of the two tiny holding cells, regurgitating his breakfast of two hours earlier into the lidless toilet in the corner of the cell. The vomit was yellowish in color, like his scrambled eggs had been; it burned his throat coming up, and a little of it got into his nose and burned the tissue there also.

When he finished throwing up, he sank back to the mattress spread on the floor and sat with his knees drawn up and his head back against the cold steel bars.

Captain Dukes, who was standing outside the cell, handed a container of coffee through the bars. "Here, drink this. It'll take the taste of that puke out of your mouth."

"Yeah, okay," Whitman said hoarsely. He took the cup with trembling hands and shakily managed to get some of the steaming liquid past his lips. He looked through the bars at Dukes. "You've hated my guts all this time and now you're being decent to me," he said, almost accusingly. "How come?"

"No particular reason," Dukes said. He would not admit to anyone that he had been receiving foundation literature in the mail. That he had been reading it. And that, incredibly, he had begun to have doubts about Weldon Whitman's punishment. "Nothing wrong with being civil to a man on the day he's going down," the bull-shouldered Death Row commander said. He avoided meeting Whitman's eyes and stepped away from the bars. Turning his back on the cell, he checked his watch; it was twenty-seven minutes to ten.

Whitman took several quick sips of coffee. What the fuck could have happened? he wondered. Cloud *had* to have seen the governor by now. His mind, sick with fear, raced anxiously for hope. Maybe they were going to make it a last-minute reprieve, so it would look more dramatic to the press and public. Sure, that was probably it. Condemned man snatched from jaws of death as new evidence is brought to light at last minute. Good. Very good. He felt better and drank some more coffee.

From around the corner of the short corridor leading to the gas chamber, came a heavy, dull thud. Whitman's head shot around.

"What was that?"

"They're testing the chamber door," Dukes told him quietly. "They have to make sure there's a perfect pneumatic seal." Dukes turned to the death-watch guard on duty. "I'm going to check the Prep Room." As he went into the short corridor, he heard Whitman speak to the same guard.

"How about turning that radio up a little?" Whitman said.

"Sure." The guard rose from the bench where he sat and adjusted the volume knob of a small radio on the floor in a corner. It was tuned to a popular San Francisco station which traditionally broadcast news of stays of execution at the prison. Every man on Death Row was tuned to the station that morning, as they were every morning that an execution was scheduled. They knew that if there was a stay or a reprieve, word of it would reach them first on that radio station.

Dukes turned the corner of the short hallway and entered the Preparation Room. Into this area protruded five sides of the octagonal gas chamber; its other three sides, with their thick glass observation windows, were beyond a wall in the Witness Room. That room was empty and would remain so for the next few minutes, but in the Preparation Room, the men of the death watch were quietly and efficiently preparing the chamber for its job. Dukes stood near the big pneumatic door and watched them. One guard was carefully counting out cyanide eggs and wrapping them in cheesecloth. Another guard, wearing double-thickness, elbow-length rubber gloves, stood next to him, waiting. When the eggs were ready, the second guard would carefully hang them on a mechanical arm under Chair A, the chair on the left as one entered the death chamber and faced the pair of death chairs. That mechanical arm under Chair A, which was operated from outside the chamber, would at the appropriate time be lowered into a lead bucket under the chair. The bucket would contain sulfuric acid, which at that moment was being measured by a third guard who would soon pour the proper amount into a receptacle which flowed into the bucket.

Dukes looked past the three working guards to still another member of his death watch: a fourth guard who was checking out the Death House telephone, on which would be maintained an open line to the warden's office in case a stay was ordered. Dukes could not help hoping that a stay *would* come through; but he could not help *feeling* that one would not. Still, one never knew.

The big guard captain walked back into the Ready Room. He saw that the prison chaplain was now talking to Whitman through the bars of the holding cell. Dukes poured himself half a cup of coffee and sat down on the bench next to the fifth member of his death-watch squad. Sipping the coffee, Dukes could not help hearing the nearby conversation.

"—haven't gotten to know one another too well since you've been on the Row, Weldon," the chaplain was saying, "but I want you to know that if there's any way I can be of help to you, I'm more than happy to do it."

Whitman looked up from where he was now squatting on the mattress with his hands closed around the coffee container. He mumbled his thanks absently and resumed concentrating on the radio, trying to ignore the chaplain.

"Is there any kind of religious solace I can offer you in these last few minutes?" the chaplain asked. Whitman looked at him again, frowning.

"What?"

The chaplain patiently repeated his offer. Whitman shook his head.

"No, I don't want anything," he said in a clipped tone. "I just want to listen to the radio."

"Of course," the chaplain said. "I won't intrude any longer. May I shake hands with you?"

"Yeah, sure," Whitman said. He rose and put one hand through the bars. The chaplain gripped it firmly.

"Goodbye, Weldon. Remember that in God's eyes your passing is as important as the passing of a king. God marks the sparrow's fall. We are all His children."

Whitman mumbled his thanks again and the chaplain let go of his hand and left the Ready Room. Whitman finished his coffee and set the container on the ledge of the holding-cell door.

"What time is it?" he asked Dukes.

"Nineteen minutes to ten."

Whitman forced a tight grin. "My people on the outside are cutting it pretty thin this time."

Dukes and the death-watch guard exchanged glances; neither of them responded to Whitman's comment.

A moment later, one of the other members of the death-watch squad came in from the Prep Room and unlocked Holding Cell B, next to the cell in which Whitman waited. Holding Cell B was empty except for two rolled-up lengths of green carpet, twenty-seven inches wide. The guard, avoiding Whitman's eyes, removed the carpet from the cell. He unrolled one length, the longer of the two, from the door of Whitman's cell to the door of the Prep Room. He unrolled the shorter length from the door of the Prep Room to the open door of the gas chamber itself.

Watching the guard perform that part of the execution ritual made Whitman feel ill all over again. He felt the taste of bile come up into his mouth, and a sudden clammy coldness came over him. With shaking hands he managed to put a cigarette between his lips. The death-watch guard stepped over at once to reach between the bars and light it for him.

At fourteen minutes before ten, the prison doctor and a deputy warden entered the Ready Room.

"The reporters outside have asked if you have any last statement for the press," the deputy warden said. Whitman looked up at him from the mattress.

"Yes, I do," he said hoarsely. "I want to deny once and for all that I committed the crimes for which I am being sent to the gas chamber. The state of California is killing an innocent man today."

"Is that all?"

"That's all, yes."

The deputy warden nodded and turned to Captain Dukes. "Get him ready, Captain."

"Yessir."

Dukes waited until the deputy warden left, then came over and unlocked the holding cell. He stepped inside the cell with Whitman. "You'll have to change now," he said.

Whitman, moistening his lips, stepped out of his felt slippers. Unbuttoning his shirt and trousers, he took them off and dropped them in a heap on top of the slippers. He stood waiting in pale nakedness.

A death-watch guard handed Dukes a new white shirt, pressed, on a hanger, and a pair of new blue denim trousers. Those were the only articles of apparel the condemned man would wear into the death chamber. No shoes, socks, or underwear. Dukes handed Whitman the trousers first. The prisoner put them on.

"Okay, Doc," the captain said.

The prison doctor entered the cell, located Whitman's heartbeat, and taped the head of a stethoscope directly over it. A twelve-inch rubber tube extended from the head and hung loosely from under the tape.

"All right," the doctor said. He extended his hand. "Good luck, Weldon."

Whitman shook hands and nodded, but said nothing.

The doctor left the Ready Room and went into the Prep Room. Dukes stepped back into the holding cell and handed Whitman the white shirt.

"What time is it now?" Whitman asked dully.

"Nine minutes to ten."

Jesus Christ, he thought, feeling sick all over again. Nine minutes. Goddamn. What the *fuck* had happened to Genevieve and Cloud?

"Put on the shirt," Dukes said gently.

"Sure." Mouth slightly agape, Whitman mechanically drew the shirt sleeves over his arms and pulled the garment around his slumped shoulders. He buttoned the shirt unevenly and stuffed it carelessly into his trousers.

I still don't believe it. I don't believe they're going to let me die. They can't. There are people behind me, and a foundation—

The radio on the floor in the corner announced the time at five minutes before ten, and the announcer said, "There is still no word of a stay of execution for Weldon Carpenter Whitman, who is scheduled to die at ten this morning in San Quentin's gas chamber. Whitman was convicted of kidnapping and sex perversion in the infamous Spotlight Bandit crimes in the Los Angeles area more than three years ago. Through clever legal maneuvers, he has avoided several previous appointments with the executioner, but never before has he been as close to death as he is at this moment—"

"Turn it off," Whitman said, a surge of emotion returning to his voice. "Turn that fucking thing off!"

The death-watch guard immediately switched off the

radio. A silence shot through the Ready Room, accompanied by such a total absence of motion that the scene was like a movie still. At that moment, that suspended instant in time, Weldon Whitman knew that it was all over.

I'll be a son of a bitch, he thought. *I'm about to die.*

At one and a half minutes before ten, the final ritual began. Captain Dukes reached into the tiny holding cell, took the condemned man's arm, and gently drew him out. As Whitman stepped forward, he realized that despite the carpet, his bare feet felt very, very cold. As if they were already dead.

It was nine steps to the Prep Room door. Dukes walked to one side of Whitman and half a step back. The other death-watch guards fell in behind them as they passed. At the door, as he passed through, Whitman saw those who were waiting: deputy warden, doctor, chaplain, the man on the telephone. He saw the open hatch of the death chamber itself, and remembered the witnesses who would be looking at him from the other side. He suddenly felt as if his bowels were about to evacuate. Mortified at the thought that he might have to walk in there and sit down in front of all those witnesses with his pants full of shit, he hesitated a step. But he was not permitted to pause because Dukes did not let him. The captain's big hand closed over the back of his arm just above the elbow, and at the same time another hand clutched his other arm. Then he was quickly guided into the chamber: stepping over the lip of the big oval doorway, being handed to a pair of death-watch guards who had come around him and preceded him into the chamber.

The room of death was starkly bright inside. It reminded Weldon Whitman of a giant steel cunt, clean-shaven, unlubricated, cold. He could not help grinning idiotically at the thought. But his grin lasted only an instant, then dissolved as he became aware of the faces of the witnesses. They peered at him through three tall windows set in three of the chamber's eight sides. Their faces were openly curious, showing no embarrassment. Curious himself, Whitman began to scan *them*, searching for someone familiar. But before he found anyone he was firmly turned around and urged into the left one of the pair of death chairs. He was seated, his back partially to the witness room, and Dukes was suddenly standing next to him, pulling a thick leather strap across his chest and fastening it, confining him to the chair in a straight upright position. And other hands were fastening other straps. Wrists, arms, legs, feet.

"Listen, Captain," he said thickly, his eyes wide and dazed, "a stay is going to come in for me any second now. I have this friend named Rob, you see, and—and this friend named—named . . ."

He stopped speaking and stared at the hatch. The members of the death watch were filing out.

Oh Jesus no don't leave me in this fucking place all alone!

He felt the captain's hands touch the front of his shirt. They attached the stethoscope head to a rubber tube which extended outside the chamber where the doctor waited with the rest of the instrument to listen to his heart stop beating. Whitman looked up, staring wide-eyed at Dukes.

"Listen for the pills to drop," the captain said. "Then count to twenty and take a couple of deep breaths. You'll go quick that way."

Dukes stepped quickly over the lip and out of the chamber. The chamber door swung shut immediately; Whitman felt a slight pressure on his ears. Then he heard a soft hissing sound as the air lock sealed the chamber.

A moment of silence followed. Terrible silence. The most silent silence he had ever experienced.

This is how it feels to be dead, he thought.

Almost at once the pureness of the quiet was broken by a subdued *plop* as the cheesecloth bag of cyanide eggs dropped into the lead bucket of acid. At the sound of it, Whitman tensed and stiffened, instinctively straining at the taut leather straps that held him. Then, as quickly as he had reacted, he *un*reacted; he realized that he had only seconds to live, and he suddenly relaxed. There was no longer any reason to be tense or hopeful, because now there was no turning back; once those cyanide eggs dropped, the state was unequivocally committed to the execution.

Weldon Whitman rested his head against the hard metal back of the death chair, closed his eyes for the last time, and waited for the gas. He thought of what Captain Dukes had said to him a moment earlier. Count to twenty and take a deep breath. One, two, three, four, five, six, seven, eight—

Fuck it.

He thought instead of that night up in the Hollywood Hills and how good it felt when he put his dick into that little spic broad's mouth and how she—cried—and kept—grabbing—at——that———fucking————cross while——————he——————

Weldon Whitman's head fell to one side and a drool of saliva trickled from the corner of his mouth and dripped down to make a dark spot on the new white shirt.

Twenty-five

Three hours after Weldon Whitman's execution, Robert Cloud and Genevieve Neller sat together in a small, private waiting room in a building across the bay in San Francisco. Cloud was clean-shaven, his hair neatly trimmed, and he wore his best suit and a tie. The room they were in was tastefully sedate and very small; large enough for no more than six persons to sit comfortably. It was furnished in velvet-upholstered Victorian armchairs and a side table with a vase of fresh flowers against one wall.

Cloud and Genevieve had been there for half an hour. They had been sitting in the little room in silence; with Weldon Whitman dead, there seemed to be little between them to say. Each of them *wanted* to talk, but neither of them wished to force conversation, and each was concerned about intruding upon the private thoughts of the other. The little waiting room soon became *too* quiet, however, and an uncomfortable depression could be sensed growing invisibly around them. When Genevieve felt it, she decided it was time to talk awhile.

"I received the most beautiful letter from Weldon this morning, Rob," she said in an almost blissful voice.

Cloud turned to her, only then remembering the promise he had extracted from Whitman to write her.

"He wrote it yesterday as soon as they moved him down to the holding cell," she said. "He felt, as we did, that he was definitely going to die this time, and he said he wanted his last written words to go to me. He wrote the letter right after he read mine to him. Then he had it mailed special delivery so that I would receive it while he was still alive."

That was a nice touch, Cloud thought. Especially since he had expected to *stay* alive. Curiously he wondered what Whitman had thought when he finally realized that he *was* going to die.

"I can't let you read the letter, Rob," she said, "because—well, it's extremely personal. But I want you to know that Weldon did not believe that the information you took to the governor for him yesterday was going to do him any good. And, of course, it didn't."

"No, it didn't," said Cloud. Because he had not taken the information to the governor. He had not taken it to anyone. Weldon Whitman's last lie had gone no farther than Robert Cloud.

Genevieve patted him on the arm. "In the letter Weldon said to thank you for trying anyway, and for everything else. He also said that he didn't want me to know the nature of the information you took to the governor for him. He said he was afraid I would be hurt by it. But he said that if on the outside chance he did get a stay, he wanted me to be the first one to visit him so that he could explain it to me personally." She paused for a moment, then gently squeezed Cloud's arm. "Can you tell me what it was that he sent to the governor, Rob?"

"Do you have to know?"

"Yes."

"All right," Cloud said quietly. "Weldon wanted to confess to all the crimes he was convicted of, except the car theft and the Calder and Luza sex crimes. He also wanted to name an ex-partner of his that he believed to be the real Spotlight Bandit."

"Is that all?"

"Yes," Cloud said.

"There was no mention of his former wife?"

Cloud stared at her, mouth momentarily agape.

"I've known about her for a long time, Rob," Genevieve said. "I obtained a copy of Weldon's complete criminal record from a friend of mine who's a clerical supervisor at the California Bureau of Investigation. It showed that Weldon was married to a Carol Whitman at the time he was sent to Folsom prison for robbery, and that she later divorced him." Genevieve looked away from Cloud. "I know a lot about Weldon that we've never discussed, Rob," she said cryptically. "I know, for instance, that he *was* a sex pervert."

Cloud looked incredulously at her. "Gen, you don't know what you're saying."

She turned back to him. "Yes, I do, Rob. I know. I know for a certainty. And please don't ask me how I know, because I can't tell you."

Cloud swallowed dryly. *Christ*, he wondered, *what had Whitman done to her?* He shook his head briefly. He would never know. He could only guess.

"The one thing I'm not certain of," Genevieve said, "is just *how* perverted he was. I don't know in my own mind if he was a *criminal* pervert or not." She paused, keeping her eyes directly and unmovingly on Cloud. "But I have a feeling that you know, Rob. I have a feeling that you could tell me once and for all. *Did* Weldon commit the Calder and Luza crimes?"

Cloud met her eyes with equal directness. "No, Gen," he lied.

Her shoulders dropped and she sat back, visibly relieved. "I'm glad for that much," she said in barely a whisper.

They sat in silence then until the door to the room opened and a short, middle-aged man in a dark suit entered. He was carrying a book-size walnut box with a silver catch on its lid. Cloud rose and stepped to the middle of the room to meet him. They exchanged quiet words and he had Cloud sign a receipt on the side table where the flowers stood. Then he gave Cloud the walnut box and left. Cloud went back over to Genevieve.

"It's time to go, Gen."

Genevieve got up. She looked at the box Cloud was holding. "Is that—?"

Instinctively she reached for the box, but Cloud held it back from her. "Wait until we get to the car," he said.

Clutching the box under one arm, holding Genevieve around the shoulders with the other, Cloud walked down a thickly carpeted hallway to a set of double glass doors. He used his shoulder to push open one of the doors and presently they were outside the building on the edge of the parking lot. Cloud led Genevieve toward her car. On the way they passed a sign that read: PARKING FOR CREMATORIUM ONLY. Cloud clutched the box he was carrying a little more tightly.

"That ex-partner of Weldon's," Genevieve said when they were halfway across the lot. "I suppose he hadn't previously named the man because he wanted to protect his ex-wife."

"His ex-wife and one other person," Cloud said, lying again. He hated to keep lying to Genevieve, but he felt he had to leave her with *something*.

"One other person? Who?"

"You, Gen," he said.

"Me?" Despite her efforts to control it, a single tear streaked her cheek.

"Yes. You especially. Whit didn't know whether the real Spotlight Bandit could find his ex-wife or not; but he *knew* that you could be found. He was more afraid for you than for anyone."

Genevieve began to cry very quietly. But beneath her tears she wore a slight smile.

When they got to the car, Cloud tried to guide Genevieve around to the passenger side, but she stopped and faced him, drying her eyes.

"I'd like to say goodbye right here, Rob," she told him. "I'm not going back to Sacramento."

Cloud saw her suitcases on the back seat of the car. He stared at her, unable to conceal his surprise. He had planned on having to stay with her for a while, until she got over what had happened. Now he realized he should have known better.

"I sold everything I had to a secondhand dealer this morning," she said. "All that I kept were clothes and personal things that would fit in the trunk. I'm going away."

"Where to?"

"I'm not sure. I thought I'd just drive for a few weeks: up the coast to Oregon and Washington; maybe on into Canada or even up to Alaska."

"And when you get tired of driving?"

She shrugged. "Find a little town someplace where they need a librarian."

"Just leave everything behind?"

"Yes." She bit her lip briefly. "Do you think I can?"

Cloud nodded. "I'm sure you can."

Genevieve smiled gratefully. "I'm glad you think so. And what about you? Will you be all right?"

"Me? Sure, I'll be okay."

"Where will you go? What will you do?"

He shrugged, as she had done. "I don't know. Maybe I'll go see Ben Droller and try to get a magazine job on *Argus*."

Their eyes met in silence for a moment. There was a suggestion of slight embarrassment, coupled with an urgency to have the parting over with.

"This is best, don't you think, Rob?" she said. "To end it once and for all?"

Cloud nodded again. "Yes, it's best."

Genevieve opened the door and got in the car. "I'll just put that on the seat beside me," she said, reaching for the box he held.

"All right." Cloud handed her the ashes of Weldon Whitman. After she took the box, she pulled his head down and kissed him tenderly on the lips.

"I love you, Rob. In a very special way."

"I love you too," he said. "Probably in the same way."

They kissed again, briefly.

"Goodbye, Rob."

"Goodbye, Gen."

He closed the car door and watched as she started the engine and drove slowly away.

It was midafternoon when Cloud got off a bus at the downtown Greyhound station in Sacramento. He walked outside and stepped into a cab, giving the driver the address of the Niebold and White law offices. It was just seven blocks from the station; when they got there, Cloud handed the driver a twenty-dollar bill.

"Wait for me. I'll be out in a few minutes and I'll want to go to the airport from here."

He entered the building and took the elevator to the top floor where the offices were. He walked past the receptionist so brusquely that it startled her.

"May I help you, sir?" she said in a perplexed voice.

Cloud ignored her and went directly down the hall toward Morris Niebold's office. On the way he passed Carla Volt's office, and noticed that the door was open and she was not at her desk. It was the same with Borden White's office: door open but no Borden White. Instinctively Cloud knew they would be in Niebold's office. A meeting of the vultures, he thought. He burst unceremoniously into the office, the alarmed receptionist close behind him.

The three of them were having a drink around Niebold's specially made desk. They all turned quickly toward the door, as startled as the receptionist had been. Carla turned so quickly that she spilled some of her drink on her dress.

"Goddamn it!" she said angrily, seeing who it was.

Niebold flushed with anger. "Your barging into places uninvited and unannounced is becoming quite tiresome, Robert," he said curtly. His eyes flicked to the nervous receptionist. "Sharon, call the police."

"Do that and I'll tell the newspapers what I came to tell you," Cloud warned.

Behind Cloud, the receptionist started to hurry back down the hall.

"Sharon, wait," said Morris Niebold. He eyed Cloud suspiciously, weighing Cloud's remark about telling something to the newspapers. "Never mind about the police, Sharon," he said. "Just close the door, please."

The woman reached in apprehensively and pulled the door shut.

"You bastard," said Carla Volt when the door was closed. "You've probably ruined this dress."

"Never mind your dress," Niebold snapped. "All right, Robert, what is it you want to say?"

Cloud stepped to the front of the desk. "I want to warn you not to try to use the Weldon Whitman case as a stepping stone to get your boy Borden elected governor."

"Why not, may I ask?"

"Because Weldon Whitman was guilty, Morris. He committed the Luza crime. And if Borden White starts campaigning on the premise that he *wasn't* guilty, I'll wait until just before the election and then blow his candidacy wide open."

Niebold's eyes narrowed to slits. "I don't believe you, Robert. I don't believe Whitman was guilty."

"I can prove it."

"How?"

"I have an independent witness who was given a religious necklace by Whitman that was taken from Glory Ann Luza the night she was attacked."

"Circumstantial evidence," Niebold said with a peremptory wave of his hand. "We can get around that."

"I can also produce, through G. Foster Klein, who is now a judge in Los Angeles, the man who *did* commit the Calder kidnapping, and who loaned Whitman the car in which Whitman committed the Luza crime. And, incidentally, Doris Calder can't refute any of her testimony against Whitman, even though it was in error, because she has committed suicide."

"What?" Borden White said incredulously. "Suicide—?"

"Shut up, Borden," Morris Niebold ordered. "If you produce such a person," he said to Cloud, "it would be the testimony of a felon. A simple matter to discredit."

"Try and discredit this then," Cloud challenged. He had

the lie fully prepared in his mind. "A confession in Whitman's own handwriting admitting his guilt in the Luza crime and several others of which he was convicted."

Sudden silence fell over the office. The eyes of Niebold, White, and Carla Volt were riveted to Cloud. Niebold's eyes were unblinking, as were Cloud's; Niebold's stare relentless, as was Cloud's. Both men, one sitting, one standing, were unflinching.

"You're bluffing, Robert," the invalid said. "If you had a story that big, you'd write it. Today."

"I *want* to write it, Morris," Cloud admitted. "I want to write it so bad I can taste it. The only reason I'm *not* going to write it is because of Genevieve. She doesn't know. And I don't intend to let her know. Unless you force me to."

Niebold leaned his elbows on the padded arms of his wheelchair. "Exactly what is it you want, Robert?"

"I want the Weldon Whitman case to die. Today. Just like the man did."

"That's absurd," Niebold blurted. "Why, that—that's a *waste*. It won't do *anyone* any good."

"It won't do anyone any more harm either," Cloud said determinedly. He bent forward and put his closed fists on Niebold's desk. "I don't want to hurt Genevieve, Morris. But I will. I'll tell her the whole story before I'll let you and Borden make a martyr out of Weldon Whitman."

"You're a fool, Robert. The Whitman story could be a goldmine for you."

"Just let it die, Morris."

"You could write your own book about it."

"Let it die," Cloud said doggedly.

"You must have enough material for a dozen magazine articles—"

"Let it die, Morris."

"I've already said you can work with us on Borden's campaign, at a generous salary—"

"*Let it die, I said!*"

"All right!" Niebold stormed, slamming a beefy fist down on the desktop. "It's dead! Goddamm it, it's dead!"

"But Morris," Borden White objected, "that's the main issue of my campaign!"

"Don't you think I know that!" Niebold all but screamed at his junior partner. "I *planned* the campaign, remember?"

He pointed a stiff finger at Cloud. "Don't you realize that if he's telling us the truth, he could destroy us?"

"But how do we know he *is* telling the truth?" Borden White whined.

"Because he has no other reason for being here," Morris Niebold said simply, his voice suddenly quiet again. "He has nothing to gain."

"I don't understand—"

"Neither do I," Niebold admitted with a soft grunt. "I never have been able to understand people who do things when they have nothing to gain by doing them." He sighed heavily and looked back up at Cloud. "You got what you came for, Robert. The Whitman matter is dead. Now get out."

Cloud walked to the door.

"This isn't going to stop us, you know," Niebold threatened.

Cloud ignored him and opened the door.

"There are other issues, other ways. Borden *will* be governor! I'll find another way!"

Two hours later, just at dusk, Robert Cloud arrived on a commuter flight at Los Angeles International Airport. Walking through the terminal on his way to get another taxi to take him back to Carol, he was suddenly stopped by the sight of the late afternoon *Ledger*. Its glaring black headline read:

WHITMAN EXECUTED!

Cloud walked over to the rack of papers and stood looking at the words. Below the headline was a four-column photo of Weldon Whitman, positioned in such a way that only his eyes and the top part of his head showed above the middle fold of the page.

As Cloud stared intently at Whitman's eyes, he reached into his pocket and touched the cross and chain he had carried with him for so long. From somewhere in the depths of his mind he recalled Josefa Luza's words about her daughter. *She had a habit of always putting her hand up and touching a cross she wore around her neck. That is why now she clutches at her throat when she is excited. . . . she has never stopped reaching up for her cross, even though it was lost the night she was attacked—*

Impulsively Cloud strode across the terminal to a bank of phone booths. He put two one-dollar bills into a changer, scooped up the coins, and found an unoccupied booth. Dropping a dime in the slot, he dialed long distance.

"Operator, I want to place a person-to-person call to Dr. Helen Jacobs at the California State Hospital in Camarillo."

As he listened to the call being put through, Cloud glanced at his watch. It was nearly six o'clock. He wondered if it might not be too late to catch Helen Jacobs in her office. To his relief he found that it was not. His call was connected surprisingly fast, he deposited the necessary coins, and Cloud heard the doctor's voice.

"Hello. This is Dr. Jacobs."

"Dr. Jacobs, this is Robert Cloud. We met several months ago when I accompanied the Luza family there to visit their daughter."

"Yes, I remember you, Mr. Cloud."

"Doctor, I'd like to ask you something," Cloud said. "Without going into how it came to be in my possession, can you tell me if it would help in your treatment of Glory Ann if she had back the cross and chain taken from her the night she was attacked?"

"It could, certainly," Dr. Jacobs said eagerly. "You mean the actual same one? It very definitely could help. Do you have it?"

"Yes. In my pocket right now."

"Of course, there's always the chance that she won't identify with it," Dr. Jacobs said, almost as if she were talking to herself. "There's the possibility that because she feels soiled by what happened that she's rejecting *all* crosses. But I don't think so. We have one doctor here who is of the opinion that Glory's clutching at her throat in the presence of a man is a simulation of tearing the cross off and throwing it away. But I don't agree. I think she's searching for the one she lost. Where are you now, Mr. Cloud?"

"L.A. International Airport."

"Could you come out to the hospital?"

"Of course," Cloud said. "I should be able to get there in about two hours."

"I'll leave a pass for you at the gate," Helen Jacobs said. "Come directly to my office."

They hung up and Cloud left the booth. He started down the terminal toward a car-rental counter.

At eight o'clock he reached the gate of the Camarillo State Hospital. The pass was waiting for him. The guard showed him where to park and directed him to the offices of the resident doctors. When he entered the building, he saw Helen Jacobs coming down the hall to meet him. She was the same big-boned, full-bodied woman of fifty that he remembered, with her carelessly clipped blonde hair, her blue eyes still strikingly direct.

"How would you like to let me use you to get another gut reaction?" Helen Jacobs asked after they had exchanged greetings.

"No," Cloud said firmly. "I came down here to bring you the cross, that's all. You find someone else for a guinea pig."

"I don't want someone else," she said, taking his arm and leading him down an intersecting corridor toward G Ward. "I want you. You are exactly the right type: neat, clean-cut, respectable-looking."

Shit, Cloud thought. He silently cursed himself for having shaved off his shaggy mustache and gotten his hair cut. "Why don't you just take the cross," he said, digging in his pocket for it.

"No, absolutely not," she said. "I insist that you keep it. I don't even want to see it. I have a very strong feeling about what I have decided to do, and I don't want the sight of that cross to influence my judgment one way or another."

She continued to lead him, clutching his arm now, walking half a step ahead of him, her low-heeled oxfords squeaking noisily on the highly waxed tile. How the hell do you argue with a woman like this? he wondered. And then he decided that you did not; you simply followed her directions, as he was doing now.

When they reached G Ward, Cloud recognized where he was. He walked with Helen Jacobs over to Room G-8 and watched while she used her master key to unlock the room's observation control box. A moment later she lighted the one-way window and turned on the room audio. Cloud saw Glory Ann Luza sitting up in bed in her nightgown, reading.

A bedside radio was playing soft music next to her. Dr. Jacobs took Cloud's arm again.

"Robert, if we can recapture this girl's mind and restore her to a normal existence, it will be a great and wonderful thing for us both."

Cloud looked down at the woman's face: it was enraptured with the thought and words she had just spoken. At that moment, her eyes shone as he had never seen any other human's eyes shine.

"What do you want me to do?" he asked.

"Open the door, walk in, and return the cross to her," said Helen Jacobs. She let go of his arm. Cloud stepped to the door of the room and entered.

Before the door had even closed behind Cloud, Glory Ann began screaming. Her face contorted in terror at the first sight of him and she dropped her book and flung back the covers, leaping from the bed. Cloud stepped toward her.

"Glory—"

The girl screamed louder. She rushed to get a chair between her and Cloud. Her eyes were wide, unblinking with fright; her slim brown body was tension-locked beneath the white nylon gown. One strap of the gown had slipped from her shoulder, partly exposing a young brown breast. She clawed frantically at her throat with both hands.

Cloud moved closer. "Glory Ann, listen to me—" he insisted. He took the cross and chain from his coat pocket and held it out for her to see. "Look!" he shouted. "Look at this!"

The girl had just drawn in her breath for another scream, but when she saw the cross and chain hanging from Cloud's extended hand, the scream broke in her throat and was reduced to an anguished moan. She stared in mute, suspicious disbelief at Cloud and at the cross. But behind the disbelief, the terror in her expression began to dissolve.

Cloud took another cautious step forward. "This is yours, Glory Ann," he said quietly. "It's the cross you lost."

She whimpered fretfully, pitifully. Both hands came down from her neck and she gripped the back of the chair behind which she stood. Her breath was labored and wheezing.

"Please take this, Glory Ann," Cloud said, raising his voice to a more conversational level. "It's yours and I want you to have it back."

She shuddered once, all over, as if a chill had stitched her body. Her eyes, fixed on the cross, blinked rapidly as Cloud brought it closer to her. The bewilderment on her face deepened. Her eyes were searching. Cloud moved up to the chair that stood between them.

"Here," he said, holding the cross and chain an inch from her hand. The girl forced down a dry swallow and her furrowed brow relaxed. She took the cross from his hand, examined it briefly, and pressed it lovingly to one cheek. Then, as if she had to do it at once or lose her chance, and despite her trembling, she quickly opened the clasp, put the chain around her neck, and fastened it. When it was on, she stood with one hand calmly touching the cross, and looked curiously at Cloud. He reached over and pulled her fallen nightgown strap onto her shoulder. She did not flinch from his touch.

"Go back to bed now," he told her gently.

Glory Ann nodded and padded barefoot around the chair to the bed. She picked up her book and climbed into bed. Cloud started for the door.

"What is your name?" Glory Ann asked before he could leave.

"Robert," he said.

"Robert." She tilted her head pensively, as if evaluating the name. Then she smiled a slight, very shy smile and drew the bed covers a little higher over her girlish bosom. "Thank you, Robert," she said.

Cloud smiled back at her and left the room. Outside, Helen Jacobs met him with a brief, solemn hug.

"Thank you from me too, Robert."

She darkened the observation window, turned off the audio, and locked the control box to G-8. Then she and Cloud walked back down the corridor together. They went outside the hospital wing and sat on a bench in the cool night air. They sat in silence for a few moments, smoking.

"What do you think?" Cloud asked at last.

"I can't say for certain," Helen Jacobs told him clinically. "The best that we can hope for is that we have penetrated the nucleus of her psychosis and can now gradually bring her out of it. The worst, on the other hand, is that returning the cross was simply *your* entree into *her* world. She may still live her life in an Adam syndrome, with you as the sole exception to that pattern. Only time will tell us. Will you continue to help me with her: visit and talk with her, and get her accustomed to you for a while, until we can test her with her father or her brother?"

"Of course." Cloud thought of Carol. "I'd like to bring my girl out when I come back," he said. "I think she would like to help Glory Ann too, for reasons of her own."

"Then bring her with you, by all means."

It was nearly one A.M. when Cloud parked in front of Carol Carter's apartment building and quietly made his way to the second floor rear. The drapes were closed so he had not been able to tell whether there were lights on in the apartment or not. He rang the bell, once, very briefly. To his surprise the door was opened almost immediately: on the safety chain first, then closed and reopened all the way. Cloud went inside and leaned back against the door to close it.

"I wasn't sure you'd be up," he said. Carol nodded an abbreviated nod.

"I've been waiting for you. I knew you'd come. I just wasn't sure when." She was wearing a short kabuki robe, belted tightly around her incredibly narrow waist. It was black, contrasting strikingly with the straight-edged yellow hair that fell past her shoulders. "You've shaved your mustache," she said.

He nodded.

"And gotten a real haircut."

"Yes." He paused, then said, "And made some decisions. For the future. For myself. And for you, if you want."

"You know I want," she said. "What kind of decisions did you make?"

"I'm going into criminology," he told her. "I want to study it, write about it, see if I can contribute something to this capital punishment thing. I'm not sure there's really an answer to whether the death penalty serves any useful purpose or not, but I'd like to try and find out." He told her then about Glory Ann Luza and Helen Jacobs, and what had happened at Camarillo. "Before I got there, I was convinced that Whit had been justly executed. Now I don't know. If Dr. Jacobs can bring Glory Ann's mind back, then we have to look at Whit's punishment all over again. Because at least Glory Ann is still alive, and if a person is alive there's always a possibility, however remote, that help can come. So what we have to ask ourselves is that if Dr. Jacobs and her psychiatry can help Glory Ann, might not someone, somewhere, have been able to help Weldon Whitman?" Cloud smiled wearily. "Do I sound very mixed up?"

She took his hand. "You sound very tired. Come to bed."

He let her lead him into the familiar bedroom. She stood him in the middle of the room and removed his coat and tie and shirt.

"Will you go with me when I go back to Camarillo to try and help Glory Ann?" he asked.

"Of course," she said, undoing his trousers and shorts. "I'd like very much to. Sit down."

Cloud sat and she removed his shoes and socks and pulled off his trousers and shorts.

"Lift your arms."

She peeled off his undershirt and he was sitting there naked.

"I want you," he said quietly, simply.

"Rob, you look so tired—" she said. Then she looked down and saw that he really did want her.

"Climb up," he told her.

She unbelted the kabuki robe and let it slip away from her flaxen hair and white body. Cloud leaned back on his elbows. Carol bent and lubricated him, then got astraddle him on her knees. Slowly, deliciously, she covered him and began moving herself back and forth in an easy, liquid motion that worked the full staff of him. She started talking, kept moving, and brought the matter that his body created to the limits of its confinement. They climaxed together, swiftly and splendidly.

Finished, he lay back on the bed and Carol lay next to him.

"That was so good," Carol said quietly.

"It was," Cloud said. But she had no way of knowing *how* good, he thought. Only he could know that.

Because only he knew that it had been the first time he had thought only of himself and of her, and there had been no thought at all of Weldon Whitman.

WITHDRAWN

DATE DUE

AUG 4 1975			
SEP 9 1975	AUG 16 1996		
SEP 27 1975	DEC 11 1996		
OCT 11 1975	MAY 20 1997		
NOV 24 1975			
JAN 3 1976			
AUG 23 1976			
OCT 19 1981			
DEC 28 1991			
DEC 17 1992			
JAN 21 1995			

75-560

HOWARD
MARK THE SPARROW

Ligonier Public Library
Ligonier, Indiana